S0-BAN-697

Bicycle Moon

By Chuck Oestreich

Prologue

Star loved the kaleidoscope. Of all the presents from her seventh birthday, it was the kaleidoscope that she played with the most.

Her mother had surprised her with a birthday party, the first one she had ever had. It wasn't a big party, just four kids from her church – and her special friend, Marcie, from school – but she loved every minute of it. And it was a classic surprise party. Her father had taken her with him as he went to the auto parts store early on that Saturday afternoon. They had walked through the store, looking at shiny chrome parts, cans and bottles of paint and polish, and even the funny tags people hang from their rear-view mirrors. But he didn't buy anything; in fact, he didn't seem to be looking for anything in particular.

But when they got home and walked through the door from the garage, at first nobody seemed to be there. Then, all at once, kids and their parents, and her mother, jumped out from behind the furniture and two of the doors, yelling, "Surprise!" She was flustered momentarily – a little scared – but then she realized it was a surprise party for her, and she broke out in a big smile and a little involuntary dance.

After the Sloppy Joe sandwiches and potato chips, and then the cake – a special cake from the big grocery store with her name on it in frosting – and ice cream, her mother said, "Let's open the presents." Star was nonplussed again; she had forgotten all about the presents. Oh, this was fun; she couldn't contain herself.

After she had unwrapped the toys brought by her friends and neighbors, and had almost rushed to put on the beautiful, taffeta dress from her mother, her father, with his hands behind his back, had said, "Here, Star, here's something special for my little Star."

It was a kaleidoscope, a cylindrical tube with glass at both ends. At first she was bewildered; she didn't know what it did. Her father put his arm around her and showed her how it worked, pointing it out the window at the clouds floating freely above the trees.

She loved it immediately. It transformed her, although she couldn't understand how or why. Looking through it, she changed from a normal little girl growing up in a small Iowa town, Owaceta, to someone out and beyond herself. The colors and patterns moving constantly through her vision whenever she gave the tube a slight movement gave her a feeling of being in a world of her own – a world that was not at all like her tree and swing and lawn, her kitchen, or her own bedroom. No, when she looked into the red and black patterned tube, the variegated facets of complex color rushed through her mind like the glittering sparkles of a transforming fairy princess's magic wand.

She was stunned. This birthday was all so beautiful – and amazing: the cake with its frosting forming "Star," her mother's eyes looking at her when she opened the package with the new dress, and her father's arm around her pointing out the window at the clouds with the kaleidoscope.

Then her father said, "Do you see anything else in the kaleidoscope, Star?"

She looked through it again. This time she noticed, besides the tumbling colors and patterns, some lines and letters that seemed to be a part of the view. "There's something else there, Daddy. Something written. What is it, Daddy? What does it say?"

"I know you can't read yet, but when you learn, maybe this year, you'll be able to read what it says. And guess what it says." He stopped for a moment, then pointing with his finger along the miracle glass, said slowly: "We - love - you, - Star."

"Look here, Dear," he spoke to his wife. "You remember Jake Domingo, the guy at work who likes to fix watches. Well, he's got a real tiny inscribing tool and I got him to put an inscription on the lens." He turned to his daughter, "That way every time you look into this kaleidoscope you can see that we love you. It says so right there."

Star looked through the kaleidoscope again, and even though she couldn't read the slightly out-of-focus words, she did recognize her name. She knew that she couldn't be happier.

That night was unseasonably warm and balmy for mid-spring, and because it was her birthday, she was allowed to stay up later than usual. In fact, she and her parents took chairs out to their back yard and were still talking, and drinking Diet Sprite in their back yard, when the glow of the dying sun completely disappeared. Soon the backyard sky was completely black, and the overhead stars, which seemed to be virtually popping into the sky, compelled their attention.

All at once her father said, "Hey, Star, go get your kaleidoscope. We'll look through it out here."

She ran into the house, and from the side table in the living room where all the presents were laid out, picked up the special tube and scampered outside. She gave it to her father, who promptly scanned the night sky with it. "Well, it doesn't work that well in the dark. You see that star right up there, Star? That's the North Star. Here look at it through the kaleidoscope."

"Oh, daddy, I can't see hardly anything. It's all dark – mostly."

While they were talking, a slight wind from the east blew a quilt of clouds away from the low eastern sky, and a gigantic full moon appeared before their eyes, perched like a magical silver ring balancing precariously on the horizon.

Star moved the kaleidoscope to the light, focusing on the moon, and was awestruck. It was even more beautiful than in the light. The moon, now filled with dancing colors, was still softly luminescent, giving a milk-pure cast to the view within.

"Mommy and daddy, It's even better than before. I can see my name better. Everything is so clear and. . ." She rushed the magical tube to her father and said, "Oh, I love both of you so much."

A month later while swinging on her backyard swing and looking through the kaleidoscope at the same time – almost mesmerized as the moving patterns moved across her vision – she fell off the swing and smashed the toy. She flattened the cylindrical tube by falling on top of it. The main lens in back popped out and all of the little particles of brightly colored glass spilled onto the ground.

She was devastated. Her first impulse was to cry – to rush into the house, into her room, and just let the tears go. And she almost did that, but when she reached down for the lens, she stopped, taken aback. The circle of glass, all by itself, was beautiful. It was a glassy crystal of shimmering depth. She had never seen anything like it before. It seemed to have a luminescence that came from within its sparkling, reflective surface.

And on its surface, now more clear than before, was the affirmation of herself as someone who really and truly counted: "We love you, Star." Her tears dried up. She took the broken cylinder and most of the little plastic particles of color and carried them out to the alley behind the back yard where there was a big trashcan. She threw them away with hardly a second thought.

But she never again in her young life went anywhere without her "Star" lens.

Star lived at the edge of town; if fact, beyond her alley was a cornfield, so close was she to the farmland of Iowa. She walked home from school with Marcie almost every day, but Marcie lived two blocks closer to school than she did. So Star had two blocks to walk by herself. But she wasn't afraid or anything like that. The first block was mostly ordinary houses, while the second block's main feature was a n old abandoned factory. Its deteriorated parking lot had a smattering of rusting machines, discarded containers, even a few old cars – with flat tires and some with broken windows. Star did not like this block and she generally went faster when she walked the sidewalk in front of it. And that's exactly what she did on an afternoon in mid-May, a few months after her birthday.

As she skipped quickly past the muddy parking lot, she almost stumbled on a pair of legs stretched across the sidewalk. They belonged to a man, his body lying half on the sidewalk and half in the mud of the lot. She was scared; she had never seen anything like it before. Why was he sleeping right out in the open – in the dirt? She wanted to run right home and tell her mother to come look and maybe do something for this man.

Then something occurred to her. What if the man was dead? She shivered, but just then the man moved – and moaned. While she looked on apprehensively, the man slowly sat up and opened his eyes.

And then he started to cry.

Star had only seen grown men cry on TV, never in real life. But this one was actually bawling, large tears rolling down each of his cheeks. She said, in a very tentative whisper, "What's the matter, mister? You wait here; I'll go get my mother."

The man looked uncomprehendingly at her, but he slowly got up and reached out his hand to her. Then in a voice cracked and filled with an echoing dread, he said, "Yes, take me."

Not really knowing what to do, but feeling very sorry for the man who seemed to be in such pain, she instinctively grabbed the man's hand and started leading him down the street towards her house.

Just then a car pulled up in front of them and the driver leaped out. He ran up to them and snatched her hand away from the crying man. The driver yelled at the pitiful man, "What the hell do you think you're doing, you drunken bum? Leave her alone." With that he pushed the man so hard that he reeled backward and pummeled to the parking lot again, his back ending up in a muddy pool of oily rainwater. Now the driver, who was a large man with a spiky, short-cut haircut, pulled Star by the hand to his car, almost lifting her into the front seat through the driver's side door; she had to scoot underneath the steering wheel.

"Come on. You gotta get outta here. That guy is no good." He started driving, but in the opposite direction of Star's home. "Did he do anything to you?"

Star just stared at him, uncomprehending.

He said it again, "Did he do anything to you?"

Star didn't answer. Things were going too fast for her. She sat in the front seat, looking at the driver, sobbing, her hand deep in her jacket pocket clutching her "Star" lens. Within a block, though, when she realized that he wasn't taking her directly home, she started crying, "Take me home. I live back there. Take me home."

But he didn't.

The road led out of the city; it became a wide, one lane county road with a gravel shoulder. The man drove at times so fast that he swerved onto the shoulder and spit gravel on the bottom of the car and into the corn on the side of the road. Not far out of the city he pulled into a cornfield tractor lane, just two tracks leading through the corn to a little grove of trees near some rocks and fences.

Star continued to sob, "I want to go home. Take me home to my mommy." The driver ignored her. He stopped the car under cover of the little group of trees, turned to Star, and said, "Quit the crying. God, I hate a crying bitch – even a little one."

"And what's that you have in your hand? Gimme it." He grabbed the lens, took a quick look at it, and snarled, "Just a piece of glass – worthless." He threw it down to the floor on Star's side of the front seat. "Now quit that crying. Quit it! Shut your god-damn mouth."

That was the second last thing Star remembered in her young life.

The last thing, while the driver's clenched hand was accelerating with unbelievable speed toward her soft and vulnerable face, was trying to find a place to hide her lens. She had picked it up from the car's floor and now was digging with all her might into the crack between the car's seat and its back, as if only there, in a crack of fabric and closeness, could she find protection.

Her dead body, raped, and with both its arms broken, was found one hour and twenty-five minutes later at the edge of the cornfield across the street from the grain elevator and seed store. The man she had almost stumbled over was still where the driver had pushed him, a sodden lump unconscious in the mud.

Chapter 1

As Dis rounded the curve at the bottom of the hill, he was almost blinded by the moon. He had been riding cautiously downhill, curving down a spiral of gradual pitch. The terrain on one side of the road slanted up into a cutout patch of the scraggly hill, the other side fell off smoothly into the river valley below. But when Dis came close to the bottom of the descent, at a speed of about 25 mph, the moon hit him.

It almost knocked him off his bicycle.

It was a bicycle moon – a full moon as big and as round as a bike wheel. It balanced on the edge of the horizon like a silver sphere, a circle of promise, mystery, and allure. Years before at some long ago campfire on some long ago bike tour, he first heard of a bicycle moon. The memory rushed over him again as he rushed almost arrow straight down the road, heading into the light from the moon's almost unnatural brilliance.

The big guy with the grizzled beard and the cotton watch cap poked the fire and said, "Listen, you get a bicycle moon and you can go on forever.

"That's right, there ain't that many full moons in the summer and most of the time there's clouds or it's raining or something. But if you're on your bike and you can see the full moon when it's rising – just a setting for an instant on the line of the horizon – why, then you've got yourself a bicycle moon. You understand what that means?"

He looked around and threw the stick into the fire. "It means you can ride forever. Just stay on your bike, dig in and go on and on. You don't have to stop; you don't have to eat; you don't even have to get water, for Christ's sake. With a bicycle moon, you got eternity just awaitin' you down the road."

The man rose then and disappeared into the darkness surrounding the campfire. He left a slightly bemused group of listeners. It's not often that evocative, even poetic, pronouncements are expressed so vigorously – especially to casual, weekend acquaintances. Although Dis remained skeptical, he remembered that he felt vaguely uncomfortable. He wanted to hear more about this bicycle moon; he wanted to talk to the man in the morning. But the way things go on a group tour, he never saw the man again. "What the hell," thought Dis, "maybe he caught himself a bicycle moon."

But now, speeding with the momentum of his hill descent and looking at the shimmering immensity of the moon balanced on the line of the river valley, Dis felt a surreal feeling of power. Gone was the ache in his back, the soreness in his legs, and the uncomfortable heaving sensation in his chest. Even his hands, covered with the leather half-gloves favored by cyclists, seemed to lose their clenching pain.

Dis roared down the last segment of the hill, then kept the same cadence when he hit the level pavement that followed the course of the river. He felt euphoric and masterful. He was a cycling machine, a synchronized flesh-and-bone, metal-and-rubber machine.

"Ah," he thought, "a bicycle moon. I love it."

He didn't really believe it, however. Dis knew better than to get hooked into things that were completely irrational. He had too much experience for that – had learned in his thirty-six years that evocation was all right for music or for the final 15 minutes of late night TV dramas, but in reality good old concrete nuts-to-butts reality was the real pattern of the world. He felt himself eminently qualified on that score.

But now he gloried in the euphoria of riding, the moon his gigantic headlight, making the pavement, even at emerging night, brighter than on a day of light rain or one heavy with overhanging dark clouds. The road, a little used country blacktop, paralleled the unobtrusive river and Dis made the most of it. He built on his cadence, spinning through the silvery dusk at about 25 miles per hour.

He was mindless, a surging, churning automaton of energy, bearing down the pavement into the thickening dark. The bicycle moon lifted from the horizon, but it still gave illumination to the sliver of roadway. Traffic was almost nonexistent; Dis kept racing forward.

Forgetting hunger, thirst, and weariness, Dis, on an emotional high, pushed almost effortlessly. He passed a rusty sign for "Garth Seeds" hanging crookedly on two posts. A few gunshot pockmarks dully glinted from the crinkled sign. But Dis hardly noticed it, except to subconsciously register it as a possible sign of an approaching town.

Around the next bend he noticed another sign, this one for "The Grand Apple Cafe – in Downtown Jeffrey." Pedaling rapidly, he knew he was coming close to a town, and realistically he also knew he had to stop someplace soon. He needed to look at his map and fix his location. He had been riding with such euphoria, that he had all but forgotten where he was, something which he could not afford to do. But food, drink, and sleep, although present in his subconscious, were way off in the distance.

However, he knew that riding in the moonlit dark was dangerous – not just because of traffic and possible accidents – but because it was unusual, and to stand out was the last thing in the world Dis needed. But he felt so good riding, not a bit tired, no worries, that he made a spontaneous decision to scoot through this town and continue on. Maybe he'd stop for a second to check his map and have a Kudo bar.

Quickly the road changed into a residential street of a small town with almost no outskirts build-up. He had been on the highway, had seen a few signs, and – boom – there he was, in the midst of the town. Small towns were like that – like magazine articles without introductions.

Most of the houses were decidedly old – possibly turn of the century – but the place had no integrity. Mixed here and there with the old were modern ranch houses or split-levels. This was a town that just grew naturally through the years. It didn't have spurts of growth, in which whole areas were built at the same time. Jeffrey, Kentucky, like its area and its people, was just a plain old small town.

Dis noticed a few lights up ahead about a block, and figured he was getting close to what downtown the little city had. He slowed down and just then she rode by. She appeared out of nowhere right next to him. He felt her presence rather than saw or heard her. But she was something: a lycra, yellow and red, bicycle vision of bliss.

She passed him quickly, but not before he caught a quick glimpse of a face, pale and softly curving like the glowing moon in the distance. Moreover, he thought he saw a momentary flicker of smile on the woman's face as she passed. It was a two part smile: at first just polite anonymous salutation, but then a hint of recognition – entered, held for a split second, and then disappeared. Did she know him?

He looked ahead to check his path, then sped up, as she was now past him and widening the gap. He slammed the pedals, really pounding, concentrating his attention on the pavement in front of him and the woman gliding away some fifty feet ahead.

And that was all he remembered.

Chapter 2

He woke up to an arm of fire and a crowd of faces – and a strange, loopy sensation in his head. The darkness gave way to pinpoints of light, which he slowly made out to be streetlights and light shining through plate glass windows. He blinked and the faces came into focus - ordinary faces, men's and women's. One in particular, a male's, was so close that he could see the half day accumulation of whiskers and smell a combination of beer and cheap bourbon spewing from the man's breath.

But this guy was helpful: "Hey, man, what the hell, you took quite a spill. You OK?"

"I guess so. Where's my bike?"

"Right here. It don't look so bad. Not as bad as your helmet. It looks like you skidded on it all the way through that intersection. Hey, man, try to move your arm. We gotta see if you can move it, right-oh."

Dis looked down, saw the blood. It appeared that his whole arm was red and bleeding, but he sat up, slowly and groggily, and twisted his arm, his right one, in front of him. It hurt, but it moved. Both he and the helpful man knew it wasn't broken.

Dis stood up now, feeling slightly faint but not in pain, and checked himself out. His right arm was torn up; it looked like a red rainy lane of gravel single-track. His right knee had a circle of red so perfectly round it might have been inscribed by a compass. Taking into consideration his arm, his leg, and what the man told him about his helmet, Dis grimly muttered to the crowd in general, "Guess I made a good three point landing."

That broke the tension. That and the fact that Dis was up and walking and didn't seem to be too injured. He looked around. He was on the side of the road in what looked to be a commercial street in the town, probably a street just off the main downtown. A few stores slouched against each other, including a closed-front bar, its overhead window glowing with the tacky pull of neon beer signs. Evidently that was where the crowd had come from. The bar had some benches and one picnic bench in front of it, and now most of the observers drifted back to the comfort of the red and green circle of light in front of the tavern and the watery gold of their Miller's or Bud Light. Dis thought, "They're probably really putting me down. Talking about this guy on a bike, comes through in the middle of the night, and lays a stripe of blood right down the middle of their beer alley."

The helpful man snapped him back to reality. "Well, man, what cha' gonna' do? You gotta have that arm taken care of, and you should have your head examined. No, wait a minute, that didn't sound right. But let's face it, you took a nasty fall on your noggin and you should have someone check it out. Why don't you come over to Stacy's here and we'll see if we can get you to a EMT?"

"Yeah, all right," Dis mumbled, as he started to follow the man. Just then he saw his bike on its side in the gutter. He pulled it upright and started an almost automatic check of its condition. The frame was straight but paint-scraped. The derailleur looked OK and the chain was even in place on the sprockets. The front wheel, however, as he spun it, seemed to be slightly out of round. It must have taken most of the shock . . . wait a minute, what the hell happened? One minute he had been riding smooth and clear and the next he was down, sliding across the pavement.

"You hit that piece of two-by-four down there," said a soft but clear voice, one that Dis hadn't heard before. He turned and acknowledged the woman in red and yellow, the bicycling moon maiden who had passed him before. "And you did a nice job of flipping almost over when you went flying."

"You saw what happened."

"I was slowing down and looking back when you took off – like ET," she softly smiled. "But look, I live right over here," she pointed over her shoulder. "Follow me and we can at least get you cleaned up a bit." The prospect of her soothing hands matching her soothing voice was much more attractive to Dis than the old-beer atmosphere of Stacy's.

So he walked with her through the crystal streets of Jeffrey, Kentucky. He limped slightly, pushing his heavy bicycle, laden as it was with almost all of his earthly possessions. She, on his right, walked silently next to her bike straight down the side street for one block and then turned ninety degrees into a street leafy with high oaks and hawthorns and nested with modest homes and big yards. With the street light and the moon's almost brilliant iridescence, the block ahead was a photographic negative of black reversed on white, an other world projection of a changeable past.

Dis glanced at the woman on his side. She wasn't smiling, but he remembered now the slight hint of recognition on her lips as she passed him earlier. Why was she helping him? Did she know him? Was he in danger? He knew this: he had never seen her before in his life. But perhaps she knew not him, but his image, his past. He had better be very careful. Hard as it as was to believe, the possibility of danger lurked in Jeffrey, Kentucky.

Softly, with hardly a flutter of her lips: "It's right over here, that yellow house. I've got the downstairs apartment." She led him down the street, through the impossible silver light – past neighbors discretely watching from their plastic K-Mart porch lounges – to the yellow house and up a sidewalk along its side. They passed through a gate and came to an enclosed yard next to a side entrance into the house. A picnic table dominated the yard. She leaned her bike on the side of the house, and said, "Stay here. I'll get something," and disappeared into the house. Dis looked around and noticed, besides the table, an inexpensive plastic splash pool, a kid's bike leaning against it, and, on a clothesline, a girl's one-piece swimming suit. His benefactor was a mother.

From the house he heard, "Damn!" It was the same voice, but it wasn't soft now. "The water – Damn – it's all over the floor. I told her not to leave her shoes all over the place. Damn!"

Dis wondered if he should go in and try to help, but just as he was approaching the door, she yelled, "Crap, hold on a bit. I have to clean up this mess." Her head poked out the door, and this time her voice was back to its pre-crisis moderation. "Chrissy, that's my daughter, left her shoes right in the middle of the kitchen and I tripped on them. So now there's water all over the place. That kid – I hope her shoes aren't ruined."

In the moonlight she saw his red-stained arm. "I'll get some more water. Wait right there." Dis looked down at his arm. It wasn't really bleeding much – just beads of drying blood mixed with dirt and sand and some loose skin. He looked at his bike. Intact – except for the front wheel, which he was sure he could fix by himself.

Maybe he should slip away right now. He could take off in the moonlight, find a camping place down the road, fix his arm and not get involved here. A swimming suit and wet shoes – and a luring voice, both soft and hard.

He was lifting his sore leg over the bike when the voice interrupted him, this time from behind the house. "Sure, go. But let me clean that up first. There could be glass and dirt, for heaven's sake. He didn't even grasp about the glass and dirt; what stopped him was the finality in the, "Sure, go" – the finality and the hard edge around the throaty syllables. He had heard the same thing before.

A suburban home, a slammed door, and a single aspirated word – "Go."

He thought, "Yes, go. Get on that bike and take off. Get away. You know you can't take this."

But she was too quick. With a fresh bowl of soapy water, a wash rag, and a couple of spray bottles garnished with kids' bandaged arms and legs, she materialized at the picnic table, a bit frazzled, but sincere. "You can't leave with your arm dripping, for Christ's sake. Come over here and let me wash it." Now he had to laboriously lift his leg back over the bike, lean the bike back up against the fence, and sheepishly mutter, "1. . . I didn't want to be a trouble. Besides it doesn't look too bad – just a bit of road rash."

But he went to her and she fulfilled her promise. Hands, voice, an aura of care – soothing. The warm, soapy water bit with a sting, but she and the spray cans of antiseptic cooled the venom of the bite. Dis hadn't been physically close to a woman (excluding convenience store clerks and a few downy café waitresses) for a long time, and this set him off. He reacted. His body tensed and seemed to resonate minutely, while his mind and feelings retracted into the protected center of his being. He was physically on edge, but mentally and emotionally hard. His fortress walls were at risk, but the citadel within was immobilized with compacted protection.

This woman who touched him with softness and cleansing was attractive. She wasn't beautiful in a classic sense, but in a mid-Kentucky sense she could brighten up a valley. Her hair was short and light; her face small and almost delicate, with a sharp nose charmed with freckly dots; but her teeth destroyed the fine line. They were nicely spaced, but the two on the top in front were a bit out of line. One slightly overreached the other. Her face was more pleasant in repose than in agitation. With her mouth closed, serenity and competency came together. While smiling, talking, or wide-mouthed with strain, her back country roots tumbled into view. But all in all, to Dis, she, in the extraordinary moonlight, had a facial beauty that left him aching within his protective containment.

Her body brought out an ache also. She wore bright yellow biking shorts that revealed a compact, trim, well-toned lower body, her hips flaring even though drawn in by the rubbery fabric. Her upper body, also slim, showed pert breasts fighting with the mainly red fabric of the T-shirt she was wearing. Dis deciphered the printing on the somewhat faded T-shirt – 'TOKRV – Tour Of the Kentucky River Valley." A stylized river profile was emblazoned in red across her chest.

"There, I think it's pretty clean. But it needs a bandage."

Dis didn't care for the idea of a bandage. It would make him stand out, in some way brand him.

"Stay here. Don't go. I've got a roll of gauze inside the house." She disappeared, again into the side door of the house. His arm and the circle on his knee were bleeding again, but only slightly, not enough to be a concern, but enough that it should be stopped. He waited.

And while he waited, it dawned on him that he had never taken off his helmet since the accident. His head seemed to be all right; at least it didn't ache and he didn't feel spacey, even though he had been knocked out momentarily. As he was taking the helmet off, she appeared again, materialized really, as quietly as a sunset breeze. "Oh my gosh, I forgot about your head. You were out, weren't you? Wow! Just look at that helmet. It's ruined. Jeez, the plastic is loose, almost coming out."

Dis fingered the shattered shield. He stared at it, but something took hold of him, immobilizing him – taking him back.

Darkness swallowed the ring of light. Through the parking lot to his train until the silver blade opened up the darkness.

"Here take it. Don't touch it!"

The glint, the push, the reeling in the darkness. Then the release, the puncture, the escaping air from the balloon. The sob with hardly a whimper. The finality.

"Cover your ass. Cover your ass."

She saw the momentary blank and it made her draw back. Apprehension, even fear, darted into her eyes for a second. She thought, "Something's wrong here. Something's out of line. Watch it, Lornaree. Keep your distance."

It was just a flash for both of them, but a flash of primary apprehension.

He came to immediately, and she responded. "There's a bike shop close to where you crashed. You can get a new helmet there – in the morning. Hey, where you from?" She didn't wait for an answer, knowing instinctively that it wouldn't mean much to her, that he was not of this area. "I mean, you can't ride without one. Just look at that helmet. You know, it saved your life. How far do you have to go?"

He shifted, not looking at her, but at the wooden side door, a door with a handle only half attached, one empty screw hole pinpointed weirdly in the combined moonlight and dim, insect-encrusted floodlight. What was happening to him? God, that had never happened before. How long had he been off? Had he really hurt his mind during the crash? He needed to get away, to rest, to sleep, but, Jesus, what if he blanked like that while riding?

He shifted his eye from the door handle, from the screw hole, and looked into her clear hazel eyes. They too were hypnotizing in the combined light. What had she asked? How far did he have to go? That was the question of his life. Just how far? "Ah . . . ah . . . actually I was looking for a place to camp." As soon as he said it, the memory of the bicycle moon came back, but he knew he couldn't explain the unexpected euphoria he had felt not too long ago in the hills before her town, the feeling that kept him from even considering looking for a place to stop. "Is there any camping place around here? Oh, I'm from Iowa." It didn't sound right, not even now after almost a month, especially with her, but it had to be.

Just then the gate in the front of the yard leaped and then smashed against the side of the fence. "Mommy, Billy Yardly said my feet were crooked . . . Oh, what happened?" The girl was perspiring, flushed from running, but she stopped at the gate's threshold when she saw the blood. Instinctively her hands went to her face, memories of TV shows and scary stories heard from friends flooding her mind. Blood . . . a strange man, big and dirty . . . her mother with a scissors.

She involuntarily yelped, "Mommy, Mommy . . . Don't let him . . ." and then trailed off into an uncomprehending stare at Dis, who, when he heard the "Don't let him," abruptly sat down on the picnic bench while his hands flew to his face, trying to cover it before . . .

Cover your ass, cover your ass.

Get out.

A shirt sticky with warm blood. Dirty pants. A wallet strapped to the chest. A quick look. Yes.

Now run, run, you stupid jerk. Get outta here. Wait, don't run. That'll give you away. Walk, but walk with a purpose. Walk to get away, to hide, to get away. You've got to get away . . . to get away.

But I don't want to get away!

Again it was she who noticed it, who held it to her reserve, who was so attuned to a basic caution, that it buried itself within her as sure as a root in the earth. But it was just a glance before she turned to her daughter. "Oh, Honey, don't worry. This man had an accident – on his bike – and I'm . . . I'm fixing it for him." She turned from her daughter and reached for Dis' arm. She could do this now. She was in control. Everything was all right. She would bandage this man's arm, see him to her door, and that would be the end of it. She knew nothing of him, except, with a surety that belied her experience, that he was troubled, but that he would not harm her or her daughter, and that she felt good in helping him.

"Come here, Chrissy, you can help me with this bandage." She folded a pad of gauze into a long rectangular shape, lay it smoothly on Dis's arm, patted it down, then taped it into place with long strips of adhesive tape. "Is it too tight? Try moving your arm." The moist-faced girl approached them, still apprehensive, still remembering warnings and words about strangers. But the man's bike clothing countered her worries. She had never yet met a person in bike clothing who she thought was "bad." Her mother had some friends and many acquaintances from the Jeffrey area who biked with her, and who she knew socially, and none of them were like the strangers on TV who were nasty and violent.

She watched as her mother tried to bandage Dis's knee. She wasn't having much success. The gauze would be flat against the circular abrasion when the knee was bent, but when he would stretch his leg, it puffed up like a sail suddenly filled with wind. If she taped it with the leg straight, he couldn't move it without the adhesive tape tearing away from his skin. She needed a circular bandage pad, but she didn't have any in the house and the drug store was closed for the night. She settled for cutting a circular pad of gauze and holding it on the knee with a roughly circular edging of tape. The woman patted the last piece of tape into place, looked into Dis's eyes and said, "This is Chrissy and I'm Lornaree. Lorn for short. Lorn McAbby. You're from Iowa, right?"

"Yeah, Iowa. Owaceta, Iowa. A town something like this. Small and . . . and . . . busy." Stop it, Dis told himself. Don't make up more than you have to. Just answer the questions and leave out the details.

"You do have a name?"

"Robert."

"Bob?"

"OK. I'm not fussy. Rob also. Robert Clemmon."

"Well, Rob, it's almost nine-thirty, too late for you to go camping, even if there was a place to camp around here, which there isn't. If you were planning to sleep in some farmer's woods, forget it. You're in no shape for that. Besides you need a helmet if you're going anyplace on your bike. Wait a minute, you can't go anywhere without making sure your head is OK."

"It feels all right – even when I shake it." He vigorously moved his neck back and forth.

"Tell you what. Come on in; I've got some Pepsi. You can call up the Forest Motel and see if they have any rooms left. Wait a minute. You're camping. Probably means you're on a budget. But, well, the Forest is cheap. I think they've got a 27 dollar special, or something like that." Dis felt maneuvered, but in a mild, nice way. He liked this gently assertive woman, even while realizing that he knew he had to get out, to not get involved. But he went into the house with them.

The girl skittered ahead of him, still wary, but happy to have someone new in the house. "Gosh, Mister. . . Mister. . . I'd be crying if I hurt myself like you did. Once I slipped off the back porch and sprained my foot. I think I cried for an hour straight. Billy Carman had a bee sting him on the eyelid, and he cried for about a week. That's what his mother said."

She would have gone on, but Lorn stopped her by asking him, "Do you want to call the motel?"

"Yeah, I guess so." The phone was on a spindly table in the hallway leading into the kitchen. It was a new Bell South one, cradled on an answering machine. She got the slim phone book out of the table's drawer, and showed him the number in the section under motels. Jeffrey had three motels, a Super 8, a Best Western, and the Forest, which advertised itself as "A downtown, hometown happy place."

She left for the kitchen where she took three glasses out of a cupboard and took a liter bottle of Pepsi out of the refrigerator. By the time she had taken an open package of cookies out of a cupboard, he was back in the kitchen.

"Yep, they've got a room, actually three. I guess I'll take your advice and stay there. Then tomorrow I can check myself out better. Besides I think my bike might need some work." Despite his rational need to be reticent, he almost couldn't help himself. "Actually, I could stand to take a break, maybe even take a job for a while. I've been on the road for about a month now, and I've spent more than I planned. I was in retail sales back in . . . in Iowa. You don't suppose there's any place around here that could use some extra help for awhile?" It was a spur of the moment thing, talking to her like this, but he liked her and her kid certainly wasn't a brat.

"Here, have some Pepsi. Sit down."

While they drank the cold, sweet drink, she mused. "You lucked out. I work at the printer downtown so I find out a lot about things like new businesses and jobs and things like that." He swirled the drink around and accepted a Hydrox, black and white cookies sandwiched together by sweet hardened frosting. "Just yesterday," she continued, "we printed up a circular for a new convenience store over on the West Side. 'We Got It' is its name. Maybe they would hire you. You'd probably have to wear long sleeves to hide those bandages though. Might not hire you if you look all beat up."

"West Side. We Got It. Got cha. I'll remember." He finished a sip of Pepsi and then became hesitant. He felt good in the rather smallish kitchen, but he knew his welcome was worn out. He did know that he wanted to return.

Dis took a long drink of his Pepsi – too long. He choked on it. The acrid liquid rose in his throat, almost going up his nose. He suppressed it, but not without the pain and the frustration caused by this involuntary action. He noticed that both of the females were looking at him, and when he could find his voice, he muttered, "My mother always told me to drink slowly."

That set Chrissy off. "My mom says the same thing. 'Chrissy, don't drink so fast. Chrissy, don't gulp when you drink . . .'"

"All right, Chrissy, that's enough. Rob – Mister . . . Mister . . . Clemmon gets the point." But she reached for Chrissy as she said this, pulling her in, hugging her.

Dis did get the point, but it wasn't about drinking too fast.

He stood up, realizing that it was time to go. He liked it here, but he was a stranger, a stranger who was new and not part of the order of things. "Listen, I really thank you. I'll make amends. I'll get back to you. Don't think this isn't appreciated. Why, these bandages alone . . ."

She interrupted, "That's all right. Real bikers around here are few and far between. We have to take care of one another, don't you think so?" She stopped, thinking that she had gone too far, had moved a little bit too much over an invisible line.

He was moving out the door now, when she thought about the motel. "Just go about three, that's right, three, blocks down the street. Then turn left for one block and you're back on the main street. The motel's right there. The Forest. It's got a big sign in the shape of an oak tree. There's a Hardee's about a block away. You can't miss it." Dis had to concentrate to hear, she spoke so quietly.

He was putting his cracked helmet on his front handle bag and starting to push his heavy pannier-laden bike towards the gate when she inadvertently blurted, "Why don't you leave the . . ." She stopped, catching herself. Let it be, Lornaree. Let it be.

He turned and looked at her, Chrissy behind her, smiling and waving. "Thanks again. Oh, and Chrissy, don't forget to not gulp when you drink."

As he pushed off down the leafy street, he couldn't conceal a grin – even though the shock from his crash was wearing off and genuine pain was appearing. Even his head was throbbing now, but it was familiar pain, a regular headache, nothing he hadn't experienced before – many times. The grin was for the fireflies arcing fitfully across the street's big, dark lawns. It was for the cicadas' rhythm-less buzz and abrupt stop. It was for the brick road's bumpy, mellow-red pool of moonlit calm. But mostly it was for a crooked-toothed woman named Lornaree who spoke as softly as she touched.

Chapter 3

The teenage girl behind the counter didn't want to be there. She was bored completely, especially with being stuck in a tiny office with a grainy 8-inch black-and-white TV without a cable connection and its MTV lifeline. The screen flickered to a summer rerun of "Cheers" while the girl inspected her toes with a fingernail clipper. Her toenails were covered with a brilliant crimson polish, which also covered her fingernails, except where it was broken off or scratched. As she clipped and filed, she became more and more perturbed. She didn't even have MTV, for Christ's sake, and she needed some more polish to make repairs. And she had to be in this stifling office until her parents returned. Eleven o'clock they promised. But they were always late. She bent down to work on her little toe, when she heard the door open. Looking up, she at first expelled a laugh, then became apprehensive. The first image to come into her mind when she glanced at Dis, his arm and leg all wrapped in gauze, was that of a mummy.

But immediately fear blossomed. Was this guy a drunk who had an accident? He looked pretty desperate. His T-shirt was dirty and he looked a little grim. What time was it? Damn, only 10:15. They wouldn't be back for at least another hour.

"I just called. Do you still have a room, one for $27.95?"

"Oh, you're the one that called. Well, no one's been in here since then. Wait a second while I get the card." Then she remembered her dad's instructions. She lied to the stranger, "Except my dad. He's in back, resting. Wait a second. Where are those cards?"

Dis didn't like motels. They wanted identification, and Dis wasn't sure about that yet. He had spent countless hours while on his bike working it out, but he still wasn't sure about how to handle identification. It didn't come naturally. So he deliberately tried to avoid identifying himself. The girl found the card and presented it to Dis. "Here you go. Just fill this out and sign down there. Cash or card?"

"Cash. How much?"

She could almost do it by heart now, but she still wasn't positive, so she checked it on the little desk calculator. "Twenty seven ninety-five plus five percent state and five percent local. So ten percent. It comes to thirty seventy-five."

While filling out the form, Dis, out of the corner of his eye, watched her bright red fingernails. They mesmerized him, not so much in their gaudy sheen, but in their nervous, involuntary rhythm as they clattered on the top of the counter. He was glad she was young and naive. It made him more at ease in filling out the details of the card. He didn't have to worry about looking guilty. But still the tap-hammer fingernails seemed to dance on his head, to drum in his brain – adding to the ache that now was blossoming into an irritating layer of pain. He finished the form and returned it to her, then drew out his wallet and took out two twenty-dollar bills.

"Hey, ain't ch' got a car? Ya gotta put the license number down right here." Her darting fingernail tapped at the empty blank.

"No, I'm on a bike. Oh, yeah, is it OK to take it into my room with me?"

The fingernails stopped. She smiled a yellow-toothed grin. "You wanna take your bike in your room? No way." She started giggling, almost uncontrollably, "Come on, ain't it kinda big for that?"

Dis had to laugh. "It's a bicycle, not a motorcycle. I'm going cross-country and I'd appreciate it if I could keep it the room – secure it."

The fingernails started drumming again. "I guess. It ain't dirty is it? We don't want no mud or anything on the rug. Grease. Ya can't get that out. Is it greasy?"

"Not really."

"Sure, then I guess it's OK. Just be careful, OK? I don't wanna have to work my ass . . . my butt off getting grease outta a rug. Here's your change and the key. Checkout time is twelve noon. Your room, let's see, number three is right around that corner and down a ways."

Thanks. Hey, how late is the Hardee's open?"

"I think it closes at eleven. Hey Mister," here she glanced at the newly written form," Mister Clemmon, you really riding a bicycle across the country?"

With the ache getting progressively worse, Dis nodded, "yes."

"Well, ain't that a trip," she blurted. Then the double meaning hit her and she giggled it again. "Ain't that a trip."

When Dis left, she was smiling and her fingernails were actually dancing on the countertop – dancing to the rhythm of a commercial weakly emerging from the forlorn black-and-white television set.

Dis rolled his bike to the room, left it leaning inside against a '50s-modern chest of drawers, and then walked to the Hardee's. He was hungry. He had had three pizza slices about five, but that was about 50 miles and one lights-out accident ago. He ordered three cheeseburgers, some fries, and since he had just had a Pepsi, a cup of water – to go. When his order came, he asked for extra catsup, stowed the little plastic envelopes into the bag of precisely wrapped burgers and cardboard protected potatoes, and went back to the motel.

Dis, not like many bikers, loved fast food. But tonight he didn't even want to enjoy any of the fat-induced flavors. He just wanted to fill the void in his stomach and then sleep – if he could. The ache in his head was increasing, now positively throbbing. He opened his front handlebar pack and took out a small plastic film container filled with aspirin, the only painkiller he ever used. He shook two of the pills into his hand and then gulped them down with a drink of the ice water from Hardee's.

He wondered if he should shower before he ate. If he did, his burgers would be cold – no major problem. But he couldn't stomach cold fries. He turned on the TV, but had difficulty finding a channel because the selector knob was missing. He could just barely move it by gripping hard with two fingers, so when he came to the first local channel, he left it there and dully watched a local news program's wrap-up. His stomach, by now, was in turmoil so he postponed the shower and made short shrift of the food, gulping it down. especially the burgers. With the fries he at least took time to dip them in the catsup from the frustrating, tightly sealed packets.

While he ate, his mind was vacant, filled with the ephemera from the TV – the usual commercials, sports (a local high school boy was trying out for the Reds), and then the weather – something which he usually listened for with interest. Now, however, he was tired, dirty, and his head was pulsating. Besides he didn't think he was going to ride tomorrow. He hadn't made a conscious decision about that, but what the woman – Lornaree, surely a strange name – said made sense. He had to make sure he was physically OK. Also he had to think about money. But he could put that off until morning. Right now all he wanted was to shower and sleep.

Sleep, with the help of the aspirin, came – but it came in fits. Throughout the night his slightly bruised brain took him to various places in his past. At one point he was following his childhood dog, Roost, around a lake shore that was alternately sandy and swampy. They kept circling and circling, chasing frogs, jumping over logs, dashing in the water. He was barefooted, but had on pants and a shirt. Way off in the distance, almost as if a reoccurring echo, his mother called him repeatedly. "Dis. Dis, come on in. Dis, it's time. Come on." But he didn't come in. He kept circling the pond, Roost leading the way, nosing through the debris that edged the pond. Just when his mother's voice became intense and irritated, Roost stopped, lowered his head, then backed off – looking back at Dis as if asking for a decision. Dis approached the spot, but in his dream never did get there. He didn't wake up, the dream just stopped and he went off into a deeper realm of rest.

Sometime later he was standing around waiting for a Saturday morning bicycle club ride to begin. He didn't know any of the other riders, who, if they were fellow strangers, were making small talk; or if they were experienced club riders, were joking among themselves about last week's ride, which evidently was a real battle - brisk headwinds and misty rain. A married couple his own age asked him if he knew the route for the day. He had a vague idea of it, since a vague outline had been published in the local paper a few days before. They mulled this over, refusing, however, to ask one of the experienced, more talkative riders about it. Eventually someone led them out of the parking area of the park they were in, and Dis started pedaling in the midst of a group of the more experienced ones. He didn't feel comfortable. They were yelling back and forth among themselves and he felt left out.

Then one of the loudest of the club riders passed him and asked him if he was a new member. Dis explained that he had just bought a bike, a Raleigh, at a yard sale, had seen the notice about the ride in the paper, and so decided to see how it would go. He had hardly ridden more than ten miles at one time before, but he wanted to see if he could do this ride's 30 miles.

The man was friendly but the he didn't stay around, speeding off with hardly any effort, while Dis started to breathe heavily just keeping up with the pack. Soon most of the riders had passed him, and he was back with the young couple he had talked with before.

They rode through a commercial area, lightly trafficked because it was still early in the morning. But the pavement was filled with cracks and broken pavement, even some substantial chunks and rocks. Just when he was responding to the woman's question about bike shops, he hit a pothole, swiveled to the left out of control, his bike edging almost horizontally to the street. The woman's husband nipped his back tire, wrenching it to the ground. He felt himself being catapulted through the air in slow motion.

But he never hit the pavement. Again he was off to a realm of deeper sleep.

And just before he woke up with a start, the real nightmare began.

He was at a table near the dark back wall of "Sam's Spinnaker," a seedy, nondescript tavern in downtown Washington, D.C. With a somewhat warm glass of Miller's close by, he kept starting at the pillar in front of him. Actually it wasn't really a pillar, but it was a central focus for the room, which was located in the basement of a four-story office building a few blocks north of the National Mall. The bar's owner, supposedly someone named Sam, had transformed the pillar to look like a ship's mast, complete with a wooden masthead table encircling it. The ceiling was covered with dingy white, looping cloth, hopefully to resemble a ship's sail. The whole scheme didn't work – instead of a sense of sea-going openness, claustrophobia cowered in the room like a prisoner in a brig.

Dis didn't like the place, but it gave him anonymity when his problems built to the point where he thought they could be solved with a beer and a blank wall - or a faded, deteriorated, fake ship's mast and sail. The beer getting warm on his table was his fourth for the night. And he still hadn't solved his problems – his wife, Ruth; his job and that bitch, Amy Jane; his boss, Silent Sam the Skulker; his daily commute by car, train and metro; his . . . he couldn't concentrate and get these problems solved because of the guy sitting at the bar across the room.

He looked just like Dis. In fact, except for the difference in clothing, the man could be Dis himself. Every time the guy looked back Dis's way, which wasn't very often because there wasn't much back there – Dis had to stop his chain of thought. The guy's eyes just quickly scurried over the people in the back of the bar – Dis, two couples sitting in the room's lone booth, and an old man just like Dis drinking by himself, except he was nursing a beer and a shot. But the guy at the bar disrupted Dis. How could Dis get any thinking done when he felt as if he were looking in a mirror and seeing a disreputable image of himself taking quick sips at a shot glass half full of what looked to be whiskey.

The man was frantic, nervous, jumpy – Dis couldn't figure out which, but he knew something wasn't right. Small arrhythmic movements periodically swept through the man, making him shiver as if involuntarily trying to shake off a blast of granulated frost. But it wasn't cold, not in the bar or outside – Washington was experiencing an early fall day with temperatures in the 70s.

After awhile Dis, slowly losing his beer-driven, light-headed driftiness because of his concentration on the man, noticed another dimension to the man's rhythm. The guy would take a sip of his whiskey, hold it in his mouth for an unprecedented length of time, sometimes as long as a whole song on the jukebox, then tilt his head back and swallow it. Then he would shift his eyes around the place, looking to the front, then twisting on his stool and searching through the back. He never stared at anyone, but his eyes took in the whole sweep of the room. His survey finished, his concentration went back to the line of bottles until it was interrupted again by the seemingly automatic reaching for the shot glass. This had been going on for about a half-hour without a break, except once when the man had to call the bartender to refill his glass.

But the remarkable thing about the man, besides his automatic drinking – what struck Dis to the point of anxiety – was the man's physical similarity to himself. Dis didn't know how to deal with it. At one point he even took out his driver's license with his picture encapsulated in plastic, and compared it to the man's face when he turned his way.

They were amazingly similar.

But Dis felt no affinity for the man. In fact, because of the nature of his clothing, he could very well be one of the homeless characters who drifted to Washington as if the nation's capital would take care of them better than any other place they could find in their wanderings. Dis had been panhandled too often to have any feelings for them. They were more of a nuisance than a problem; slight annoyances that he had learned to disregard in his daily hurrying to work. He never gave them money, just a slight negative nod – and he never looked them in the eye.

Thinking about panhandlers set Dis to musing about his commuting. Why did he do it? The ten minute drive from his home to the commuter station; then the 25 minute train ride into Union Station; and finally the bus – 15 minutes or so – to Tilden's Department Store. Almost one hour each way every day. Two hours a day. Ten hours a week. Jesus, for working forty hours a week, he was spending a quarter of that time just getting there.

God, he would like to bike it. Just thinking about it blew away more of the alcohol weariness he had been drooping under. Two hours a day on his bike – doing something useful – not just taking off by himself for a country ride, escaping. He'd be saving money – train fare, gas, deterioration of his slowly-falling-apart Chevrolet Impala. And all that god forsaken time.

But biking to work!

Why didn't he do it? There was just no way. He could probably get through the suburbs. He was sure there were roads that paralleled the multi-laned, bicycle restricted highways which were the most direct route. In fact, he had once bought a detailed, large-scale map of Washington D. C. and vicinity just for the purpose of sketching out routes to work. It could be done, but he didn't know about the condition of the lacy, intertwined roads he would have to use. He had never really given them a test.

But riding in the central city . . . It was the city that stopped him every time he thought of commuting. My God, you just can't ride a bike through Washington, D. C. It wasn't so much the crime-infested inner city that concerned him. He could handle that – his department store was edging it now, about to be engulfed, some said – and he had learned to survive. After all, he wouldn't be biking through the tough areas at night – just early in the morning and in the evening rush hour. And there was something to be said for safety in numbers.

No, mainly it was city biking itself that stopped him. He didn't think he could survive that. The congestion, the rumbled-up streets, the erratic pedestrians and car drivers, the peripatetic teens and kids, the taxis from hell, the stopped-cold-in-the-streets delivery trucks, the J-walkers, the . . . Hell, he wasn't a bike messenger, willing to risk his thirty-five year old body for a teenage thrill or a few extra bucks.

Besides, what would he do when he got to work all sweaty and . . . He would have to change clothes. He couldn't bike in his Stacy Adams leather shoes, cotton-polyester slacks, and white shirt and tie, his standard working uniform at Tilden's. They had a lunchroom with some small lockers, but no place to shower and hardly enough room to keep a change of clothing.

He also didn't have the right kind of bike. He would have to buy a mountain bike or, perhaps, a hybrid, one with wide tires and quick shifting ability. His bike, his lovable Diamondback Master, was a road bike – meant for speeding down the relatively smooth roads of the countryside. And then what was he to do with his bike? Sure there were back rooms all over the aging department store, but they were constantly in use, stock constantly being shipped in and then moved out into the display areas.

Maybe if he didn't live where he lived. If he lived north of the city, he could use the Rock Creek Park trail and bike most of the way into the city without all the traffic and congestion. But to do that he would have to get Ruth to agree to move. Well, it just wasn't possible. No way!

The negatives kept adding up in Dis's mind, but even as he piled them up like beer cans at a fraternity party, he knew they didn't hold up. It wasn't the routes, the traffic, the clothes, the time, or anything – it was himself. He; the big, macho biker; the guy who liked to brag at parties about his long, 100 mile, weekend "centuries"; just didn't have the guts to ride his bike to work. What would people think? What would his wife say and do? How about his boss, Silent Sam? The other guys at the department store? And Amy Jane? He could picture her upturned nose moving in disdainful circles when he came in dripping with sweat.

But still . . .

About then Dis noticed a distinct change in the atmosphere of the place. The low-down sleepy ambiance was subtlety being shaken into focused, red-tinged activity – and the destitute-looking man at the bar had broken his rhythm and was now staring directly at him. He had spun around on the bar stool and was almost glaring at Dis, who through the man's scowling face and unkempt hair could clearly see the almost identical image of himself. Maybe the man could see the same resemblance in Dis. Maybe that was why he was looking so hard, was so intent in almost boring holes through Dis's head with his now suddenly clear blue eyes.

Abruptly the man stood up, turned toward the bar, swept up the loose change in front of him, and wheeled out the door. Without a word or a hint of recognition, except for the stare, he was gone. Dis wondered if he should follow, should holler after him, "Hey, buddy, stop. We have to talk. We look so alike, we could be twins. What's your name? Where you from? Are you related to me?" But he didn't. He just sat still – good, old indecisive Dis. No wonder he wasn't getting anywhere in his job, his marriage, his . . . But, hey, the man was a bum, a disreputable part of the Washington homeless army. Who the hell cared if he looked like me? He was staring because of envy. Me with my white shirt and Tilden silk tie special; with my blond, blue-eyed yuppy looks; with my in-shape body; my soft, alluring young wife; my baby who . . .

Shit! Dis stood up and was about to go, not to follow the man in hopes of meeting him, but to follow his lead in leaving the suddenly cold, dark, and uncomfortable bar. But then his caution took over and he sat down again. He didn't want to meet the man. He would wait awhile, give the guy some distance. Then a thought came into his head. He gathered his things and walked – a little shakily to the bar. When the barkeeper turned to him and asked, "Another?" Dis shook his head. "Naw, that's enough for the night. But, hey, you know that guy that just left, the one who was sitting right here?

The bartender with his frizzy crew cut nodded.

"Do you know him? He acted as if he was on to my case. What's with him anyway?"

"Hey, Sonny, what do I know? Don't get on me. He comes in once in a while. Always alone. Just sits and drinks – cheap stuff. He's losing it, though. Looking worse and worse every time I see him. Could be homeless, the way his clothes are. But, no, I don't know him. Don't know his name. But you know, you two do look alike, now that I think about it. You related?"

"No, no. I never saw him before in my life. Well, I just wondered. No big deal. No problem. Listen, I'll see you, OK?"

Dis left after stopping in the club's dirty washroom and relieving himself. Even though he had had four beers, he wasn't feeling tipsy. Maybe studying the rhythmic man had sobered him up. Maybe his mood this depressing night was so sour that not even four beers could lift his spirits. Whatever, he felt almost normal as he walked down the side street away from the bar. He came to a parking lot, almost empty now, on a corner where he had to turn to get to his Metro station. With the wariness of a seasoned big city worker he knew he should avoid such places, but it was almost clear of cars and there was still a little light left in the evening sky. What the hell, save a few steps, maybe make an earlier train, get back to Ruth quicker – but she wouldn't even be home, at some meeting probably.

Dis gingerly hopped over the wire cable surrounding the lot and started across it diagonally. Even before he passed the first car, he could feel it. Something like a sixth sense ripped through him. Protect yourself. Go back to the sidewalk. Get away.

But it was too late. He was there. The man from the bar. The man lurched towards him, a strange, gurgling voice rasping from him, "Here, take this."

Dis dodged him, but saw a knife, not in the man's outstretched hand, but in his other hand, next to his side. The knife glinted in the semi-darkness. Dis's instinct was to turn and run, but the surprise held him, froze him like a cartoon character stranded in mid-air.

The man lurched closer, stopping just in front of him. Still Dis didn't move. He could now see the man's face – his own face, scruffy and dirty, but his own face. The man's eyes appeared huge, and Dis stared into their blue depths. Behind their blankness was fear; but behind that was something that took Dis aback – a cold desperation, an almost physical determination darted from the man's eyes. Then as Dis breathed rapidly, the eyes seemed to cloud over and merge together into one huge circle of chalky white, a ghastly full and pitted moon and Dis was inexorably heading right for it.

The man lurched again almost pushing his outstretched, clenched-up hand into Dis's face. "Take it, God damn it, take it!"

But Dis was distracted by the knife in the man's other hand. It also was moving – moving towards him. The movement triggered something hidden within the hard closeness of Dis's being. He swung both of his arms up, trying to knock the knife away, but somehow the knife didn't move. It hovered in the air, a slow motion enigma of silver and bone. Then it hit the ground and spun in an slow motion circle. Hands reached for it, but only one found it – Dis's.

Almost immediately the man's body crashed into Dis. His head smashed Dis's collarbone. But Dis held the knife between them. There was little space, and in an instant there was none.

Dis could feel the knife enter the man, at first with slight resistance, then as smooth and as slick as a snake sliding into a wood pile. The man slumped, and as he fell, he slid off the knife, still held in Dis's hand. When the man hit the pavement, Dis thought he heard a hiss of air – of life – sputtering from the knife slit.

The man moved on the ground; clutched at his chest; tried to use his mouth, but could only manage an unearthly, unclear, rolling sob. Then with a last spasm of energy and control, he lifted his clenched hand up to Dis, who stood towering over him. "Here. Take this. Star. Star Oatage. Don't touch it." And then next to Dis's lightly polished brown leather shoes, the disheveled man moved no more. Ever.

Dis could not believe what had taken place. He was standing over a man who looked just like himself, but who nevertheless was dead. He was dead from a stab wound just below his breastbone from which blood was still flowing, and which had been caused by Dis.

Or had it?

All Dis could remember was the miraculous appearance of the knife in his hand and then the man lurching against both him and the sharp point of the knife. He knew instinctively that he was not guilty of anything and that right now, with a bloody, death-causing knife in his hand, he was in inexplicable trouble.

His first thought was of escape. He should drop the knife, turn and run, never looking back – just go. But wait a minute, he wasn't guilty. He had been attacked by a mugger in a parking lot and had successfully defended himself. He was a hero, a goddamn urban hero.

Were there any witnesses? He looked around. He and the body were fairly close to a car, but the parking lot, with only a smattering of cars, was empty of people. Dis could detect no movement. He searched the sidewalks within his sight and they too, surprisingly, were empty. A few cars were moving on the streets, but they were far enough away that precluded their drivers having seen the death. The parking lot and the street corner were surrounded by store buildings and warehouses that were either windowless or had windows obscured and dark, or, in one whole building, boarded up. Dis, somehow, was alone in a very public place with a knife in his hand, in the middle of millions of people, none of whom had witnessed his act of personal valor and self-defense.

"Damn," he whispered to himself. Then it hit him. Because there were no witnesses, the next person to see him under the present circumstances would automatically jump to conclusions and see him as a murderer, see him as a man holding a knife standing over a bloody body. "Run, you fool! Get the hell out of here before what you're thinking makes itself painfully true. You don't have much time, Go!"

But Dis was still rigid. His legs held him as if they were sculptured from tarred Washington D.C. parking lot pavement. He bent down and looked at the man. A nucleus of an idea pinged in his head before compassion led him to seek for the certainty of death. Even though he could see that the widening circle of blood had slowed; maybe the man was still living although he was rigid and not breathing. Dis reached for the man's shirt collar and with both hands on either side, tore the buttons apart, opening the man's chest to view. The bleeding had indeed almost ceased and there was no movement of any sort from the man. Dis slapped him and met the resistance of flesh deepening into tightness. Not even an involuntary flicker escaped. The man was dead all right. So dead that ever so quickly he was thickening into ashen indifference.

It was then that Dis noticed the hidden wallet strapped to the man's chest. Looking around him again, Dis reached down to the wallet strap, gave it a yank, and with a swift movement, removed it. Hardly taking time to think, he wrapped the strap around the wallet and put it into his pants pocket. As he did do, he noticed his own hand reddened with the man's blood.

Then he remembered the man's clenched hand and the awful, gurgling message that erupted from the man before he died. "Here. Take it." And then something about a star. A star and an outage, outrage, something like that. Something very close to that. And what was that warning? "Don't touch it." Dis grasped the man's dead hand and saw that something was clutched in it. He used both hands to force open the hand, and quickly extracted a small package – flat and covered with a foam wrapping held in place with rubber bands. Without stopping to consider what it was, Dis put it also into his pants pocket.

Did the guy have anything else? "What," Dis thought to himself, "the hell is going on? Am I the mugger? What am I doing going through this guy's stuff?" But somewhere in the back of his brain a complex shift of basic living patterns was starting to precipitate, and Dis knew he wanted to find out everything he could about the man. But when he looked around and could almost feel that someone had to be approaching the area, apprehension took over. The winds of exposure blew through his consciousness. He knew he had to run. He looked down once more, noticed the knife, wondered if he should take it, and then almost instantly, grabbed it, folded it, and pocketed it also.

One quick last glance at the man's face again startled him. Dis himself lay there – bleeding and dead in a parking lot. His own face contorted into a death grimace stared grimly at him, the eyes empty – no defiance, no fear, no hate – just two blue moons now glassing over into opaqueness. "Get away. Now. Cover your ass." Dis wrenched himself into action. With the surety of an urban worker, he strolled at a fast pace across the parking lot, knowing that actual running would cause attention, even though there didn't seem to be anybody around. Scanning his field of vision as rapidly as possible, he fast walked down the street leading to the metro. Two phrases assumed a mantra in his brain: "Don't touch it," and " Cover your ass, cover your ass."

Softer phrases – meaningless to him – also floated within his memory: "Star. Star outage. Star Outrage. Don't touch it."

The closer he came to the metro entrance, the more agitated he became. Someone had seen the whole thing he was sure. How could they not. Washington was filled with people – everywhere. Surely someone had seen it. And even worse, what if someone had seen just the aftermath – seen him standing over the body, seen him open the man's shirt, seen him take the man's wallet, seen him walk away from a dead man. God Damn, he was stupid. Why did he do these stupid things? Some consciousness within him came slightly together, but his surface anxiety became perfervid.

He found himself sweating as he walked. He knew his face must be red, his clothes damp with perspiration, his eyes enlarged and extended. He noticed his hand, red with almost dried blood, and quickly thrust it into a pocket. He would wash it off at the train station's washroom.

At one point about a block from the metro entrance, on a street of stores and slowly strolling pedestrians, he checked himself, forced himself to stop, turned to a store's plate glass window and looked at himself as if in a mirror. What he saw was a contradiction: his face was alive with unconscious action, sweat oozing from forehead and chin, but his eyes were just the opposite. They were the eyes of death: cold, hard, and becoming obscure as if from an encompassing membrane. Yet even as he watched, the two eyes merged into one, becoming a calcified full moon of escape, of search, of ultimate solitude – and this moon dully shone from his own reflected face, his own dead face.

As he awoke in that broken down motel room, his body covered with a fine sweat, and the bed clothes damp from his fitful nightmarish exertions, he could still see, just for an instant through the space between the two curtains of the room's only window, an eye-like full moon. Then a cloud melted it into mist.

Chapter 4

It was seven-thirty in the morning and Dis sat with a Styrofoam cup of Hardee's coffee at the out-of-balance table in his room at the Forest Motel in Jeffrey, Kentucky, wondering about his next step. He ached, almost all over, and though he knew he could start biking if he had to, he just plain didn't want to. But he also didn't want to stay at this "downtown hometown happy place." It was cracked and used, boring and artificial, cheap and ammonia-dusted rather than scoured – just like the girl's ten carmine fingernails, cracked and drumming, going nowhere but active as river flies after a flood.

He thought of the woman with the soft hands and voice. What was her name again – Lornaree – Lorn. Her mouth of beauty, cracked into authenticity, glimmered in his memory.

He took out his wallet and toyed with it. A fleeting memory of the last dream he had last night erupted when he opened it. The wallet wasn't really his, Hal Disberry, recent Washington, D. C., suburbanite and shoe department manager for the respected downtown flagship of the Tilden Department Store chain. (The two suburban stores; one in Annandale, Virginia, and one in Rockhurst, Maryland; were not losing money as his store was. They were successful – if breaking even could be called that.) Yes, Hal Disberry, supposedly happily married to an attractive, socially rising real estate agent.

Hal Disberry, Dis for short – Dis for all time. All time except for never. Would he ever be Dis again? Ridiculous, he would always be Dis, the man who went through 35 years of life with that name. But now he was Rob, Bob, Robert, whatever. He was Rob, but all he knew about his present self was in this wallet and in a seared mental image of a dead man in a parking lot who was his own mirror image. In the wallet, the two cards, one a driver's license and one a social security card, showed him to be Rob, Robert Clemmon, a 33 year-old man whose last address was in Owaceta, Iowa. Also in the wallet, hidden in the bill section under a leather flap, was a picture of three people standing in front of a one story bungalow in a place surrounded by trees, bushes, and, in the distance, a flat horizon. A man almost identical to himself stood facing the camera, a faint smile tracing his nondescript, but not unpleasant face. Next to him was a young girl of perhaps five, a gap-toothed smile beaming from a face whose classic symmetry gave signs of rich beauty in the future. And next to her, arms entwined, was a woman whose face had that beauty underneath a mop of disheveled hair. The man was Robert Clemmon, Dis was sure of that, and he assumed that the woman and child were his family and that they lived in Owaceta, Iowa.

Why Robert Clemmon would give up this classic, American family and end up a drunken, homeless murder victim in Washington, D. C. was beyond Dis's ability to figure out. What had happened? Was it something like his own small domestic tragedy? How could that be with a daughter as pretty and full of life at the one in the picture? And the woman a combination of classic beauty and somewhat rough edged wholesomeness. Why would he give up these to drift through the sour underside of big city life and end up as a question mark on a morgue attendant's data sheet?

Dis was intrigued by these questions. In off-moments on the road he fantasized finding out the answers – of going to Owaceta and seeing if the woman and child were still there – of discovering why the family broke apart. But then he always came back to the warning to himself to stay away. After all, he had killed the man. The farther away from the man's previous life, the better. Who knows what was hidden beneath the tranquil happiness that the camera lens had picked up on that sunny day in what he assumed was Iowa? Still Dis had to confess that he would like to know. After all, for all practical purposes, he was Rob Clemmon. And even now he was slowly, erratically moving west – getting geographically closer to Iowa, even though that was not his intention.

But in reality he wasn't Rob Clemmon. To himself he was still Dis, and would always remain so. However as a living person in America, all that was left of Dis was a small piece of paper laminated in plastic, confined now in the down tube of his bike, pushed down by the seat post, possibly never to be resurrected again ever. The immortal remains of Dis Disberry: simply words on a driver's license.

    Hal Disberry
    1846 Hankin Road
    Rockhurst, MD 12654
    SS# 546-78-9837
    Birth: 3-14-64 Sex: M Ht: 5-11 Wt: 165 Eyes: Blue

When he made "the break," he had wondered if he should keep anything. He wanted to make a clean break, to never be connected to his past again. But on the other hand, he was Dis. Could he just simply let himself go? It got down to a locked toilet booth at the Charleston, West Virginia, train station. There he took every remaining piece of paper that had his name on it, tore it into shreds, dropped it between his legs into the toilet, and then reached behind himself awkwardly and pulled the flush lever. He didn't even watch them go because he was staring at the driver's license. It was the one piece of himself left. Should he cut it into shards with his key chain knife and then toss them into the next trash bin he encountered? Everything told him to do just that. "Make a clean break." And also the constant chant: "Cover your ass."

But he hesitated. What if somehow, somewhere, he needed to prove that he indeed was Dis. Oh, his fingerprints were on file somewhere, a number of places actually; but what if he needed immediacy, what if he couldn't wait? So he kept the license. He stuffed it securely into his front pocket and walked out of the toilet not completely someone else now, still the old Dis, even if just through a thin piece of laminated plastic. Later the license in his pocket became too heavy a burden to bear. A minor slip-up, an accident, and the game was up. He would be back to Ruth and Hankin Road, but certainly not Tilden's Department Store. At least he knew he was through with that store forever.

After he bought his bicycle in a downtown Charleston store – one distinguished by a dusty assortment of old bicycles hanging hit-or-miss from the ceiling – and had spent some time adjusting the seat on it, he realized that the tube directly below the seat could accommodate the license, if he bent it into a half tube. He had trouble doing this, though. When he bent it far enough, the plastic snapped. He had to snap it two more times, forming a small square shape before it would go easily into the tube.

He opened his wallet. Actually the wallet wasn't his; his was probably in a landfill somewhere near Charleston, West Virginia, after he had pushed it into the slot of a trash receptacle at the train station. The wallet he was using was the same one he had taken from the dead man in the parking lot, minus the strap. If he was going to take the man's identity, he would do it completely. Actually the cloth, Velcro-closing wallet was nondescript; it could hardly be linked to anyone in particular. His own wallet, on the other hand, was given to him by Ruth three Christmases ago and he was sure that she would remember it.

He took a sip of coffee and then checked the bill section of the wallet. He knew his money supply was down, so he wanted to check it exactly. He counted three twenty dollar bills, one ten, a five, and four ones. When he took them out and opened the concealing flap of the secret compartment, he confirmed the two hundreds that were all he had left. Being on the road on a bicycle was great as long as the money held out. He had reined in his spending, but still $279 and some odd change was all he had in this world. Maybe it was time to stop and see if he could stockpile some more.

He had started out with almost exactly $1,750 all but $350 of it in one hundred-dollar bills. The saving began almost three years before he left, right after he had come home early from a Saturday morning bike club ride on an out-of-the-way route and noticed Bill Gerlock's car parked about a block away from his house. As he was riding up his block, he caught a glimpse of Bill, the owner of a local furniture shop who was a golf fanatic, a real tee-head in Dis's opinion. Bill was leaving Dis's house – walking down the side sidewalk – and this didn't seem right. No one was supposed to be home. His wife was out selling houses.

Dis braked discretely and pulled over to the intersecting side street, behind Junior Buckrupt's pickup truck. Bill continued to his car, not noticing the staring bicyclist. Soon, sure enough, the garage door on Dis's house swung up and there was Ruth, backing out a little faster than ordinary. She swung away from Dis's vantage point, and took off, leaving the door to descend with, what seemed to Dis, a sudden clank of finality. Later when he asked her how her morning had gone, she crisply said, "Oh, you don't really want to know. I almost had a sale, though. Out near Hillcrest Heights. A nice, old colonial, but they're still asking too much."

"Oh, you weren't in town then. I thought I saw your car."

"No, it must have been someone else. Where'd you see it? Weren't you out biking?"

"Yea, but I came home early – about eleven." Here Dis lied. He was really home by ten-thirty.

"No, I was still out in Hillcrest Heights. Probably someone else around with a car like mine."

After that every time he took his pay check to the bank he made out the deposit slip for $25 less than the amount and asked the girl for the twenty-five in cash, knowing that his monthly statement would only record the deposit. His wife usually just glanced at the statement when it came every month; she had her own income and checking account and she really didn't care about his as long as he paid the household bills and kept her generally aware of their financial situation. He didn't really know why he was doing this, but somehow it seemed necessary to him. A secret nest egg of readily available cash became, just like that, a minor obsession to him. He kept the money between pages 36 and 37 of the June, 1994, issue of *Bicycling Magazine*, about half way down the stack on his bookcase shelf, a place he knew she would never notice. Three times he took the accumulated small bills, because of their bulk, to the bank and exchanged them for $100 bills.

By the time he left he was able to retrieve $850 from the confines of an article entitled: "Self-contained Bike Touring for Beginners." He almost reread the article, but he didn't have the time. Another $650 came from his last check. Instead of his normal deposit, he had the entire check cashed. The girl looked quizzically when he asked for that much cash, but he explained that he was going on a business trip and he needed it to impress some clients. The business trip was halfway correct, but he didn't have any clients, had never had any, and, besides, throwing money around to make an impression was not his life style. The girl gave him the money, six hundreds and the rest in small bills, and said, "Well, I'm impressed. Have a good trip." If only she knew the irony of her statement, issued with just a hint of a smile, as if strained through her net of unruly hair.

The last of his money came from a cash advance from Tilden's. To them and his boss he was going on a business trip the next day, the annual buyer's trip to New York. They begrudgingly had provided him with airplane tickets and confirmed hotel reservations. Also tradition at Tilden's called for lower level managers to have some extra ready cash when they went to New York; Mr. Tilden himself remembering in a famous internal communication when he accidentally spent all his cash in a restaurant and had to walk up lower Broadway instead of taking a cab.

So Dis, with $1,750 on his person about five weeks before when he had left his house on Hankin Road, was left with $270 now as he sat in a decidedly run-down motel near the downtown of Jeffrey, Kentucky, nursing an extensive case of road rash and in need of a new bike helmet.

He had taken his time that Wednesday morning, which seemed so long ago that he had to search to bring it back. He was flying to New York; or so everyone, especially his wife, thought; so he could take his time at breakfast; he didn't have to be at the store as his usual 7:30. He had a 10:30 a.m. flight out of Dulles. Surprisingly, his wife was up and cheerful that morning, and she actually touched him when she appeared in the kitchen in a cream colored wrapper which he had given her for her birthday the previous year. His mind was feverish with what he was about to do, but since the night of the death in the parking lot he had had much practice in keeping a calm outward appearance on top of turmoil inside.

With his toast before him and a cup of coffee in his hand, he felt her two hands on his shoulders almost before he sensed her coming down the stairs or smelled her faint morning scent. He steeled himself and didn't move. She hadn't touched him for at least two months; what was going on? Her voice was light, which he knew came only when she was either completely at ease or just the opposite: working so hard at flirting that her voice became unnaturally becalmed – a whisper of girlish coquettishness, instead of her normal hard-edged, almost shrill tones.

"That's right. You're off on your buyer's trip today, aren't you?"

What could he say? A myriad of responses fluttered in his head. This was it, the last time he would ever see her, talk to her, smell her fruity essence. After nine years – actually almost ten – of marriage, this was the end. Should he be nice to her? Sarcastic? Bitter? Unresponsive? Or just plain nasty? He would try nice, although he didn't know if he could control himself. "Yep, Off to the big one. Gonna take the 10:30 from Dulles and should be at Kennedy in about an hour. Got the first meeting this afternoon at three."

"Well, aren't you going to have fun; three days in New York City." She fussed with a grapefruit, slicing it in half, and then started to separate the sections.

He almost jumped at her softly uttered bait, but held himself in check. "Yeah, I should be back on Saturday – Saturday morning. I'll leave my car at the airport so you won't have to bother." He couldn't resist. "But you'll be working Saturday morning, right?"

She paused at her grapefruit and turned to him, a slight edge in her voice. Why had he put that slight emphasis on the phrase, "Saturday morning"? "Right, I'll be working this Saturday. But, hey, go to New York. Work hard. Have some fun.

Are you going to be able to take in any plays? Remember when you took me with you and we went to see "Evita"? That was fun."

Change the subject, Dis thought. Don't get caught up in sentimental reminiscences. It's too late. Still, he did look up from the magazine he was reading. She was an attractive woman. Her broad face, now without any trace of makeup, was regular with wide spaced eyes, somewhat squinty; beautiful full eyebrows, one of her best features; and a mouth that danced when lively. Her body matched her face; she had a big frame and she, in her mid-thirties, was just now settling into it, hips spreading into her mid-section like a mid-summer stream slowly weeping through a break in its bank. But she knew how to hold herself in and dress effectively to emphasize her maturing figure. Now on an ordinary morning in just pajamas and a wrap she was attractively rounding.

Her breasts, concealed somewhere behind the soft layers of cloth, were ample, but seemed to be decreasing as she filled elsewhere, perhaps in some obscure symbiotic relationship. Yet Dis knew their softness and symmetrical beauty, and for a second he wanted to brush them with his fingers before he gave them up forever. The last time he saw them was three nights ago, when, in a huff, while he was trying to get to sleep, she rushed into the bedroom, pulled off her lounging clothes, except for her panties, and stood before him. "That son-of-a-bitch, Danny. He wants me to check the figures on that house I sold yesterday, and he wants it right now. I gotta go down to the office for just a little bit. I won't be long."

Danny was her boss, a string-bean pill-popper with a bad case of acne, even though he was almost sixty. He was also compulsive about reports being absolutely correct and he had a habit of working on them at any hour of the day or night.

Dis opened his half sleepy eyes and was taken aback by how beautiful she was. It wasn't lust that stirred him, although it should have been. He had been without sex for some three months. No, what made him almost shiver was something akin to looking at a well done nude painting or sculpture. Especially now that she was thickening out, his mind clicked to Delacroix or Raphel, but not quite to Rubens. Actually for a germ of time, he held in his mind Thomas Hart Benton's "Persephone" as he gazed at his wife's unblushing beauty. He felt like the man in the picture too, even though he was married to the beautiful subject standing almost naked in, not grass, but his own bedroom. But she quickly put on a pair of slacks, a bra, and a slipover sweater, and breezed out with hardly another look in his direction.

Now at breakfast on his last day with her, he took a last bite of toast, reached for his coffee cup, and said, "'Evita', yeah. But this time there's no time for plays. Old Henry says I gotta cover both shoes and underwear. Jim Garvey, you remember him. He used to have men's clothing. Well, they never replaced him so we all have to share a part of his old responsibility. Shoes and socks – and now underwear. No, I don't think I'll see any plays."

He knew she'd be bored with his work talk and he was right. She had stopped in the middle of serrating the fruit and was studying the calendar hanging down from one of the lower cabinets. "Jesus, today is the 25th. Shit, I forgot all about that appointment with the bathroom man. You know, about the hot tub. And there's also some houses that I want to drive by and talk to their owners." As she brought the two halves of grapefruit to the table and gave him one – an unexpected gesture because breakfast for them was usually strictly get-your-own-and-like-it – she continued to babble on about housing sales prospects. "You know that house on Kilmore, about . . . between 6th and 7th . . ."

Dis turned her off. He sat almost slumped in his chair, morosely looking down at the grapefruit. Despair swamped his mind and threatened to flood his body. It was almost too much to bear. Her breasts and now a goddamn grapefruit. His eyes became watery as he realized it all came down to this. He really should pull a Jimmy Cagney act and push the grapefruit in her face, do something that would mark a finality, that would bring this whole thing to an end with words and action and emotion and rage.

But he was Dis – Hal Disberry – and he just didn't act that way. He talked about men's shoes and underwear. He took off on a bike, for Christ's sake. He calmly observed the garage door descending on his life, and when he looked down at his Tilden Department Store shoes in a parking lot all he saw was a goddamn full moon becoming more and more opaque.

She touched him again. This time on the sleeve of his Windsor weave shirt. "What's the matter? Are you crying?"

He was crying, for Christ's sake. But how could he explain it to her? He wiped away a tear, pulled himself together, and said, "It must be the grapefruit. I got some of the juice in my eye. What were you saying?"

"Just that I have to get going. Busy, Busy. I'll drink my coffee while I'm dressing. Are you packed? Do you have enough clean shirts? Oh, don't forget your electric razor. Remember last time you had to buy one of those Jiffy ones and you cut your chin . . ." By this time she was in the bedroom and he didn't have to face her scrutiny, something which neither of them had been doing for the last few years.

So Dis ate his grapefruit. By the time he finished and was taking the last, lukewarm swallow from his coffee cup, she raced in and was just about out the door before she remembered that he was going to New York. For formality's sake she returned to him and almost ceremoniously pecked him with her lips as she said, "New York, whoa. Well, don't work too hard and have a good time. I'll see you sometime Saturday, right?"

"Right."

And she was gone – in a soft rustle of skirt and blouse and a clicking of small-heeled shoes on the garage floor. Dis could hear the car door opening, but when he didn't hear it close, he looked up. She was at the interconnecting door. "Hey, don't forget Danny is throwing that dinner party on Saturday, and we've gotta be there. I think it's at six-thirty." And she was gone with not even a pause for a reply.

Dis got up, put his coffee cup in the sink, then took the remains of the grapefruit to the cutting board, sliced it into small sections, turned on the sink water and the garbage disposal, and very deliberately pushed each small section into the obliterating opening.

That was five weeks ago – when he had $1750, a job, a wife, a house, and a life, of sorts, in one of the great metropolitan centers of the world. He was Dis then. Now he was someone who he didn't know called Robert Clemmon. He had about $270, a bike, a few clothes, some camping gear, and a few hours left in the Forest Motel. Maybe it was time to shift. Five weeks on the road on his bicycle had turned from solitary escape to apprehensive independence, sometimes even joyful independence; but now he felt the need to restock, to open up, to replenish. And, obviously, he had to get some more money.

He opened his left rear pannier and carefully took out his one set of "civilian" clothing. The long, light blue summer-weight pants and the red and yellow plaid sport shirt were both of "wrinkle-free" polyester material, and, as he hung them on the motel's hangers, he noted that they were not badly crushed from the many days in the tightly packed bike bag. He had only one set of shoes, except for the canvas slip-ons which he wore sometimes at night or when his riding shoes were wet. His riding shoes were not "official" biking shoes, but merely a good set of Rebock walking shoes that slipped easily into and out of the clips with which his bicycle was equipped.

Having worked with shoes for the last few years, Dis knew that much of the shoe business was filled with hype. Biking shoes were especially guilty. In essence, they were almost all the same – a number of brands even being made by the same slave-labor factories in Southeast Asia. And they weren't that much different than other running or walking shoes. Comfort, quality materials, and careful construction were the keys, not the bewildering quirks of styling or gimmicks.

Biking shoes were bad, but kids' athletic shoes were hopeless. It was all hype. Pumps, humps, padding, neon, air injectors, gel pads – Dis had been inundated with these minute variation on the basic athletic shoe while he had been working. He had had to put up with innumerable salesmen spouting this trick tab or that plastic sac. On more than one occasion, he was tempted to grab a salesman, spin him around, make him face the big advertising sign that hung over his shoe department, and yell "Get Real!" into his face, but he didn't. He listened to the salesmen, agreed with them, bought from them, and sold their products. God, he was glad to be out on the road away from "Get Real!"

He took his toiletries kit from his left front pannier, went to the motel's bathroom, a gray and dingy room with a lone sink and a small mirror above it etched with wrinkles of age. The sink's bowl had one particularly distasteful blemish that had been patched over with some sort of pseudo-ceramic white material. It hardly covered the stain, merely adding a lumpy chalky texture to the off-white bowl. The shower-bathtub was a twin to the sink bowl, except that its seams were cracking into powdered lines of brittle caulk, some of it gritting beneath his feet when he stepped in. But he showered, taking extra care to protect his bandage from the spurting water. He shaved with the decaying mirror, and even felt good about himself when he finally dressed in his at-home outfit. His shirt, however, was short sleeved, exposing his bandage.

Since it was about ten o'clock, he had to make a decision about staying for another night. The place was cheap enough, but hardly the place for an extended stay. What if he found that he didn't like Jeffrey, that he didn't want to stay, or, even worse, the reoccurrence of his constant traveling fear, that he couldn't stay? Also what could he do with his bike? For the last five weeks all he did was get on it everyday and ride: he had no need to store it. He decided he'd check with Miss Fingernails at the desk. Maybe he could leave it at the motel while he checked out the town. The girl, however, wasn't at the desk. Instead, an enormous man filled up the cramped office, almost swallowing up the office's only piece of furniture, the tiny chair that the girl had been sitting on last night. As soon as Dis entered, the man's face lit up. "Well, hello there. Good morning. What can I do for you? We're downtown; we're hometown; and we're happy."

Dis looked at the man sharply. Was he putting him on?

But no, the fat man couldn't be stopped. "You look like you need some assistance on this beautiful day here in Jeffrey. Well, you came to the right place. I'm big, but I'm full of help. What's that you need now, old buddy?"

The man seemed to be genuine, but still Dis couldn't be sure. "Well, I'm down in number three, and I was wondering . . ."

"Oh, you're the man who came in late last night on a bicycle. God almighty, that's terrific! My daughter couldn't get over that. 'He came in without a car, just a bicycle, Dad, a bicycle. Not a motorcycle. And he wanted to put it in his room. Said he was riding it across this country.' Every once in a while we get someone like you, but you're the first in a long time. Hey, you don't look so good. What did you do to your arm?"

Dis didn't want to get too friendly with this man, but the man appeared to be unstoppable. He seemed to be either completely loquacious, almost compulsively so; or, to the suspicious Dis, somehow very interested in him. Dis decided to be wary. And he made an immediate decision. He would stay at the motel another day. "Oh, I had a little accident yesterday in town here. Say, is it all right if I stay another night down there in number three?"

"Sure enough, my buddy. Let's see." He shuffled through some cards on his desk, all the while sputtering with labored breath and oozing around on his fulcrum of a chair, which was almost completely invisible beneath him. "You paid for last night – twenty seven ninety five – cash. We have a deal here. Second night in a row to our cash paying friends is one dollar off. We like to encourage people to stay with us here in Jeffrey, you know, to get to know our little town instead of just rushing through it going someplace else. And we also don't like to pay that little extra charge to the credit card companies. 'Course most people still use plastic, but we're old fashioned here; we like you cash paying customers. So we give you a buck off if you pay cash and stay another day. Wadda' you say?"

"Sounds fine with me." Dis didn't want to encourage the man too much, but at the same time the guy probably knew everything possible to know about the town and the people in it. He might be handy to get to know. But that was jumping the gun. Right now all Dis wanted to do was to walk around a bit and see about making a little money.

Dis had his twenty dollar bills out and was handing the payment to the fat man when the phone rang. The man took the money and did some writing on Dis's card while he talked. "Hey, Frank, old buddy. I'm glad you called. Besides that we got a busted door and lock in one of the shacks. You gotta get over pretty quick and get to working. I'd like to do it myself, you know that." Here the man started laughing, almost bubbles of mirth popping from his mouth in a stream of hiccuping hilarity. "Oh, bull shit, this can't wait. You can go to Tumphrey any time you want, but I need you here. You know I can't do it, and my beautiful Doreen just ain't fit for doing that kind of work, and Calleen was right in this office all last night while we was at the square dancing so she's still sleeping. So, Frank, I'll be looking for you. You get over here. Tell her that Tumphrey can wait. OK, old buddy?" He listened for awhile, at one point erupting again in a bubbling stream of laughter, and finally gave Dis his change and waved him to go. Dis walked out, leaving the man stuffed in the tiny office, looking like a huge melting golf ball slowly engulfing its tee.

Chapter 5

In front of the motel, Dis moved in the opposite direction from the Hardee's toward what appeared to be a smattering of commercial buildings. He was looking for a bicycle shop, a clothing store, where he could buy a long-sleeved shirt, and, of course, what did she say its name was? "We Got It?" But that's out on the west side, he remembered she had mentioned. He also, almost subconsciously, kept attuned for a printing company.

He started walking past modest wood-frame residences mixed with some turn-of-the-century, more imposing homes. Some of the homes were in disrepair, but most were tidy and neat; not showcases, but well lived-in homes. A few commercial structures, generally on corners, interrupted the flow of residences. After a few blocks, homes gave way to businesses, but Dis noticed even more businesses down the side streets to the south. At a street called Clayton, Dis followed one of these streets for one block until he came to Main. This street was evidently the heart of the downtown, for in both directions from where he stood, commercial establishments lined the somewhat narrow street. Beyond to the south, Clayton veered and on its east side rose a multi-storied, glaringly white, gingerbread-trimmed courthouse. Other streets to the east and south formed a square around this classic courthouse.

Down Main, about half a block, an old fashioned sign proclaiming "Clark's Department Store," protruded at right angles from the line of buildings. Dis thought, "Yeah, sure, that's all I need, a failing department store. Well, I could probably get a job there. No, wait a minute, don't even think about it. It's too close to the past, too connected."

However, it might be a good place to buy a long-sleeved shirt.

Clark's was neat, slightly decrepit, but also halfway up-to-date. Dis felt good in the place and he found exactly what he was looking for – a broadcloth dress shirt, on sale for just $9.95. As he walked through the men's clothing area, he noticed a display of ties on sale. Should he buy one? They were cheap enough, only $4.95, and a tie would make a good impression at a retail store. But no, he had had enough of the life of ties. A dress shirt was close enough to a return to the past as he could take. He walked right by the ties.

Nearby was a Walgreen's multi-purpose drug store. He thought of bandages. The mild pain that Dis felt from his arm and leg reminded him that he would need to change his bandages. He went in, and acting like a citizen of the town, strolled through the aisles looking at items of a more permanent nature than could be carried on a bike. He ended up, however, buying just a box of gauze and a roll of adhesive tape.

Then, out in front and looking up and down the street which fronted on the imposing courthouse, Dis felt a sense of satisfaction. He felt a degree of livability about the place. The town certainly wasn't spectacular, but it had its sense of time and place. It was unhurried. It was reasonably sure about itself. And if it was a backwater compared to Dis's suburban life outside of Washington, it certainly wasn't a swamp – foul, still, and rank. At least it didn't seem that way to him on first impression.

He took his two purchases and retraced his steps to the motel, going through the parking lot to avoid the gaze of the fat man, or so he thought. He changed into his new shirt and set off walking again, this time to the west. As he walked, he rehearsed what he would say to the convenience store manager. He had to get all the things about his new identity right – all the details he had planned hour upon hour while riding his bike. A slip-up might cause suspicion, and, ever the possibility, a question to the authorities. Just remember, he told himself, "Cover your ass." If anything goes wrong, just walk out. Nothing would ever happen. He, himself, as manager and in charge of hiring for his department, had had innumerable people abruptly leave in the midst of interviews or while filing out application blanks. What could he do? They walked; he went to the next applicant.

The street, which Dis realized was the main highway lacing through the town and which was probably designated as such because the old main street was too narrow to be enlarged, changed from strictly residential to newer commercial buildings. Used car agencies led the pack, usually crammed into what had probably been a vacant lot next to a residence, now the agency's office. Then came a strip mall of a video store, a local instant pizza shop, and a launderette complete with game machines. This gave way to the ubiquitous national franchises for hamburgers, oil changes, ice cream, tacos, all-you-can-stuff steak, and hair care. A little farther on, he skirted a car dealer, walking on a thin strip of grass, just enough for a mower, between the curbing and the highway. After he passed a line of vans, parked so close they looked like a shiny, multicolored insect segmented into globular body parts, he came upon his target.

The "We Got It" was new, gleaming, and ugly.

Its parking lot wasn't even paved yet – its gravel base lay baking in the late morning heat. But the orange and green plastic sheeting which covered the building was blinding in its reflectorized brilliance. A sign, poking from its shiny facade, featured a caricatured male face with an enormous mouth from which blasted in a comic book balloon, "We Got It!" Below it, taped to the front window, hung a temporary banner, flapping in the slight breeze, announcing "Grand Opening." Below it in smaller letters were: "We Got: Pepsi - 24 cans - $2.95."

Dis walked to the entrance without hesitation. He thought he would look foolish to stop or turn around and retreat, since he had no car. His first impression of the place was of repugnance, but then he thought that its very assembly line, stamped-out appearance would add to its anonymity, and that's what he was looking for.

Next to the entrance was a small, hand-lettered "Now Hiring – See the Manager" sign, which made Dis mentally thank the woman who had tended him last night. Lornaree. . . ree . . . whatever, she knew what was going on. The woman behind the island-like checkout counter, however, was someone whom Dis would probably never thank. She was a skinny, wizened, witch-like woman, dressed like a scarecrow in a one-piece house dress that looked as if it had come from a Sears Roebuck catalog of the 1930s. She had a lit cigarette dangling from her tight lips, even though a sign facing the customers proclaimed, "Please – no smoking." Since no one was waiting near the counter, he spoke to her. "Could I speak to the manager?"

"Guess so. You're speaking to her."

"Oh, well, I saw the sign on the door about help wanted and I'm interested."

"You are, huh. Well, lemme see." She rumbled around behind the counter searching for something. "Here, take this over there and fill it out." She had pointed to a small alcove where four new video game machines blinked mechanically, occasionally erupting in a cavalcade of light and subdued sound. Dis leaned over the glass of a "Galactic Exploiter" machine and started to fill in the application. When he came to the address line, he hesitated momentarily. What address should he put down? The motel? He didn't even know its address. But then he thought, what the hell, I've got to put down something and wrote in "Forest Motel, room 3, Highway 84, Jeffrey, Kentucky." His name, of course, was Robert Clemmon. And his social security number, according to plan, was that of the dead Robert. Under "Previous Employment" he put down "Emory Steel Company, Pittsburgh, Pennsylvania – Shipping Clerk." There was no Emory Steel Company that he knew of, but if she asked, he would tell her that he was laid-off without benefits and was now traveling, searching for new opportunities – and that he liked Jeffrey and thought he might settle here. The other details of the applications, such as references and education, were also all made up. He gave up his three years of college and his associate degree in marketing for the simple, "Diploma – Central High School, Flagtown, Pennsylvania."

When he had finished, he returned to the counter, where the woman was lighting up a new cigarette. Dis noticed that the cigarette was a misshapen, lumpy, paper-flapping mess, held together mostly by her fingers – she evidently was making them from scratch, rolling her own. Without a word, he gave her the application. She didn't even glance at it, simply stuffed it somewhere behind the counter and then said, "Can you work second shift?"

Taken slightly aback, Dis hesitated, "Well . . . I . . . I guess so. Second shift means what hours?"

Holding the cigarette in front of her lips, she replied: "Three to eleven. Eight straight hours. You gotta eat on the job, cause we ain't got nobody else. 'Cept I'll come in from about five to seven when it gets real busy – if it ever does, that is. So far there ain't hardly been enough business to stir a hunk of melted Jello."

The hours were not what Dis wanted. In fact, having worked regular day-time hours all his life, he hadn't even considered anything else. But it made sense. Off-shifts were undesirable; any new help would have to take them. He replied; "Well, I guess three to eleven sounds OK. When can I start?"

"This afternoon."

"Whoa. That's pretty quick. But, what the heck, why not?"

She let out a stream of smoke, almost into his face. "I'm so sick of working twelve, thirteen hours a day. It's ridiculous. My husband runs the farm all day and then comes in here for twelve hours every night. I don't know why we even built this place. It's a bunch of pig shit, pardon the expression, but I'd rather be home cleaning up for those pigs than here wading around in this pig shit. I'm just about to scream."

The burning end of the cigarette was dangerously close to her lips; but evidently long practice let her almost spit the tattered remnant of paper, tobacco, and glowing end into an empty Disney glass (Goofy chasing Mickey) on her right. The glass was filled with water and other bits and pieces of cigarette butts. To Dis it was disgusting.

"You come in about two this afternoon and I'll show you the ropes. The old man won't be happy about the money we'll be paying you, but, Jesus Christ, we gotta have some relief."

"Aah, what is the pay?"

"Minimum. You know what that is?"

Dis had hired enough stock boys so he knew all the ins and outs of the minimum pay law, but he had to remember the lie he was living. "Well, it's been a while since I worked minimum wage. What is it now?"

"$5.15 an hour. Shit . . ." She started almost talking to herself. "What with all the bookkeeping, I don't know if we'll even break even. The old man will be uptight, that's fer sure, but I can handle him. We shorely need some help; that's fer sure." While she was carping to herself, she almost automatically started rolling another cigarette. Dis watch in awe as the various ingredients appeared out of nowhere, were assembled by her marvelously dexterous fingers into a recognizable form, and then with a quick lick from her tiny darting tongue and a quick flick from a plastic lighter, the finished cigarette, reeking and glowing, was dangling from her lips. The process was so mechanical that Dis wondered if she even knew that she was doing it. "Anyway, you be here about two. I gotta show you a bunch of stuff. Let's see, what's your name?" She started shuffling around behind her, but Dis came to the rescue.

"Rob. Robert Clemmon."

"OK, Rob. About two. All right?"

Dis left, feeling slightly punched in the gut. Minimum wage - around 200 dollars a week. He'd have to find someplace real cheap to live if he wanted to save anything. He couldn't continue staying at the motel at about thirty dollars a night; that'd be more than he was making – too much.

As he retraced his route back to the motel, Dis made a mental list of things to do before two o'clock, in just about three hours. He should find some inexpensive place to live; check his bike out thoroughly; find a bike shop and get a new helmet; get something to eat, probably a restaurant meal because the "We Got It" lady had said he'd have to eat on the job; and he'd really like to talk to Lornaree – Lorn – again.

"Wait a minute. I'm working nights. I'll probably never get a chance to even thank her because she works days. Hey, I can't even return the bandage stuff she used on me – shoot, why didn't I even think of replacement stuff when I bought my bandages at Walgreen's this morning. Maybe I'll just walk down there again and go a little further and see if I can find her printing shop and a bike shop."

So about 11:30 Dis found himself in front of a rather imposing building – solid stone, turn-of-the-century, beau arts architecture, with a sign over an impressive arched entrance which read, "Charles Smath and Son; Printing and Publishing." It was more than the one or two employee, quick-print shop that he expected. He went in and asked a pimply young man at a front desk, " McAbby, Lornaree McAbby. Could I see her?"

Within 30 seconds, Lorn, looking absolutely refreshing in a flowing skirt and silk blouse, breezed into the room. Her hair seemed fuller than the night before, and the subtle makeup she used emphasized the naturalness or her freckled nose and cheeks. An off-color shade of lipstick blended nicely with her off-blonde hair coloring. To Dis she seemed transformed from a helpful, sympathetic fellow biker to an independent woman of business – efficient and effective. And very attractive to him.

"Hi," he almost stammered. "I wanted to replace the bandages from last night, but I took your advice and got a job at that convenience store. Second shift, so I probably wouldn't have a chance to bring them to you until my day off, which I don't know when it'll be . . ."

She interrupted, "How are you anyway? How's your head? Could you sleep? You don't suppose there was any real damage to your head?"

"Hold on. Hold on. I'm OK. Just a slight headache – I didn't even take aspirin this morning. So I guess the head is OK – it must be, I was able to deal with that lady who runs the "We Got It.""

"Yeah, she's something else, isn't she? Deep down she's OK though. You'll find out when you start working for her. Her husband. Well, I don't know about

George."

"Oh, you know them?"

"Just for business. They had some fliers printed up when they opened and I helped them out with it. Also some newspaper ads."

"I see. Well, I don't want to take up any of your time. But I would like to thank you again. You really helped me last night and I appreciate it very much."

"Hey, that's OK. You're a biker. We have to stick together and help each other out."

"Right. Well, thanks again."

Things were a bit awkward. It was obvious that they both felt an attraction to the other. Dis was certainly drawn, but he didn't know how to continue. She, however, very naturally picked up the continuation. "A bunch of us go biking almost every Sunday morning. If you're not working this Sunday, why not join us? We meet at 8 o'clock at the Hardee's on highway 84, you know the one close to the Forest Motel. This week, let's see, Frankie is going to lead us up and down the bluffs. Come on, join us. We have a good time and – well, you know – get some good exercise."

Dis replied, "Well, right now I think I'll take a rest from biking, but by Sunday maybe I'll be able to move my arm." He laughed. "Heck, by then I'll probably even be using it for things like shaving, eating – scratching my neck."

She laughed with him, a melodious riff on her normal soft voice that seemed to enter also into her eyes. They danced with the music of her laughing lips. "Well, I have to get back to work. Sunday at Hardee's, right?"

"Right."

Dis left, feeling happy, almost buoyant. Here he was stranded in a backwater town, his body itching with road rash, about to take the lowest paid job in his life, without a regular bed to sleep in, and he was walking down the street with a big, shit-eating grin on his face. Damn, he felt good talking to her. Damn.

Chapter 6

Sunday couldn't come too quickly for Dis. He was settling into a new life –
one that was a couple of notches lower than anything he had ever experienced or
contemplated, but one that was strangely comfortable to him. It shouldn't be, but it
was. His job at the "We Got It" was almost fun, except for the eight straight hours of
standing and the occasional problem customer. Surprisingly, most patrons of the
convenience store were friendly, honest, and helpful. They knew what they wanted,
they knew its price, and they didn't want to spend time pondering it. They weren't
like the finicky shoe customers back at Tilden's, forever sending Dis or his fellow
clerks on search-and-locate missions to the back room for that elusive exact style or
size. At the "We Got It," contrary to the implied guarantee of the store's name, if the
product wasn't in front of the customer, it wasn't there – period. They didn't have it.
The customer knew there was another similar place down the road a bit, so no big
deal.

Also, the place wasn't that busy, although it had a steady stream of cars
pulling up and customers popping in. The flow was small enough that Dis was never
overwhelmed by people waiting overlong for service. Marge, the smoking woman
who hired him, even gave up coming in around the late afternoon "rush hour," since it
wasn't that busy. Dis was happy about that; it was difficult for two people to work
behind the counter without getting in each other's way, especially when one had a lit
cigarette constantly hovering in the air. Marge did, however, drop in throughout his
shift, just to keep an eye on things. Dis knew that she was watching him, but it didn't
bother him. He'd do the same thing if he were in her situation. Besides, as Lorn had
said, Marge wasn't a bad sort. Except for her smoking and her taciturn manner, she
was generally agreeable. And she was very decisive. Snap, and her mind was made
up. With Dis, she had evidently evaluated him when he walked in the door on the day
she hired him. And her judgment was positive. He had proven to be honest,
responsible, and not lazy. Beyond that, she didn't care.

Also, Dis was still living at the Forest Motel. When he returned that first
day after accepting the job at the "We Got It," the fat man was gone and the teenage
girl was back in the office. As he was going to his room after an unsatisfactory meal
at a downtown cafe, she yelled out the door at him, "Hey, you, Mr. Biker, how's your
arm?"

"It's just hanging there. I can't feel a thing – except the pain."

That broke her up. The fingernails came up to her mouth as she almost
yelled an uncontrollable laugh into her palm. Finally she looked him square in the
face and said, "Show me your arm."

"Well, old Doc Clemmon would like to open the operating theater to you
while he changes bandages, but he's in a bit of a rush right now. Got to be to work, so
the bandages will have to wait."

"Wait a minute," she giggled. "You got a job. I thought you were on a
bicycle trip?" Dis was standing next to her now, smelling the fruity, almost
overpowering scent which she had liberally doused on herself that morning, and
noticing without being obvious that she had a burgeoning figure struggling through
the straight plains of pre-adolescence. Her face, regular and up-turned cute nose, was
also in a fight – with blemishes and a few slight skin eruptions. Once she survived
nature's shift from furious growth to future maternal maturity – and learned to live

with all the superficial beauty aids thrown at her by teen culture – she was going to be an attractive woman.

"I am on a trip, but I need some cash. So I'm starting work today at that new convenience store out on the highway. Say, you don't know of an inexpensive place to live do you? The "We Got It" doesn't pay even enough for your twenty-seven ninety-five special."

"Hey, what about the shack?" she said almost to herself. "Well you know, Ol' Dad says the shack's available."

"The shack?"

She was picking at her little finger now, pulling a tiny piece of skin from the side of her fingernail, worrying it. Dis noticed that she was wearing a pin-on button that read "Do It." He also noticed that she had put too much rouge on one cheek, giving her face an unbalanced appearance.

"Yeah, didn't you notice that ol' shack in back down there? We rent it by the week – or even the month, I think. To tell you the truth, it's kind of nasty, but it's got a kitchen in there – and a separate bedroom. Three rooms, I guess."

"Really?" Dis looked out the back window to where the girl was pointing. He noticed a tiny, freshly painted, miniature house straight out of old pictures he could recall of 1930s "motor courts." He had seen it before, of course, but never really gave it a thought.

"Can I take a look?"

"Right. I'll have to ask Ol' Dad or Emma Jane. I don't even know how much it costs. Go over and look it over – I think it's open. I'll be right there."

She was right. It was "kind of nasty" – everything in it was old and didn't match – but it was clean, deceptively accommodating in space, and its working kitchen had pots and pans, even silverware. Dis was testing the bed, lying on it full length, when she reappeared in the doorway. He jumped up, but not before he caught a flicker of mixed feeling on her face – impulsive attraction and embarrassed reaction.

"Boy, you must be tired or something. For a minute I thought you were sleeping. Can you fall asleep just like that? My friend Marcie can. She does it in class all the time. One time . . . oh, well, you don't wanna know about that." She paused to get back on track. "Ol' Dad says this here shack is empty right now, and it goes for 50 bucks a week or 150 a month."

Dis jumped at it. It was just what he was looking for, and he could handle the price. "Let me take it for a week then. I'll see how it works out; maybe then I can go for a month or more. Here, I think I have just about fifty in my wallet."

"OK. Ol' Dad said he wanted to talk to you if you took it. So I'll try to get him down here. How long you gonna be around?" Now she was nonchalantly spinning her necklace pendant with one hand as she leaned slightly forward and accepted the money, almost every cent Dis had, except for the 200 dollars hidden away. As they started walking together back to the main motel, Dis replied, "I have to be to work in about an hour, but as to how long I'm going to be around, I just don't know, I just don't know."

That was about a week ago, but now it was early Sunday morning, the weather looked promising, and Dis had his first day off since starting at the "We Got It." He found that he was expected to work six days a week. Marge and George shared the Sunday work; but they closed down at eight in the evening, so even they had a little break.

During the previous week Dis had spent one entire morning cleaning his bike and truing up his front wheel. He had also, after he got paid (in cash - he wondered if

Marge was doing some creative bookkeeping), found the town's one bicycle shop, a laid-back place called "Spoke 'n Chain," and bought a new shiny red Bell helmet. Now, on Sunday morning, he was back in his biking clothes, on a pannier-less bike, and ready to roll.

When he rode into the Hardee's parking lot, about ten people were in various stages of preparing their bikes for a ride. Some were taking them off car racks, adding air to tires, and making adjustments. Others were grouped together, chatting and kibitzing together. He did not see Lornaree.

Just then Lornaree rode up on her classy Trek 1100. Everyone's attention turned to her, the attractive new arrival. After she had said her hellos, she immediately rode to Dis and asked him how he was feeling, not having seen him since the morning after his accident. Then she, in a surprisingly commanding voice considering its softness, introduced him to the crowd, which had now grown to about fifteen riders.

"Excuse me, everyone. We've got a new rider with us this morning. Rob here – Rob Clemmon, right? – is new in town. He's staying here for awhile, but he's really touring the country on a bike. Rob is from . . . where did you say you were from, Rob?"

She would ask that, Dis thought. He couldn't say Washington; it might provide some subtle link to someone there. On the other hand he didn't really know Pittsburgh, having only been to it a couple times on buying trips, and once on a weekend vacation with Ruth. He compromised, "Oh, I'm from a number of places. Virginia, Maryland, Pennsylvania. I was in Pittsburgh for awhile before I started this trip." He looked around, wanting to divert attention. "This looks like a good group. You must have a good club here in Jeffrey?"

Dave, about three bikes over, jumped at the bait. "One of the best. We call ourselves the "Chained Knights" 'cause our high school teams are nicknamed "Knights." We have lots of fun and do lots of rides. If you're going to be around for awhile, you gotta join us or we won't let you even ride through town."

A balding older man with a potbelly spoke up. "Ah, leave him alone, Dave. Come on, let's get this started. Anyone who's late will just have to speed up to join us. Or they can join us out at Mindy's. We're gonna stop at Mindy's, everyone. Out Raintree and then south on 13 to Mindy's. Let's get going."

As they took off, Dis found himself comparing them to the club riders whom he had ridden with in Washington. These people were more down-to-earth, more basic. For one thing they weren't dressed to the brim in the latest fashionable shorts and jerseys like the D.C. crowd. Club rides there seemed at times to resemble fashion shows; people much better at showing off their latest purchases than at having a brisk, friendly ride. Here catalog clothing was the order of the day – that and some local T-shirts commemorating rides, tours, and events. The Washington crowd were really into expensive, multicolored, spandex jerseys; Dis didn't know what they did with their T-shirts, probably used them to clean their RX-7s and Probes. But in Jeffrey, Kentucky, from what Dis could see, people wore run-of-the-mill four panel shorts and T-shirts from the last ride they were on, the more local the better. A number were even wearing "Chained Knights" T-shirts, logo-ed with a humorous but attractive jousting knight on a bicycle, complete with spear and chain armor.

In the fifteen riders there were two couples. The fat, balding man and a very short, thin, leathery faced woman were together. Another woman, very tall and muscular, was with an even taller man, more thin than muscular. These two were dressed alike in the same tour T-shirts from an across-Tennessee ride of the previous year. The other riders were a variegated mixture of mid-America: three or four young "racers," one female, who took off together and within one block were almost out of sight of the majority of the riders; some young adults, moderate riders like himself and, he was glad to notice, Lornaree; and the middle aged and older crowd, including one 84-year-old, Vern, who according to the chatter hardly ever missed a club ride.

It was Vern who actually led the ride, the racers becoming rapidly invisible in their haste to outdo each other. He climbed on Raintree Road away from the highway, past Main Street, through a few other parallel streets of quiet residences, to another area of more settled commercial build-up. Here on the outskirts, on what was evidently a county road, were located the town's lumber dealer, soft drink distributor, and florist shop, along with other businesses and a few small factories – sheet metal works, plastic fabricators, and such. The road, Raintree, here was in need of repair, with gravel on the thin width of shoulder and constant patched and unpatched potholes. None of the riders talked much as they threaded through this section; riding through the lazy Sunday morning traffic in a long line, each intent on the vagaries of the road immediately ahead.

Finally, as they started climbing a moderate hill, the businesses dropped off. At the top, a major intersecting road cleared the way for Raintree to become an enjoyable biking road – two fairly recently blacktopped lanes with a slight shoulder. At first they passed a few scattered residences with front acres shaven and trimmed meticulously, like moss on alpine rock. These gave way to farms, some huge and prosperous; others, unkempt and slovenly; still others, boarded-up wrecks waiting for wind and rain and entwining vegetation to return them to a more natural state. In short, Raintree Road was a typical country road, interesting but not exceptionally so.

Dis found himself riding behind a woman of about his age whose Lycra bicycle shorts seemed to increase rather than decrease her considerable mid-body bulk. Although she seemed to be of average weight, she had an out-of-proportion behind. Dis mused, as he churned through the pleasant countryside, about the unflattering effect of biking clothes on people even a little overweight. Especially from behind, fat people's buttocks on bikes looked grotesque, twin hams pivoting on an all but invisible fulcrum or twin wine sacks overfilled with undulating sherry or merlot. Even legs from behind were not that attractive: sinews and tendons flexing under strain; shifting from concave to convex behind the knee; bulking out, almost deformed into bursting tear drops through the calves. The typical rider's position, with upper body leaning down and over the bike's top tube and handlebars, stretching the butt at the pivot point, simply did not present a pretty picture from behind.

Of course, being slim helped immensely. And the quest for a sleek body was one of the driving forces behind many cyclists' willingness to pour themselves into tight pants and jerseys and then ride furiously for extensive lengths of time and mileage through sometimes miserable weather and road conditions.

The woman slowed down a bit and Dis started to pass her, hoping actually to move up to Lornaree, who was near the front of the group, talking to the tall couple. As he moved around, the woman glanced at him and said, "Hey, you. Don't cha work at that new convenience store out on 84?"

Dis nodded, not really happy to be associated with such a low-life job.

"I thought I had seen you before. I was out there the other day, getting some aspirin, and I remember you because you were being pestered by some Kentucky redneck about the price of a six pack of Miller Lite."

Dis remembered the incident, and, as he looked at the woman's face, he remembered her also. At the store she had been behind a guy with tattoos up and down his arms, some handmade, who insisted that the Millers should be cheaper since it was warm. Dis hardly remembered details of the incident; what he did remember was the kind, almost laughing lips and eyes of the nicely dressed woman as she followed the action in front of her.

"That's right, I think I remember you too. You were laughing at me, weren't you?"

"Laughing at you? No way! I was laughing at that poor, gut-busting sack of tobacco trying to wheedle you out of 22 cents or something."

"Yeah, what was that all about? Cold beer or something. Right! Now I remember. He had seen a sign in another store about warm beer being only $2.39 a six-pack."

"Oh, you were good. Comin' on as his buddy, telling him he didn't want any of that luke-warm, piss-water stuff, when he could have a cool one sliding down his whiskery throat. You got him so thirsty that he forgot all about his extra quarter or so. When I went out to the parking lot, he was sitting in his pick-up drinking away like he had just come in from a whole day of dunking hot pigs in cold mud."

Dis had to laugh. He remembered the incident and was even a little proud of how he had handled it. "We get some strange people in there. Yesterday we had a reverse flasher."

"What? A reverse flasher?"

"Yea, this old geezer wearing a long coat came in and stayed back by the freezer too long. I wondered what he was up to. Pretty soon a girl came over laughing and told me to watch the old man back there. She said, 'He's showing his butt.' I looked up in the mirror and sure enough, he had some sort of slit in his coat and, I guess, his pants too. He was standing facing the freezer, looking around at a mother carrying a baby, and holding the slit open. Then he leaned over, and there it was, his bare behind poking out."

"No kidding."

"The mother evidently didn't see him 'cause she didn't do anything. I quickly called the cops, then went back to where he was, looking at the freezer all innocent like. Get this; he said he was looking for frozen moon pies!"

The woman let out a yelp, "Moon pies, no; I don't believe it."

"Yeah, moon pies. Crazy. I had to half drag the guy up to the front, but when I got him there, he didn't try to run or anything. When the cops arrived, they said, 'Oh, Uncle Paul's at it again.' Evidently this Uncle Paul is OK most of the time, but every once in a while he does some strange thing and has to be institutionalized for awhile. One time they found him sitting up in a tree in the park, just sitting there refusing to come down. They had to get the fire department to lift him down with a ladder. I guess he's harmless."

"Sure, harmless. Seeing some old fart's bare behind in a convenience store is just about as harmless as the covers on some of those magazines you guys have staring at us as we wait in the check-out line."

"Hey, don't look at me. I only work here." Dis threw one arm up in mock innocence. There hadn't been any cars passing them all through the conversation, and most of the riders were doing what Dis was doing – chatting with fellow riders, keeping up a leisurely pace while enjoying the easy morning ride. With the light wind coming from the west, Dis hardly knew that he was riding. His five weeks of constant riding up and down the countryside, through some formidable hills, even mountains, roughly following the Appalachians down into Georgia and back (to be evasive as possible), had built up his riding muscles and aerobic capacity to a sharp touring level. Even now after his accident, his arm and knee had healed enough that he felt only an occasional ache as he got into the rhythm of the ride. He wasn't even bandaging them anymore, just still wearing a long sleeved shirt to work.

Now he slowly overtook a middle-age man dressed all in florescent neon – bright green top and blazing yellow shorts. He even had socks with two lines of neon encircling each ankle. Dis wondered momentarily what the man thought about as he put those clothes on in the morning. Was he thinking safety, visibility, fashion? Was he reveling in the chance to act like an adolescent again? Or did he just stand in front of his mirror and glow? His bike, a Kline, was also neon, a swirling, merging combination of greens, yellows, and oranges. It evidently had been custom painted.

On the back of his florescent orange, hard-shelled helmet he had stamped out his name in bright green plastic letters: KNOBBY. From behind he didn't look particularly bony or angular; perhaps it was just a nickname based on his last name.

"Hey, Knobby, how's those knees holding up?" someone yelled.

Knobby, the supercharged surge of color, was visibly limping. He appeared to have overextended himself. His cheeks were red and he could hardly talk because of his out-of-breath wheezing. Sweat covered his forehead like water on a suddenly emerging seal. The front of his green jersey was etched into an oval pattern by his body sweat.

He glanced over to them, and said, "Gall dang, those people take off. I was up there riding with that second group and all at once they was gone." He had to pause to catch a breath. "I mean, we went up a little hill, and it was just like they was going downhill and I was going up. I don't know how they can go so fast." He reached up with one of his neon-gloved hands and wiped a layer of sweat from one side of his forehead to the other.

Someone made an introduction: "Rob, this is Knobby, as you could tell from his helmet. Actually his name is Herman Knobinsky, but everybody calls him Knobby – except those guys at the fire station, right Knobby?"

With a pained look of actual distress, Knobby said, "Oh, forget about those guys for awhile. What do they know."

Dis had the feeling that Knobby was one of those persons who is always setting himself up to be knocked down. Dis didn't know about the fire station, but he could imagine the jokes and put-downs that the other firefighters would pull on this ostentatious gadfly. And sure enough, it wasn't long before Knobby was telling an involved story about how some firefighters secretly rubbed starch and alum and some itching powder they got at a joke store into his biking shorts on a 100-mile ride. But he got his revenge, he loudly proclaimed. "But I fixed those sons-of-b's. I swore I'd do something to them, but I waited a couple of weeks, you know, sort of lull them into complacency. I knew that these guys rode to the station on nice days, so I had my plan. One day when all their bikes were there, they all went out on a fire call. Well, I snuck and took all of their bike seats. Then I put them in this canvas bag from work and hoisted them to the top of this tower where they dry hoses. But I rigged the rope with a slipknot, so when they was at the very top, a good yank left them dangling all by themselves with no way to be lowered. I got my revenge. And guess what? It took them three days before they found that canvas bag – and then one of them had to shimmy way up there and loosen it."

They had now reached the first real hill, and it didn't take long for Knobby to lose his audience – or, more accurately, for his audience to lose him. Dis found himself in the front of the group, leading, and not really exerting himself too much. Some of the others were keeping up with him, but by the time he reached the top of the hill, the group was strung out in an elongating line. Dis found himself unconsciously content. He was enjoying himself on his bike, not riding to get away, to hide. He was getting to know some interesting people, including women; and with his job he was finding himself becoming attuned to the non-urban ways of this likable small town. He rode along by himself now; riding for the sheer joy of it.

The day was becoming bright, clouds shifting into wispy patterns of floating contrails, a crosswind picking up slightly on his right. The road, still Raintree, became a series of hills, most rather steep but short. The terrain on both sides of the road became more rugged and wooded, farm fields being replaced by humps of tangled trees and bushes: obviously they were approaching a river. Dis spun up one long but gradual hill, and there below, indeed, lay the river. It meandered before him at the bottom of a long, sharply declining bluff, sparkling like a silver-dewed cobweb dancing in the morning breeze. The road before him was a biker's dream: a downhill, smooth and softly curving; almost seductive in its femininity.

He jumped at its promise.

He quickly zipped into his highest gear and, at the road's gradual downturn, sped up as fast as he could – before the decline took any reason for pedaling away from him. Now it was just momentum, steering, braking, and balance. He sped through the first gradual curve, air rushing over him like mountain rapids over river boulders, his computer hitting 40 - 43 - 45. He kept his eye on the road, only looking occasionally at the entire river and valley scene, and also at the bike computer. God, this was great. Leaning forward, bending down, hands gripping the down-turned ends of his handlebars, he felt himself at one with the world – with himself, his bike, this road, and his existence. He couldn't express it, and it went so fast, but something spiritual, something eternal rushed through him. He was lifted. Ecstatic.

The road leveled out somewhat. He lifted his head – took a slight breather. He took the chance to flick his mode button to "max speed" and read, "47 mph." But then, as he passed a small parallel creek channeled under the road, he found himself descending more, almost flung again into a downhill – into speed, into wind streaming around him, into vibrations resounding through his bike and himself, into an almost hypnotic state taking him from his normal existence – into a oneness with his entire environment, an acute awareness of his senses at a frenzied pitch of feeling and awe.

He was into and out of himself simultaneously, hardly aware in the swiftness of his descent, of his concentrated pleasure, of his thrill in being completely alive. One last down, short but extra steep, ended with a sweeping 90 degree turn. It took all his pinpointed effort to negotiate the turn without braking, something he normally didn't do, loaded down with panniers and the heavy weight of mundane reality. But now he was on a lark, just he and his bare bike and a beautiful Sunday morning. He let the hill and the road take him sweeping around the curve, the bike leaning into it, hardly upright, but at a precarious slant. He had the sensation of barely skimming over the surface of the road, his elbow almost touching it. But he hardly had time to notice, so fast and compounded were the sensations shooting through him. He was a bullet of concentrated physical pleasure shot from this mighty rifle of a hill.

As he rounded the last part of the curve and the road lost its downhill angle, Dis's mouth, a line of steel, relaxed into a curving grin of satisfaction. He looked up from the road and saw the bridge rapidly approaching. No wonder the hill was so steep. It was almost right next to the river, which had dug itself so deeply into the ground, like a knife-line in a hunk of cheese, that its bluffs hugged their maker, first on one side than on the other, alternating with gradually inclined flood plains as the river meandered through the sharply cut landscape.

Dis sped across the bridge, a sign telling him that the river was the "Beartree." On the other side, three or four bikers were stopped, watching the road and the hill which Dis had just descended. He didn't want to stop, knowing from experience that a tough uphill was looming, and wanting to keep his momentum going for it. As he passed them, however, he saw Larnaree smiling her pursed smile and waving at him to stop. The bikers with her took off as he went by, but she stayed where she was. He braked, looped around, and pulled in next to her, still flushed with the excitement of the downhill. "Wow, what a hill! You didn't tell me you guys had a downhill like that. That was terrific!"

Again smiling faintly, Lornaree replied. "Yeah, Beartree's great. I just love it – especially since they resurfaced it two years ago. Before, you had to be real careful. But now you can just let yourself go. There's hardly any traffic, ever. How fast did you go?"

In his euphoria, Dis hadn't even thought to check his computer after the last steep incline. He punched it. "God, I don't know if I've ever gone so fast – fifty-four miles an hour – Wow!"

"Fifty-four, that's great. You beat me, but I hit fifty coming down that last stretch."

Dis was still beaming, "Fifty-four. That's amazing. This must be something like the Grand Canyon. Oh, wait a minute. How do we get out of here? I don't know if I want to climb back up what I just came down."

She smiled and Dis could see her slightly uneven row of teeth, "I'll tell you a secret if you promise not to tell anyone else. We never go back up Beartree – that's its name, by the way. Oh, sure, there's some macho-honchos who have to showoff, but most of us just keep going down the road, and then guess what happens?"

"There's a giant crane?"

"You wish! No, we follow the river for a couple miles – it's kind of pretty, woodsy and . . . uh . . . uneven – and then we come to Verhoven, a grungy little river town that we avoid. They don't even have a convenience store, just convenient dogs. But outta there the road starts going up, but it takes its time about it. I guess we go back to about as high as we were before, and it takes awhile to climb it, but it's a gradual climb, not like Beartree."

"Have you ever tried to climb Beartree?"

"Do you think I'm a macho-honcho?"

"Well, you were doing all right as we were riding out."

"Hey, I can keep up with the group, but I'm no Tour de France climbing freak. I did climb Beartree once though. Went down to bottom granny and just zipped up that ol' hill at a fast clip of maybe three miles an hour. I mean, I was dangerous – weaving over that blacktop like a zoo lion in a hot cage."

"Yea, I know what you mean. It's possible, but it "ain't" fun. One time out East – in Vermont, I think – a long time ago. All I had was an old Schwinn ten-speed. I swear going up one of those mountains I was standing on the top pedal just watching the wheels turning backwards. It took me half an hour just to go backward to the bottom of the hill where I started."

"Oh, come on," she arched her eyebrow, "you're putting me on now."

"You think I am? You really do, huh? Well come on with me. We'll go back to Beartree and I'll show you what I mean."

Laughing, she replied, "No, no, I believe you – well, not really. But I'm not ready for Beartree today. What I am ready for is some food. And you know what's at the end of the climb out of here? Of course you don't – it's Mindy's. And Mindy's has some good grub, some Kentucky breakfast fixins, and I can't wait."

"Are you serious? A real Kentucky breakfast? You mean a can of Mountain Dew and a Hostess Twinkie. Wow! What are we sitting around here for? Let's go."

In the back of his mind as they rode through the willows and cottonwoods close to the gently riffling river and as they started the moderate climb out of the valley, was a sense of a quickening of his senses brought on by this woman. She was a physical gal, accepting the challenge of keeping up with him; although he moderated his pace, gained through all his recent hours on the road. She seemed to relish the chance to pedal harder at the slight upward shifts of the road, and an almost exuberance came upon her when the road leveled or shifted down slightly. She rode with determination, but Dis couldn't discern it on her face. Instead there was a calmness, an almost bland sameness with just the hint of a smile. She seemed to be at peace with her basic nature, at one with muscle and gain and will.

She was also fun to be with. They bantered up the road, not talking about anything of substance, but exploring each other in an informal, unconscious manner. They went back and forth lightly, using humor to touch upon each other's background, intelligence, feelings, and motivations. They had a good time. Dis, so used to traveling on a bike by himself, hardly realized he was moving. It wasn't so much that he wasn't exerting himself physically, he was – it was still a good, long, pull. It was just that he was so involved with the woman with him that she commanded his attention: his body and its physical demands went on auto-pilot. She also seemed to be heightened by his presence. Her legs churned – she had her derailleur set at a higher gear than his – and sweat beaded from her forehead, but her soft grin never became a grimace, and she kept up her end of the bantering with as much aplomb as a guest on a late night talk show.

They were a good match. From afar they could be mistaken for a spindly four-wheeled oddity, tires next to each other and synchronized as if by one drive chain, propelled by out-of-sync but compatible motion from each side. Up close their heads belied the axiom about "eyes on the road." Both of them rode with heads turned, eyeing each other as they chatted. They were both proficient enough riders to almost automatically check the road ahead for traffic and surface hazards, to listen and occasionally skim their eyes to the extreme left corners in checking for vehicles coming up from behind, while all the time riding very close together in safety and intense conversation.

It was this quality of being actively and completely alert - as they climbed the gradual valley bluff with its hardwood oaks and maples and variegated underbrush - that spread like an endless, interconnected bicycle chain through the gearing of their individual selves. When he pulled into the hard dirt-and-gravel parking lot of Mindy's Bar and Grill, Dis felt both buoyed and content. He had had a good first leg of the morning ride and he was now with a woman who spread anticipation throughout his body and mind.

He went into Mindy's hungry, but more alive than any day since way before that fatal day when he walked through a Washington D.C. parking lot.

Chapter 7

Dis was in his shower singing. He didn't realize he was singing; in fact, he hadn't sung in the shower since way before he left Washington, his job, and his wife. His shower was a miserable little "tin box," in which he banged his elbows almost every time he lifted his arms. But he was getting used to the confining space and it was clean. He knew it was clean; he had spent almost all Saturday morning cleaning the "Shack," which, given the small size of the place, meant that he had been actually meticulous in searching out undetected dust and grime accumulated not so much from deliberate misuse but from simple neglect.

The place hadn't been used much recently; its last tenant Dis estimated to be a large, middle aged woman who smoked: this based on three lipstick stained cigarette butts he found behind the toilet, an old yellowing Clark's Department Store sales tag from a size 14 blouse which he found in a back corner of one of the three drawers of the dresser that was squeezed next to the bed, and a page from a magazine – still taped to the side of the apartment sized refrigerator in the kitchen – featuring six pictures of Elvis from teenager to puffy Vegas headliner.

The girl with the fingernails – what was her name? Calleen? – evidently did much of the cleaning around the Forest, and while being halfway responsible, she was erratic and superficial. Since Dis had moved into the shack, she cleaned it once a week, on Saturday, bringing in clean bed linen at the same time.

Dis, while scrubbing himself, was singing "Looie, Looie" for no particular reason, getting through some of the words, but having to hum just as many as he knew. Nevertheless, the song's nervous energy and optimistic melody perfectly fit Dis's mood. He was having a great Sunday so far, his first "day off" from his job. He had had a brisk, invigorating ride; had met some interesting people; and had ended the ride with Lorn.

When the two of them – the other riders strung out the length of the road – wheeled into the Hardee's parking lot at the ride's end, he suggested they stop for a curlicue cone of frozen yogurt. She had done him better, inviting him to her apartment for a special "treat," which turned out to be a root beer float, a summer post-ride tradition with her. While they were slurping up the last creamy-brown mixture of fizzled-out soda and melted ice cream, her daughter Chrissy burst into the house, all a-buzz with gossip she had heard after church while riding back on the church bus. She hardly noticed Dis, so caught up in telling her mother about what happened at a pajama party held the night before, a party to which she hadn't been invited.

She, of course, had to have a float too. And while she was gulping it down and talking at the same time about what Susie Langley said about Jill Jacobs, she finally acknowledged Dis's presence. "Oh, hi there. You had the bike accident, didn't you? Are you cured yet . . . no . . . I mean are you all right?"

For answer, Dis held up his right arm and showed her the lattice-like washboard of scabs up and down his upper and lower arm.

"Oh, gross. Anyway," she turned to her mother, "Sarah says we gotta be at practice a whole hour before the game starts because coach is mad and we're gonna have extra drill and . . ." She was off again, this time about the softball game her team was playing at four in the afternoon. They were playing the Ramsey Square Rams, and they were going to kick their butts.

Dis figured it was time to leave. He and Lorn had something more than just friendship between them, and he enjoyed the pre-adolescent antics of her daughter, but this was just the second time he had been together with the two of them and he didn't want to be pushy. He sensed a thin line down the right side of this little family's highway and he wanted to ride smoothly but squarely right down the middle of it. So he had left, after vaguely mentioning another ride next Sunday. Lorn, however, had said no. She only missed church once a month to go biking. Other biking times were in the evening or on Saturdays. Dis, of course, worked evenings, but his mornings were open. They both tentatively agreed to look for each other next Saturday morning at the start of the usual club ride.

So with "Loo-E, Loo-I" reverberating through the small "shack," Dis finished his shower, dried himself, wrapped the towel around his waist and inspected his face in the mirror. He knew he wasn't bad looking, his Germanic blue eyes and light brown hair – disguised now with dark brown dye and a lower face with a now nicely cultivated beard and mustache - adding a bit of distinction to his regular features. In actuality, he was bland – neither handsome nor homely. Just a regular face attached to a regular brain attached to a regular body. So why, he mused, did he end up here?

"Looie, Looie," trailed off into the discolored ceiling of the little bathroom. He stared into the eyes of the regular face in the mirror and could almost see the warm feelings of the morning trail off like tendrils of smoke from a lonely trash fire of the heart. What had he come to? He was thirty-five years old, working in a dead-end job, living in a time warp of a cheap "shack," with hardly a cent to his name and almost no possessions. Moreover he was nobody – a man without an identity, without a real name, without a past. Who was he?

One central fact was that he was a killer – a killer by accident – but still a killer. He couldn't escape that. He, Dis . . . Rob . . . whoever he was, was a killer. He had been the prime agent in taking a fellow human being's life. He had felt the knife slide in and had seen the life stagger out. That was incontrovertible. And because of that he assumed he was wanted. And he wasn't sure about his fingerprints. Maybe in his haste to rip open the man's shirt he had left a blood smeared print somewhere on the man's body or clothes. Even though he had seen no witnesses, had noticed nothing in the papers, and no one seemed to be following him or asking questions, he knew that murdered people, even murdered homeless people, are not just forgotten about – are not just pushed into pauper's graves and covered over forever without even a cursory investigation. He didn't feel remorse about the killing. After all, the man was a mugger and would have used the knife on him. And the killing itself had been an accident, so filled with darkness, alcohol, and vagueness, that Dis still did not know what actually happened. All he knew was that he was technically guilty of a crime that he didn't consciously commit.

He did commit the crime of home desertion, however. That was premeditated.

He wondered again – as he had done so many times on the road – what Ruth had done when he simply never appeared that Saturday afternoon, which seemed so long ago. He knew, for one thing, that she had to be furious. They were supposed to go to one of her boss's end-of-the-month parties, something she was always adamant about. She felt they helped her career, and he supposed they did. But he was usually bored, never really relating to the real estate pushers with their appraiser minds and local boosterism – not to mention their hardly undisguised lust for the almighty "million dollar" month. Dis sold for a living – shoes and socks, to be sure – but he found he had almost no affinity with this group of supposedly super salespeople.

Would she have called the cops when he didn't show up? Maybe not – at least immediately. Ruth was smart. She would have checked with the airline first. Did she know which one? He hadn't left any information about that or his flight number, but she would probably remember that he always flew the United shuttle from DC to New York and back again. She would have checked and found that he wasn't on any flight that Saturday afternoon. Then by checking with the hotel in New York or the Wednesday flight out, she would know that he hadn't appeared in New York. Actually Tilden's might have called her, wondering why he hadn't shown up in New York – but probably not. In all likelihood his fellow managers wouldn't question his absence until he didn't show up for work on Monday. They were usually so concentrated on their own departments – what with salesmen, displays, and individual invitations to sales receptions, parties within parties, and the whirlwind activities of a major sales fair – that he would hardly be missed in New York. But on Monday in Washington, he would be. Old Silent Sam would be fried.

Dis smiled in the mirror as he pictured his grumpy boss looking at his watch, pulling first one finger than the other, getting more and more agitated with every minute that Dis didn't appear. Then when he found out that Dis hadn't been in New York, he would be livid. His ear would jump. Dis had seen that happen two times. The man's right cheek would become redder and redder and then the color would spread into his right ear. Almost immediately the ear would start jumping, twitching and moving like a fish on a stringer. Dis would have loved to have been there to see it happen again, but, of course, the two events were mutually exclusive.

No, Ruth probably had been in a dither, really angered, explosively bothered, but Dis felt for sure that she had still gone to the party. She wouldn't have missed it. She would have made up some fake excuse for his absence and then, while she lightly clawed the linen suited arms of the various gray-templed men invariably grouped around her, she would be plotting a suitable revenge when Dis, the prodigal New York pilgrim, would return.

But he didn't return. And he would never return to his big money-down, all interest payments, suburban shell of a home; his side of a satin-sheeted, cold, and hardly rumpled bed; or his satin-clothed, cold, and hardly rumpled wife.

He missed her, he had to admit to himself. But the missing had more to do with long acquired habits developed over a period of years. How could he not miss her? She had been a preoccupation for the major part of his mature life. She had shared the immediate scope of his existence for more than nine years. But now, with his life completely changed, his lifestyle upside-down, she had become just one other aspect of a life dimming and receding, like the slow fading final shot at the end of a grimly realistic, made-on-a-budget movie. He missed her; but now he was missing her less and less. And, he said to himself constantly, he felt no remorse in leaving her – and in leaving her so abruptly. Their marriage was finished. They both knew it. Two dissimilar plants had intertwined but the intimacy had choked rather than nurtured. He wanted a baby, a family, the proverbial happy hearth roasting with gentle satisfaction. She wanted wealth, honor, self- realization; a baby could wait.

Two weeks after he was promoted to department manager at Tilden's – after they had been to "The White Cellar" for Spanish tampas, and later had "crawled the pubs" up and down P Street NW in Georgetown; after they had made happy, skin-smooth love in their satin-smooth sheeted bed; and while he was resting on one elbow soothing her cheek while his forearm hairs caressed the curve of her breast; he had said, "You know, we ought to have a baby."

Immediately the soft afterglow faded into something that both smothered and withdrew into a red-hot core.

She shook his hand away from her face. "No, let's wait. Let's see how your job goes. What if it doesn't work out?"

"What can I say? It's working. I know the place, the people involved. They need me."

Now she was on an elbow, her slightly wide face slowly moving away from his in the soft dark. "I don't want a baby."

"Now, Ruth."

"I don't want a baby." She caught herself. "I mean not now. Come on, I just started with Harry. What about me? I made some commitments."

"I know that, honey, but we should have a baby."

Now she was out of the bed, almost running to her closet for her wrap. "No, not now."

And that was that. She controlled their birth control and he could do nothing to circumvent it. He envisioned substituting placebos in her round plastic container of birth control pills, but he knew that wasn't the answer. For their baby, she had to be wholly and completely child-ready. And right now she wasn't ready. He knew that she was in charge and she didn't want a child – not now, at least.

But he did. Deep down he could feel both he and Ruth shifting away from each other into separated independence, into an accentuation of their different natures. A child, perhaps, would mend the rift. But even more than that, he wanted a child because a child was bedrock, the foundation of life, the reason for existence – he knew to his core that he had to be a father. That was the simple truth.

But you don't run away from a marriage – completely disappear like a rabbit in a magician's hand – because you can't agree on an admittedly important part of the fabric of life. If it gets down to it, you divorce.

And when they did get down to it, she would have nothing whatsoever to do with a divorce. She was even more adamant about divorce than motherhood. "Just try it, you bastard, just try it!" she screamed. They were in their combination kitchen-dining room where he was heating up scampi in one of her new copper-clad pans. She had purchased the set with part of the commission from her sale of a particularly ugly ranch house to a new assistant superintendent of the Rockhurst school system. The entire set of pans hung inappropriately and randomly in any open wall space in the small kitchen area – too many of them for the available space.

"Just try getting a divorce!"

It was the first time he had brought up divorce; actually all he had mentioned was separation. He had come from work late, having stopped at one of the downtown bars, not Sam's Spinnaker, but another of the same character. He had had a few beers, but the sight of an old re-run of a "Honeymooners" program on the hazy bar television was what made him determined to confront his wife. Ralph and Alice Kramden were certainly not he and Ruth, but underneath the TV buffoonery and pratfalls, Dis saw only the basic incompatibility that was similar to what was making his life miserable.

All the way home on the train he kept saying to himself: maybe we should split for awhile and see what happens. And that's what he told Ruth, who was reading the newspaper at the Formica covered table in a sullen mood and a formless running outfit, while he reheated the leftovers from her earlier meal – a shrimp and white sauce mixture over leftover rice. "Maybe we should split. You know, separate for awhile and see what happens."

"What did you say?" She had her back to him, but she knew every word he spoke.

"Oh, come on, Ruth, you know what I said." He shook his head, "This just isn't working out."

"Just try it, you bastard, just try it." She paused. "Just try it."

Even though her back was to him, he could almost see her determination squaring – her feet pushing forcefully harder on the floor, her shoulders widening fractionally. She turned slightly and almost barked, her eyes not on him, but on the shinny copper pan that he was holding over the stove's front burner. She yelled, "Jesus, I don't believe you. Just when things are working out. I mean, look at these pans." She jumped up and whisked the hot pan, filled with the lumpy shrimp mixture, off the stove and stood with it in front of her, her eyes now mesmerized by the shiny copper swaying in her hand.

"You wanna split." She paused – for effect or for inspiration, he couldn't tell. "Well, split this." And she flipped the contents of the pan at him. He couldn't believe what was happening. She was normally not a demonstrative person, and now various pieces and clumps of food were flying at him, propelled by her fury. She, however, was not a good marksman; most of the scampi, especially one large, coagulated mass of it, landed on the floor in front of Dis; but a few pieces of it did hit him, one landing on the collar of his off-blue shirt even though he instinctively jumped out of the way to avoid it.

As he staggered backward, she stood, fuming in front of him, her hand still grasping the pan, looking unbelievably, to him, like a caricature of Jayne Meadows glowering at Gleason. He couldn't help it. He smiled. He thought, "Scampi. No way. Alice Cramden and scampi. No, no. OK, Ralph, you want scampi, I'll give you scampi." He started laughing hard now, almost uncontrollably.

It was the wrong thing to do.

She lurched at him, pan in hand, but her foot hit the warm mass of food and she fell. She fell roundly; feet spread, arms akimbo, pan hitting the side of a cabinet, the scampi coating her pants as she slid through most of it.

He stared, unbelieving, but then, again uncontrollably, the "Honeymooners" zinging through his head. He yelped with laughter, yelling, "How sweet it is! How sweet it is!"

She sat there, the warm goo slowly seeping through her pants, waiting for his laughter to die. When it did, she slowly pronounced, in tones so chilling that it froze the scene forever in his memory, "No separation . . . No divorce . . . No nothing . . . Never . . . If you even think about it, you bastard, I'll get you . . . You won't have anything. Not a thing . . . anywhere . . . anytime. I'll take you for everything, you bastard."

He almost laughed again, her last phrase hitting another trigger within him. "I'll take you for everything." This was moving from a TV re-run to a B movie. "I'll take you for a ride. I'll take you for everything." But right then he knew that she would. He stifled the laugh, realizing in a flash that she wouldn't let him go without making the entire rest of his life miserable. And coupled with this was a realization almost as bad: if he did stay with her, their life, after this, would also be miserable.

That's when he retreated, running to get his coat and take off in his car. She jumped up, chasing him, still with the pan in her hand, yelling, "Don"t do this to me! Dis, you bastard, don't do this to me!"

Two unfortunate events happened together right then. She fell again. She still had scampi on her shoe and she slipped again, this time on the hard wood floor of the living room. But when she fell this time, she banged her face into the magazine stand, battering her nose, and sending blood streaming down one side of her face. The pan went skittering across the floor to Dis's feet, where he almost automatically picked it up. And then, unrelenting, she continued after him, her face a bloody mess. He retreated to the side door, where, inexplicably, he fumbled with the knob, turned his back to her, and walked out, still holding the pan. She followed, crawling on her hands and knees, sobbing between licks of blood, "Don't do this to me! Don't do this to me!"

Unfortunately, at the same time Anne Calbert, their next door neighbor, was just returning from one of her mid-evening shopping excursions and had just opened the trunk of her car which was parked in front of her garage door. When she heard Ruth's piercing, "Don't do this to me," she at first jumped – startled – and then turned and stared. What she saw was a bloody, distraught Ruth crawling – disheveled - out the door, Dis standing over her with a copper clad frying pan upraised in his hand. Annie let out an involuntary, "What?" Dis looked over to the sound, saw what Annie saw, and as he lowered the pan, knew he was locked in. For the rest of his life. Forever. The copper pan, the setting sun of his existence.

He, of course, had rushed to Ruth, comforted her, driven her to the hospital, tried to make amends. And strangely enough for a short while after this incident their life together had become almost happy. They both apologized fulsomely to each other, said they would forget the ugly happening, and the next night even made love – for the last time in their lives, as it turned out. Still two things bothered him: the bandage on her nose and the knowledge that in a court of law, with prissy Anne Calbert in attendance, Ruth had his being in her tendoned grasp.

The sheer sexual pleasure of the lovemaking was marred by the realization that she was being so nice because she had him. He was locked in, and the damn bandage on her nose, which he had to be so careful about, was the key. It was ironic, but in this their last intimacy, when they were as physically close as any two people can be, when he was poring seed into her chemically and physically unreceptive reproductive organs (she was both on the pill and using a diaphragm), at that very moment of frenzied love and pleasure, he realized that he had to run. He had to make a clean break and take off.

He didn't know why or wherefore, but she was pure possession. He knew she wouldn't give him up. She wouldn't accept separation or divorce. There was no way out. She had him – in submission – forever. As he lay, upraised a bit over his beautiful wife's heaving chest, inspiration hit him. Maybe it was the mini-death of his orgasm that made him think of death. But death it was. If he were dead, wiped off the face of this earth, he would be free of her. She would have no control.

If he were dead, he could live.

But, obviously, he didn't want to die. But what if he could just disappear so completely that for all practical purposes it would be the same as his death? From that moment on, as he was withdrawing from his wife for the last time, he started plotting his disappearance from her forever.

Now, as he looked into the mirror of the tiny bathroom of the shack, he gave himself the luxury of a small smile. He didn't have much going for himself, to be sure, but he had whipped her. He had disappeared without a trace – as far as he could tell. Perhaps she had hired someone to search for him, but if she had, that person wasn't successful. Oh sure, there was the slight chance that he really was caught, that he was under constant surveillance and that she was just waiting for the proper moment to pull him in. But that was the stuff of movies and TV, not of ordinary people in the real world.

He wondered what her life was like now. Actually, because they had been so distant to each other for the last years of their life together, things probably hadn't changed much for her. She had the house. It was in both their names. She very likely still had her job. If she managed right, she could live appropriately. She probably still had her lover, Bill Gerlock, the golfer. Maybe by this time they would be living together – except Bill was married to Jane, also a golfer, albeit a morning-with-the-girls type.

And Ruth would be pissed. Where was her husband? Oh, it would stick in her craw; it would twist and squirm constantly. He knew this; but it did not make him particularly happy. He was not that vindictive. Perhaps he thought of the future too much. Maybe that is what made his life unique. Other people just kept plugging away and things eventually gave way or worked out. He saw into the future – into a lifetime of unhappiness, of incompatibility. And his plans, by accident, sheer accident, worked out.

He turned away from the mirror and said out loud to no one but the tiny room, "Sees into the future, bull shit. What about Amy Jane?"

God, yes, Amy Jane. The toucher. How wrong he had been about her. She appeared at Tilden's just after the fight with his wife, but before he had observed Bill, the golfer, sneaking away from his home on a Saturday morning. She applied for a job as a salesperson in his shoe department, even though they usually were unconsciously sexist - men in men's shoes; women in women's. Amy Jane had experience, however, even though she hadn't worked for the last seven years because of a marriage that had recently broken up, and the women's department was filled. Betsy Pickford, the aging woman in charge of women's shoes immediately liked her, and since she couldn't use her, sent her to Dis, who she knew needed another shoe clerk. He hired her.

Amy Jane was about 30 years old; not pretty, but cute; short and a little bit chunky; with large pouty lips, a little too much makeup, and a bouncy upbeat personality. During the interview Dis had to stop himself from asking if she had been a cheerleader in high school, although later she told him she had been the president of her high school's pep squad – the Boom-Boom Boomers of Bradford High School. She also had a tendency to wear somewhat low cut, flashy blouses, and skirts and dresses an inch or two shorter than the norm, two habits that vaguely troubled Dis. He knew he should say something to her for the good of the store, but at the same time he caught himself looking more than he should. In fact he found himself looking forward to her arrival each day, not so much for her clothing, or lack of clothing, he told himself, but because she did add friendly cheer to the usually reserved shoe area of the store.

After two weeks on the job, she promoted a "let's have a couple of drinks after work" with the sales staff of all the clothing departments. They took over the back room of Roonie's, a nice bar and grill trying to survive on a seedy street near Tilden's. He somehow found himself sitting next to her and also found that she was a "toucher." Her hands could not keep away from someone she knew fairly well. She gripped him by the shoulder when making a point, brushed lint from his back, even at one point straightened his tie - all done innocently and seemingly unconsciously.

So Dis and Amy Jane had a friendly relationship, the same as she developed with almost everyone with whom she worked. Even though Dis's home life was going downhill faster than a mountain bike without brakes on a 22 percent single track, Dis was very discrete at work. Tilden's was a conservative store - from old

Nathan Tilden, the 78-year-old son of the founding father, down to the rule that bra ads must feature drawings, not photographs of women. Employees who fooled around with other employees somehow found themselves out on the street, working at a five-and-dime or worse. Even he, as a minor manager, had been told to watch his employees and report them to his boss, Silent Sam, if they were involved in any hanky-panky on the job. So Dis enjoyed being friendly with Amy Jane, and that's all.

But three days after the "few drinks at Roonie's" she did present him with a problem. When she took off her light coat in the morning, he knew he had to do something. She was wearing a blouse she hadn't worn before, a loose fitting, beautifully silky white garment that scooped low across her chest, revealing the curves of her bust. She evidently was wearing a modified push-up bra because her breasts and the crevice between them were very apparent. Dis held his breath. Maybe she would catch herself in the mirror, realize that the blouse was "too much," and make some adjustment in the back, raising the bust line. But no, her first customer, a young black man looking at wing tip cordovans, got an early morning eyeful when she leaned over to help him take some shoes out of their box. Dis, in the back of the department, found himself getting the same eyeful – as if magnetically drawn to the shimmering silk and the plump flesh behind it. But as manager, he had to do something. He knew that the cut of her blouse was a violation of the store's informal dress code and that already tongues were probably flapping around the floor and beyond. So after she had made the sale he called her to the back room.

"Well, Dis, that guy wanted top-of-the-line and that what I gave him. He's walking away with a pair of Gorman Elites in brown and burnished leather."

"Listen, Amy Jane, I have to talk to you about something." God, Dis said to himself, what a cliché. Can't you come up with something a little bit more original?

"Oh, you do? What's wrong?"

Dis started to reply when she interrupted.

"Oh I know, you don't like my shoes." She lifted her leg and pointed her foot at Dis, in the process lifting her already short dress to above her knee. "I know they're tacky – I got them at Walmart – but I like them. They're a little bit . . . smart . . . you know, with-it."

"No, Amy Jane, it's not your shoes. It's your . . . blouse. It's a . . . how can I say this. . . it's a bit loose. Now don't get me wrong, it's extremely attractive, but . . . ah . . . you know Tilden's is a very conservative company . . . and . . ."

"Oh, Dis, don't be such a beat-around-the-busher. I get the point. You think my blouse is kinda low, don't you. You know, it looked so smart and smooth in the mirror when I put it on this morning, but you know what my problem is? I'm still too new on this job. Dummy me, didn't think ahead and remember that I'll be bending over old shoe boxes all day long." She reached out and touched Dis's arm. "But don't get all up-tight. I'll take care of it. A few pins in the back and I'll be able to do cartwheels in it."

"Now you realize, Amy Jane, there's nothing personal about . . ."

"Nothing personal, really Dis." She was gripping his arm now. "I find this very personal. . . and I thank you. You're such a nice guy – and a nice boss. Lot's of people I know – including some of those women over there in jewelry and perfume – are probably wagging their tongues right now, but you, you're so cool and compassionate." Here she let go of his arm but not before running her hand down his sleeve. "I'll go fix it, and Dis . . . thanks, thanks very much." She turned and left the little room that was overfilled with shelves of shoe boxes. Just as she slipped through the slit of the curtain which made up the door, however, she turned to him with a slight smile and said, "You can help me, you know."

Dis was stunned. What did she mean by that? Help her pin up her blouse? My god, the image leaped into his mind and refused to budge. His hands from behind pulling her blouse out of her skirt, then grazing the bare flesh of her waist as they reached around to her front and slowly moved upward to her constrained bra and the plumpy softness underneath.

Stop it, he told himself. She didn't mean anything. It's just her way of talking. She's as innocent as this . . . this shoehorn, which he had been lightly turning and twisting in his fingers. She was just saying that I could help her learn how to act and do a good job here at the store. Still what about that smile? What did she mean by smiling like that while she said, "You can help me."?

Just then Bill Bronkly, one of the two other shoe clerks, whipped through the curtain looking for a size 13 brogan in black, effectively interrupting Dis's quandary about Amy Jane's possibly provocative statement. Bill said, "Boy, you must have really said something to Amy Jane. She tore out of here a few seconds ago looking meaner than a senator left out of the pork-barrow. Never saw her look so angry."

"Are you serious?" Dis replied. "Shoot, I didn't think she was mad. She sure didn't act that way to me."

When she returned, with the blouse as demure as her extenuated superstructure could make it, she was as friendly and as breezy as usual. Dis wondered about Bill's comment, then almost forgot about it as they went about caring for a raft of customers' demands, brought on by a special sale of mid-priced shoes.

And then there was the "Rock and Roll Bicycle Tour."

This was an upcoming weekend bike ride that Dis had been chatting about with his staff during coffee breaks and when no customers were around. Sponsored and named after his club, the Rockhurst Rollers, the Rock And Roll Bicycle Tour, or RARBT (called "rarebit" by everyone associated with it) went up through the gentle hills and valleys between Baltimore and the Potomac River to Harrisburg, Pennsylvania. It was about 80 miles one-way, although a 40-mile short route was also available. Riders stayed overnight on Saturday at Global College, just to the south of Harrisburg.

The motif for the ride was Rock and Roll music. Each refreshment stop played recorded Rock music and a '60s music dance followed the meal at the college. Some of the riders got into the spirit of the ride by rigging their bikes with miniature speakers and tape players so they could blast out Three Dog Night or Jimmy Hendricks as they pedaled down the road. It was a fun ride with lightly traveled roads and lots of easygoing camaraderie along the way and at the college.

Dis's male fellow workers were not serious cyclists, although they listened to his tales of rides and tours, one of the few times he became really animated and spirited. Amy Jane, also not much of a cyclist, although she had an old steel Schwinn 10-speed rusting away in her garage, showed more interest than the others, asking for details because, according to her as she patted Dis on the shoulder, she had "never even known they had such things."

So Dis was almost bowled over on the morning of the first day of the ride, as he pulled into the second rest stop, located about 40 miles from the start – at the point where the short route started. There she was. She was bouncing around the picnic tables, wearing a bright blue pair of skin-tight biking shorts and an abbreviated yellow halter that made every movement of her full breasts and nipples obvious to every rest stop onlooker, which included almost every male, and many envious females. She ran up to him as he was leaning his bike up against a tree, and gasped into his face,

"Surprise."

"My god, Amy Jane, what are you doing here?"

"Well I'm going on the ride, don't cha know. I'll bet you can't believe that, right?"

"You're going to do Rarebit! But you're not a biker, you don't have any experience."

"I told you "surprise," didn't I? Hey, you're the cause of this. You talked so much at work, really getting excited about it, that you got me going. So I said to myself, 'I'm going to try it, but I'm not going to tell Dis because what happens if I chicken out or the weather is putrid or something.'"

"Wait a minute, wait a minute. I can't believe this. You – dressed like a biker – hey, neat outfit, by the way – are going to do Rarebit. Fantastic!" Dis was caught up in her enthusiasm.

"Well, I'm only doing the 40-mile section. I haven't even started yet, haven't even been on my bike. In fact, it's still on the car."

"Well, let's go get it.. I have to see this old baby Schwinn that you've talked about. That's the one you're using, right?"

"Well, no. My friend Marcy – she and her husband Jack live right down the street from me – well, anyway, Marcy just got a new bike last year. When I told her what I was planning, she practically forced me to take her bike. She hardly ever uses it; she doesn't like to be sweaty."

They almost ran to her car, a red TRX, a few years old and looking somewhat ragged. On the back, mounted on a trunk rack, was a spiffy Bridgestone RB-2 looking ready for action. As Dis was taking the bike off the rack for her, she inadvertently brushed his sweaty arm with her tight but resilient halter-top. The physical contact made Dis wonder what exactly this was all about. Should he be suspicious, or what? But in the excitement of the tour and with the prospect of riding with this attractive and fun-to-be-with female, he let caution fly away like a goldfinch disturbed by bikers rolling down a hill.

Actually he had a ball that weekend. They rode together, ate together, danced together, and spontaneously got into the spirit of the tour. Strangers who saw them probably thought they were a couple; but in talking to club members and acquaintances, both she and Dis were quick to disavow any relationship. They were both workers at Tilden's, both had significant "others," and both were just out to enjoy a good time this weekend.

She turned out to be a halfway decent rider, although Dis had to slow his usual pace to ride along with her, something which didn't bother him because they got on well together. She was inherently bouncy and optimistic, and seemingly without guile.

Except, well . . . Dis couldn't be sure.

When they had arrived at the college, and were looking for their baggage in the huge pile of bags, suitcases, duffels, etc. that the rented Rider trucks had deposited in front of the school's gym, Dis jokingly said, "What are you looking for, yellow? I bet you have a yellow tent to go with your yellow outfit."

Amy Jane replied, "No, just a green bag and a brown suitcase. I don't have a tent."

"You mean you're not tenting. What are you going to do, stay in the gym?"

"I thought of that, but the guy I talked to on the phone said they had some extra dorm rooms, so, hey, why not? I'm in a room, a room with two beds."

"Well, you lucked out. Usually they're out of rooms two weeks after registration opens up."

"Yeah, that's what he said. Hey, you want to stay in the room with me?"

Again Dis was taken aback. Did he hear that right? An invitation to share her room? Wait a minute, he couldn't do that. What was going on here? "Sure, I can pitch my tent right between the beds. But how do I put the tent pegs through the floor?"

"Oh come on, Dis, you silly guy." Here she couldn't resist giving him a sham punch to the chest, her hand lingering a split second longer than the action called for. "You wouldn't have to put your tent up. That's the point. Why go through all that work when there's an extra bunk?"

Dis wasn't quite ready for all that the invitation stood for – if it meant anything. Was she Miss Innocence or Madam Temptation? Whatever, he wasn't going to push his fate, not now at least. He pulled at an imaginary mustache and said with an exaggerated western accent: "A'm sorry, Miss Amy Jane, I'd shore like to share your domicile this here night, but, truth to tell, I snore so bad, especially after riding that there doggie all day, that you wouldn't be able to sleep a wink. So, shucks, I'll just amble out to the barn and sleep with those critters out there. They won't mind my snoring. Shoot, those pigs can out-snore me – not out-grunt me, but out-snore me – that's for shore."

"OK, Dis," she laughed. "OK, I get the point. I didn't really expect you to agree. You're too nice a man for that." She spied one of her bags, "Oh, there's my brown case. Now where's that green one?"

Partly out of being fatherly to this woman, who was probably here because of him, and being drawn to her vitality and, yes, her at times barely masked sensuality, Dis said, "A'm goin' ta pitch ma tent right over yonder." Then he reverted back to a more normal tone, "Should we eat together?"

"That would be great, Dis. You know I don't know hardly anyone else here."

"Well, let's see. It's about four right now. Get the tent up – shower – shave . . . How about around five-thirty. I'll stop by your room about five-thirty."

"Five-thirty . . . well, maybe six . . . sounds just about right. Oh, there's my green bag." She retrieved it and was about to leave with her luggage when she returned to him. She grabbed his arm in her normal way, but then with an extra pinch said, "Seriously, Dis, don't take me wrong about that room sharing. I was just thinking about you out here with the chance of rain."

"Rain? Did you say rain? Well, in that case forget this tent. You said you've got extra space in that room?"

"Oh, Dis, you goof. You know it's not going to rain. Go set up your old tent." Then she did it again – the same smile that he remembered from the blouse incident crept to her lips and she almost whispered, "But you better watch out." Here she did a modified hootchy-cootchy dance fluttering her hands in front of her face and almost singing, "I'm the sheik-ess of Araby, and into your tent I'll creep."

She turned, picked up her bags, and left him, her tight buns under the blue Lycra sash-shaying up and down, her bare midriff, faintly glowing from the day in the sun, curving with provocative flesh, and her auburn hair, held with a clasp in back, bobbing happily.

Dis didn't know what to say or think. All at once he yelled, "Hey, Amy Jane. What's your room number?"

She didn't even turn, but he could hear over the low din of bike tour sounds, "One-three-two."

Unfortunately, also hearing these last few exchanges was Eric Yowder, a fellow Rockhurst Roller who had ridden with them through a long, boring cornfield stretch outside of Shippensburg. Eric was one of those good looking guys who somehow always ended up talking about themselves. But he was single, and by his looks and actions, obviously found Amy Jane extremely attractive. He was looking for his bags also, and when Amy Jane left, he pushed someone's duffel bag at Dis and said, "Hey, married man, better watch out. She wants "you" in one-three-"two.""

"Naw, we're just friends – she works in my department. But, hey, you know that."

"Yeah, I know that, but I also know what my eyes saw and ears heard. And I'm envious, old buddy. Those blue shorts are something, right? Hot. Well, Dis my friend, don't get burned. Or be like me, always have the hose ready to put out the fire." With that and a roaring laugh and a knowing nudge to Dis's side, he left.

As Dis walked to his potential tent site, he was slightly troubled. He was absolutely innocent in his mind about his relationship with Amy Jane. But now there was a public witness of talk that could be misconstrued, although probably nothing would come of it because his wife, Ruth, hardly ever showed up at any bike club function. But what about Amy Jane and her intentions? Why did she suddenly, out of nowhere, pop out of the hat at that rest stop dressed all bright and itchy and waiting for him? Why didn't she even mention that she was also going to do this tour, especially when she made it known that she hardly biked at all? Also she worked under him; he was her boss, technically. The whole thing seemed vaguely like a conspiracy against him, and, as he started to put up his tent, he wondered if he should subtly alter his behavior with her – become more cool, reserved, stand-offish – introduce her to single guys and make sure they realized that she was not "his."

But on the other hand, he was having a ball and he didn't feel guilty. And she was above board with him. Sure, she had ridden with him, but she didn't know anyone else and he was the real reason for her presence on the tour. He had made it sound so appealing that she wanted to join in on the fun. She didn't tell him – made it a surprise – because she didn't want him to feel responsible in any way. Besides she, being a new employee, didn't want to appear to the other shoe department people as being too pushy. She just wanted to have a good time doing something she had never done before with someone whose company she enjoyed. That's why she waited for him. She didn't want to ride alone, that's for sure. But she also got along well with him and had fun – and was certainly not interested in a more serious relationship with him, a married man.

So Dis put off his reservations and had a blast. During the meal, the tour meeting that followed, and the '60s music played by a local DJ, he and Amy Jane and a host of other club members, acquaintances, and newly met people had a lively time. They ate well, talked fulsomely, and let themselves go during the dance. Dis found himself dancing all night – with Amy Jane, with fellow women bike club members, and with women he had only met in passing. And Amy Jane was in her glory. The men were almost literally lined up to dance with her – single guys, married guys, youngsters in their teens, and even some old farts. Even Vern, the 84-year-old "rock" of the club, the man who was always on every club ride, took his turn in holding her hand and leading her through "Me and Bobby McGee."

And nothing happened that night. They went happily to their separate beds – he to his tent and she to one-three-two.

The next day they rode together to the short route starting point where she loaded up her car and he took off for a fast and sweaty final 40 miles. When he got home, Ruth was in one of her foul moods – no one had showed up to an open house, even though she had been there for five straight hours. When she coldly disappeared into the bedroom without even saying goodnight, Dis tried to read the week's copy of Time Magazine. He stared at the pages but couldn't concentrate on them. The words kept blurring, because of tiredness or something else. And the blur kept turning into the number - one-three-two.

Chapter 8

Two weeks later Amy Jane organized another after-work get-together, this time for a Tuesday. But Dis was surprised when after closing up his department and arriving at the bar-restaurant, Tommy's on E Street, to find his boss, Silent Sam, sitting with the group. Bouncy Amy Jane had somehow conned the usually extremely taciturn man to join them. The store group, about ten people, was around a circular table, some on chairs and some on a soft cushioned extended bench. She was sitting right next to Sam being her usual lively self – but with a subtle difference. Was she or was she not was acting toward Sam the same way she had acted toward Dis on the bike tour and sometimes in private moments on the job? She wasn't exactly flirting, but she was obviously focusing more sharply on Sam. And, while not blatantly so, she was working her sex appeal.

The effect on Sam was almost astonishing.

Silent Sam suddenly became Silly Sam. He didn't come out of his shell; he climbed on top of it. Dis had never seen – or heard – him like this. He laughed uproariously; he told jokes; he gossiped – inconsequentially, of course; if there would have been dancing, he would have danced. At seven, when three fellow workers left, the Karaoke machine went on the line and Amy Jane, with her cheer-leading voice, started following the words on the screen and smiling at Silent Sam like a model in a new car commercial. A tiny thought buzzed like a bee into Dis's brain and then expanded into a full-blown colony: he was being set up. Why did he feel so suspicious about her when she had always been so nice to him? Why did he feel that she was after his job?

Was he being paranoid – converting a guileless, vivacious young woman into a predator stalking the corridors of Tilden's Department Store? Was he reacting to what he subconsciously felt was his own inadequacy as shoe department manager? And even more, was he really up-tight about his inadequacy as a man – his sour marriage, his almost non-existent sex life, his loneliness, his frustration on a job that didn't mean that much to him?

After that evening out, a subtle change took place in the relationship between Dis and Amy Jane. The joy and fun just weren't there. Dis found himself studying her more, but not openly – on the sly. She almost gave up her touching, although she appeared as friendly and funny on the surface as before. They still joked around with the other members of their crew between customers. They even shared lunch breaks together when the schedule allowed for it. But something was different; something that both of them knew but could hardly put into words.

Then about two weeks before Dis made his decision to disappear, his world of work started falling apart around him. It started with the women's washroom. At Tilden's the two employees' washrooms for the first floor were back-to-back in an area behind the elevators close to the loading dock. One day about two o'clock in the afternoon Silent Sam, followed by an entourage of all the other heads of departments on the first floor, marched through the shoe department and summoned Dis to follow. The group – six strong, including Sam – scurried through the store to the women's washroom. There, after knocking on the door and making sure it was vacant, Silent Sam pronounced, "Ladies and Gentlemen, we have a problem." He opened the door and led them in. When they were all assembled, staring absently at their reflections in the large mirror behind the two sinks, he abruptly about-faced and pointing over their heads, said: "And the problem is right there."

He was pointing at the water pipes from the two toilet stalls that they were now facing. Dis looked but could see nothing out of the ordinary. Then Sam took one of the room's stools, stood on it, and with a bony finger pointed to a space next to where one of the pipes entered the wall. Dis could barely see an opening; just a little light appeared on one side of the pipe.

Sam spoke: "Ladies and gentlemen, if you examine where that pipe enters this room, you will find an opening, an opening fairly recently made, and an opening that allows someone standing on a chair in the men's washroom which is directly on the other side, to see into this room, in fact to have a rather commanding view of this room. This pipe, you see, doesn't go through to the other side. It turns in the middle of the partition and goes upward, allowing someone on the other side plenty of head space to do his sickening viewing. Now, about an hour ago, a young lady employee of our shoe department, Amy Jane Andover, to be exact, was sitting before this mirror adjusting her makeup and clothing when, as she told me, she had a feeling, a perception, if you will, that she was being watched. She didn't look around, instead she looked into the mirror, and while scanning the room behind her, she noticed a movement right here." He pointed again at the opening.

"She focused on that movement and told me that she could clearly see an eye. Yes, ladies and gentlemen, an eye – a blue colored eye. While she was watching the eye, it disappeared. Miss Andover quickly jumped up and left, with the intention of seeing who was in the men's washroom. But she was too late. Within a few seconds Clifford Ford, from small appliances, entered the washroom. But before he did, she asked him to check if there was anyone else in the room. He reported that it was empty. She immediately went to her supervisor, Mr. Disberry, but found him busy with a customer, in fact a family of customers. Then, seeing me, and being very distraught about the incident, she brought it to my attention. I examined the hole from the men's washroom and found that it indeed offered an extensive view of the women's. I also noted that the hole appeared to be recently made, since the plasterboard was clean and there was even some plaster dust around it. I then went to Clifford Ford and asked him if he remembered who had used the washroom before him. He, unfortunately, did not know; he had simply walked from his department and found the room empty – as he told Miss Andover. So I would like all of you to do two things immediately: interview each of your male employees and find out when they used the washroom last; and secondly, ask them if they observed anyone except for Clifford Ford using the washroom around one-thirty or quarter-to-two. When you're finished, report back to me. I'll be with Warren here – helping him check out the loading dock area. Someone could easily have observed something from there."

All of the department heads dutifully did as instructed, but the results were nil. What with customers and varying duties, all any of the employees remembered was when they themselves had used the washroom – and even then they weren't sure about the time. At least that's what Silent Sam reported to the group of department heads after the store closed down that evening. All through the meeting Dis felt that Sam was looking at him much more than at the other department heads. When the short meeting was finished, Sam came up to Dis and pulled him aside. "As you know, I let Amy Jane go home early. She was very agitated – as were many of the other women. God, this is upsetting! But we've got to find out who did this. You'll do your best, won't you, Dis?"

Dis nodded – and wondered why he was being singled out.

"She's in your department, boy. Take special care these next few days. I hate to see someone so disturbed."

What is this "boy" stuff, Dis thought. He's never called me "boy" before. Dis felt a slide, a soft, evasive shift, in the almost nonexistent relationship between his boss and him. Something slipped into place.

Dis, however, was absolutely innocent. He knew nothing about the hole or the spying. He had used the washroom at lunch and while he was there, Frank Jasper, an effeminate snit who sold housewares, had come in complaining about the smell. All Dis would say was, "Yeah, when I came in, I needed a gas mask."

By the next day, Amy Jane had recovered. She was almost her usual self, except not quite as open and sportive as before. She was also dressed more conservatively, with a skirt that actually concealed her knees. But a rift was apparent between her and Dis. On the surface they were friendly and warm; underneath, however, Dis sensed that what had before been a crack was now a chasm.

As for the "incident," nothing came of it. Workmen appeared and fixed the hole in the wall. Employees received a memo about "respecting each other." Men noted at what time they used the washroom and didn't linger there. Women did even less lingering. In fact Dis heard from the grapevine that Gladys Southy didn't use the washroom at all any more. She went out to lunch just to use other facilities.

But, nevertheless, Dis felt that he was under suspicion.

And, as it turned out, he was.

At first it was just little things – minor changes in behavior that had no normal explanation. Amy Jane, while not consciously avoiding him, approached him cautiously now. The men in his department seemed to be wary. It seemed to Dis that if he joined a conversation during a slack period, the men either quickly moved off to "take care of my shoes" or something, or they awkwardly paused and searched for a new topic of talk. Silent Sam, formerly a shadow occasionally moving through the department, became a ubiquitous ghost; he seemed to be mysteriously present every time something untoward happened. The store's security personnel, usually not floorwalkers but floor-loungers, spent much time walking back and forth through his department. And he also noticed another "customer" who seemed to be constantly in the store, reappearing to examine the same shoes over and over again.

About three days after the washroom discovery, Dis was waiting on a customer, a young stockbroker from Miles and Miles down the street. He was on his knees reassuring the man about the toe space in a classy wing-tip from Italy when he looked up and saw Amy Jane leaning over a changing bench to reach some open boxes of shoes on the floor. Her flared skirt opened, and Dis found himself almost automatically looking at the sudden display of usually concealed flesh and underwear. Almost as soon as he noticed where he was looking, he felt a presence behind him. Sure enough, Silent Sam was right behind him, noticing where he was looking, his face looking slightly ironical and very arch.

A few days later while looking at sweaters during his lunch break, he overheard two sales clerks talking at the cash register kiosk about 30 feet away.

"It looks like the ol' stringbean is about to grab him."

"Are you serious. What happened?"

"Well, not much. But I heard from a guy in luggage that the gal knows for sure that he's the one."

"Come on, how could she know?"

"I don't know, but according to the luggage guy – you know, the guy with the big glasses – she was around here about a half an hour last night after everybody left, talking to the big bosses. All the department heads were there for the meeting. This guy in luggage didn't know what actually came about, but the idea is that they're about to put the old kosh on him."

"All really . . . ah, check sweaters out . . . we better be quiet, what do you think?"

Dis almost panicked, but he very discretely replaced the sweater he was looking at and left the store for a hurried stroll outside. Thoughts tumbled through his brain. They had an after-hours meeting with department heads and he wasn't included. What gives? What the hell is going on here? I'm innocent, for Christ's sake. What kind of evidence could they possibly have? It has to be me they were talking about. I'm a department head, for Christ's sake, and I wasn't told about that meeting – and she's from my department. It's her, I'll bet. God, maybe she's been setting this up all along. If I'm out, who are they going to replace me with? Not any of those other guys could handle it. But she could. God yes, she could. That's it. She's not after me – she's after my job! The hell with it, I'm going in to see Silent Sam and find out what's going on.

But he didn't. Sam was out and, according to his secretary, wouldn't be back until later that afternoon. But when Dis returned to the shoe area, one of his clerks, Gary Wright, a young, hairy fellow who always looked like he needed a good scrubbing, pulled him into the back room. "Listen, Dis, I have to tell you this even though they told me not to. You've always been square with me, so the hell with them. I don't care if they see me. They questioned me over my lunch hour. You know, about that washroom bit. But most of the questions were about you."

"Oh, Christ, what is this?" Dis felt the bottom go – he was screaming down a hill on a bike and hearing the snap of a broken axle; he was in the middle of a highway hearing the fearsome roar of a big truck on top of him, a quick glance in his mirror . . .

". . . Enough. Stop it, Dis. Stop it." It wasn't Gary Wright talking. It was he, Dis, talking – talking to himself. He looked into the mirror in the tiny bathroom of the shack and saw his face, suddenly strained, his eyes almost matching the round, moon-shape of his bicycle rear-view mirror.

To himself he said, "Put it behind you. It's finished. Gone forever. You're history there, a forgotten cipher. Who cares if she has your job – jumping around guys' feet all day long. Who cares. Forget about it. You're someone else now. It's a brand new world – a new one. And, hey, it's Sunday afternoon and you've got nothing better to do than go to a baseball game – a girls' softball game. What time did she say they played? At four? Heck, maybe at about four-thirty he would stroll past . . . what was it, Ramsey Square? . . . and get involved in watching a little softball."

Chapter 9

Dis lazily moved his leg, stretching as he lay wonderingly awake in that instant when the phantoms of night shift fitfully into the realities of wakefulness. Things were not right. The bed was not his bed, not the lumpy tilting washboard of springs and mashed cotton of the shack. The smell was not the antiseptic, bleach aroma of institutional sheets and pillowcases into which he subsided every night. And the foot which his stretching leg met was certainly not the emptiness with which he had been sleeping for so long.

The foot was Lorn's, and after touching it lightly, Dis quickly moved his foot away from it. Let her sleep. Let her sleep.

He didn't open his eyes, instead he simply let his mind remember where he was and what had happened:

The peach walls, bordered with tendrils of fruit and flowers squaring the room into definition.

The modesty with which Lorn had left him on the living room couch only to reappear from her bedroom wearing a slip of a silk robe, standing with the bedroom door half way open, looking squarely at him and saying simply, "Come."

His eruption, which was quick; a sharp, almost unexpected and involuntary tremor of pleasure, leaving him almost instantly at the lower end of the rainbow arc of sexual pleasure; and her, he was sure, still hovering over the cache of gold.

The start of his wistful, apologetic explanation – "God, I'm sorry, but it's been so long" – which she cut off completely by nipping the tip of his nose with her wayfaring teeth and saying, "Be still. Let me enjoy you now. I can wait."

Earlier, when they first kissed: the softness of her cheek on his. It had been such a long time since he had had this elemental human closeness that he drew away, turned away really, to mask the involuntary moistness coming to his eyes and the tightness pulling at his throat.

The simple beauty of her up close. Her tongue wiping her lips as if to completely savor every vestige of their kiss. Her forehead, spotted with a spattering of freckles. Her nose, upturned; but blunted, not sharp, ready to burrow. Her teeth and mouth, slightly out of skew, breaking the placid mold of the rest of her face, turning her into a one-of-a-kind, setting her apart with an offside distinctiveness. And her eyes – with lashes that brushed the world into clarity – transparent and tentatively green on the surface, but deep set with rock solid surety within.

The feel of her breasts on his chest as they lay in bed, side by side, kissing; twin extensions of her form and passion, trying to burrow into him, but soft – too soft – wonderfully soft.

The feel of her lower back as he skimmed it when he embraced her. Rounded but firm, resilient to his circling caresses.

Her humor as she gave him a Kleenex from her bedside table and said, "Here, my sweet Noah. Use this to clean up after the flood."

And above all, the contentment he felt as he drifted into sleep, her hand lightly touching his side, her smell brushing his consciousness, and the memory of her shift of passion when they made love, measuring his convex need and emptiness with a concave sheath of expectation and satisfaction.

Dis tentatively opened his eyes but could see nothing. The room was still in complete darkness; evidently it was still very early in the morning. He moved his head slightly, remembering with a faint smile how a winning hit in a girls' softball game led him to be here, warm and content, sleeping with a woman who, if he did not love, he certainly cared for overwhelmingly.

He had gone to the game and had quickly, with Lorn's open acceptance, become a member of the little group of parents and adult fans sitting behind third base and cheering with eager enthusiasm every nuance of girlish achievement on the part of Chrissy's team, the Central Wildcats. They had had a good time, partly because the other team had some definite weak positions, which allowed Chrissy's teammates to get on base more than their skills allowed. However, the opposing team, the hated Rams, reversed things at the plate. They kept pace, keeping the score even through inning after inning until it all came down to the last crucial and cliched moment – Chrissy at bat, her team down by one, two base-runners on, and the last inning of the game.

Dis smiled to himself in bed as he thought of the dribbling ground ball that Chrissy tipped from the side of her bat on a bad swing of a bad pitch. However, the ball eluded the third baseman and, beyond her, the left fielder was a decided Ram liability. When she eventually found the ball, she threw it to second rather than third or home plate. Chrissy's teammate, Debbie, crossed home plate with the winning run while the Rams' second baseman was grappling in the dirt with the under thrown ball.

But Chrissy was the heroine, and part of her glorious prize was the unprecedented permission to stay overnight at her best friend Janie's house, even though the next day, Monday, was a school day. Actually Janie's mother was the moving force, insisting so adamantly, especially since Janie needed some help with the last page of a weekend math assignment, that Lorn had relented – but only after making Janie's mother promise that the girls actually get some sleep.

Needless to say, after the game, the ensuing obligatory pizza party, and the early organizing of clothes for Monday morning, it was ten o'clock before Lorn knocked over a wooden chair in her kitchen after offering Dis a nightcap, a Lornaree McAbby special – Kahula over vanilla ice cream.

As she picked up the chair, she said, "God, you were good tonight, Rob. How you put up with a bunch of screaming pre-teenage girls for two straight hours just creases my Levi's. I'd have a number one, back-of-the-eyes headache if you hadn't been around."

"It was kind of fun. I enjoyed it." Dis hesitated. He didn't want to get into specifics about his past, but he said, "I've never done anything like that before."

She let a beat pass before she looked around from the ice cream container and dishes and said, "Anything like what? I'll give you your choice of three. Cheered a girls' softball team to victory; ate pizza and drank Coke-Cola with a noise level higher than the noon siren downtown at the fire station; or seemed actually to be enjoying yourself."

As he accepted the ice cream covered with the golden liqueur, and dove into it with a zest belying the pizza feast he had just finished, he replied quickly, "No, really, I had fun." He was about to say that he had never had an experience like that with a bunch of pre-teens, but he hesitated again. Let the past lie still. Celebrate the present. "I mean I like chocolate syrup glopped on my pepperoni pizza and flying paper drinking-straw covers in my eye. Oh, yeah, and singing "We are the champions" forty-three times straight. And trying to have a conversation with the woman with the red turban sitting next to me. And I really admire the incredible ability of the ordinary thirteen-year-old girl to hit high-Cs while saying, 'Oh, yuck'. Seriously though, two things were the best for me. Want to know what they were?"

Lorn pulled a blank. "What do you think? Naturally I do."

"OK then. One was you letting me share this day with you. I mean, going down Beartree and then the amazing victory of the Central Wildcats. I'm full . . . I'm content and happy and all those good things."

Another beat filled the Kahula charged air. She stopped it with, "And . . ."

He filled his spoon with a great lump of silvery ice-cream, dipped it into the thin reservoir of liqueur on the side of the dish, and brought it to his mouth. Mumbling, with his mouth full, he said, "De othure best ish zish ash crem. Ish topping." With that he lifted his chin to the ceiling, and gulped down the mouthful of sweet confection.

Lorn was beside herself with laughter, but Dis got up from his seat and went to her, behind her. He gripped her back and turned her around in the chair. "No, Lorn, you're the topping." Looking her straight in the eye, he said, "The best, I think, is being with you all day."

She deliberately placed her spoon in her dish, gently rose, and put her hands on his chest. "You're fun to be with too, you know." With that, she lifted her head up to his and kissed him, a simple touch of the lips, almost virginal, soft and pure. He moved his lips slightly, then drew back and looked at her again.

"In my need; in my loneliness," was all he could utter before he wrapped his arms around her, she nestling her head between his head and shoulder. He whispered in her up-close ear, "God, I haven't been close to anyone for so long. I haven't held anyone, kissed anyone, made love to anyone. Hold on . . . hold on. My legs are trembling so much, I could fall. Hold me, Lorn, hold me, please."

She did. She folded her arms around him, herself also relishing the contact, so needful, so true. Then she moved her hands from his mid-body to his neck and on to his head, one hand on each side. Holding his head, she eased away from him so she could see his face.

All she could do was look; words were meaningless. Light was purer than air and sound.

But touch was physical – had texture . . . reality. She slowly pulled his face to hers again. This time their lips clasped . . .

Dis, in his memory, as he lay in the dark in what was probably morning, thinking back, could not place time. He did not know how long they had stood, embracing, in the cozy kitchen of her apartment. He did know that he almost lost control of himself as the intensity of their kissing increased. He had been overwhelmed by the sheer physical rapture that built up, like clouds before a late afternoon thunderstorm, between and within them. He remembered sharply that he was ready to explode when she abruptly left him and disappeared into her bedroom – only to reappear in silk and with that one word, "Come."

It had been less than wonderful, however. He was too quick – an adolescent without control, a schoolboy erupting almost spontaneously at the first contact with warm flesh. But she, in her knowing and loving, had taken it in stride, and had been content to hold him silently, cushioning him in the warmth of her arms and bed as they drifted into sleep.

But he was awake now, savoring the softness of her bed. He wanted her softness too, though. Slowly he stretched out his foot again, this time deliberately touching hers, rubbing it, and wrapping his instep over its top. She surged slightly, next to him, waking with a start. He did not know this since it was still absolutely dark; he could not see her face flutter as she became consciously aware of his presence in her bed. He could not see the slight smile on her lips as she turned to him and moved into his sleepy embrace. But he did feel the wonderful fullness of her as she slipped into the warm depression shaped by his body. He instinctively wrapped his arms around her garment-less body, almost surprised at the sheer pleasure to be touching flesh – warm, soft, and smooth flesh. He drew her closer, her head below his, his nose breathing in the unique scent of her hair. With slight pressure he both lifted her up and lowered himself so that their faces touched. He brushed her lips with his, then said, "I'm dreaming. This can't be real."

With his lips on her nose, she murmured, "Keep dreaming," and surged against him, this time her lips finding his – soft lips that became hard – lips that opened to liquid tongues.

He reached lower. This time, he thought to himself, is for both of us, not just me.

And it was – for both together in need and urgency.

He was helpless, his body in control of his mind, and all of his body concentrated into his sex. And he was within her, and she was in rhythm with him, and all was right, all was perfect, all was one.

He looked down in the darkness, and although he could not see her, he could feel her face, her pleasure, her acceptance of him – but her love . . . he did not know. She lifted her head and brushed his face lightly. She whispered, "Oh, Rob. Rob. I know you now. I know I like you very much, but I need to know all about you. Oh, I can't wait. You know what you are? You're a map. That's right, a map to be unfolded." With her hand she brushed his face, feeling its surface, touching it lightly, like a furniture maker feeling a newly sanded surface.

"Yes," Dis said, almost to himself, "I need to be unfolded." He loved the contact of her hand. He put his arm up and used it as a pillow for her head. With his other hand he explored her belly randomly but with keen interest, like a prospector in a virgin mountain valley. "You know, you're right. I have been a map."

He thought quickly about the lies that he had told her about his supposed past. He was a shipping clerk in Pennsylvania with a high school diploma, a mother and father at home, and a great compelling need to get away, to change, to find himself by setting off cross country on a bike. He was unencumbered by a wife, girlfriend, or children. In short, he was as free as a highway, snaking up and down through the hills of Kentucky. But, God, how could he be intimate with her, intimate beyond sex, and not get caught up in an increasingly complex web of lies and fabrications? What he wanted to do, needed to do, was to spill the whole story. But how could she live with that – murder, desertion, alienation? He couldn't put her through that – his own particular ring of hell. She didn't deserve that.

But she didn't deserve lies either.

Then it hit him. He couldn't tell her the truth because quite simply, she would make him face up to it. He knew to his core that Lorn was a woman who could not live a lie. If he told her, he would be back where he started – only it would be worse. He would have to face Ruth; perhaps, he would even have to face the management and his co-workers at Tilden's; and, for sure, he would have to face the Washington D.C. criminal court system.

He didn't think he could do that. Lying was easier – and it worked. At least it had so far. By himself, on his bike, these last weeks, he had found it easy to do, in fact, he even enjoyed it. It gave him at times an exhilarating sense of being completely himself – self contained and self sufficient. We was truer to himself by lying.

Or was he?

He did know that his past was leaving him, becoming dim, indistinct. The minutia of detail that he had lived with for so many years was drifting from his memory, replaced not by details, but by emotions and feelings, dispositions that were hateful to him, that he did not ever want to face again:

Take it, God damn it, take it.

Dis, you bastard, don't do this to me.

He moved his hand upward and cupped her breast, feeling its roundness and its slight nipple with the tips of his fingers. It was then that he realized that he had never seen it, in fact, had never seen her naked. Last night he had walked into her darkened bedroom and closed the door. Now the night still lay like a velvet canopy over them, taking away sight, but heightening the other senses – touch, smell, taste, speech.

He spoke – whispered. "You know, Lorn, you're a map too. A map that I want to explore. Let's see. I want you on my front pack; that way you will always be in front of me, right. I would be able to see you constantly. You'd be my guide, my reference, my. . ."

She softly interrupted, "My cue sheet."

He laughed, "Right. And then, now get this, then when I've gone through this section of my life, I'll unfold you and there'd be all kinds of new territory. You'd be a brand new, unexplored area. . ."

Laughing, she took his hand in the dark and moved it lower towards her navel. "Sure, a country with valleys, some strange and unexpected." Here his hand met the bud-like depression. "There'd be hills." She moved his hand upward to her softly complacent breasts. "But not mountains," and she lifted her face up and kissed him quickly. Then she again moved his hand downward. This time pushing it below her navel. "And there'd be unexplored country – well, not quite – but country of . . . complexity . . . of risk . . . of pleasure . . . of . . . But enough of this, it's Monday morning, at least I think it's morning."

She leaned out of the bed and reached to the bedside table, pushed a button, and a clock lit up. After her eyes adjusted, she spoke, "It's about five-thirty, Rob. A little bit early for me; I usually get up at 6:00. But we're awake now. I think I'm going to get up and make something special for breakfast. Let's see, do you like . . . meat-loaf and gravy?"

"What? Oh, well, yeah . . . covered with catsup, with lots of greasy fried onions on the side. . ."

"Got-cha. Coming right up. On the other hand, how about some French toast? French toast made the McAbby way?"

She rolled out of bed, and still in the dark grabbed her silk robe. Slipping it on, she went to the window, the robe still opened slightly. Dim light from a far off streetlight crept through a narrow opening between the curtains, giving Dis, who was watching intensely, an image that he would remember for the rest of his life – her breast, framed in silk, and bathed in powered light. In an instant the silk covered it, but not before it registered in Dis's mind as pure beauty – soft, white, symmetrical, and something else, something unworldly, something celestial – something unearthly.

French toast the MacAbby way turned out to be a modified strata – a bread and egg mixture, baked and topped with gooey American cheese. That and a pot of coffee and beautiful Lorn, with her freckles and slightly crooked teeth, were the components of the best Monday morning breakfast that Dis could remember. Small talk and no talk was the conversation, but when she had finished eating and was sipping her coffee, she reached for his hand and said," You know, Rob, last night was really not me."

Bantering, he said, "It wasn't? Well, I wondered about that. I told you, didn't I, that I thought I was dreaming."

"No, I mean, the sex. . . hell, I was probably more horny than you. It had been a long time for you, I knew, but I'll bet even longer for me."

He grasped her hand tighter, "I think I know what you're trying to say, and I think it's the same with me. I don't want just a roll in the hay."

"I got carried away last night. I mean, I just don't do things like that. Don't get me wrong, I have no regrets. In fact, to tell you the truth, it was damn wonderful. I love you as a lover. But I guess you captured something of me – something that said, 'Let go.'"

He shifted and looked her straight in the eye, "No regrets. Lorn, I didn't plan on anything; I didn't have any ulterior designs; I just know that what happened, happened – and it was an unexpected gift – a great and wonderful gift that I feel so good about that I just can't explain. I do know this: I'm not leaving this town." He let go of her hand, and said, "Now if you will please pass the syrup, I'd like to finish this here Kentucky special, McAbby toast."

"Wa certainly, Sir. Syrup comin' up. Would cha lak me to pour? We aim to please."

"Well, I'll have to say this. You sure do. That's right, you sure do please."

Dis ate his breakfast with consummate pleasure. Then he left on foot, discretely, popping out from her side yard onto the street, trying to appear as if he had been naturally strolling down the street. Lorn had neighbors who talked to each other about such things, and she told Dis she would just as well not like to be the center of their conversation this week. One neighbor in particular, a red-wigged irascible old lady whose brain seemed to be softening into lard, had her face plastered against her front door window pane every time Lorn started her car. The situation as she explained it to Dis was, "Listen Rob, I'd give you a ride to your place, but as soon as I start that little old car of mine and you're in it with me, they'll be so much noise from telephones ringing in this neighborhood that it'll drown out the MTV in all the teenager's bedrooms all cross town, causing them to wake up and get to school on time, and then what would happen? Who knows?"

So Dis made his escape. As he strolled past Mrs. Red Wig, he noticed no discerning eye following him. He spent his morning at his "shack" cleaning his bike, whistling and singing to himself, and saying "Hot Damn" to his reflected image every time he passed the stained mirror in his bathroom.

Chapter 10

Dis went to work at about a quarter to three feeling pretty good about himself and his world. He had had a good Sunday ride, had enjoyed being part of a family through the evening, and had lost himself in the warmth of Lorn's wonderfully charged bed that night. He had even escaped the wrath of Mrs. Red-Head, he hoped. God, it was good to be alive.

He even had some positive feeling about the next eight hours at the "You Got It." He really didn't mind the work, even though it was strictly dead-end and he was just barely making enough to support himself. "You know," he thought to himself as he waved through the tobacco smoke to Marge, "if I'm going to stay around here, I should start looking for a better job."

He and Marge got along, after a fashion. He liked to kid her about her smoking, making exaggerated fan motions with his hands, clearing the air symbolically, when they chatted in the absence of customers. Through her smoke screen, they spoke most of the time, however, about the work details of a clerk changeover at the convenience store: the changed prices of this or that, the need to keep an eye on the supply of milk or a particular brand of beer, the items that Dis could put on the shelves if he had free time. Dis made a habit of jotting these things down on a pad which he kept in his shirt pocket, a practice which always threw Marge for a minor loop.

"God damn, you're acting like a reporter again with that little book pad."

"That's right, and I'm about to conduct an interview with central Kentucky's supreme champion cigarette roller."

"You don't say," she muttered to him, blowing a mouthful of smoke into his face.

"Is it true that you roll cigarettes in your sleep? That you keep the pouch and the paper on old George's fat belly? That you can roll a cigarette while giving change? That you can . . ."

"OK, OK, you got that little paper book, well you listen to me, and take this down – A'm gonna roll all right, A'm gonna roll right out of here. A'm gonna roll right home and make me and George a big pot of chili – you oughtta taste my chili, it's got more bite to it than . . ."

Dis interrupted. "Bite? It probably tastes like smoke. *Marlboro* chili. Hey folks, try this new special we got for you today, *Marlboro* Chili – chili that not only bites but smokes."

She interrupted, "Hey, Rob, I thought you was interviewing me. Put that little pad away and listen. Anyway a'm going home, gonna have me some chili, gonna sit back on my big ol' couch, put my feet on big ol' George's big ol' belly, and watch the TV. And you know what you're gonna be doing? You're gonna be stocking this here store with *Marlboros*. That's right, a case of 'em just came in and you need to get some of 'em on the shelf."

"*Marlboros*, watch this now, Marge, I'm writing this down. How do you spell it?"

"Oh, hush, you, and get behind here. Ahm gonna take me some of these kidney beans and . . . boy, I can taste that chili right now.

She left – a skinny, wizened lightning rod amid a cloud of smoke – a woman whose public face was cracker-wrinkled, indistinguishable from thousands of others behind the miles of counters that lined America. Privately, however, and underneath her taciturn facade, Marge was a hoot.

Her husband, George, was the owl. Dis didn't really know him because he swooped in only occasionally during Dis's night shift, never saying much, but noticing everything. He did come by most nights at a few minutes before eleven to check the receipts before the change was locked in the safe. A security truck picked up the day's large bills earlier in the evening so usually there wasn't too much cash around the store, a fact that gave some comfort to Dis. He hoped all of the desperate, gun-and-run, hold-up scum of the area knew it too, although they probably could not read the notice about the store's absence of cash that was posted on the main entrance. Tonight, however, when George materialized about eight-thirty, something was different about him. He seemed to be more flitty than usual, sweeping around the store like a darting hummingbird, constantly at the counter for a few seconds and then gone somewhere else in the store. When Dis did catch his eye, he would turn away quickly and then disappear. Finally, right after a young mother and her two-year-old had left with a package of Twinkies and a copy of The Globe, Dis could take it no longer. Instead of tidying up around the counter area, which he usually did when the place was empty of customers, he deliberately put his elbows on the plastic surface and waited, looking out over the store. Sure enough, like a fish rising to a bait, George materialized right in front of him. "Caught cha," Dis blurted before he could stop himself.

All George did was look at him, his eyes hardly visible behind his great glass spectacles.

"What's going on tonight? You're running around here like a snag in a pair of women's nylons. What are you doing, checking up on me or something?"

"No." Then he said nothing more.

Dis waited.

Finally the man put his hand up to the counter and said, "Shake."

After a beat, Dis said, "Shake? OK, I'll shake." He grasped the man's hand and they shook. That seemed to be that. George withdrew his hand and remained where he was, placidly looking at Dis. Finally George broke the silence. "We're going to give you a raise."

"What? A raise? God, you had me going there for a second. A raise, hey, that's all right. But I've only been here for about a week."

"Marge and I have talked it over and we're going to give you a 25 cent-per-hour raise starting today." With that he turned and walked away as if, like a balloon losing its air, he had exhausted himself and was now completely flaccid. He walked, not swooped, to the door and disappeared.

Dis looked after him with a mixture of disbelief and satisfaction. Twenty-five cents an hour meant, let's see – two bucks a day, ten bucks a week – big deal! However it did mean that Marge and George thought well of him and had come to rely on him. His own personal money matters were improved, but not by much. Right now, after getting his weekly check on Saturday, he had a new hundred-dollar bill in his secret compartment next to the two that were there before he hit town. In his wallet he had sixty-three dollars, and his pocket had a smattering of small change. After paying for his rent; basic, inexpensive food – much from cans and the produce department of an "Eat Well" supermarket down on the highway, but also much from the Hardee's – and for some necessary clothing, Dis had managed to save about half his first paycheck.

It wasn't much, but he wasn't in debt and $350 was probably enough to get by on for awhile if he had to leave. But he wasn't planning to leave – he now had a raise, ten bucks more a week, and there was Lorn, of course. But who was he kidding? He was going nowhere here. And in the big world he was probably a wanted man, a man who couldn't make waves. Subconsciously, Dis let things slide. He would stay just where he was, build up a little savings, sit tight, be ready to move, and, in the meantime, have the excruciating pleasure and possible pain of expanding his relationship with Lorn.

Chapter 11

Around 9 o'clock he had another surprise – this time from a lone male customer who Dis recognized – a bicyclist who had been at the same table with Lornaree and him when they breakfasted at Mindy's Bar and Grill out on Beartree Dis thought his name was Tom . . . Tom Mitton. The man rummaged around in the back grocery section before coming to the counter with a half-gallon of milk and some cottage cheese.

As he presented a five-dollar bill to Dis, he said, "I think I know you. Were you riding with us out on Beartree yesterday? Sure, your name's Rob and you were sitting at the same table with me." He laughed, "You weren't paying much attention to me or the other guys at the table. I don't know why. Could it be Lornaree?"

"What do you mean? Your name is . . . Tom, Tom Mitton. Am I right?"

"Damn. How'd you remember that?"

"Hey, we were talking back and forth." Dis smiled, "Was there a woman at our table?"

"Come on, man, give me a break. Listen, Rob, you the owner here?"

"Come on, Tom. Nope. I just tend the bar. Sell a little milk, a bit of bread, and a whole bunch of condoms."

Tom laughed and then paused, getting serious. "That means you're a clerk, right?"

"Just what I thought." Tom paused, then tossed off, "Minimum wage, I bet, right?" After Dis nodded, "Listen, Rob, you're a guy in good shape who looks like he could handle some real work, some outdoor work. I'm a contractor; got a small construction company down on Doubleday Road, and right now I need someone to help out – do some digging, some dirty work, that sort of thing. Weak mind, strong back sort of stuff, you got me? Now, I don't know your situation here, but if you were to show up at Mitton Construction, Doubleday and the Highway, tomorrow morning at six, you could work for a good ten hours at twelve-fifty an hour – six days a week, for awhile at least."

"Jeez, Tom, I couldn't do that and leave Marge and George – you know, the owners of this place – just like that, with no warning . . ."

Interrupting, Tom said, "I was hoping you'd say that. Actually it was a little test. But I'm serious about the job. I do need somebody – and soon. I'm using temps now, but, Jesus, you gotta spend half your time with them, just to make sure they're working – and haven't run off with most of your tools, wood, whatever. So if you can work it out with . . . with whoever is running this place, come out and see me. You'll have to work hard, but you'll be making what – twice as much as you make around here?"

"What can I say, I'm interested. I did do construction work a long time ago. Probably my legs are up to it, but I don't know about my arms."

"That's right, you're the guy that was biking cross-country at random. Shoot, you oughta be in great shape – and the way you were riding out there on Beartree, I know you are. Hey, a little construction work will do you good."

"What do you mean, I really get a work-out around here. Lifting packs of cigarettes, shuffling candy bars, even making coffee means I have to haul all that water. But, yeah, I'm interested. I'm going to have to think this over. Tell you what,

I'll get back to you one way or the other. Mitton Construction, right – at Doubleday?"

After Tom left, Dis almost caught himself hyperventilating. A decent job offer, a raise, and Lorn, all in the same twenty-four hours. Was he living right, or what? Without question he would take the construction job. It sounded ideal. This Tom seemed like a good man to work for, and with all that money he could really load his secret compartment. Besides with construction there wouldn't be much of a background check, probably nothing at all. Laborers were a fluid commodity.

The only problem was quitting on Marge. George, he could care less about, but he had developed a certain affection for the acerbic co-owner. She had grit, determination, and, behind her blank-faced facade, a lively, intelligent sense of humor. Oh, well, they could go back to longer hours while trying to find someone else to do what he had been doing. Shoot, just when they had given him a raise. He wondered if Marge was behind that. Probably. He couldn't conceive of the Owl having anything to say or any opinions to express. She probably brought it up, and ol' Owl had to come a-flitting over here to check me out – again and again. I hope they didn't get into an argument over giving me a raise, with Marge for it and George saying no. God, that would be bad, if she finally won and then I go and quit on them. But, on the other hand, I don't owe them anything. I've done my job, put in my time, and received very basic compensation for it. Opportunities arise. You can't say no to that open door.

He had to stop his inner monologue because suddenly the place was filled with customers. A mother was trying to explain to her two adamant kids that there was no Bubbleific; that they would have to take Bubble-Gubble instead. The kids would have none of it, insisting that they should look through all the packs of gum in the display boxes. She said, "Let's go," but the kids wouldn't budge, their searching hands making a mockery of the geometric, rectangular order that Dis had established during some of his low-traffic time.

A man was looking over the magazines, reading the back cover of each one.

Two young, yuppy types were having an animated discussion about fishing lures in front of the coffee machines, taking tiny sips from their steaming paper cups between lively retorts.

Three teens in "grung" clothing were looking through the videos, giving loud critical summaries of every one they had seen – which seemed to be the entire collection displayed by the store. "Oh, yea, I seen that at my girl friend's. A couple'a heads roll, and one guy, man, gets it in the face with a spade. It's not bad . . . well, kinda boring actually."

A woman dressed as if she had just come from an office – suit, white blouse with neck scarf, goin'-to-work shoes – was at the counter, buying thirteen lottery tickets: ten "Box o' Funs" and three "Majestic Madnesses."

All at once two teens, a boy and a girl, burst into the store. The girl's blouse was miss-buttoned, causing a bunched-up bulge in her mid-section; and the boy had lipstick stains all over this chin. The girl clutched the boy and almost pushed him over to the snack food aisle. She started looking over the array of fat-saturated potato products when surprisingly her boy friend attacked her. "Come on, Teresa, you old left legger. You got one leg longer than the other and you know it." She was standing there, in front of the racks of snacks, when Billy slammed her. He chopped her from behind on the leg, her left leg, and whispered hoarsely as he did it, " I said, 'Let's go, Left leg.'"

Her hands went out, pushing him with all of her outraged, teen-young force. "Don't call me that, Billy-baby!"

He staggered backward, almost falling over the metal greeting card rack. To steady himself, he grabbed at the rack, crushing some of the cards in the top row, ironically the Sympathy ones. Suddenly with a movement evidently learned from Chinese action movies and practiced for hours, he kicked his leg in a circular whip that struck her leg on the side, the left leg again. He started the same chant, "Left leg, left leg, left leg," kicking her each time.

She started moaning and swinging her arms randomly in front of her, trying to reach him as he backed away down the aisle, all the time kicking with his right leg. "Left leg, left leg, left leg."

Dis skittered around the counter and out the locked half-door of the counter area. Enough was enough. They were going too far and he had to stop them before this developed into chaos. In the periphery of his eye he noticed the three teen guys edging towards the battling couple.

Suddenly the man at the magazine rack appeared as if by magic in front of Billy, dodging his kick and grabbing and stopping the offending leg, leaving Billy stupidly pinioned on one leg, like a scruffy dancer on a yard sale music box. Without a word the man heaved Billy's leg to the floor – it almost bounced – and then backed away so he could see both of the fighters. All he did was glare – no words, no admonitions. But it was enough.

Teresa edged closer to Billy, almost seeking protection from the glare. Then she looked around and suddenly noticed that the entire store was looking at her. Her cheeks became red and she seemed to wilt, her body nervously twitching, especially her abused left leg.

Dis rushed up and yelled, "O K, you two, you better get out of here. On second thought, you miss, you better stay here for awhile. Do you have someone who can pick you up?"

In a tiny voice, a high-pitched whisper, she said, "I'll go with him. Hey, no big deal. We was just having it out, that's all. Billy gets that way every once in awhile. Come on, Billy, let's get out of here. I'm going to take the Doritos. Yea, they'll be good. You gonna get anything?"

"Naw . . . well, I guess I'll have to get these cards." He still had two cards clutched in his hand.

The man who had actually stopped the fight was nowhere to be seen. But Dis, in the back of his mind, knew he had seen the man before . . . at least he thought he had.

George didn't come in at eleven that night. But before that Dis made his decision. He would tell either George or Marge immediately that he was going to quit. After he had talked to them about it – he owed them that at least – he would contact Tom to see when he could start construction work. As he locked up the store that night, he decided to ride out to Doubleday and check this construction company out, even thought he knew he wouldn't be able to see much in the dark.

Next afternoon, about two-thirty, Dis walked into "You Got It" determined to tell Marge about his decision to quit. Two customers were in the store, but almost before he could say hello, Marge stopped him with one of her typical squinty-eyed comments, expelled between puffs of smoke, "A guy was in here asking about you."

"Jesus. What?" It slipped out before he could control himself.

"Yeah, a guy came in about ten, wanted to know, you know, stuff about you. Your name, where you lived, stuff like that."

"What'd you tell him?"

"Wadda you think?" She lifted her eye at him through the smoke. Dis thought he could detect a hint of a smile.

"Well, I don't know, I hope. . . " A customer who wanted a pack of Camel Straights interrupted them.

When she had rung up the man's purchase, she said, "Not a god-damn thing."

"What?"

"That's what I told him – not a god-damn thing."

"Jesus, Marge, I appreciate that. Not that I'm wanted by anyone or anything like that, it's just that . . . What'd this guy look like?"

Her fingers were rolling again, automatically stretching the paper and pouring a neat line of tobacco perfectly down the middle. "You know, Rob, I like you. You're a good clerk. So I don't want any strange bastard comin' in here, asking questions, and gummin' up the works. I told him nothin'."

"Great, Marge, great. What did he look like?"

"Average"

"Average?"

"Yeah, white, about six-feet tall, brown eyes and hair, bushy eyebrows, hair thinning a bit, cut short, but not a crew-cut, wearing a . . . let's see . . . kind of an off-blue jacket – almost gray, sports shirt, dress pants, leather shoes, not sneakers, had a ring – looked like a wedding ring, talked soft with kind of a hushy voice, low not high, didn't have any warts or anything like that, but had lots of hair in his ears, some in his nose."

Dis couldn't believe her; that was the most she had spoken at one time since he had known her. But her description didn't trigger any identification in Dis's memory. Who was this man and what did he want? "So, you didn't even tell him my name?"

"Nope."

"Did he say why he wanted to find out about me?"

"Nope."

Dis said distractedly, "Hmm, well it's probably nothing. Maybe an old friend or someone back in Pennsylvania."

"Nope. He did ask about Iowa though."

"Iowa?" Dis was in a quandary. He had told Marge that he was from Pittsburgh, Pennsylvania. The only persons in town who had heard him mention anything about Iowa were Lorn and her daughter, Chrissy, and that was the first night when he was drowsy from crashing his bike. He had never gone into his past with Lorn since then. Iowa, that was the state on Robert Clemmon's ID. Someone was looking for the dead man, not Dis. But he effectively was the dead man.

"Iowa. I don't know anything about Iowa . . . never been there. What did he say about Iowa?"

"Didn't say, just asked."

"Go on."

"Is your night clerk from Iowa?"

"What?"

"That's what he asked, 'Is your night clerk from Iowa?'"

"Iowa, that's strange. What did you tell him?"

"I told you – nothin'."

"Well, thanks, Marge. I don't know what's going on. Must be a mix-up somewhere. Did he say he'd be back?"

"Nope. See that box over there. Those are What-Nut Cups, some kind of new candy bar. They gotta be shelved. Also see this check here. No more from him.

We just got a debit notice from the bank. And . . ."

Marge continued her end-of-the-shift routine, but Dis was hardly listening. What the hell was he going to do? He couldn't very well tell her right now about quitting after she had gone out of her way to protect him from this questioner. Yet he needed to get over to the construction company quickly or the job would be gone. But, what the hell, someone was hot on his tail. Jesus, all at once he had problems. What should he do?

Nothing, except the routine, was what he ended up doing. Marge left and he took over the store, but he did the work automatically, his mind in a multi-faceted quandary. He wanted to stay in this little town. Lorn was a gasp of air into suffocating lungs. He had the real possibility of a decent-paying job. But someone was after Robert Clemmon . . . wait a minute. Marge didn't tell the guy anything, not even my name. The guy just wanted information about the night clerk. But he knew Iowa. Jesus, how did he connect me and Iowa? He's got to have something substantive because people from Iowa are a rarity down here. He's not just looking for haystack needles; he knows about me.

Dis realized that his little world of Jeffrey, Kentucky, was disintegrating, that, in fact, if he didn't get away, the rest of his life could disintegrate. *Someone is still looking for Robert Clemmon and I killed him.* This hit Dis as he was going over cash register totals during a lull after the dinner hour. He was tempted to let out a loud "SHIT," but as he looked up, the door opened and the man who had stopped the fight the night before walked in. The man was wearing a light blue jacket, a sports shirt, and dress pants over leather shoes. He looked around, glancing momentarily at Dis, then went over to the magazines and looked through them, paying particular attention to their back covers.

Dis almost panicked. His pulse rate went up and he could feel his cheeks getting red. This guy could be some kind of a detective and he could arrest me right now. Jesus, I can't leave. There's no one else here. What the hell am I going to do? Again, the answer was nothing, because nothing happened. After about five minutes, the man walked up with a TV Guide, paid for it with a five-dollar bill, and left. He didn't even mention the fight the night before. Dis breathed easier – but only momentarily. Through the store's window, Dis watched the man get into his car – a fairly new gray, common model, perhaps a Ford Taurus or something like that – but he didn't leave. The car with the man in it just remained in the lot, out past the light, in the slot closest to the highway.

He's waiting for me, Dis thought. As soon as I get off work, he'll grab me. He can see me from here, can watch every move I make – except when I go to the back of the store. Keep calm and figure out a plan. How can I get away from here without him seeing and following? Lucky thing I ride my bike and keep it in the back room. I can leave from the back. Does he know where I live? Probably not since I didn't see him last night.

Wait a minute. Last night. Was he out in the lot? No, I would have noticed him if he hung around the lot. What about when I left? Come to think of it there was a car that followed me for awhile last night. I remember being bugged waiting for it to pass me – and it was light colored too. Hey, last night is when I rode out to the construction company – and I took a short cut through that barrier where they're fixing Whilhelm Road. I probably lost him there. Damn, and I didn't even know I was doing it. He probably thinks I live out there somewhere. I could leave now. Go up in front and secretly lock the door, leave the lights on, and sneak out the back. Boy, that would really piss off Marge. She and George might even get the local police involved. In fact, Bill Effingham, the cop who regularly stops in during the night shift, would probably notice my absence and start all kinds of checking, including getting George and Marge out to the store. Of course, Marge knows there's something funny going on – what with this guy asking about me. And she knows where I live . . .

Just then the door opened and George, the Owl, swept silently in. He pinioned around the coffee machines and swooped to the back of the store near the frozen food cabinet. George immediately made up his mind and grabbed the opportunity. He left the counter and sauntered to the back of the store, out of sight of the gray car. There, he almost had to trap the elusive George, who without looking at him tried to keep away from his approach.

"George, stop and listen, OK? I got a real problem, George, and I'm sorry, but you're going to have to help me out. I'm going to have to take off right now. Can you take over the store?"

The glass-eyed George said nothing, just stared.

"Also, I'm going to have to quit. I appreciate your offer of a raise, but I got a much better job offer and I just can't turn it down. Besides you knew I was just temporary, didn't you? I mean, I liked this job, but, come on, a man can't live on minimum wage forever. Anyway, I have to leave right now. I . . . ah . . . just got a phone call from my . . . girl friend. She's got an emergency and, what can I say, I just have to go and help her."

In the front of the store, the door opened. "Damn," Dis thought to himself, "I've been too long in the back. The guy's getting suspicious." But it was just two teenage boys who entered and started over to the magazine section. "So anyway, George, everything's balanced behind the counter. I'm really sorry about this, especially such short notice. I know Marge'll be pissed, and I'm really sad about that, but a man's got to do what he's got to do, right? Here's the key and . . . I'll be back next week sometime to collect my pay, all right?"

With that, without waiting for a reply – and without getting as much as a question on George's placid face – Dis walked through the back employee's door of the "You Got It" for the last time. He picked up his bike in the storeroom and then left through the delivery door, which locked automatically behind him. He walked his bike across the slender patch of blacktop behind the store, keeping the store between him and the front parking lot with the gray car. Typical of new edge-of-the-city businesses, the "You Got It" was backed by a fenced farmer's field. This one was corn – half-matured corn. Beyond the field was a small suburban development of about ten homes. Also typical was that the kids from the development had opened a small section of the fence and in their comings and goings had even worn a semblance of a path through the field. Still keeping the store between him and the car, Dis quickly walked the bike to the right, parallel to the fence, searching for the opening. Just when the rear of the car started to come into his view, the fence opened up, and Dis was off. He walked – ran, actually – the bike down the slight path, bouncing it both because of the rough terrain and because he was constantly looking back to see if he was observed or if there were any sign of the car leaving. Within 300 yards the path veered and he was protected from being observed, but of course he also couldn't see the car. Dis wondered how long it would take the man to discover that he wasn't in the store anymore. Headlights sweeping in an arc through the soybean field put an end to the question. The man, who because of the night before knew Dis used a bicycle, was evidently driving around the store to see if Dis was in back or if there was a back exit.

Would he see the opening in the fence?

Dis didn't have time to consider. He had come to the end of the path, a corner of the field that abutted two fairly new suburban yards, both expansive and clear – not a tree in either. He jumped on his bike and surged through the closest yard to the street, jumping and veering through the choppy grass. The development's streets corkscrewed to one main exit to the highway. He would have to take the highway, at least for about six blocks. At the edge of the older part of the town the streets branched out and he could slip down a side street. But now he could only hope that if the guy was out looking, he was looking in the opposite direction, towards the construction company.

Glancing left and right, and not seeing even one car's headlights, Dis raced through the stop sign and on to the highway. Then he poured it on. It was only six blocks, but within the first block, he had snapped through to the smallest gear on his rear, and was standing and pushing as fast as he could. With one block to go he picked up a headlight behind him, in the distance but approaching rapidly – too fast for the 45 to 35 mph decreasing speed limits as the highway entered the town proper. Dis laid it on. He could possibly turn off into someone's driveway or hide behind a roadside shrub, but it was too dark, he was going too fast, and he was almost to the side street – Third Street. Luckily he needed to take a right; he wouldn't have to veer across the road, possibly attracting the eye of the looming motorist.

He had to brake when he hit the side street, which was illuminated by an arching street light. Slowing, he noticed a hedge along a curving driveway that would hide him from both the highway and the street. With a quick decision, he turned into it and positioned himself to watch the approaching vehicle. Soon the slowing, but still speeding, car came into Dis's view. It was gray, but it wasn't the guy. Dis could discern two teenage boys, smoking and laughing as they roared past. The kid in the passenger seat lifted a magazine as the car sped under the street light. Dis relaxed a bit. They were probably the two kids from the store. Probably had a Playboy or a Hustler.

Dis took off, building up speed as he left Third and followed Collins, which paralleled the highway almost all the way to his motel, which lay across from the highway stretched out like a supine Cyclops, its neon one eye blinking erratically in front of its darkly diminishing bulk. As he slowed for the now busier highway, Dis was glad that the shack was so isolated; he could pack his bike behind it with some degree of protection. "Damn," he said to himself. "I like this town and now it's all gone bust. I have to sneak out in the middle of the night and leave behind people who mean something to me. And it's forever probably. I'll probably never return. But Lorn – Damn, sometime I'll come back. I just have to. I will."

He wheeled to the back of the shack, and quietly entered his little home. He hoped no one would notice his presence – and his absence – at least for awhile. It didn't take him long to collect the things he needed to take with him. It was down to essentials again – the few "civilian" clothes he had bought to wear at work had to be left hanging in the shack's one closet. He did find room in one of his panniers for the dress shirt he had bought his first day in Jeffrey. Even though the night was chilly, biking shorts were in order. Dis knew he was going to ride like hell and he wanted to be as comfortable as possible. He also put on a T-shirt along with the wind jacket that he bought way back in West Virginia. He didn't have much, but his camping gear – tent, sleeping bag, and some essential cooking items – did take up some space. He would probably need them more now than before.

Should he leave a note to Ol' Dad and Calleen? Why not? It wouldn't hurt and he could lie about where he was going. Perhaps it would throw whoever it was who was after him off his trail for awhile. He didn't have any writing paper so he tore a page out of a magazine and used a fiber-tipped pen to write in large capital letters, "I HAD TO LEAVE. MY SISTER HAD AN ACCIDENT. SHE LIVES IN FLAGTOWN, PENN." He had paid for this week's rent but he wasn't about to go around and ask for a refund.

He knew he had to write to Lorn, but he didn't have time for that now – besides he didn't even have paper or an envelope, much less a stamp. And as for stopping and seeing her before he left, he quickly dismissed that. He needed time to explain himself to her, and a hasty middle-of-the-night departure with all kinds of unanswerable questions was beyond him right now. He wanted to get away, quickly, cleanly, and silently. If he escaped, he would have ample time on the road to compose a letter to her. He knew her address, having checked it more than a number of times in the store's phone book. He wondered if he should add a little to the note he was leaving here. After all Lorn knew he lived here. When he disappeared, she just might become concerned and ask about him. He picked up the note and added underneath what he had written, "IF A WOMAN NAMED LORN COMES AROUND, TELL HER THAT. . ." He hesitated. He had never said anything to her about love, but he knew he was as close to love with her as he had been with anyone else in his life, including his wife. But still they had really just met, and . . . and did he really want to leave her, possibly forever, with "love" as a last word? He finished the sentence with, "I'LL BE BACK."

After he had packed his bike with his small front panniers and his camping gear bungied on top of the back panniers, he made one quick scan of the shack's room and one quick look at the note. Wait a minute, if the guy found out about this note, he would also find out about Lorn. Who knows about the implications of that. Dis didn't think there would be any danger, but he couldn't take the chance. He tore the bottom section of the note off and stuffed it into his jacket pocket. With that, he was off, snaking through the streets of Jeffrey, Kentucky, with only a half moon to light his way through the black countryside and his dreams of Lorn crushed like the fragment of paper in his pocket.

Chapter 12

Dis rode swiftly and invisibly through the night. He had avoided the highway, going out on Raintree, following the route from the previous Sunday. He had studied the area, both from the county map posted at the store and the state highway map. He knew that a myriad of county roads branched south past Raintree, any of which he could take out of the river valley and into the central spine of the state. His plan was to meander through county roads and then go vaguely northward or northeast toward Indiana, or perhaps even Illinois. He would stop for food only in larger towns where he could retain his anonymity, and sleep in campgrounds or in the open to save money.

Right now he rode without a light, although he had his flashlight bungeed on the handlebar. He used it only when he could not make out the road ahead, especially when he went through sections of woods or forests, or when he came to intersections and stopped to check his map. It was after midnight, and what few cars he encountered betrayed themselves with their headlights and especially their noise long before they could see him. He had time in every case to find some roadside concealment until the car was past him and out of his horizon. None of the cars that passed him, in either direction, was the gray car that was becoming more and more ominous in his memory.

The wonderful hill leading down to the Raintree River bridge was still wonderful, although with his bike loaded and in the half-moonlight, he descended it much more subdued than the one time he had done it before. When he crossed over the bridge, the memory of Lorn waiting on the side of the road for him flooded through his being. He thought of her – riding with her, being with her, making love to her, being accepted as a part of her little family – and a physical ache ran through him from the back of his throat to this spine. But he kept on pedaling. He had to. It was either that or be confronted by the man who was looking for the man he killed. He could not face that.

Instead of turning with the river and riding down to Verhoven, he continued straight back up the other side of the river bluff. It was steep, but not as steep as Raintree; with the added weight of his gear, however, he was sweating by the time he reached the top. The roads here, through the cross-hatched pattern which he followed, climbed, but more gradually. He rode them with hardly a pause, fast and without detection as far as he could discern. He had taken along a bag of Snickers bite-size candy from his shack. They now kept hunger from seriously limiting his speed, but after a couple of hours of biking he could feel both the lack of sleep and the need for a good meal . Occasionally he crossed major highways, and twice he even rode on them for a few miles – very warily both because of cars' potential speed and the difficulty of finding cover in case of a gray car sighting.

About 5:30 in the morning, when the sky was lightening up slightly in the east to his left, he came upon a bridged interstate intersection that was lit up like a block of Broadway billboards. He had second thoughts about riding across the overpass – he certainly would be visible – but since he didn't want to backtrack, he put his head down and sped over it. On the other side he found a miniature village of gas stations and fast-food restaurants, including a McDonald's. It was brightly lit, with a smattering of cars parked around it. Dis was tempted. An order of pancakes, or maybe even two, would ease his stomach pains and give him energy for what lay ahead.

As he rode by it on the county road he considered using its drive-in facility, but rejected that because he was sure to be noticed at this hour in the morning on a bike. Instead he eased back, entered the back part of the parking lot, parked his bike beyond the lights, and, making sure there were no gray cars about, walked to one of the side entrances. The few customers hardly looked up from their coffee, biscuits-and-whatever, and newspapers. The sleepy girl behind the counter looked a little surprised when he ordered two pancakes-and-sausages and a cup of coffee, but succumbed to somnolent normality when he said, "To go." He doubted very much if she had noted that he had appeared without benefit of a car appearing in the lot. He took the breakfast and all their plastic paraphernalia out to his bike, and since it was still almost completely dark, he sat down on the edge of the back parking lot and devoured them, soaking them first with the sugary but flavorful syrup over a couple of molded mini-mounds of whipped butter. They never tasted better, and Dis had had many occasions to taste them on biking excursions. The coffee, fiery hot and sharp with flavor, was almost as good as the cakes. Yes, Dis thought, some fast food was great!

With his belly full, and the coffee keeping him awake, Dis headed north from the intersection. He was now in north-central Kentucky, a land of gently rolling hills, trim but sparse farms, and many patches of trees and woods. He had ridden all night and was, he figured, about 80 to 100 miles from Jeffrey. He could probably ride more, but he knew that he should at least take a nap now in the early morning before riding more during this day. He needed to get on a normal daylight riding schedule.

He stopped at a turn-off to a cornfield and checked his state map for possible public campgrounds, but there were none in the vicinity. But when he looked around, he could see that the turn-off led to a corn crib some 300 yards off the road. Growing corn surrounded the crib and no other farm buildings were visible. It looked like a handy place to catch some sleep. Soon Dis was behind the crib, stretched out on his sleeping bag, his bike lying close to him. Only when he lay down did he realize that he indeed was fatigued. Even though it was light, he slept immediately and soundly, thinking fitfully before he blanked of Lorn and of what he must write to her.

The noise of an engine woke him. He sat up quickly, looked around, and saw that a tractor was moving around in a neighboring field. It was harrowing between the rows of corn and at every pass swung around to the edge of the field where Dis lay. The sun was overhead and warm, and a glance at his watch told Dis that he had slept about three hours, enough to satisfy his need for rest. He could ride the rest of the day and look for a good campsite for the night. A quick survey of the map showed a state park with many camping sites on the Ohio River about 50 miles away. He would use that as a destination.

Riding now, easily, down a deserted county road, Dis's mind was preoccupied with both Lorn and avoiding detection. He began many letters in his head, but could not settle on any. Perhaps if he waited until he could sit down in camp with pen and paper he could express himself the way he wanted to.

As for detection, he realized that he must use camping sparingly. The man in the gray car knew that Dis had a bicycle; he most likely had followed him out to the construction company. But he didn't know that Dis did not have a car. He had never told Marge or George that he had arrived in Jeffrey on a bike. In fact he had talked "car" with Marge occasionally, calling the Impala he had left back in Maryland "my car" as if he had it with him in Jeffrey. The people at the Forest Motel would, of course, know that he had appeared with a bicycle loaded with camping gear, sans car. But how would the man find out where he lived? Dis didn't think that Marge would tell him. She was just ornery enough about people nosing around to tell him flatly, "Don't know." But if the guy made a systematic check at all the motels, he would probably find the truth. Ol' Dad would have no reason to hold back, and Calleen probably would happily blurt out almost anything she knew about him. Dis remembered her look of surprise and compulsive question when they first met: "You really riding a bicycle across the country? Well, ain't that a trip."

So, if the man got that far, and Dis could not assume otherwise, Dis would be easier to locate than if he were in a car. People at campsites would remember a lone bicycle camper more readily than a lone car camper. Even people in and around stores remembered people on loaded bicycles, at least fleetingly. So Dis changed his mind. He wouldn't plan for the state park this night; he would use it as a fall-back in case he couldn't find a place similar to this morning's – concealed, fairly comfortable, and away from whoever owned it. That meant he would have to be wary with fire and cooking, but that wasn't much bother; he could live for days on cold canned food, vegetables, sandwiches, and, his old stand-by, fast food. However, he'd better be on the lookout for an average sized town with a fairly large supermarket so he could get some of this food he was thinking about – also some paper and a stamp.

God, he was glad he hadn't left a message for Lorn in the shack. If he had, the guy would probably know about her right now and would be trying to get information from her. What would she tell him? *Did she really know that much about me?* Would she tell him that she had slept with, had made love with, a man whose past was as unclear to her as the muddy water in Raintree River?

And what would the guy tell her about me? Just what did he know? That I am from Iowa. That my name is Robert Clemmon. That he wants to talk to me because . . . yeah, because what? Because I was a homeless drifter, a barroom souse in Washington, D. C.? That I was killed – yeah, killed, get that – in an encounter with a depressed yuppie shoe clerk? No, it doesn't make any sense.

Just what the hell is so important about me that someone should be on my tail for so long and so far?

It has to be the law. They finally identified the body and confirmed that Robert Clemmon was dead. Then that name came up on computers because I used his social security number. Or maybe they did have a verifiable fingerprint?

But, Jesus, why all the big fuss about a long dead homeless drifter?

OK, so Mr. gray car driver knows I'm on a bike. That makes me conspicuous and easier to find. All he has to do is drive around and ask at groceries and convenience stores -- and motels and campgrounds -- and if he gets a positive answer, he knows when and where I've been there and gets a clue as to which direction I'm going. I've had it. How can I possibly keep ahead of this guy?

Maybe I should get rid of this bicycle and get a car. That way I become just one of the anonymous drivers up and down the highways. I could take off for anywhere -- the east coast, the west coast, hell, I could lose myself in Florida, what with all the tourists driving around there. And there's California where the car is king. But, Jesus, all I have is $350. What kind of car can I get for $350? No, I couldn't get one even if I had the money. I'd have to use my license – show identification – get a title. I do that and I'm gone – back to D.C. and whatever awaits for me there.

The truth of the matter is that the bike makes me stand out. What if I abandon it and take a train or a bus? They don't ask for identification as long as you have the cash. Let's see, but if that makes sense, the guy has probably thought about it too. Obviously he'll check with all the possible ticket sellers, bus drivers, and others who could possibly remember me. If he gets lucky, I've had it because he can get a line on where I'm going and then he can zero in on me -- maybe even be there waiting for me at the end of the trip.

And whenever I get to, wherever I go, I'm going to have to find a job pretty quickly. It'll be hard to camp without a bike, and motels will eat up my $350 as quickly as Marge rolled a cigarette. So I'm stuck at some minimum wage job without my bike or a car or any way to leave quickly -- except by bus or train. But then I'm back on the same treadmill. In fact he'll be able to follow me pretty easily once I give up my trusty steed. But what if I took this old bike with me? I could box it up and ship it with me on a bus. I'd stand out, that's for sure. And there'd be documentation. He could find out exactly where I'm going. All right, what if I bought a bike for cheap after taking a bus or train? I'd still have my camping gear; I could carry that with me. Then when I get to wherever I'm going, I can go out on the road again and stay away from Mr. Gray Car. That just might be the thing to do. I don't really need a good bike. A $25 used Huffy from a Salvation Army store will get me where I want to go -- wherever that is?

Dis pulled off the road into a small park, almost a roadside park. This one was really a trail head for a nature walk to a small waterfall. At one of the picnic tables, he took out his Midwestern highway map and tried to figure out where would be a good place to pick up a bus. He wanted a fairly large city, one with enough traffic at the station so that he wouldn't stand out. The closest large cities to him were Louisville, Owensboro, and Paducah. Louisville was probably too large, with too much traffic, and he knew nothing about Owensboro. That left Paducah, a city in the general direction he was traveling anyway. He also didn't know anything about this city, but since it was right on the Ohio River, it probably had buses or maybe even trains going in all directions. When he got there, he would have to make the decision of where to go next. He could wait. He would have to.

But when he looked up, he noticed a small sign at the edge of the small picnic area. It made mention of a walk-in camping site a few hundred yards down a path off the main path. Dis's stomach was starting to bother him, and as he looked at his watch, he realized that the heft of the afternoon was behind him. Besides that, he now could feel the fatigue from last night's riding pressing upon him. Maybe he could camp here for the night?

Taking his bike with him down the path until he found some bushes he could park it behind, Dis explored the camping area on foot. It was just what he wanted -- small, empty of campers, and with almost private campsites separated by trees and bushes. He knew from the map that he was within one or two miles of a small town, so he wheeled his bike to the campsite, took off his back panniers and camping gear at the most isolated site, and set up his tent, a small, light, two person number. That finished, he put all of his gear into the tent and started off with his almost empty front panniers for the town and some food.

The town was Bullville. It had a convenience store on its outskirts, which he passed by, and a surprisingly well stocked grocery and general merchandise store in its downtown, in the middle of a block fronting on a classic small town square. He bought a bag of apples, four cans of baked beans, two cans of ravioli, a loaf of wheat bread, a healthy chuck of cheddar cheese, three small cans of tuna, two cans of sweet corn, and since he planned to cook dinner tonight, a pound package of spaghetti and a jar of Ragu spaghetti sauce. Then he found a note pad, and was about to buy a whole pack of envelopes when he noticed the greeting card racks. He could buy a card that came with an envelope, but, on the other hand, a whole pack of envelopes cost less than one of the cards. He bought the pack. While waiting to pay, he grabbed a pack of chewy candy bars. He had nothing classy, just good camping food that would satisfy him for the next few days at least.

He asked the clerk if she sold stamps. The answer was, "No way, Bub. Over there's a machine, though." Dis had to buy a small packet of stamps.

When he returned to the park's parking lot, it was deserted. He hoped it would remain that way for the rest of the evening and night. To Dis's relief, no one else was at the campsite. He got out his cooking gear, had to walk back to the parking lot for water, but soon had a pot of water heating up. When Dis purchased his camping gear way back in West Virginia when he started this odyssey, he wanted lightweight, reliable items. One that he was particularly happy about was his Gaz stove. It was little more than a burner and a holder that screwed onto a small can of pressurized gas. It was simplicity itself.

Now when his pot of water was almost boiling, he replace it on the stove with a smaller pan filled with the spaghetti sauce. He let it warm up and then covered it and let it simmer for a few more minutes. After a quick taste, Dis replaced the sauce on the burner with the pot of water, quickly got it boiling, and dropped in the spaghetti -- breaking each handful neatly in half. He opened one of the cans of tuna and got out the bread.

Waiting for the spaghetti to cook made him realize how hungry he was. But soon his hunger was behind him as he almost ravenously devoured the food, eating every bit of it, including four slices of bread and one of the candy bars for dessert.

After he had taken the dishes down to the parking lot and cleaned them, and had disposed of all of the used packaging in the lot's heavily lidded trash containers, the evening's light began slanting to the west and losing its intensity, lengthening both shadows and beauty. Dis sat at the picnic table and started to compose a letter to Lorn. He found it hard to begin, but he knew what he had to say; he had been composing it in his mind all day.

"Dear Lorn,

I will be as direct as possible; perhaps it will be easier.

I'm gone. Something of absolute importance came up unexpectedly and I had to clear out in the middle of the night. I can't tell you why I left or where I'm going -- or, for that matter, when I will return. There is a good chance you will never know the answer to any of those questions. But I hope, with all my soul, I will be able to answer all of them for you sometime in the future.

One thing is certain: My departure had nothing to do with you.

I'm sorry if this sudden break in my life causes you discomfort. No excuses, but my past is my past and it cannot be ignored.

Lorn, I am shattered to have to leave you. Do know that. Also know that I did not "use" you. I hope that I am above that. We had sex -- fine, grand sex, but it gave me more beauty and comfort than mere sensation. It was a completion, a whole, in a life that had been too long solitary.

Above that, I felt better with you and your daughter Chrissy than with any other people in my entire life.

As to the future, I'll repeat what I wrote above: I'm gone. Somehow I'll have to put you out of my mind; you will need to do the same with me. We will probably never meet again. My problems are complex and I will never involve you in them. But you will be with me forever -- in my memory, in my heart, in my soul.

Lead your life; I will lead mine. Who knows what the future will bring. But don't depend upon me. God, I hate to write that; I want so much to have you depend upon me, but it is not to be -- at least for the foreseeable future.

Lorn, I never told you that I loved you. I wasn't sure; I'm not now. We just didn't have enough time. But what I felt for you in the few moments we were together was as close to love as I have ever been in my life.

Love, Rob

P.S. Please do a couple of things for me. Number one, destroy the envelope this comes in and never tell anyone the postmark. I'll be gone from here immediately; but, still, destroy and forget where this comes from. Number two, and pretty obvious -- if you do keep this letter, keep it secret. And number three, don't try to find out about me or to follow me. If someone comes around asking questions, answer them truthfully (except for the postmark) to the extent of your knowledge. You will not hurt me."

In the dying light Dis read the letter over again. He knew it wasn't beautifully poignant, but it was truthful, direct, and he hoped it would be appreciated. Lorn had accepted him wholeheartedly – completely and intimately – and she deserved something other than an unceremonious, secret departure. He hoped that it would not get to her too late; that she would not have done anything that could possible jeopardize herself in any way. But he could not think of any possibility of that; the worst thing that could happen would be for the man (or someone working with him?) to intercept this letter and gain his whereabouts at tomorrow's date. If that were to happen, would she even see this letter? Probably not, if they were going that far. With that in mind, he took out another piece of paper and copied the letter. Even if he never used it, he wanted to have a copy. How would he know if she never got the letter? Probably he wouldn't, but who knows, he still wanted a copy of it. Then Dis took one of the envelopes, wrote Lorn's name and address on it, and pasted on one of the stamps. In the space for the return address, he simply wrote, "Rob." Then he thought better of that and wrote another envelope without his name. Who knows?

Crawling into his sleeping bag, Dis couldn't believe how tired he seemed even though he had slept about three hours that morning. He felt reasonably safe at this site, this "lucky find," but he didn't want to stay around very long; it was too close to Jeffrey. He wanted to get some distance between himself and the innocuous man in the gray car. As he drifted into sleep, his mind chased two images, both sharp in his memory, but both taking on nuances of added detail above his first impression. The images were the gray man leafing through the magazine rack and Lorn's soft white breast in the dim morning light. Somehow, as hard as he tried to concentrate on Lorn, his mind transformed her into a middle-aged, sedate male calmly flipping pages in the store. And somehow that image became more and more ominous, however unprepossessing its outward appearance.

Chapter 13

He was up with the first hint of light; actually he was awake even before when he thought he heard something close to his tent. However he couldn't be sure; perhaps it was nothing, perhaps a small animal – it could be anything else, right? He waited in the stillness for another sound – anything. But nothing came, not even the wind moving through the trees. Eventually he reached for his flashlight and checked his watch: 4:07.

Not bad. He had had about seven hours of good sleep, enough to carry him through a day that he hoped would be full of intense riding and one which would increase his safety. When he opened the zippered flap of his tent, he could barely make out the trees at his campsite, but a semblance of light filtered through the darkness of the grove, enough for him to get moving. His breakfast was two apples and some water from his water bottle. He thought of the instant coffee that he usually had every morning, but even though he could make some for himself now – he had a small jar of Folgers and, of course, his Gaz stove – he declined. He wanted to get on the road while traffic was minimal. Later he could stop for breakfast and some coffee.

If he could get to the Carbondale, Illinois, area during the day, he would have time to scope out the city. He vaguely knew it to be a college town, which would mean there would be many bicyclists. There he would see if he could effectively hide or if he would have to make the break by a bus or train trip. He knew he was probably wasting his time even thinking about staying in this sparsely populated area, but he came to realize that he really didn't want to get on a bus or a train. For one thing he liked his bike. Oh, he didn't have any sentimental attachment to this particular Trek, although it was certainly a good bike. But he liked the concept of biking – the freedom, the mobility, the ability to be unencumbered by the usual. Also, deep down, he felt he was safer with a bike. Somehow a car – or being at the mercy of buses or trains – was a limit rather than an extension of his feeling of freedom.

As he biked through Bullville, he stopped at the storefront Post Office and deposited his letter to Lorn in the slot on the outside collection box. What would she think when she read it? Would she even know he was gone? – they were not to the point of daily or even regular meetings.

You know, he thought momentarily, maybe my smartest move would be to circle back to Jeffrey. Gray Man would certainly not be there anymore; he'd be out looking in an ever widening circle while I'd be sitting pretty, right at the heart of things, at the core of the target. And I'd be with Lorn. I could tell her the truth about this whole mess and maybe she could help me get through it and have some kind of a real life. With her.

No. His problems were his, not hers. Now was not the time for him to get her involved. Time, that was it. Time. If he could run, could stay ahead of whatever was left of his old life, time would come to his aid. Time would kill the old – give it a natural death. He could run with time, could live with time.

By studying his maps last night he realized that the only bridge across the Ohio at Paducah was an interstate one. But if he traveled further west he would get to Cairo, Illinois, on country roads, and it had a bridge.

He found a road west out of Bullville that was as quiet and as clear as a passage through a desert, except that this road was gently rolling and surrounded by fields and woods. It passed through some small towns, towns that seemed to get increasingly more ragged the closer their proximity to the river. About seven o'clock his stomach started its usual biking message, and he started looking for a likely breakfast stop. He checked his map and noted that he was close to Hoopston not a town, but a city of about 6,000. Surely a town of that size would have a Hardee's, or at least perhaps a bakery. It also very likely could be a magnet for Gray Man, but Dis didn't plan to stay long, and he would avoid the main streets and downtown. He continued on and soon was riding a street parallel to the main street through Hoopston. Dis had almost traversed the city when he came upon a tiny storefront brightly lit up and sporting an aging sign hanging in its plate glass window: "Alma's Cafe and Bakery."

The place had a big counter, a glass case filled with various baked goods; a few tables and chairs; and Alma. Dis carefully didn't park in front of the store, where perhaps his bike would be noted and remembered. After passing it on the street, he rode in from the side, divested himself of his more obvious riding paraphernalia – helmet and gloves – and strode into the cinnamon smelling place. An elderly couple occupied one table. But no one else was present except the formidable woman behind the counter, who Dis took to be Alma. He ordered a cup of coffee and two of the large cinnamon-raisin rolls glistening behind one of the case's glass. As he waited for his food, the woman behind the counter boomed, "Where you from?"

Startled, Dis glanced at her to see if she was talking to him. She was – and staring. She repeated her question, "Where you from?"

Dis hemmed a bit, thinking he didn't want to be too exotic – not New Jersey. Why not some place in Kentucky? "Where am I from? Well I . . . Louisville . . . north Louisville. Got me a little place."

The woman blinked her eyes, taking in the information. Then she asked, "You know Freddy Spraig?"

Freddy Spraig? No he didn't. She must take him for a local. "Sorry, but I've never had the pleasure." Dis didn't really want to get into a conversation with the woman. He didn't want to be noticed, to be remembered. He turned away from her and walked to the furthest table in the place with his food and coffee.

Her booming voice followed him, "Well you sure look like Freddy. Course they's some other people around here that look like him too. Junior Ivy and Sharon Will, to name a few. You sure you ain't related to Freddy Spraig – or any of the other Spraigs? Damn, you sure look like him."

Dis glanced her way, made a quick "no" shake of his head, and rushed through the food and drink and then left quickly. He was glad to be out, although the bakery and coffee had been excellent. She was overbearing and it was quite obvious that he would be remembered. But, hell, if ol' Gray Man came around these parts with a picture, he might be chasing look-alikes all over the county if what she said about Freddy Spraig was true.

Later that day, Wednesday, Dis reached the Mississippi River in the Cape Girardeau, Missouri area , more specifically a town on the Illinois side called Eagles Gap, a city bordering the river. As he rode in from the north on one of the county roads, Dis sensed that something out of the ordinary was going on in the small city. It was about 4 o'clock and the place was bustling with bicyclists. They were everywhere, streaming through the city's blacktop streets, zipping back and forth and around in circles at the city's outlying strip mall. As he rode with the traffic, watching for gray cars particularly, Dis caught a sign which read: "Eagles Gap College Straight Ahead." However as he went on and bike traffic picked up, he realized that something having to do with bicycles was happening at the school.

Dis pulled over – off the street and onto a side street – to get his bearings and to scope out the situation. It didn't take him long. Almost every bike that passed him had a cardboard placard attached somewhere reading, "BTMRV." Dis was astute enough about bicycling to realize that he had stumbled into a group bicycle tour. He knew the RV at the end of the acronym stood for River Valley, and it hit him immediately that he was with a Bicycle Tour of the Mississippi River Valley.

He started riding with a small group of bicyclists and as he turned a corner near the center of town, he noticed on his right, spread out over a series of softly rising green hills, the Eagles Gap campus, a series of turn-of-the-century Gothic classroom buildings now dominated by two very large, modern, glass and brick buildings. One of these was certainly the college's gym, while the other Dis took to be the student center. The two buildings were literally swarming with pedestrians, bicyclists, and bicycles. In every direction tents radiating from the buildings, covered the grounds. There was no doubt that this was the tour's overnight stop.

Dis could hardly contain himself. All these bicyclists. As soon as he could get his gear off his bike, he would blend in as one of them. He would be almost impossible to spot. Dis made an immediate decision: he would "bandit" this ride – at least overnight. He rolled his bike to an outlying section of grass, and then decided against being so isolated. His anonymity depended on being swallowed up as a part of the group. So he moved into the mass of tents until he found a small open section, hardly more than enough for his tent and bike. However, most of the other tents were just as closely spaced – people did not like to carry their sometimes heavy camping gear farther than they had to.

He pulled into the space and dropped his tent, sleeping bag, and mattress pad to the ground. Now, except for his panniers, he was indistinguishable from any of the other bikers whose gear was carried to each overnight location by a truck or trucks. He quickly set up his tent and stowed his panniers in it. Then he set out to find out everything he could about this BTMRV.

He strolled to the gym first because that seemed to the main focus of most of the riders. The side doors were wide open and people were massed around them, shifting and moving individually and in groups. Dis looked in and wasn't surprised to find the gym floor covered with sleeping bags, camping gear, bicycles, along with many bicyclists. Riders evidently had the option of tent camping or sleeping in gyms or protected places.

Dis looked around for information or printed material, but could find none, although he did spy people sitting or lying on their sleeping bags reading what looked like tour information. Then he found crowds of people milling around an area close to the back wall of the building's expansive foyer where a table and a large bulletin board were set up. Discretely, Dis checked it out. The bulletin board was filled with individual messages from one biker or group to another, most of the messages out-of-date. "Mamey, call your mother. John, Wednesday, 4:30" and the like. But some had more general information – the location of restaurants, showers, and the like. The table also had more specific information about the ride itself so Dis sidled up to it and slowly took a selection of the material lying there.

Back at his tent, he quickly found out that BTMRV was a week-long tour which followed the Mississippi River on a general south to north route. Participants stayed at colleges or high schools, had their bags carried each day, had breakfast supplied each day, but were on their own for lunches and dinners. The ride ended on Saturday at a large medical center across the river from St. Louis. Buses had carried most of the riders to the starting point. Tomorrow's ride was 60 miles long, Friday's about 40 but Saturday's would be only 30. He didn't like the idea of banditing. In other circumstances he would have talked to the organizers in and possibly worked out a daily fee arrangement, but now his reduced money situation and the overriding need for secrecy forced him to try to sneak through. On the other hand, he wasn't going to take much from the ride except for the security of traveling with numbers of bikers.

However, a shower did sound nice – especially since he didn't know when he would be able to take the next one. So he found his toilet kit, zipped up his tent, and headed for the gym, where a moderately hot shower amid the camaraderie of tired bikers made him almost happy. Back at his tent, however, he pondered this latest twist to his situation. He would like to stay with this tour until it ended – it certainly offered safety in numbers. However, ol' Gray Man, once he found out about it, would probably think the same way. He could start systematically looking for Dis's familiar face in the crowds. But that's all the man had to go on; he didn't know Dis's tent, or his bike, for that matter. Dis doubted that he came close enough to identify the bike on the night he followed Dis to the construction company. To the casual observer, most bikes looked pretty similar, especially in the dark.

One thing Dis did know: if he stayed with this tour, he had to always stay with groups. Being alone would make him stand out like a neon light in a marquee of light bulbs. If he stayed, he needed to study the cue sheets of previous days and get a handle on the small talk of the tour. To his advantage, Dis knew that since the tour was past its mid-point, bicycle stories were becoming passé. However, he would have to come up with some basic biographical data in case he was asked. Maybe he'd use the "person" he made up at the bakery – from suburbia north of Louisville, with the added information that he had just moved there and didn't really know the area yet. He got out his highway map and decided on either Indian Hills or Windy Hills, flipped a mental coin, and settled on Indian Hills.

By now Dis's stomach had set up its distress signals, so he roused himself to deal with supper. He knew he couldn't cook his own meal; that would really make him stand out. He also knew that he wanted large quantities of food, carbos particularly. Knowing that with many rides civic groups set up special food facilities, he wandered over to the student center and looked over the bulletin board again. Sure enough the Eagles Gap Women's Club was serving meatballs and spaghetti at the American Legion Club downtown for $4.50, and the Giant Boy Restaurant had an all-you-can-eat buffet at someplace called the Turnaround for $5.95. Having had spaghetti the night before, Dis immediately opted for the buffet, a selection which seemed to be popular because while making up his mind, Dis heard a woman behind the table give directions to the Turnaround to three different people. It was within walking distance – about five blocks – and yes, they served drinks.

The Giant Boy proved to be a good choice. The management had set up a special serving area in the basement for the touring bikers. The food was plentiful, if not particularly distinctive – although they did serve some fritters made with local cherries that everyone raved about – and the place was crowded enough that Dis was happily obliged to sit at a long table with a random assortment of fellow bikers. Sitting across from him were a middle aged married couple who were nice but overtired, and three men from Nashville who had somewhat guiltily taken a week from their wives. Next to him was a young couple from Ohio who were quieter than he was, and a father with two pre-teenagers who, both boy and girl, ate like horses – both in quantity and in manner. While Dis ate – again with one eye constantly on the door – he abstractly participated in the small talk of strangers randomly together for a shared social and physical purpose. Besides the route tomorrow and the two major up-hills of today, the talk roamed from the ecology of dammed rivers turned into lakes, through the best brands of ice cream, to how to help the Mid-East turn completely capitalistic. Dis enjoyed a good meal; interesting conversation, for the most part; and a subdued sense of security. He even walked back to the college with his meal-mates, blending in again with a group. He saw no sign of the Gray Man.

Before returning to his tent, Dis strolled through the student center, where many tourers loitered, some watching either of two video tape players, one showing *Breaking Away* on one side of the lounge and the other featuring a video of last year's BTMRV. Since it was still too early to spend the rest of the evening in the tent, he settled on the floor to watch the tour video. It could possible arm him with some important information. The video, unfortunately, was not too much better than a home movie – interesting to the participants, but deadly to outsiders.

While keeping one eye on the video and one more active eye on the people around him, especially the constant flow of people in and out of the area around the large TV screen, Dis noticed a woman in front of him with obvious dyed hair – blonde strands emerging from a dark, almost black, crown. This set him to thinking about his own hair. Should he dye it another color, or perhaps let it go back to natural? Way back then, when he had broken away from Washington and his wife, one of the first things he had done was to dye his hair a dark shade of brown – almost black. At the same time he had also started a beard and mustache. The beard, kept neatly trimmed, was lighter than his dyed hair, but occasionally he would add some of the dye to the beard to darken it. Sometimes it looked pretty blotchy close-up, but at normal distance, Dis was convinced, the old Dis was hard to discern through the "disguise."

But, still, the Gray Man had somehow recognized him. How? That was the question that Dis had lived with constantly for the last few days. So what if he changed his facial and head hair again? Went back to the original? Shaved his face and dyed his hair back to its natural color? It probably, however inconceivably, wouldn't make much difference to the Gray Man, but it might confuse witnesses who the man would interview. What about doing it right now? The showers were probably just about empty by now. All he would have to do is find an open drug store or even a grocery store and buy some dye. In fact he had passed a Walmart as he was coming into town. Should he do it? Why not?

He got up, noticing that it was still light out, although the light was suffused, presaging the advancing darkness. Just as he was passing through the still crowded door that led from the lounge area to the entrance, he felt something hit him on the back of the right shoulder.

"What the?" He turned and was face-to-face with a small, squat, middle-aged man whom he instantly recognized but could not place.

The man hit him again on the shoulder and said, "What the hell you doin' here? You on this tour?"

As soon as Dis heard the voice, a high-pitched, aspirated whine, he recognized the man. He was Knobby – from Jeffrey! Knobby, the guy who told the story on himself about the itchy shorts on the Raintree ride. Damn, how am I going to explain my presence? Besides this guy is a creep and a bore; if I acknowledge him, he'll probably latch onto me and never let me go. I have to ignore him; that's the only possible escape.

Dis abruptly shrugged his shoulder, then moved his eyes off in the distance. He then faked a big smile and moved off to the right, as if seeing a friend and rushing to him. He continued in the direction right out the main entrance and down the steps, not looking back once. He prayed that Knobby wasn't following him. Half way to his tent he stopped near a large stone monument and looked back. Knobby wasn't there.

Now he had to get the hair dye. And stay out of view as much as possible. Damn, why had he even gone to the student center? He should have holed up in his tent for the whole night. This guy Knobby was a loud mouth who wouldn't hesitate to blab to the Jeffrey bike group, and especially to Lorn, that he had seen me on this ride. Well, maybe if he never sees me again, he'll think it was a mistaken identify and forget about it. Fat chance. Hell, as soon as he gets back he'll probably run to Lorn, asking her about me. Damn!

Back at his tent he angrily grabbed his bike and soon was roaring down the street in the gathering dusk of the small town. At the Walmart he bought a box of Clairol blonde hair coloring and a box of pop-tarts, which would serve him for breakfast. He wasn't going to chance eating with the tour group. He had a razor and a small pair of scissors in his toilette kit.

Soon he was under the shower of the gym massaging great spurts of the dye into his hair. Without washing the dye out, he took the scissors and started chopping away at his neatly trimmed beard and mustache. He almost held his breath for fear that someone would come in and say something, but the place was empty and remained so, except for an occasional man using the toilets, which were off in an alcove. They hardly even looked at him. Finished with the cutting, he took his razor, a Bic three-blader, and neatly trimmed his facial hair from his face. Then it was back to the shower to rinse away the dye. When he looked in the mirror after the shower, he didn't even hesitate in recognizing his old self. He was Dis again, his bearded, dark head already a fading memory. Had there even been a picture taken of it? He couldn't remember one, thank goodness.

Dis left the gym through a side passage, avoiding the main basketball court floor, which was now in almost-darkness, only one soft night light illuminating sleeping sites scattered like playing cards throughout the main floor and into almost every available ledge, corner, or alcove of the place. These sleepers sought out infinitesimal cubicles of privacy like otters in a riverbank. They were at odds with themselves: loving the tribal camaraderie of their spread-out institutional tepee, but protecting themselves with tacit shields of crawl-in-the-corner, cover-with-a-blanket privacy.

As he walked through the gym's foyer and out through the randomly scattered melange of tents, Dis felt eyes searching him. He wanted to run to his tent. He forced himself to be calm; after all, just one man had recognized him, and that man was inconsequential. But, nevertheless, he couldn't avoid the feeling that he had blown his cover, that he was vulnerable, that somehow his links with the past were being strengthened, not diminished.

When he found his tent, he quickly entered it and stowed his things, undressed, and squirmed into his sleeping bag. He had forgotten to zip the tent flaps, so he sat up and before zipping, took one last peek out of the front of the tent. At that moment, a slow moving cloud finally opened up and the edge of the moon slipped through, giving Dis a fleeting glimpse of a curved half circle of softness emerging from the silken garment of darkness.

Dis stared – rapt. Then the light shrunk, covered by unseen and unknown vapors of night. In the darkness, peering from his little tent, Dis hoped – but with a sense of sadness and distance - that he was not alone.

Chapter 14

Dis spent Thursday riding from groups to groups. To be alone was to be avoided, so he would move up to a group, possibly as few as two riders, stay with it for awhile – as long as he could, until he thought the people were becoming bothered – and then speed up to the next group. He watched ahead for anyone resembling Knobby, remembering that he had worn a particularly garish combination of neon Lycra on that Sunday ride, but was confident that Knobby was behind him. Dis had started early, had not eaten breakfast with the other riders, and was a good, swift rider. He had no trouble loading his panniers stuffed with his tent and sleeping gear into the baggage trucks. A truck driver was there to help stack the bags, but he didn't take the time or the bother to check baggage or wrist tags.

About 20 miles into the ride Dis realized that he was running out of groups. He had started about 6 o'clock, had been passing a number of groups, and now the groups and individual riders were diminishing. And some of them were the true "speeders," the young racers who vied with themselves as to who would come in first – would be the first to find his or her baggage, to lay it out at a prominent place in the gym, and to laze around very conspicuously in front of everyone else who came in later.

He pulled into a small town that had made some preparations for the influx of riders. Two civic groups had taken over the town's one park and set up tables with breakfast items – coffee, sweet rolls, and the like. Dis rode to the back of the park, got off his bike, and approached the stand warily. Only a few riders were sitting around eating, so Dis bought some coffee and two gigantic, homemade cinnamon buns. He didn't want to isolate himself too much, so he sat down at the far edge of one of the benches, close to two youngsters who were still breathing hard, sweat beading from their foreheads. They had juice and some granola bars, and seemed to be still racing – gulping down their food and drink almost between gasps of air. He could probably ride with them, but he decided not to. He didn't want to get too far in front of everyone else. He had joined this tour to lose himself in the masses.

Consequently he loitered. The two racers left, but Dis remained. If fact he stayed around for about an hour, watching the stand get more and more busy, and also watching for the rumbling appearance of Knobby. Dis planned to leave as soon as Knobby appeared, knowing that Knobby would probably make a beeline to the food tables and not start looking at fellow riders until his hunger was slaked.

Sure enough, just when the long wait really started getting bothersome to Dis, a conspicuous bubble of almost glowing neon rode into the park and pulled up directly in front of the stand. It was the whale-like Knobby, by himself, but spouting and steaming to those around him about his need for food and drink. Before Knobby could get off his bike, Dis was on his feet, retreating to the back of the park, keeping people between himself and Knobby. He quickly mounted his bike and instead of wending through the park, went off in the opposite direction, down a town street. He would circle back to the main route, avoiding the mass of riders in the park's front.

Back on the route, Dis was not isolated. Riders in pairs and larger groups commandeered the road. Dis had no trouble riding with various groups of people, although he deliberately did not get into conversations with them. He was not rude, just taciturn – a bland rider, unremarkable, and – he hoped – easily forgotten.

As the day progressed, riders became more and more stretched out along the road. Many raced ahead, but many more took their time, stopping at every possible rest stop, pulling over at even minor sightseeing opportunities, or just stopping under a tree to relax, even nap. Dis again ran out of groups, but he used his same strategy throughout the day. He would wait, inconspicuously, at major rest stops until Knobby appeared lumbering along in a cloud of color, and then Dis would take off in the security of many groups.

The ride followed the west side of the expansive Mississippi River through Illinois, generally moving north, but occasionally going up to the east and then returning to the river. The terrain was definitely mixed – flat, river bottom land with occasional upswings over bluffs into roller-coaster hills. The riding was interesting – not easy, not hard – but captivating in its constant call for different riding techniques. Dis found himself racing along perfectly straight, perfectly flat country roads, breezing through small towns. But then, at the sight of water, he turned with the land, rising up on undulating, ever increasing lifts and dips. It was beautiful riding for those on vacation, for those with nothing on their minds but the enjoyment of the day and the anticipation of the evening's food and rest.

Dis had other things on his mind. He decided he would remain with the tour, but just today, and not follow it to its end on Saturday. There, everyone else would be switching to cars or public transportation. A man on a bike, loaded with panniers, leaving the area would be very obvious. Besides the ending location – a large hospital's parking lot, he had learned – was just across the river from St. Louis and its horrendous traffic problems. No, if he left the tour at today's ending location, a town called Hickcomb, and headed northeast, he could be in Carbondale by nightfall easily. On a Thursday afternoon the traffic going into the city shouldn't be too bad and he should be able to get a bus with no problem.

But now Dis was having a good day. But then about one o'clock, with around 15 miles to go before Hickcomb, he pulled into Stringer, Illinois, and almost ran into the gray car.

It was empty, however. But that didn't alleviate the sudden rush of adrenaline or the flush of fear that overcame him. He was riding through the town's main street, watching carefully for gray cars, both moving and parked, when at the town's one stoplight he found himself in a group of about six bikers waiting for the light to change. Before the green came on, however, the rider in the lead, seeing no traffic, moved out and turned to the right. The whole group, Dis included, almost by instinct followed – down a hill, squeezed in by construction barriers, and, at the bottom, almost literally into the nondescript rear end of the gray car parked on the side of the street. Dis, at the back of the group, was so preoccupied with not hitting the other riders that he didn't notice the car until he was almost upon it.

He didn't hit the car, but he did stop abruptly, just barely avoiding it – luckily no rider was immediately behind him. He didn't stay around to make detailed observations, taking off instead with the rest of the group until he found an alley between two business buildings about a block away and pulled in to figure out what to do. He had noticed two things about the car, however: it was indeed a Ford Taurus, not new, but a fairly recent model; and it was from Iowa – the license plate that he couldn't make out before was an Iowa one.

This was the car in the "We Got It" parking lot. Dis knew it with no qualifications.

He leaned his bike against one of the building's walls and peeked out into the street. A few pedestrians were on the sidewalks, but they ignored him, thinking, perhaps, that he was just another one of those crazy bicyclers. He could see that the car was empty and could not discern anyone remotely resembling the gray man on the street. When he looked the other way down the street, however, he saw many bikes scattered around a swatch of greenery. From where he stood, Dis had a hunch that the greenery was the town park and that it contained refreshment stands of some sort, although the town was not listed as an official route refreshment stop.

The gray man was probably down there, watching every bike that came down the street to the park. God, thank goodness I almost hit the car; if not, I'd certainly have ridden down and been identified. I've got to get out of here, but quick – and obviously avoid the park.

Dis returned to his bike, and went through the alley to a back street that paralleled the main highway. Cautiously he rode down the street, past impassive small cottages and bungalows, watching constantly for the park to his left. Within a few blocks he could see that the street he was on bordered the hillside of the park. He turned right and moved a block over; luckily the town was large enough that there were a few streets behind the park which he could use. They stopped, however, quickly enough, and he was forced to turn left and reenter the county road which the tour was using.

As he turned, he entered a steady stream of riders, which was good. Looking back, he saw that the park was about two blocks behind him, and that many people were milling around a square group of tables. Dis was sure that the gray man was there somewhere, anxiously waiting for Dis to appear.

How had he found Dis? The first thing that came to his mind was Knobby. No, that's too far out. How could Knobby communicate with his pursuer? Impossible: well, maybe not quite. What if the gray man had put an ad in the Jeffrey paper – a reward ad asking for information about Dis, giving a cell phone number? What if Knobby had called home yesterday and mentioned that he had seen someone who looked like the new guy he had ridden with that recent Sunday, the guy who worked at the convenience store? And what if whoever he had talked with in Jeffrey had told him about the ad and the reward and given him the number to call? Knobby could have called and said that a guy who looked like Dis was doing BTMRV? Jesus, maybe it wasn't completely impossible.

But no, why would he publish an ad? He knew Dis was gone – or did he? Could he have thought that there was a slight chance that Dis might be hiding out somewhere in Jeffrey and he wanted to cover every possibility? Cripes, he just might have done that. After all, he had never seen Dis leave. All the man probably knew is that Dis had left the motel in the middle of the night unexpectedly.

And what about Lorn? God, what would she be thinking? What would she have done? If the ad was published in the next afternoon's paper, Lorn was certain to have seen it – or heard about it – before she received Dis's letter. Jesus, why didn't he send it earlier? Or left a warning at her house that night? Or woke her up and told her what was going on?

She wouldn't have any crucial information to give the man, but if she called the ad's number, the man would find out about her. And if he was dangerous in some way – and Dis was more and more convinced he was – she would be linked with that danger.

But this was all speculation. The gray man had probably stumbled on the tour just as he had – and realized that it would be good cover for a bicyclist riding across country who didn't want to be noticed. If fact he might have come across the tour at that last town, Stringer, and started checking immediately. If he had gotten word from Knobby, he probably would have gone ahead to Hickcomb, the tour's destination for the evening – or maybe even had driven to last night's overnight. If he had done that, he obviously didn't find me.

Well, what do I do? I have to get to Hickcomb and pick up my gear – that's a certainty. In fact, I better take off, but fast. If the gray man would stop and think about it, that's the best place to find me. I have to pick up my gear.

But maybe I should wait until Knobby rides by – he's not that far behind me, although he'll undoubtedly spend some time at that park – and find out if he indeed did call home. But what would that get me? I'd know what happened, but I'd also absolutely confirm my presence here with him. Right now I don't think that Knobby could positively swear that he had seen me.

So, I'll bust my ass right now and at least get my gear before the gray man gets there – I hope. At least I'll know because he'll almost have to take this road to get to Hickcomb; from what I remember of the map, there's no other decent alternate route.

He was off. The wind was moderate and mostly crosswind; the road gently up and down with many long curves and only moderate traffic. Without loaded panniers, Dis was soon up to 20 to 25 mph on the flats. He ground into it, pushing himself at his highest gear to spin his chain rings as fast as he could. The energy came partly from release, partly from frustration. It was good to take off and leave this lazing crowd behind – especially Knobby; but he was also propelled by the exasperation of so many locked and crucial mysteries that he was deliberately avoiding rather than facing. While he raced he pondered what to do on the upcoming evening. The gray man would be at the overnight stop for sure. Dis needed to get his gear and take off, perhaps sleep in a farmer's field as he did before. On the other hand, If he got there before the gray man, he could pitch his tent close to the baggage area, get in it, and watch him through the tent flaps. If Dis never left it, the man would never be able to identify him – the man can't know what my tent looks like. That way Dis could get an idea of what he's up to. Dis had food in his panniers; he wouldn't have to go out to a restaurant.

No, that's too dangerous, he told himself. I'd be too close to him and, who knows, what could come up? Besides, what about tomorrow morning? He'd be around when I'd have to take the tent down and be out in the open. That settled it in his mind. He would race to his gear, load it on his bike, and take off to somewhere else for the night. He had thought that hiding in a group tour would protect him because of its anonymity. But safety in numbers didn't work if all the numbers, one by one, had to pass a certain point where a discerning observer could locate himself.

Within half an hour he was zipping into Hickcomb, following its circling streets to its central high school, perched on an uprise behind the waterfront business district. No gray car had passed him since he had left Stringer. He fairly raced to the side of the school's gym, where in the parking lot, the two 26-foot trucks had unloaded the collective gear of the tour. The gear was strewn, in an almost orderly fashion, on two separate sections of the pavement leading into the gym, each section for one of the trucks.

Dis had loaded his two sets of panniers into truck A, and because his gear was panniers not luggage, bags, or sacks, it was easy to spot – even in his haste. A few other riders milled around the baggage, looking desultory for bags that they knew must be there but just could not identify no matter how many times they looked. But Dis quickly loaded his bike, and with a quick glance at his highway map, was soon on a county road traveling northeast from Hickcomb. Only a few cars were on the road; not one bike. It was getting to be late afternoon. Dis could probably try to find a campsite in a park somewhere, but he decided against it. No, he would ride until twilight and then find a place off the road. The weather was great and he had food in his panniers. No problem.

He was, however, getting tired. He had ridden all day and raced for the last 15 - 20 miles, and now he was loaded down with all of his possessions. He slowed his pace, but still the increasing number of hills seemed to be getting both longer and steeper. In fact they were: Dis was leaving the river valley by country roads that were not engineered for modern, high speed usage; instead they followed every movement of the land, the pavement seeming to be lightly painted on the rolling surface of ancient, tumultuous upheavals.

In about an hour, after going through a series of small hamlets, Dis noticed the traffic picking up on his two-lane county road. Soon he came upon a larger community, one with two strip shopping areas on the southern outskirts and a two-block long downtown business section. The downtown area was teeming with traffic, both motorized and pedestrian. Dis wondered if the stores were open here on Thursday nights. But then he caught a sign hanging from a rope between two buildings announcing "Glory and Fiddling Encampment – Douglas County Fairgrounds."

The word "Encampment" locked into Dis's mind. Maybe here was another chance to escape into anonymity, at least to be able to set up his tent legally and without much of a chance of discovery. He would check it out.

It was almost impossible not to find the fairgrounds. The major road through the town led right to it. Dis pulled off the road and left his bike propped next to a tree in front of a bright yellow frame house. He crossed a side street, now choked with traffic, and examined the admissions area. The event seemed to be a general "olde tyme" gathering of musicians, crafts people, campers, and people waiting to be entertained. General admission was $3.00, with camping available for $5.00 per tent or vehicle, with one admission free for every tent or vehicle. That sounded good to Dis; five bucks for a hassle free tent space in the company of a large group of unquestioning people bent on having a good time.

The problem was his bike. Having his bike with him would set him apart. He needed to park it securely away from the camping area. Inside, past the admissions gate, he could see a bike stand, now almost filled with bikes chained to it. Why not there? Probably not much of a chance of it getting stolen in this small town, besides he was going to junk it in the near future anyway. So he bought a camping admission, locked his bike to the rack, and carrying his bags, located the tenting area. Soon his tent was up and he was in it, wolfing down two of his cans of tuna and half of his loaf of bread. When he got out to fill his water bottle, he noticed that showers for campers were available in the back of one of the fair's exhibition buildings. Why not? So after he had finished his meal and put his gear in order, he was soon standing under the warm spray of a shower head lathering his hair, which was, he noticed, getting long.

Two other men were in the shower area, one of them complaining to the other. "Damn, that Billy just up and left. Just like that, he walked out and said, 'Hell, I ain't comin' back.'"

The other, a middle-aged redheaded man, replied, "Well, what you gonna do? You can't run it by yourself, just you and your Rosie, can you?"

"Hey, if we have to, we have to – but the wife, she ain't feeling so good right now. But we'll do if we have to. That's all there is to it. It's the breaking down that's the trouble. We gotta be on the road for up north early Monday, and how am I gonna break it down with just me and the missus and be out of here Monday morning?"

"I don't know, Carl, it looks like you're gonna have to find someone around here."

"Yea, I know, but I hate to do that. These small towns hardly ever have decent workers just sitting around waiting to take off all over the country. Oh, you can find someone to work a weekend, but that's about it. They never want to leave where they're from."

"Yea, I know what you mean. Well, put up a sign on your wheel, and see what comes up."

"Oh, dang, this is going to be a long weekend, with just me and my sick Rosie running that wheel."

Dis had to stop and think. What was this "wheel?" And did he want to work? He could use the money, whatever it was, but what was the work and would it give him any protection? What the hell, it wouldn't hurt to ask.

"What kind of wheel you talking about mister?"

The man who had been complaining – whose only distinguishing feature since he was naked under a running stream of shower water was the fact that his ears were about two sizes too big for his head – looked at him critically, sizing Dis up. "Wheel? – a Ferris Wheel, my friend. Wife's running it now, but she's not feeling good – been working all day setting it up. The young fellow who was helping us just took off about two o'clock this afternoon – just left without even taking his pay for the last two days. You wanna work?"

Dis didn't know what to say, "Well, I don't know. What's it all about?"

The man was now washing – actually scrubbing – each of his almost flopping ears. "All you gotta do is sell tickets for now. One of us – looks like it'll be me, what with Rosie sick – collects the tickets and puts people into the buckets. Selling tickets ain't hard work – hell, we got a nice ticket booth, even got a fan in it – but the hours are long. Later on when you get to know the job maybe you can help outside, but now all you gotta do is sit and sell tickets. I'll be working outside. Rosie helps out some when she's feeling OK, but she's really down right now. You know what that Billy did, you know why he up and quit right in the middle of the afternoon?"

Dis gave the expected nod.

"He was gonna win the lottery. That's what he told me. About one o'clock when we had the axle up and was takin' a break, he just told me he was gonna win the lottery, the "daily dumb-dumb," he called it. He said he had a feeling. He had a couple bucks and he wanted to go downtown and buy a daily dumb-dumb. Said he knew for sure that he would win 500 bucks. He knew it deep down in his heart."

The redheaded man with him interrupted, "What did Rosie say about that?"

"Well, I tell you, Rosie just sneered. You know how Rosie sneers when she's against something? Well, I guess you don't know too much about that, but I sure do. Anyway this young fellow, Billy, just grabbed his things from the back of the trailer, said, 'Hell, I ain't comin' back,' and we ain't seen him since."

He looked at Dis, "The big thing is putting up and taking down the wheel. Workin' it is easy work; it's only a matter of putting the time in. But come early Monday morning we gotta take it down, load it up, and take off for up north. You interested?

Dis still hadn't made a decision. He was definitely interested. For one thing he needed the money. With only about three hundred dollars and the possibility of spending about half of that on a bus trip, he really didn't have much to fall back on. If he could get through the weekend, he'd be off away from the gray man with his bike and some extra dough. But the main consideration was that the crowds again would cover him, would give him that layer of anonymity that he need for self-protection. Even working on the ride would add to his protection, especially being in a ticket booth. The gray man, if he chanced to come to this fairground, would be looking for someone in the crowd, not a worker. Dis's perception of carnival workers was that they were invisible – nondescript people without individuality. He would be better off here than on a confining bus, heading off to a specific spot where he could possibly be located. He told the man, "Yea, I'm interested. I'm out of a job right now; I'm actually traveling. And I could use the chance to earn something extra. How about the pay?"

The man was drying himself, "I'll give you 40 bucks a day and a place to pitch your tent. You got a tent, don't you? On take-down and put-up days I pay 60 bucks. You travel with me and the wife for free, but you gotta pay for your own food and everything else. And" - here he grabbed Dis by the arm and leaned close to him - "it's in cash. Get that, cash. No red tape."

Dis caught the drift and then some: cash meant no forms, no tax, no making up names and numbers. He could be someone else. Who this time? How about Gary . . . Gary Frank, from . . . from Virginia. Yeah. He said, " I'm interested, very interested. I could use a job for awhile."

The man stuck out his hand, grabbed Dis's and they shook. "Well, son of a gun, I got me a helper in the shower. Wait 'til I tell Rosie about this. She'll really be relieved. When she gets down, things get real tough for me. Oh, she does her part, but when she's not feeling good – well, it's hard to put up the wheel by yourself that's for darn sure."

"I'm sure of that," Dis replied. "But I never worked on a . . . wheel . . . before. Is it pretty hard to handle?"

The man was drying himself. "Well, I'll tell ya – Hey, what's your name anyway?"

Dis had to stop and think. "Gary. Gary Frank. I'm from Virginia."

"Gary is it, heh? Well, Gary, glad to have you with me and the missus. My name's Carl, Carl Breezeny. And I guess you know my wife's named Rosie. About the work, naw, it's not bad. People are good for the most part, especially people out to have a good time. Hell, they don't want to make any trouble; they just want to pay their money and go for a ride. Sure, sometimes someone has had a little too much to drink – especially late at night, right before shutdown, but usually there's so many people around that the drunk guy ain't got a chance. The worst part of the job? You know what it is? Listening to that darn organ music all day and night – the same thing over and over again. But you get used to it – sometimes you don't even hear it."

Dis laughed and said, "Organ music . . . it's not my personal favorite."

"Well, come on, get finished dressing and I'll take you over to meet the missus and show you what you gotta do."

Chapter 15

Within an hour Dis was sitting in a narrow wooden ticket booth, a wire grid in front of him and a threadbare mesh curtain behind him, selling tickets almost as fast as he could count up the change. The wheel was a gold mine. People paid a dollar a ride – fifty cents for kids – and the wheel almost always had a line of people, ticket in hand, waiting to get on. Carl was right; the work was easy and the people almost invariably were pleasant. Oh, a few of them complained about the line, but they could see the length of it when they bought their tickets so they weren't surprised when they had to wait a bit.

Dis knew that Carl was checking him out for honesty. He would too, given the case. After all, Dis was handling money and he had stepped into the job right out of the blue – or in his case, the shower – no recommendations, no background check, no nothing. So about every fifteen minutes Carl stepped into the booth to collect the extra money – the big bills usually. Also Dis could see him counting the tickets he tore up at the entrance to the wheel. Through the torn curtain, every so often when he had a lull, Dis could look back at the operation of the wheel. A couple of times he caught Carl making marks on a sheet of paper he had on a little clipboard next to the bucket of torn tickets. Carl probably knew the exact number of riders every minute of the evening, and if he slipped up, he could always count the ticket stubs he meticulously deposited in the bucket. So Dis knew he had to be honest; but that was no problem for Dis. For the most part he was the epitome of honesty.

Dis liked the protection of the booth. From it he could keep an eye on the constantly moving swirl of people in front of him, and he knew they had a difficult time in seeing him. The green wire mesh that covered most of the front of the booth let him see out, but deflected light from outside so that he was just a shadow to someone walking in front of the booth. Dis noticed, for instance, when Carl gave him a toilet break, that when Dis returned, he could hardly make out Carl's features behind the screen. All he could see were Carl's hands at waist level in front of the opening. Carl had a goose neck lamp angled down over the money counter, and that helped too. But when Dis was in the booth, he could see all about him very clearly. And he was on the alert – for a nondescript man in a light blue jacket who, if here at all, would probably be on the edge of the area, carefully screening everything – and especially, everybody.

No man – no gray man – appeared, at least as far as Dis could observe. But he did see a wild and assorted mixture of people from his Ferris wheel booth vantage point. For one thing, people were dressed in just about anything that the human mind could fashion for wearing apparel. Swirling silks, tie-dyed Levi's, top hats, handkerchief bikini tops, tuxedos, Victorian dresses, obscene T-shirts, tutus, even a swashbuckling pirate suit appeared to Dis's extra alert eye during the course of the evening. Of course the Ferris wheel was a part of the "Glory and Fiddling Encampment," and that obviously added immeasurably to the flamboyance of the dress.

Dis couldn't really figure out the "Glory" part of the name, but the "Fiddling" took no guesswork. Much of the crowd was decidedly "old-timey;" the men with beards and long, flowing hair, and clothes that somehow never seemed tucked in; the women, red-scrubbed and freckled, in dresses that collectively formed a catalog of frontier fashions through America's formative years. Some of the people were performers at the "Encampment" – Dis could tell this by the random comments that filtered through the green mesh of his booth – but most were spectators, appreciators, or the merely curious.

At about seven-thirty, when the sun's rays started to get slanty, and off in the distance Dis could hear the dim notes of country music starting to echo through the variegated sounds of the carnival, Carl appeared and announced to Dis and the flowing crowd in front of the wheel that he was going to "disorganize the organ music." A few seconds later much of the sound component of the Ferris wheel experience ceased, replaced by human words and calls, the underground buzz of machinery and electricity, and the incessant music of the fiddles from the bandstand somewhere off in the distance. Carl yelled from the wheel, "Now that's my kinda music!"

Dis didn't completely agree with him, but he found the fiddle music very pleasant, even satisfying. It had a current of subdued energy, a sweetness at it core, a sliver of pure color – red and blue, and, yes, silver – that pulsated on thin wires of resonance. But Dis didn't have too much time or leisure to listen to it; he was busy taking care of the demanding constant line of people queuing up in front of the booth – and sweeping the area with his eyes, searching always for the looming gray man.

He wasn't to be found, not at the "Encampment." Dis hoped that he was still with BTMRV, trying to find the Dis needle in the haystack of bicyclists.

On this, the opening night of the fest, the bandstand music stopped about 11 o'clock, although random snorts of fiddling music pierced the dark occasionally in the next few hours. Dis guessed that the amplified stage show was over, but that impromptu fiddlings were going on throughout the fairground's camping sites. After eleven o'clock things got very busy for Dis and Carl. People evidently wanted to enjoy the warm-cool night with a ride through the sky in an electric-bright cylinder of spidery steel and classic wooden beams. They streamed to the wheel, dollars clutched in their hands, many of them towing sleepy-eyed kids. It was a friendly, peaceful crowd – people who had had a good time with something they loved and were still within its spell. Dis caught the feelings and the camaraderie and felt good himself.

He went to bed in his small little tent still feeling good. He was filled up, having eaten the last two hot-dogs from a van converted into a food-stand whose smell had been seducing him all night. He was twenty dollars richer, his pay for the evening's work. His relationship with Carl was nice and easy, although he hadn't yet met Rosie – she had been sleeping when Carl took him to see her. Working on the wheel was easy and, at least for now, interesting. And he hadn't seen the gray man.

The rest of the weekend was music of the same pitch. The days danced through Dis with the air of a fiddle. Although confined most of the time in the tiny booth, he felt secure and protected within its walls. It was almost the same as being behind the shell of a mask. The grounds were filled with low-keyed people feeling mellow about life in general. No one gave Dis a hard time over tickets or waiting in line; just the opposite, they were invariably pleasant and patient, many of them singing quietly to themselves or with the omnipresent music that wafted through the area.

Dis met Rosie, an enormous woman who rolled from her trailer to the wheel on Saturday morning about eleven o'clock, when Dis was just starting to sell the first tickets of the day. She waddled up to the booth, smiled and said, "You must be Gary. I'm Rosie. You'll see me around some today, but not much. I still got these tremors and I'm not going far from my home. Carl tells me you're all right, so you just keep doing what you're doing and don't pay any heed to me." Having said that, she disappeared surprisingly quickly for a woman of her girth. She was so big around and only average in height, that Dis wondered how she could ever help with the heavy work of putting up and taking down the wheel. He would see what would happen on Monday.

Carl's Ferris wheel wasn't a part of an organized carnival company. Carl was an independent. He didn't have the security of a regular series of big stops all through the carnival season, but he also didn't have to pay a large percentage of his take for that privilege. Actually since Carl was an old-timer with a proven record, his schedule almost took care of itself. Rosie made sure of that. She kept up a constant series of telephone calls and letters, making sure that the event they worked the year before would be in existence and would accept them again. She also had a network of carnival people through the country who invariably knew of alternative events when one of their usual stops either folded or for some reason didn't want them to return – something that was extremely rare.

Carl and Rosie worked mid-sized events, not the big state fairs or – on the other hand – the small town church festivals. They loved alternative events – entertainments that drew people with some degree of commitment, with some degree of being part of a group that had an image to project. Their best ever, as Rosie told Dis on Sunday, was years ago in following the Grateful Dead rock group. They loved it; the fans were united and furiously loyal; and they made a mint. But the Dead had become too big for them, had started performing in massive municipal auditoriums and arenas, graduating from the county fair grounds with a small carnival on the side.

Now Carl and Rosie took pains to hook up with Harley Davidson ride-ins, jazz and blues festivals, Renaissance fairs (they had to be away from the grounds, however), three-on-one basketball tournaments, innovative art festivals, old car and farm vehicle shows, soap box derbies, boy and girl scout jamborees, New Age and Seth gatherings, and similar events. One time they had even done a week-long nudist convention, but Rosie had nixed any more of that; she had stood out too much since she adamantly refused to bare herself, and she became almost physically sick after looking at naked people for a whole week in a row.

Two types of events they refused to do were rock festivals, especially ones that featured heavy metal, and Revolutionary and Civil War enactment encampments. For the one, they couldn't handle the rowdy spin-offs of the hugely amplified music, and for the other, they just didn't think that people should get enjoyment out of recreating a war. As Rosie said, "Celebrate a war. Nonsense! War's about killing. Only place to celebrate it is in a cemetery – and then don't celebrate. Just bow your head and pay heed. That's all: pay heed."

They were both in their fifties and they were "doing very well, thank you." They liked the constant traveling, had a comfortable and serviceable trailer and a small bungalow in Florida, didn't mind the long hours, and were taking in more money than spending it. Carl told Dis while they were cleaning up their space on Sunday morning that everything they owned was completely paid off. "We don't owe a cent to anyone, I'm proud to say."

On Sunday afternoon, just out of curiosity, Dis kept a record for an hour of the number of tickets sold: 67 adults and 43 children. They took in $88.50 on a relatively off-hour; Dis was sure they doubled that at the peak hours of Friday and Saturday nights. At that rate they could be collecting almost a thousand dollars a day during their weekend engagements. Sure they had some overhead – Dis's pay, carnival space rent, electricity charges, gas and travel expenses – but still they were able to keep a good part of almost everything they took in. They did have weather problems occasionally – an all-day soaking rain meant a day without income, but also a day in the trailer reading, watching TV, visiting with other ride people, or just catching up with loose ends. On the whole, Dis surmised, they were doing pretty well.

Dis kept his tent in the camping area, but – except for sleeping - he didn't spend much time in or around it. As for food, he reveled in the spicy, odorous fast food of the carnival, but it didn't take him long to have his fill of it. By Sunday night he was actually throwing away a half-full paper plate of French fried onion rings. But before that he had crammed himself with frankfurters slathered in steamed onions, hamburgers heaped with melted cheese and pickles, gooey slices of pizza, tacos overflowing with lettuce and sour cream, little doughnuts fresh out of the hot fat, gyros dripping with lamb and lemon juices, and spicy and hot shish-kababs. He went crazy with the mostly fat-fried, pungent offerings, but he told himself that he was making money now and he could splurge a little – especially after the sparse eating earlier in the week.

By Sunday Rosie was up and running, recovered from whatever had been ailing her. Actually she hardly ran – oozed was what Dis thought she did. But still she went where she wanted to go and did what she wanted to do without any ostentation. She took her time, but invariably she always seemed to be just exactly where she wanted to be just when she needed to be there.

And she quickly became almost a grandmother to Dis. When he first met her, when she appeared behind the curtain of his ticket booth, she carried a plate of just-out-of-the-oven cinnamon rolls for him. Almost her first words were concern about him – where was he sleeping? How long had he been on the road? Did he have family? Did he know the best place in the fairgrounds for pancakes? Dis's mind had to work fast to keep up with her questions and to remember the lies he had to make up. He assumed her memory was computer-sharp so he had to be on his toes. He hated that. He would have wished he could be up-front with her, but he couldn't, at least now. On the other hand, she probably had met like this with literally thousands of "helpers," many of them with more lies in their lives than miles on Dis's bike.

He couldn't figure out Carl and Rosie. In the rough and tumble, low-scale, scruffy world of carnival ne'er-do-wells, they were Norman Rockwell icons of respectability and decorum – besides being exceedingly nice. They were caring and concerned about him as a person, not just as a worker. During the course of the weekend, Carl – in a very pleasant way – had made sure Dis knew who, of all of the people working the "Encampment," to avoid. Most, the ones who hardly ever shaved and whose clothes always looked slept in, he dismissed with a laugh. "Ha, stay away from him, Gary, he doesn't care about himself." For others he had one-word summaries: drinker, card-shark, ho-mo, the clap. One even was "bad-breath."

Rosie, on the other hand, was a matchmaker. Unfortunately there were very few unmarried women within Dis's age working this event. Rosie had one woman, the owner of a soft drink-cotton candy venue, over to the wheel's ticket booth almost as soon as she was up on Saturday. The woman was friendly and funny, but she was running a little too cotton-candy plump and she had a disagreeable habit of clicking her teeth together as she talked and laughed. She and Dis joked about being locked in their respective jails, but after an initial flurry of repartee, she drifted away and never returned – and Dis never felt the inclination to hang around her open-sided van, with its saturating smell of Pepsi and cotton-candy.

Dis wondered why he was getting all this attention; after all, to them he was just a drifter. But they evidently could see through his life on the road to his basic stable nature beneath. Dis was comfortable with them; perhaps he would remain with them for awhile.

Early Sunday afternoon, before the customers started massing, Carl took Dis out of the booth and showed him how to load the customers and to control the wheel's movements. After about 15 minutes of showing and helping, Carl took off, leaving Dis alone with the customers and Rosie in the booth. Dis didn't like being out in the open; he felt exposed and vulnerable, especially since the weather continued to be exceptionally sunny and bright. He felt he was a conspicuous target for anyone's stare, especially for an unobtrusive man in a blue jacket. When Carl came back about an hour later, Dis feigned a headache from the sun and Carl took over the outside duties. Dis went back to the booth, and his contentment, while Rosie disappeared – lumbering here and there in Dis's periphery, talking to other carnival people around the area, always just seeming to ease into his vision just when her presence seemed to call for it.

Sunday night was slow. The performers had one last early-evening show, but many campers had taken off during the course of the day, especially in the late afternoon. The carnival stayed open until a little after sundown, but then with only a few spectators wandering around the grounds, and many other vendors packing up, Rosie came out of their trailer and said, "That's it." Physically, she seemed transformed. Maybe, Dis thought, it was the clothes. She was wearing a pair of bib overalls, large enough for two and a half people, a tent-like blouse of plain, plaid material, and a large plastic helmet. She was ready for work.

And work she did. In tearing down the wheel, it was Rosie who took charge, who did most of the heavy work, who drove and maneuvered the flat-bed truck which carried the wheel, who was Dis and Carl's taskmaster, driving them almost with no letup until three in the morning when Carl pleaded with her for a short sleep break. "Come on, Rosie, we got to drive all day tomorrow. I don't want to be falling asleep over the steering wheel."

By that time they had all of the swinging benches half dismantled and carried and lifted onto the back of the truck. Rosie carried one end of every one; while the men alternated in this heavy work. Dis would have taken her place, but she insisted, squatting down with her expansive legs, resting the axle-rod of each bench on her shoulder, and lifting it before either of the men could get the other end out of its break-apart, circular holder. "OK, Carl, you get in there and sleep; I'll just finish knocking down the booth and then maybe I'll be tired too – maybe."

She turned to Dis, "Gary, go sleep. You're going to have to drive some tomorrow 'cause we gotta go all the way to Peoria. When you get up – and I'll be over to wake you – make sure you pack up your tent and gear and bring it all over here." A big question came over her pleasantly dimpled face, "Hey, I never asked you how you came to this town. You don't have a car, that's for sure. What were you doing, hitching?"

"No. I've got a bicycle."

"Oh, for pity's sake, a bicycle." She paused, looked him straight in the eye and Dis could almost see equations, suppositions, and determinations flying around and dropping into place in her mind. "Well, we got room for it on the truck. Bring it too."

By noon the next day, Dis was exhausted, Carl was sweaty and cantankerous, but Rosie, from her commanding position on the bed of the truck, was still a demon of energy. The men's job was to dismantle the wheel piece by piece, taking one elbow or girder or strut from one side, then moving the massive axle 180 degrees and removing a counter piece from the other side. They then carried the sometimes weighty parts to the truck where Rosie took over, moving them around almost like chess pieces being replaced in a storage drawer, each in its precise position. The parts, so strung out and expansive when assembled, formed a compact interlocking block after Rosie was through with her work. Eventually the heavy engine and the massive main axle riding on its supports were the only parts still on the grounds. For these the truck had to be maneuvered to a precise position from which they could lower the axle inch by inch to a permanent support on the truck immediately behind the cab. The engine, which was on wheels, had to be winched up a ramp and strapped tightly into place. Rosie and Carl worked together beautifully doing this. Carl, especially, getting his second wind, seemed to love the precision of the work and the synchronization of the action.

By two o'clock in the afternoon Rosie had Dis's bike strapped down under canvas on the truck, they had eaten meatloaf sandwiches from the trailer's refrigerator, and they were ready to roll. The fairground amusement area was basically deserted, most of the other carnival attractions having packed up and gone in the morning. The wheel, being the largest ride, took the longest to break down. A kiddy camel ride, its owner sleeping off a drunk, and the cotton candy-Pepsi van were the only attractions left on the lot. Two people were searching the area – one with a sack for aluminum cans and the other with a metal detector and a long screwdriver looking for coins and anything metallic of value.

Dis has his choice. He could ride with Rosie in the flat-bed truck or Carl in the pickup truck which pulled the trailer. He wasn't familiar with driving a big truck so, since he would be driving the pickup, he elected to start the drive with Carl. They had about 300 miles to go, their destination a small town, Kickapoo, just west of Peoria, but very close to a state park – Jubilee College State Park. It was the site of an annual "Jubilation" festival. They hoped to be on the grounds of the festival late that night, Monday, so they would have a whole day, Tuesday, to set up the wheel in preparation for a long Wednesday-to-Sunday gig.

Rosie led the way in the flat-bed, Carl following behind, making sure the canvas was secure and that no parts shifted around because of road vibrations or the impact of the occasional pothole. Carl, despite having working hard early that day, became loquacious. He told Dis his whole life story – how he had broken into the ride business by working just as Dis was doing as a hire-on; how he had met Rosie, a caramel-apple maker and seller; how they were married at a carnival in Pokatensy, Pennsylvania, with a preacher from a revival tent operating next to the carnival; how they suffered through a flash flood in the hills of Tennessee, losing a leased Tilt-a-Whirl and almost their lives when a wall of water rushed through the fairgrounds; how they had scrimped and saved to get enough to make a down payment on their wheel; and how they had meticulously paid it off over a twenty year period. Carl was particularly proud of that. "It's all paid for, Gary, every last cent. We own it clear and free."

They rode through lovely country. Illinois was green and growing in this, the mid-season of the year. It was flushed with the sun and the results of past rain. Rolling hills rumbled to their right and left, washes of undulating color under a blue and wispy white, full-crowned sky. Near the road, which led them north and a little east, an abandonment of flower-weeds tossed pinpoints of blue and red and yellow to their eyes. Even the ubiquitous roadside trash - Bud Light cardboard wrappings and convenience store plastic cups being the most visible - became softened and blurred as they sped through the afternoon countryside.

"Well, Gary, what do you think of this carnival business?" Carl asked, out of the blue.

Dis blurted out before he really thought, "I like it – I assume you're asking about your Ferris wheel and not about the whole carnival economy, right?"

Carl turned his head slightly and looked at Dis, "Come on, Gary, tell me the truth. The way you talk you can't have been drifting around the country all your life. I bet you went to college, right?"

Dis didn't say anything, mulling how close to the truth he should go for this genuinely good man. But still caution rode on his conscience like the heavy Ferris wheel on the truck bed just ahead. "I've been around. I went to college, sure . . . for a little while, and I've been knocking about, doing this and that all my life. I need to settle down, I guess. But I don't like being in one place for a long time – I tried it a couple of times and didn't like it."

Carl interrupted, "You ever been with a carnival before?"

"No."

"Well, think about it. You got both things you need: a nice home all the time and you're always traveling. Can't beat it. Home and travel all the time."

"Yea, I see what you mean. It sounds good. Actually I didn't mind those days back there at the fiddlers' fest. In fact, I kind of liked it. The work was easy – selling tickets certainly is better than digging ditches or cleaning porta-potties. And even last night and today wasn't that bad – tearing down the wheel. Hard work, to be sure, but I've had worse, that's for sure."

"Well, you gonna stay on with us for awhile then?"

Did had to stop and think about that for a beat. Why not? He would be making – and saving – some money. He would remain rather inconspicuous, even if he had to leave the confines of the booth and work outside on the wheel. He would be traveling away from the gray man, he hoped. And Carl and Rosie were decent people who would treat him honestly, he thought.

He smiled at Carl, "Does that mean I passed the job interview?"

Carl's eyes swayed from the highway. "Yea. Rosie likes you. And I depend on her, you know. Hey, I think you're all right too, but the real test is Rosie. If she's on your side, you're OK, get it?"

'I can understand that. Rosie is quite a person. She makes some mean cinnamon rolls too."

"So, what do you think? You gonna stay with us for awhile or not?"

"Sure, why not. I'll have to check out northern Illinois, right? But I think you can count on me for awhile at least."

"That's good, Gary, that's good. You need to stop and settle down. You know Rosie's looking out for you in the sweetie category, don't cha?"

"She's looking to fix me up, is that what you're saying, Carl?"

"You stay with us, Gary, and she'll find someone for you, someone just right for you. You know, we know lots of people – we meet lots of them on our rounds – and Rosie has a sense about them. She knows quality, even if sometimes it may not be on the outside, you know what I mean?"

Dis thought for a moment and then said, 'You get some people who are down and out but are still decent, right?"

"Right."

Dis didn't care for the match-making talk – a momentary flash of Lorn's face leaped through his memory – so he deliberately switched the talk. "You know your wife is one of the most decent people I've ever met, and I was surprised at her capacity for work. She's a glutton for hard work, isn't she?"

Carl looked straight ahead at the rumbling truck ahead of him. "That she is, my boy, that she is. But I know what you're not saying." He turned his head and looked at Dis, "How can she be so fat and work so hard; that's what you're thinkin', ain't it?"

Dis smiled and affectionately hit Carl of the shoulder with his left hand, "Hey, Man, I didn't say that, but, you know, I was really surprised that she could work so hard. She carries a lot of weigh, right; but, boy, can she work!"

Carl, watching the road carefully, said, "She's my lifesaver, Gary, my absolute lifesaver. You know it's not the wheel, or the trucks, or the savings I send almost every day to my bank in Florida. Those things are about contentment . . . about, well, I don't know how to say it . . . about being satisfied with your work. But Rosie's about life – about havin' a life that's worth something, you know what I mean?"

Dis nodded, thinking of two people, Ruth and Lorn. His world of "worth something" was a momentary cloud filling his memory for just an instant before Carl began again.

"Sure she's a big lady – always was and probably always will be, but, you know, when you get right down to it, looks don't really mean that much. At a carnival you can really see that. I don't know how many slim and pretty and, you know, really attractive ladies I've met working in carnivals all these years that turned out to have as much value as . . . as . . . as the give-away prizes at the win-every-time booths. Most of them have been hard, really hard – and it almost seems that the better looking they are, the harder they are. I could never figure that out. I mean, they got everything in the looks department, but they're so hard. I don't know, maybe it's men that make them that way . . . most of the men aren't much better."

He paused, maybe thinking about someone in particular, "Now Rosie is hard when it comes to work, but she's soft when it comes to being decent. She's a big lady and," here he looked critically at Dis, "a real lifesaver. That's it, a real lifesaver."

A smile appeared on his face as he looked forward. He seemed to be staring so hard at the back of his wife's head through the back window of the flat-bed truck, that she was probably involuntarily thinking "lifesaver," so hard was the quality of his stare.

They drove in silence for awhile through the speckled late afternoon light – a light filled with flying things, some living, some the growing earth's discarded detritus now windblown in freedom. After about two hours, Rosie's brake light started blinking and she started to wave her right hand, a signal that she was about to pull off the road. They were near Springfield, Illinois, now, riding the interstate north. Carl flipped his headlights on momentarily to acknowledge, then slowed and followed her off the interstate and into a vast ocean of a parking lot with an archipelago of service buildings rock bound in the middle. They followed her around to the back of the parking lot where there was enough space for Carl to pull beside her. Soon, after using the facilities' restrooms, they scrambled the driving. Now Dis took over driving the pickup with Rosie taking up most of the space next to him.

The wheel truck, with Carl driving, led the way as usual. As they pulled out of the parking lot and onto the road that let to the interstate intersection, and Dis was struggling mildly to adjust himself to driving – and to driving a pickup carrying a trailer – Dis caught a glimpse, just a momentary flicker at the periphery of his vision, of a gray car - THE GRAY CAR - parked in front of the restaurant building.

He knew it instantly. It was unmistakable in his memory and it caused his heart to sink. But just as quickly he was rolling through the intersection and concentrating furiously to merge easily with the interstate's heavy traffic. Once driving in crowded but calm traffic, he almost succumbed to panic. Was he on to me? Is he right on my tail? Dis swept the rear view mirror minutely, looking for the car following him. Thank God it wasn't there.

From his side Rosie spoke. "I thought you said you were a good driver. I hate to tell you, Gary, but you look scared – positively white. What's the matter, you don't like interstates?"

Dis glanced at her quickly, his mind working rapidly. "Well, it's just that I haven't driven in awhile . . . and I don't know if I've ever towed anything. Don't worry. I'll catch on and get settled. I don't have to worry about the route, just follow Carl, right?"

"That's right, Gary, just keep behind him. Carl's a steady driver. He won't be making fast passes around trucks and such. We want to get there tonight, but Carl's not the one to make a fool out of himself in doing so. He just takes it easy and we get there in good time."

"We're going up this interstate until we get just east of Peoria, right? Then we go west on 74, looking for the exit to Kickapoo."

"I guess that's right, but that's Carl's business. He takes care of the driving – the direction that is." She paused, looked closely at him, and then said, "So you're going to be with us for awhile?"

Dis wondered how she knew that. He hadn't seen them talk privately when they had gone to the toilets and exchanged driving back at the stop. Maybe they had been together so long that they could communicate without words. "Well, I'm not going to make any long range commitments, but, yeah, I'll stay on for awhile at least." He glanced at her, "I like you two. The job's not bad. And I can use the money."

She looked quizzically at him. "'Long range commitments'. Come on, Gary, tell me the truth about your past. You didn't learn to talk like that traveling around the country on a bike, now did you?"

Damn, Dis thought to himself, all these lies. What did he tell Carl? Evasive. "Yea, I've been to a little college – just enough to know that it wasn't for me. Too much maneuvering for position, if you know what I mean. Then I guess I've been just knocking around for awhile now. Oh, I had a couple of steady jobs over the years, but one thing or another came up, and since . . .yeah . . . I had no commitments, I decided to go on the road – to see this great country."

He glanced at her and what he saw was skepticism. Her eyes, shining from the puffy contours of her ruddy face, told him that she knew he had specifics that he didn't want to bring up. Did she even have an intimation of his guilt, of his killing, of his desertion, of his disappearance into anonymity?

She spoke first. "You got a lotta things you're not saying, I know. But that's OK; I guess everybody does, everybody on the road. But, Gary, you're a good worker and honest – that's the problem we have with most helpers. They just can't stand, somehow, to have all those dollars flowing past them without them taking any, you know, secretly. We gotta watch that carefully. We've been watching you, you know."

With his eyes on the road, Dis nodded, "Sure I knew that – right from the start. In fact I was surprised you put me in the ticket booth so quickly. Was that a test?"

"Well, yes and no. I really was sick, and selling tickets is a lot easier than running the wheel. You gotta be proven responsible to run the wheel. But you're right, we did want to test you. We need someone like you, and we saw quickly that you were a cut above the usual roustabouts that we can find. So stick around with us for awhile, Gary." She put her soft hand on his shoulder. "Maybe you'll find something with us that you've been looking for."

Dis gave her an oblique glance and a smile.

She continued, "But I'm tired now. I'm gonna close my eyes and rest a bit. Carl's gonna need a break when we get around Lincoln. We'll be stopping there for some food. So just let me rest; but if anything comes up, you just give a holler."

She closed her eyes and was quiet. Dis thought back to the rest stop. He retraced his steps in the parking lot and the john. Was the gray man there, and if he was, had he seen Dis? He and Carl had walked together with Rosie leading the way through the parking lot. No, he didn't remember anyone remotely like the gray man in the lot. They went through an automatic door that wasn't working. He remembered that Rosie had some trouble in getting it to open. Carl and he both gave it an extra push to make it move. Then they walked through a sort of hallway to the john. One side of the hall was open to the restaurant – it was a Country Kitchen – a divider about belt high, topped by plants and some ceramic statues, shielding the eatery's booths and tables from the general public. They could have been seen from the restaurant. Dis, however, remembered sweeping the place with his eyes – it was a standard practice with him now – and he didn't recognize the gray man. However, as he remembered it now, he wasn't that careful. There might have been people with their backs to him, or people hunched behind someone at the counter . . . or – it hit him almost with the physical force of a whiplash from a rear-ender – someone sitting directly next to the divider, someone with a clear view through a break in the greenery, watching everyone who walked down that hallway.

Damn, why had he been so open; why had he let his guard up so?

But wait a minute. Had the car been there when they went in? They walked around to the front – it was the only entrance. Had he scanned the parking lot for the gray car? He was talking to Carl and Rosie, but, yes, he did remember looking at the lot, and there was no car in the area where he later saw the car. Could it be that he had lucked out and just missed the gray man? God, he hoped for that.

But what was the guy doing at the stop? I assume he knows I'm on a bike, so what is he doing looking for me at an interstate rest stop near Springfield, Illinois? Let's see, the bike tour broke up on Saturday and he missed me on the last nights of the tour. God, I hope he had to wait until every piece of luggage was picked up on those nights. Today's Monday; yea, I guess someone traveling on a bike could be about here in a couple of days.

But what's he doing? Asking people about me, just as he did back at the "You Got It?" He has to have a picture of me – well, not of me, but of Rob Clemmon. So he's probably asking people, especially the waitresses and such, if they've seen a guy on a bike who looks like this, then he shows them the picture.

Well, I'm not on a bike now – and I'm not in a car. Driving this pickup is a real stroke of luck. With the bike under canvas up ahead, he can't even follow the bike, if he knows what it looks like. Yeah, he probably does. There were enough people on the tour who could probably identify me – and my bike.

I'll bet he got to that Knobby and gave him a real song and dance about me. By now Knobby will have told Lorn – shoot, I'll bet he called her up as soon as he got home. Well, if she received my letter, I hope that at least she'll be cool and not say a word about this whole thing – about me and her. Damn, the one thing in life I really want, and both she and I have to be absolutely silent about it.

Forget it Dis, forget it. It's over and done with. You're in trouble enough without getting her involved in it too.

By now they were traveling through central Illinois, heading away from an increasingly glaring sun that was burning through the powdered haze of the late afternoon-early evening. But he couldn't think of the sun; it was the moon that surfaced in his memory. The moon and Lorn. So soft, and silver, and pure. So desirable – and now gone completely.

Because of a goddamn gray man – and Iowa. What had Marge, back at the store, said the guy had asked? "Is your night clerk from Iowa?" Well, hell, of all the states in the world, somehow I'm connected with Iowa. What is it anyway? State fairs, cornfields, small towns, hicks, the Iowa . . . what is it? Big Ten. University of Iowa . . . Hawkeyes, that's it, Hawkeyes. Damn, maybe that's what I'm going to need – hawkeyes – if I'm ever going to see my way out of this mess. We're going to western Illinois, right next to Iowa. Iowa. What if I were to go there?

His racing mind stopped. Could he run forever? Could he keep avoiding a showdown? Or did he eventually have to face whatever he had to face? Rosie had just been talking about commitment. Maybe he had a commitment to himself – and, hopefully it wasn't too late – to Lorn and even Chrissy, for that matter.

The sun was almost blinding. He reached up and pulled down the truck's sun visor, almost at the same moment, checking the rear view mirror automatically. Just at that moment with the sun's rays slanting into his eyes, he caught just a momentary glimpse – no, not of a gray car – but of the rising moon.

It was then that he knew that he had to go to Iowa. Maybe not right now, but some time in the not too distant future.

Chapter 16

Dis and Carl were working on the engine. That is to say, Carl was working on the engine and Dis was watching and being the "hold and run" man – "Hold this a minute," or "Run get me the. . ." They had just set the wheel up again for the second time in one week, and since the McDowell County Thrashers' Reunion wouldn't open until the next day, they had a whole day to just take it easy and do some necessary maintenance. Dis could do most of the ordinary mechanical adjustments on his bike - adjust the derailleur, for example – but he was no mechanic and he knew it. Once back in Rockhurst he had taken his back hub apart, and then had to cart it sheepishly to the bike shop to have it put together again properly.

They had been working in northwestern Illinois for about a month now, usually moving only short distances between weekend stays – although they did play one Wednesday downtown festival. They also had a very successful full week at an antiques and wine festival in the old Mormon settlement Nauvoo on the bluffs of the flood plain of the Mississippi. Carl had given Dis an extra day's pay – a full $40 – just because they had done so well, and because they had to work so hard and steadily. But also during the month they suffered a full weekend of constant, driving rain, forcing them to close up on both days after only 15 minutes and no customers. Dis did get paid for those days.

Carl paid Dis every day – in cash, usually ten-dollar bills. And by now, Dis had more than a thousand dollars hidden in his toilet kit in his tent. Usually when he had more than 20 or 30 of the ten-dollar bills, Dis converted them at a local bank to 100-dollar bills just because of the space problem.

After about two weeks, when he could see that Dis was not drinking or gambling his money away, Carl suggested that Dis should start a bank account or some safe savings plan somewhere. Having lots of cash around was an invitation to disaster. Carl, himself, each day wired the previous day's cash to his bank in Florida, but he knew that Dis couldn't start an account down there. Carl volunteered to bank Dis's money in Carl's account – "I keep very good records; you know that." – but Dis wanted to keep his money on hand, and graciously declined. Carl would have been honest with it, Dis knew, but Dis also knew that he had to have it available in case he had to leave quickly – in case, obviously, the gray man showed up.

He hadn't. In fact the last Dis had any contact with him was that fleeting glimpse of his car at the Interstate rest stop near Springfield. Dis hoped the man had given up on him. After all what was he worth? How could a man spend so much time in tracking down another man unless there was some money involved? And Dis knew that he had no real money; in fact he felt rich with his thousand dollars – a piddling amount, he knew, in the middle years of a man's life. He didn't like to think about other reasons for the man stalking him. It was obviously connected to Iowa somehow – and to Rob Clemmon. Was Rob Clemmon wanted by the law? The gray man didn't seem to be a police officer. Dis felt for sure that he wasn't. The law operated out in the open; it didn't act so secretly.

Then what was it? Revenge? Jealousy? Righting a wrong? Many nights Dis drifted to sleep pondering these questions. He also told himself that the only way to find the answer – and to resolve many of his problems – was to go to Iowa, to go to the town on his driver's license, Owaceta, and confront the truth. But he knew so little. What could he do? What would happen? Would he be in danger? Not likely, since he really wasn't Rob Clemmon. But if he did go there, he would have to give up Rob and become Dis. And he would have to confront his sad past – the killing, Ruth, his old job, his desertion, his running away.

In many of his bouts with his conscience, it came down to money. He decided he didn't want to visit Owaceta unless he had a car and a relatively healthy clump of 100s in his toilet kit. He would need the car for mobility and in case he had to get away quickly, and the money to give him basic anonymity in shelter and clothing and other incidentals. However, now that he had more than a thousand dollars and had seen no signs of the gray man for about a month, he was becoming less resolute in coming to terms with his past. He was actually enjoying his work with Carl and Rosie. He found that he liked the customers - mostly youngsters and young marrieds with children - who were the mainstay of the Ferris wheel business. The more aggressive and potentially disruptive teenagers and young unmarried stayed away from the wheel, for the most part. It was too tame, too babyish, not enough thrills or imagined danger.

In early summer they were setting up for an extended weekend at the fairgrounds of Illinois' Whiteside County, just outside the small town of Morrison. The town was a beautiful place with a homogeneous mixture of people, homes, and stores. Unfortunately, a state highway filled with looming trucks ran right down the middle of it. And only a block away and parallel to the highway, a major railroad trunk line carried long lines of freight cars five or six times a day and night.

The town was bisected, to be sure, but not divided.

Inn the middle of the two major transportation arteries, a lovely throwback to an earlier time still survived. Main Street still had its turn-of-the century buildings, most of them occupied by small stores that, while not thriving, were nevertheless still viable. About the only intrusion by modern impositions was a Hardee's fast food-ery, but even it was becoming acceptable since it offered senor citizens unless cups of coffee and didn't make them move through the also endless and lazy afternoons.

A row of stately mansions looked down upon the highway just to the west of the downtown and on both sides of town many impressive and well kept-up middle class houses flourished.

The fairgrounds at the town's southern edge now held – beginning on Wednesday - "The Good Ol' Railroad Days" fair, with a somewhat small carnival dominated by Carl and Rosie's Ferris wheel.

To the north about a mile and a half, a state park – Morrison/Rockwood State Park - surrounding an archetypical fishing lake, serene in its setting, lay among a dammed-up river's once valley.

Late Tuesday afternoon the wheel was up and just about ready to be tested. Carl was at the controls and Dis was taking it easy doing some paint touching-up to the fare booth.

All at once a man and a woman, middle aged, and wearing typical bicycling gear appeared in front of him.

"Can we take a ride on the Ferris Wheel?"

"I . . . a . . . don't think so. I'm sorry, the fair doesn't start until tomorrow, so I guess that we're not open for business. Looks like you'll have to come back tomorrow afternoon."

The woman, cute and trim, responded, "Oh, we'll be gone by that time. We're only here for the night."

"Oh, you're on vacation? You're on a bike trip, I bet?"

"You guessed it," the man replied. We're on GITAP – he pronounced it "Git-ap", a week long bike ride, and we're staying tonight up at the state park. In fact, we stay the whole week at state parks, camping – in tents."

"Hey, that sounds like my kind of trip."

"Well, it's a good deal – a week of carefree biking, sleeping outside under the stars and usually in a woods, good food – we have prepared breakfasts and dinners at the parks' pavilions – and we ride with some real nice people."

"It sounds like a lot of fun. I'm a bike rider myself, when I'm not making this big wheel go around. I've been to a couple of long rides. Is this ride you're on a big one?"

The woman, looking closely at the mildly handsome Dis, said: "Well, you'll have to come out to the park . . . let's see, it's Morrison. That's right Morrison-Rockwood . . . and see what it's all about. Hey, this evening after dinner, they're going to have some kind of music I heard – blue grass or something like that. You oughta come on out and meet some of us. I'd be fun for you – get you away from this carnival for a change."

Dis couldn't resist kidding her a little. "You mean to tell me there's something wrong with the music around here. Why I can't get enough of this pipe organ tooting, these Scott Joplin rags, and especially the merry-go-round nursery rhyme music. Blue grass. Isn't that banjos, guitars, and squeaky voices singing about ol' Pa down in the valley?"

She gave him just as much. "Well, come on, ain't chu heard that dat blue music is classical. Violins instead of banjos. And 'Oh sole la me-o' up in the air instead of down in some nasty valley."

"You're a treasure, lady." Dis looked at the man. "You keep her wrapped up. She is a genuine treasure. What ever you do, don't take her out on any country roads on a bike. No, she deserves a stretch limo. Oh sole la lim-o."

But Dis never made it out to the state park and the blue grass music, although the invitation was in the back of his mind. A small ride, overnighting in state parks, with friendly people, wow, that was the stuff of some far-off future when his life was sorted out and he would have the freedom to go and do what he wanted.

But what kept him from biking out to the park was Gloria.

Gloria ran the spook house. She was the sole owner and operator of it. Her mother, who lived with her and sold tickets and collected the dollar admission charge, was a wizened old lady with curly gray hair, which looked like a vaudevillian fright wig. Gloria was the inside-person of the attraction. In jeans and frilly blouse, she was there to protect people from themselves – and also to boot them out when they were deliberately causing trouble – something that happened with more than occasional frequency.

The spook house was basically just an ordinary truck trailer with many extensions. Metal porches expanded the size of the truck; painted flats attached in front gave it the appearance of large height; and a honeycombed interior of heavy black drapes made up an intertwining maze that was the heart of the spook experience. Lighting and sound, along with mechanical "spooks" – ghosts flying on a wire overhead, witches rising from a black box, a gelatinous brain melting into nothing, a corpse floating above its coffin – all provided the shocks, surprises, and scares that the customers loved and paid for.

But sometimes people, especially teens and pre-teens, went a little crazy in the spook house. They transformed into spooks themselves. They would become part of the action, for instance, lurking along a drapery wall and jumping out at customers who followed. Sometimes they staged faked fights and murders for the benefit of the unsuspecting. They were known to lie on the floor and reach out and grab people's legs. They loved to wait for little kids and deliberately torment them. They also sometimes were destructive, trying to knock apart the mechanical spooks, to make holes in the drapery walls, to splatter the place with their drinks and food.

So Gloria had to be in the place – or at least close to it – during operating hours. She could handle the job, there was no question about that. Although slim and average in height, she was absolute boss of her domain. Let a hulking high school football player start tearing up one of her spooks, and in an instant she had him marching out, his arm bent painfully behind his back, shuffling sheepishly to the local policeman stationed at the event. When kids started grabbing others, she grabbed them – and tossed them out.

She could have dressed as a spook – a witch, or a ghoul, or some other heinous fiend – and add to the scares of the ride, but that would reduce one of her chief jobs – calming frightened children. When she saw tiny kids entering the ride, she was especially alert because she knew that most of them couldn't handle the intensity of the darkened scares. Although she had a rule that little kids had to be accompanied by their parents, she knew that many of the parents couldn't handle their own kids; it was up to Gloria to remove the kids, console them, and get them laughing again.

So Gloria was good at her work; she made money, and except for the long hours and constant attention to human irresponsibility, she was pleased with her lot. But she was tough! At least she appeared so. Although physically she was only average, she projected a disarming, unsuspected toughness because she didn't hesitate to jump into potentially troubling situations and because of her mouth. In fact Dis heard her before he saw her. On this off day with the Ferris wheel already up, he was walking back from the fairground's crumbling toilet barn when, as he passed a nondescript trailer truck, he heard:

"Get your ass over here right now. Will you huh?"

Dis looked around. The high-pitched, cutting sound came from the truck.

"What are you, blind? And deaf at the same time? Get in here right now."

So Dis skirted the truck, found an opening in the back, and entered. He saw the back of a neat and slender woman. She was standing on a small ladder, putting some black drapes up and having problems. The hooks weren't catching and she was in danger of having the entire wall of drapery tear away.

"That box, Blondie, grab it."

Dis thought, "Blondie? Where is this woman coming from? Sure my hair is light, but I'm not a blondie."

"Come on, Pooka brain, get up here and hang on to this drape while I get some more hooks."

Obediently, Dis did what he was told to do. But he wasn't going to take her lip – not quietly at least.

As he mounted an upturned wooden box, he said, "OK, OK. Mighty Mouth, I'll help you out, but you should have taken care of the hooks before you got on the ladder."

"That so?" She was on the floor now, a box of hooks in her hand, looking up at him. "What do you know about this job anyway? You can't even put up a Ferris Wheel without Rosie leading you every step of the way, and you have the awe-das-i-tee to come in here and try to tell me how to do my job. Well, Buster Buns, I just might leave you up there all day, looking like a ballet dancer or something, holding that drape."

"Hey, Spook Lady, your whole upside-down just might go crashing to the floor if you don't get up on that ladder like about right now. What do you think I am, Atlas or something? I can't hold this up forever."

She laughed, "Atlas. That's funny. Well, you got the buns for it, but that's about it." She moved her stool close to his and jumped to its top. "Now hold it steady while I attach them."

Dis was immobile, balancing on top of the box, arms – holding up a not inconsiderable weight – stretched overhead. She was right next to him now, also stretching to reach the hooks. Dis noticed three things about her almost immediately. For one thing, she smelled unique. Dis couldn't figure it out. Perfume had to be a part of it, but just a part. She had been working all day – physical work – yet the smell wasn't offensive, as he was sure his probably was. It wasn't overpowering – just a unique outdoors sweetness mixed with a feminine acuteness, a tang, an edge.

He also noticed a somewhat plain but not unattractive face underneath an overlay of creamy, flesh colored makeup and some more deep color underneath her eyes. Dis was very close to her. He could see the texture of the makeup, and under it, the smoothness of her cheek skin. Her eyes, outlined in mascara and various tints, were active and dark, almost black; penetrating, alert, glimmering. He glazed his eyes a tiny bit and found it easy to envision the real woman under the artificial; and what he found, appealed to him. But he couldn't understand why she was wearing the makeup on this, a workday, a set-up day.

The other thing he noticed about her, and this almost immediately, was that she wasn't wearing a brassiere. The fluidity of her breasts through the T-shirt emblazoned with "Wonderland Park and Expo" was too free for them to be confined. This turned Dis on ever so slightly, even though he realized that it wasn't that unusual, and that it didn't have anything to do with sex or being sexy. She probably just wanted to be comfortable while she had to do a demanding, hot, and sticky job.

She placed the last hook and nudged Dis in the side, "OK, Blue Eyes, you can let go now. Gloria's got it all hooked up. You don't have to hang out here anymore. Get it?" She slapped Dis on the chest before she stepped quickly backward down the ladder.

Dis let out an obviously faked groan, "Ohhhhhhhh, that's bad." He dropped to the floor. "I'm glad that's finished, but hang tight, Gloria. . .Gloria it is, Glory be!" He was about to slap her in the chest, when he had second thoughts and held back. He did feign a punch-motion to her shoulder.

They stood eying each other, laughing and enjoying the back-to-back repartee. Instinctively they knew that they both were attractive to each other. She broke the silence. "Glory Be? Really? Well, Gary – yea, I know your name. If it's one thing Rosie's good for, it's cluing you in on what's going on with all the rides and workers on the grounds. She thinks you're a bunch of crap, don't you know?"

Dis stiffened. He didn't believe that. "Wait a minute. Wait a minute. Rosie said that? Well, wait till I get to her. If that's really true, I just might have to switch my allegiance from Ferris Wheels to spook houses, except these spook houses are. . ."

Gloria interrupted. "Hey, come on. Can't you take a joke? Naw, you come highly recommended. Rosie's working on your case, did you know that? She's been urging me to sashay down to your wheel so she can formally introduce us. But wait a minute, what were you saying about spook houses?"

"Well, I was going to say that they are a complete sham, an utter artificiality, nothing in them is true; they're a fraud and a scam and. . . they're. . . fun."

"God, Rosie, was right. You don't talk like a ride-person. You must be flying from a college somewhere, right? Either that or you work cross-word puzzles all day long."

"Neither. If you must know, I'm the leader of an international consortium seeking to determine if and where alien presences have landed on earth. And, guardian of the spook palace, with bright and shinny eyes like a redbird's, I think that everything seems to indicate. . ."

Gloria interrupted, "God, you can go on and on, can't you?"

"That aliens are hale and healthy right here in spook heaven!" With that Dis turned and walked out the back entrance. When he landed on the ground after jumping off the truck's bed, he turned back and said, "I'll be back later for my pay, Alien Lady."

"Sure, and I'll have the puddin' cookin' too. But what'd you say before that? What'd you say about my eyes?"

In a stage whisper as he was moving away, Dis replied, "Come on over to the Ferris Wheel. It's leaning and we need someone to hold it up while we find the anchors."

So it was this strange, verbally assertive and imaginative carnie woman who kept Dis in the fairgrounds that night rather than roll his bike out to the state park. But also, always lingering in the back of his mind, was the slight possibility that the Gray Man might have heard about the ride and would make a move to be in the vicinity. Dis didn't want the Gray Man to see him on his bike.

That evening with the wheel up and ready, the park closed until opening day on the next evening, and Carl and Rosie reading lazily in their deck chairs under their trailer's canopy, Dis did wander over to the spook house. He knocked on a back panel, but no one answered. He was about to turn away when a strong blast of rich coffee scent hit his nose and Gloria's high pitched voice assailed him, "Hey, Batless Atlas, the cappuccino's ready."

The voice came from the vicinity of the truck's cab, which was parked behind the spook house and pointed in his direction. He walked to it and found that the cab almost transformed itself as he walked around it. From a traditional highway vehicle it became a neat, and very feminine, house-tent. And now this living space was filled with the powerful aroma of rich Italian coffee. As Dis came up, Gloria was just putting the finishing touches on the frothy milk into which she would pour the thickened black coffee. "Here's your pay, Stoolie. Better compensation you won't get this side of Jefferson City, Missouri."

Dis took the offered cup, raised it to his lips, said a quick "Ciao" before taking a tiny taste, and then smiled at her. "Hummm, good stuff, Glorioso. You know you could go into business selling this." He took another sip, this time a healthy one. "You could bring Italian coffee culture to the great western prairie. Think of it, you could combine your ride here with a cappuccino stand. Let's see, coffee and spooks. . . spooks and . ."

Through her own mug of coffee, Gloria replied, "Somehow I get the impression that you don't respect my spook business. Well, Tarry Gary, have a seat over here and let me tell you a few things. This is one of the few rides on the circuits that is making more money than a fleet of Tilt-A-Whirls, even in times like these, when people don't seem to have that much. This is pretty good coffee, isn't it?"

In answer, Dis blew a little into his mug, spattering a little of the air-filled milky foam, "I haven't had any better since Starbuck's in East Orange, but that's another story. . . go on."

"I'm taking in more money because of the JCs. That's right, the JCs and Halloween. You know everyone of these little towns sets up a haunted house every Halloween. The JCs put on costumes and rent an old house or a storefront and do a land-office business doing essentially what I'm doing – giving people a quaint, harmless scare. Make it dark; give 'em some shocks – some surprises; and, I guess you could say, ugliness, grossness. Anyway, all these people who in the past never went into a spook house at a carnival now have experienced them in town. So when I come to town, the ice has been broken, don't you see? They come to my spook house because they want to recapture those thrills of the past."

Dis mumbled, almost as an afterthought, "Don't we all want to."

"Hey, Buster Buns, if you're thinking about 'recapturing' some sleazy thrill from your checkered past right here and now, you just better put down that cup and take that walk right now." Gloria's normally high pitched voice strung itself even more tightly as a lifetime of fending off sexual innuendo and advances automatically cranked into usage.

"Oh, just hold on, little coffee lady, I'm not about to cop some cheap thrill – besides I know for a fact that this coffee isn't cheap. It tastes to me as if it is a French blend with vanilla and just a touch of cinnamon. It's not Starbuck's, but it could be Encardif's. Am I close?"

"Not even in the fairgrounds. I bought this at the Hippity-Hop Supermarket back in Moonover last week. It's a nothing brand, but you're right, there's vanilla and cinnamon in it. It's good, isn't it. Hey, listen, sorry about that jumping on your case about thrills, but I guess it's almost automatic in my case. Carnie ladies are supposed to be hard, but easy, right?"

Dis looked up from his cup and replied, "Yea, I heard they go down a heck of a lot faster than those bowling pins where you knock-em-over-with-a-baseball. And hard. Carnie women are harder than the enamel on their fingernails. And hot. Well, they're hotter than the afternoon sun on cotton candy in. . . Where's your mother?"

Gloria looked at him real quizzically. "You are a weird man, Gary. . .Gary ? What are you doing playing at being a hired man on a Ferris Wheel? My mother, by the way, is where she is every night when she gets the chance – at the movies. If we're not working, she's downtown at the Bijou – if the town we're in still has a downtown movie theater left. She doesn't like those new mall theaters. She likes the old fashioned ones that are falling apart. Claims to feel right in them. Anyway I'm not fast, and I'm not hot, and I'm not. . . hard."

"You aren't? Well then what am I wasting my time here for, sippin' at this cotton candy coffee? I mean, fast and hot I can live without, but not being hard. Well, I can't take that."

She looked at him for a long time before she said in a slow, almost hushed tone, a changeover from her usual soprano, "Carnie women are hard – hard on the outside, but inside, well, we're different – most of us at least."

Dis matched her tone. "I think I know that." He paused. Then, more brightly, he said, "However, some carnie women I know can brew up a classy cup of coffee, and I thank you very much for it. I think it's worth hanging on for two hours holding up the "Wailing Walls." He stood up to go. It was then that he noticed the pistol lying next to a four-in-one spice container on top of the fold-down board that served as the kitchen counter in the portable home. She noticed his glance and dismissed it with a quick, "I was cleaning up the piece before I got the urge to brew up some coffee. Any problems with a lady having a little protection?"

"Hey, no. Not me. A good looking gal like you could probably use a piece of artillery."

She looked at him quizzically with a hint of a smile on her lips before changing the subject. "You know, Gary, haven't you been around these parts before? How long you been working on carnie stuff?"

"Oh, not long. I just started with Rosie and Carl a couple of months ago – over in Kentucky."

"Really? I know this sounds like an old song, but I could swear that I've seen you before – maybe not met you – but, boy, you look familiar."

"Well, shucks, I just bet you use that line on all the guys – on all the guys that Rosie sends to you."

"No, really. Something to do with cars. Cars and a river bank. You ever sell cars?"

"No, not ever. Can't stand the pesty things myself."

"Well, cars. I've got a fleeting memory of someone, somewhere who looks just like you. Cars. How about a mechanic? You fix cars?"

"Nope, drapery is my spech-e-ality."

"Oh, get outta here. Drapery. But I've seen you before. Maybe never talked to you, but I've got an impression of you in my memory. Somehow, we've met before . . . and it has to do with cars – and a river – and . . . this is the truth, Gary. . . somehow it's not very pleasant."

Dis jumped in, "Ah, the history of my life: racing along like a speeding car, getting dumped in a surging river, and as I'm drowning, finding out that the whole thing is not very pleasant. Well, Miss Memory, thanks again for the Java. You're a fun person to talk to, even if you have some flawed memory cells in your pretty head. Come on over some time to the Ferris Wheel and I'll give you a guided tour of my pup tent and I'll maybe even make up my special cosmopolitan recipe: macaroni and cheese, Gruyere cheese. Ciao." With that he left and, indeed, went back to his pup tent. Actually he grabbed a news magazine from his tent and sat with Rosie and Carl on their "patio" reading it in patches and talking to them, desultory, at the same time.

Rosie wanted to know what he thought of Gloria and Dis wouldn't give her a straight answer. He knew Rosie well enough by now to mildly tease her. He told her that Gloria was all right, but too thin for him; she was cute, almost beautiful, but too much out of control; she couldn't keep her hands off him.

Rosie rose from her canvas and aluminum seat when she heard this. She almost floated to Dis and punched him weakly in the soft of his stomach, saying, "Yeah, Gary, just the opposite is true, isn't it? Isn't it? Tell me the truth. Gloria is a classy dame and she doesn't counter any truck with pawing - guys pawing her or her pawing guys. She's independent. Maybe that's her fault. She's her own person and she can handle it." Seriously, Gary, Gloria is a good woman. She works hard and doesn't play around. And she comes from nothing. If you get to know her, she'll tell you her life story. I'm not about to tell you it, but I will say she's come from nothing. She's risen by herself alone. And risen is accurate – because her family was down there and most of it still is. Just for one example, she has a brother under life imprisonment right now. A murderer, Gary, a child murderer too. She won't tell you about him unless she really gets to know you, but he really gets to her, tears her up. And her father, well, let's not even get into it. Let's leave well enough alone. Gloria, somehow, gained strength from it all. I don't know how, but she did."

"She lives with her mother, doesn't she?"

"Oh, Minnie is a character. You meet her yet?"

"No. She was. . . at the movies."

"At the movie is right. Well, you'll meet her when things get rolling tomorrow. This should be a nice gig. The weather looks promising and we always do well here in Morrison – at least the last couple of years. Dang, these mosquitoes are at it. I'm going to go in for the night. You just remember, Gary, that Gloria's all right. She's a strong woman, and she's all right." With that, Rosie got up and with a nod to Carl they both went into their trailer. "Good night , Gary."

Dis read his *Time* for awhile; but then even he was bothered by the insects – and by Gloria. He was impressed. She was feisty and independent for sure, but he sensed that underneath her carnival bravado lay a resilient, cornbread foundation of care and concern. He didn't know if he really wanted to find out about her personal life. Her mother seemed to be no problem, but what about her father – and her brother. . . a murderer, a child murderer, a convicted one, in for life. She probably has other skeletons in her family closet – old boy friends, even husbands, perhaps – who he didn't particularly want to know about, not even in passing. Later as he drifted to sleep in the turgid, humming Illinois prairie air, her slim, energetic form, her cute-but-plain face brushed with artificial color, and her ironic, zippy wit refused to go away. At one point he consciously brought up his standard mental picture of Lorn – her eyes looking up at him as she washed his injured knee – but even that faded into a composite Lorn-Gloria as his eyes and mind joined the blackness of the tranquil night.

Chapter 17

The next morning as he drifted around the Wheel, not really doing much of anything, while Carl was giving each of the seats a detailed inspection and Rosie was mysteriously concocting something that smelled of vinegar and thyme in her trailer when she wasn't dropping in on each and every citizen of her fairground's world, Dis caught himself unconsciously focusing on the spook house. Gloria was retouching the paint of an aluminum panel depicting a woman in medieval dress with her amputated head, neck trailing bloody connecting tissue, securely in her arms. The woman's tiny waist contrasted grotesquely with her more than ample bosom; her breasts hardly constricted by the dress, defying gravity as only cartoon characters could. Gloria's mother, coffee cup in hand, was telling her about the movie she had seen the night before. More correctly, from drifting swatches of sound that the wind blew to Dis, she seemed to be more intent on the theater than the movie.

"Yeah, that's right, two box seat sections on each side of the screen. But they were closed off. They wouldn't let me sit there."

"But how was the movie?"

"It was OK. That Denzel Washington is a hunk. Is that what you say, a hunk? Well, whatever, he is."

"Mother, what do you know about hunks?"

"Hunks; bunks. But there were these cherubs on the ceiling holding garlands of flowers, and these garlands hung down over the sides, looping over the exits."

Dis was supposedly inspecting and repairing the fence that encircled the Ferris wheel for both safety and crowd control reasons, but he was in reality just enjoying the fresh morning breeze, lazily listening to the fairground's sounds, and keeping a watchful eye on everything associated with Gloria. Carl eventually gave up on him. "Go over there and help her paint, why don't you? At least then you won't strain your eyes so much."

So Dis walked over to the Spook House and asked Gloria if he could paint her breasts for her. Gloria's mother, Minnie, cracked up at that. She had never met Dis, but had seen him around the grounds on the day before and wondered if he liked movies.

"There's a matinee this afternoon, wanna go?"

Dis didn't know what to think. "Hey, I have a job. I can't just take off anytime I feel like it and run to a movie, even though I wouldn't mind going. I haven't been to a real movie is a long time."

But he could take an afternoon off, so the three of them went to the movie at the Isle of Avalon Theater of Morrison, Illinois, an old neglected dame of a theater with an immense, old-fashioned, burnished aluminum popcorn maker that stood behind an ornate, carved counter-top in the lobby. They saw a forgettable movie, but Minnie enjoyed the ambiance of the theater, and Dis and Gloria enjoyed the intimacy of sharing both fresh buttered popcorn and each other's closeness.

That night turned into one of those perfect Mississippi valley nights, enhanced in many of the carnie's minds by what they brought to the evening – lights, sounds, smells, and the aura of excitement, danger, romance, and fanciful glitter. The shoddy facades that masked the cheap, manufactured rides and games became just for a moment almost romantic and daring. The sweet, oily, steam-enriched smells of the heavily fried foods pulled, for one more time, palates into unexpected yearning. Even the old, constantly repeated recordings became more musical and crystalline in the still, dry night. But it was the lights – multicolored, flashing, and haloed with glowing rings – that transformed the mild and windless night and the stubble filled fields of the county fairgrounds into a true but temporary city of wonder.

And the Ferris wheel provided much of the light.

Dis loved it. He was helping Carl load and unload the riders, while Rosie was in the booth selling tickets. The crowds, heavy and still awe-struck on this the first night of the engagement, were more than friendly, almost jubilant. They waited patiently, laughingly, in their roped off waiting line for their turn to arc off into the dark night on this gleaming and glowing ring of circular motion, all the while jumping to the syncopated music, smelling the pervasive hot-dog spiced aroma from the food concession stands, and noting, sometimes with wonder, the fantastic variety of people, clothes, and mannerisms.

Most people waiting for the Wheel had lived their entire lives in the Morrison area of the extended Mississippi River valley, had mixed with the same people in all of their activities, but on this night everyone was different. They hardly recognized acquaintances or even friends. Everyone was strange to them – friendly, different, and marvelously interesting. Where did all of these aliens come from? Why were they dressed so weirdly? Why were they so happy and full of life? And why am I the same?

When eleven o'clock came and the temporary police officers came strolling through the grounds, shoeing people to the exits, people only reluctantly moved. The revelers wanted to continue enjoying the illusions of the night, but they didn't protest – only withdrew slowly, with occasional backtracks and returns.

By midnight when the grounds were settled and the Wheel was wrapped up and tucked away for the night and Rosie and Carl had said goodnight and disappeared into their trailer, Dis was still too wound up to crawl into his little tent. He took a stroll through the grounds, conveniently just happening to pass the spook house an inordinate number of times.

Finally, when he decided that he had better get to sleep, and headed one last time past the spook ride to his tent, he almost bumped into Gloria. She was seated on a canvas chair next to her ticket booth with her long legs stretched to a peach crate, her temporary footstool. Her right hand held a tall glass, tinkling with ice cubes.

"Hey, night wanderer, watch where you're going. You wouldn't want to spill my drink, would you?"

"Well, hello. Hey, what is this a toll road or something? How am I supposed to get through your legs." Dis hesitated, "Your slim, and I might add, lovely, legs? What's it going to take for you to let me through?"

She stared at him and then laughed, "That depends. I might lower or raise them, but, watch out. You just might get caught between 'em."

"Well, I . . . in that case, I think I just might not pay the toll. I might have to let myself be captured and then suffer the consequences."

"Suffer? Is that what you say, suffer? If that's your attitude, you'll never be able to get through. You'll have to go around or back up and retreat."

"No, that's not like me. They don't call me Stonewall Gary for nothing. 'Damn the torpedoes, full steam ahead."

"Hey there, Stonewally Bally, you try to get through my legs and I'm the one gonna' be damning your torpedoes. I'm gonna' be damning 'em right up your . . ."

"Hold it there. Hold it right there. Girl, you get uptight quickly, don't you? Here I'm just enjoying the night, strolling around the park here, taking life easy, looking at the lights and the stars, smelling that little bit of corn perfume . . . you smell that?. . . above the hotdogs and the barbecue sauce . . . that little bit of sweet pollen of corn?"

"Sit down, Gary. What would you say to a drop of Jack Daniels?" She shook her glass so the ice cubes clinked against the sides. "Want a nightcap?"

"Well, let me ponder that for a minute. I normally don't drink much, never have. But, on the other hand, I don't normally have pretty, sassy mouthed women offer me drinks on quiet, starry nights after we both have been working our tails off all evening and been to a movie together all afternoon . . . Sure, I'll have a taste."

Gloria disappeared into the general vicinity of her cab-trailer while Dis looked up into the sky and appeared to be studying the stars. The moon was just a glint of a crescent off to the east, but it still reminded him of Lorn. What was he doing here, bantering, and waiting for a drink, and who knows what else, with another pretty woman who he was starting to care about? And who appeared to have some empathy with him? "Dis, don't do it." he told himself. "Hold back. You're on the run."

But as more of the lights of the carnival went out, and the stars became brighter in the dark, he didn't move.

He heard the ice before she appeared. Then she materialized out of the darkness and out of his star gazing posture. He was sitting on the ground, his back against the ticket booth, her chair empty.

Without a word, she gave him a tall glass of Jack Daniels, ice, and water. Then she grabbed his other hand and pulled him.

Dis was surprised, "Hey, watch out. What are you trying to do?"

"Come on, Gary, let's take a walk around the grounds. We both have been cooped up all night in our rides. Let's do a little walking and sipping."

"Sounds good to me, even though I've been around this place a few times tonight. I'll show you the ropes. Stick with me."

They walked through the dusty old fairgrounds, filled now with machines, and tents, and all manner of attention-getting contrivances. Hardly anyone was around, but both of them knew that their walk was not unnoticed. Carnie people didn't allow strangers to wander around their grounds at night. Yet they were not challenged. Carnie people knew.

They ended up kissing – like a couple of teenagers, in the shadows behind the spook house, out of sight, they thought, of both her mother and other nearby trailers. Their kissing happened quite naturally. They drifted closer and closer as they wandered around the area. Soon his hand was on her shoulder and he could smell her perfume above the carnival smells and the corn.

After their first kiss, Dis drew back and said, "I was wrong yesterday. I said you were hard and you said you weren't. God, Gloria, you were right. Your lips, your face, your body. I can't believe they're so soft."

"Didn't I tell you that I wasn't hard. Sometimes," she leaned into him resting the side of her face on his chest, "I appear that way, I know. God almighty, working in a carnival, you have to, but deep down, you know, I'm as soft as a bunch of cotton candy."

Dis blew into her hair, "You know, I think I knew that when you first yelled at me from your ride. I said to myself, 'Here's a very pretty lady with a rowdy mouth who's putting on an act. I wonder if she knows it.'"

Gloria pulled away and put both of her hands on his shoulders, "Thought you could see through me, eh? Well, listen, my shoulder man, rowdy mouth or not, nothing gets through me without me knowing it and wanting it. Hear?"

Dis kissed her again. This time hard. He pulled her body close so he could feel her shoulders and breasts and hips – and the strain of her legs on his. He reached down and put a tentative hand on the small of her back and pulled even more. She responded with fever. Her soft lips became hard, a living line of pressure straining to connect with him.

She snuggled. Her body became an insulating, inflated pillow of down, inundating him, filling all his crevasses, vibrating softly and slowly, infiltrating and filling his space and his surface. He pulled even harder, wanting the closeness, wanting the blend, the mesh.

But she pulled her lips away and leaned her face to his neck, her body still undulating slowly, not letting the closeness go. "Gary, I want you in the spook house."

Dis, with his lips blowing slightly on her light brown hair, his chin resting on her forehead, said. "Really, babe? But I've got commitments and . . . well . . . a looseness. How can I explain it? A need to be loose."

She shifted her head and looked up at him, her dark eyes surveying him fixedly. "I think I know what you mean. Besides Rosie would never let you go. If I took you away from her, I'd be drummed right off the route. I'd be poison. You know, Rosie's powerful. She's in charge. Things go through her and that's how they get done or don't get done."

Dis whispered, "Don't I know the woman's power. But I love her for it."

"Anyway, Gary'" Gloria pushed herself from him, grabbed his hand and pulled him along with her, "when I said I want you in the Spook House, I wasn't thinking of hiring you. I just wanted you to come with me into the place. So, come on!"

Dis couldn't resist. He let himself be swept up the front stairs, through a curtain and into blackness. The stars gone now – along with the sliver of moon. Sight disappeared – but touch, and smell, and hearing became acute. Her hand in his became warm urgency. Her smell – of makeup, a touch of perfume, a night of activity, and a surging femininity – locked him into her individuality. And he heard her breath whistling through her lips like cottonwood down swirling through a river creek bed.

She stopped and he walked into her, and she into him. They intertwined and gave themselves up to texture, and undulation, and gentle friction. Kissing, they found themselves falling – first to their knees, then to the floor. They rotated over each other, surging and rolling. They felt drapery over them, edges and corners, but they spun uncontrollably across the floor, clutching, caressing, arousing.

Dis was out of control. He pushed her on her stomach and frantically pulled her blouse from her blue jeans, sweeping his hand up her sublime back to her brassiere, where he deliriously tried to undo the clasp. Whispering hoarsely, "Damn these underwear makers, haven't they ever heard of Velcro," he swept his arms skyward – and all hell broke loose.

Sound blared through the chamber. A staccato, hoarse, and ugly laugh erupted with dismaying volume. "Ha ha; ha ha; ha ha," reverberated, stopping Dis, making him jump with arrested anxiety. "What the hell is going on?" he rasped at the completely dark world around him.

The sound continued, "Ha ha, ha ha, ha ha." It was piercing, almost trumpeting; it blocked his senses like a sudden police car's siren unexpectedly erupting on a crowded city street. He knew the harsh laughter must be echoing through the grounds, perhaps even waking people up.

Through the laughter he heard a slight giggling. "Hey, hey, hey. We hit the trigger. We moved." The giggling gushed into a full high-pitched laugh. "I can't believe it. We rolled around so much, we're way over in the mirror room. Oh, Gary, Gary, Gary, don't move. It'll stop, but you can't move."

"What the hell is going on, Gloria?" he whispered into where he thought her face was.

"There's a motion detector." She couldn't continue, convulsed as she was with laughter. "It. . .it. . it makes laughter. The mirrors; it laughs at you." She broke up again, almost sobbing. "The mirrors; we were in front of the mirrors."

In a flick the annoying laughter stopped. They were back in silent blackness – except for Gloria's subdued sobbing, her almost choking hilarity.

Dis whispered, "Jesus, all I wanted to do was open your bra."

Gloria whooped.

She kicked - and again the ruckus blared. "Ha, ha, ha, ha, ha, ha," blasted from the speaker somewhere overhead. Gloria couldn't stop laughing, and now Dis, rolling from her over on his back, joined her in laughter. Together they lay next to each other and roared.

Through his convulsions, Dis managed to get out, "The mirrors. The mirrors. Ha, ha, ha, ha. We should have had the lights on. . . ha, ha, ha. We could have watched ourselves rolling around in front of the mirrors." The mechanical braying continued, almost drowning out Dis's opened mouth declaration.

Gloria joined in, "Yeah, then you'd been able - ha, ha, ha, ha - to unhook my bra."

Abruptly the repetitious laughter stopped. The place was silent and dark, except for the diminished laughing of the two of them. They lay, arms on each other's sides, laughing into each other's face, almost kissing, communicating with soft bursts of comical breath, not pressure. Then they heard something outside – a murmur – another murmur – then a bang on the side of the truck.

Gloria knew the story. She slithered to the side of the truck, clutching her blouse back into place with one hand and pulling Dis with the other. "We're caught. Our neighbors heard the ruckus. Let me handle this. God, I hope nobody has a gun."

She led him silently through the completely darkened maze of partitions and drapes. Now, walking, she knew her way explicitly, having chased teens, drunks, and frightened kids through the place countless times. They emerged at a slit in an exterior drape, a secret, emergency exit.

Three people were standing in front of the normal entrance, and a few more were back in the shadows. Gloria strode up to the three. "Well, I got that fixed. God, I'm sorry if I woke you up, but that darn detector's been going off on its own for a week now and I finally figured what the matter was."

One of the three, a whiskered fat man, said, "Oh, it's you, Gloria. We heard the laughing and just wanted to check. Everything all right?"

"Yeah, Pete, I think it'll be quiet now. Gary, here, and I were sitting talking when I finally figured out how to fix that relay in the mirror room. Well, you know me, I just had to fix it now – and Gary was here to help me. So we did. But, shoot, I had to test it, you know. That's when it started, and I couldn't get it off right away."

The fat man said, "Well, I tell you, Gloria. I like a little laughter as much as the other fellow, but the next time you wanna test that there outfit, you wait till daylight – either that or get a helper with some experience." He jokingly pushed Dis in the chest. "If everything's OK then, we can go back and get some sleep."

"Yeah, it's set. I'll leave it alone now. Thanks again, you guys. I appreciate."

When they were gone, she looked at Dis and said, "Well, one thing I'll have to do tomorrow morning is get up and bake up some peach pie. That's my specialty. I think Pete and his buddies are gonna have pie for lunch."

But between the two of them, that was that. Their passion had been broken, if only temporarily. There would be a time and a space and the stars would shine for them. Dis left her, not discontented or frustrated, but light, floating . . . What did he tell her before? Loose.

When he crawled into his tent, the stars were floating like silver birch leaves through a dark and still forest.

When he awoke the next morning it was from a rough shove. Rosie was at the flap of his tent. "Gary, get up. Something's wrong. There's a man here asking about you. He's got a picture."

Dis almost hit the top of his tent. To himself he thought, "Damn, the gray man." To Rosie he said, "What's happening? What time is it?"

"It's still morning, but this man was at the gate when I was coming back from downtown. He asked me if I knew the people who worked here. Then he showed me your picture and wanted to know if you were here."

"Oh, God, Rosie, did you tell him?"

"Are you kidding, Gary. You know me better than that. Listen, I don't know what this is all about, but I spread the word. No one's going to tell that guy a thing. But you have to do something, and you have to do it quickly."

Chapter 18

Dis was working hard. He hadn't ridden for a month and it showed. He was out of shape so he was pumping.

But it hurt. The calves in each of legs were aching and he could consciously feel the difference in his breathing. He wasn't gasping; no, but his breathing was strained – he felt as if he were sucking air. Before, breathing had been natural, something he wasn't even aware of. Now his open mouth quivered as he compulsively pulled in the air.

It was about ten in the morning and he was riding west on a silent county road through low hills, wooded valleys, and fields of corn and soybeans. Occasionally, near the isolated farmsteads, cattle drifted through tightly cropped pasture, and dogs barked an exclamation point to his passage. Only three cars had passed him since he had turned off on this road, and none of them had been gray or a Taurus.

As he spun his crank arms, he had time to think about the hectic moments after Rosie woke him so roughly. First he got a description from her of the man who had the picture of him. It indeed was his gray man, and he was still driving the same car. At least Dis would be able to recognize his pursuer.

Rosie was smart; she knew immediately that her Gary would not want to be found by this man, who she also knew through her years on the carnival circuit to be a cop. So she lied. The photograph the man showed her was of Gary sure enough, but not quite the same Gary she knew; somehow something was different. She couldn't quite place it, but it was another reason for her suspicion.

She told the man that, indeed, a man who looked like the picture had worked on one of the rides, the Caterpillar, she thought, but he had left about a week before. She remembered because Tim and Sally, the owners of the Caterpillar, were fit to be tied when he walked off on a Saturday evening right before the big nightly rush. They said he told them he had had enough squealing and was going back to McDonald's. This had happened, let's see, last Saturday; that must have been Lowevale, about 150 miles south. But Tim and Sally were, let's see, they were in Kerry this week, working the Sandman Shuttle and Capworks Festival.

The man had thanked her, but she noticed that when he returned to his car, he didn't drive off. She knew he would ask other carnival workers, so she walked casually out of his sight and put her network into action. Within minutes every carnival worker had the word: Gary had been here – on the Caterpillar – but had left at Lowevale.

When, sure enough, the man returned and cornered Bill McGinn at his corn-dog booth, everything went smoothly. In five minutes the man was back in the car, and the car was speeding away.

Dis was appreciative – not fulsomely – his thanks were in the hard glint of his eyes as they communicated with Rosie. But he also couldn't tell her what the man was after. In fact, he didn't know for sure himself. So he told Rosie, "Damn, I have to go, and just when things were looking up. But you know the past; it's going to catch you, and I'm not ready to be caught yet."

He knew he had to take off, so he almost ran to the flat-bed trailer and pulled his bike from under a canvas. As he was attaching his panniers, Rosie and Carl both appeared. Carl said, "Here's the money you've earned – up 'till today. In cash. Looks like you'll be needing it."

Rosie added, "There's a little bonus there too. You've been a good worker, Gary, and you've earned it. We, the both of us, just wish you could stay longer. You're a good worker and a good person."

Dis was working furiously, tying on his sleeping bag, pad, and tent. "Ah, shucks, I bet you say that to all of your hired hands."

Rosie had a paper bag with her. She handed it to Dis, saying, "Here's some food for . . . well, for today at least." Then quickly for someone of her enormous girth, she grabbed his shoulder, squeezed it, and looking him squarely in the eye, said, "Whatever happens, Gary – or whatever your real name is – whatever happens, you can come back here and we'll take you in. You know that. You just look for the red and yellow Ferris wheel, and you'll know you're home."

She looked at him intently, then said, "Come on, Carl, let's make sure everything's smooth on the grounds. Gary, just cut through that gate back there." She pointed to the rear entrance that led to a gravel perimeter road. "Billy Joe said that if you go straight on that road for about four blocks, if becomes blacktop and heads west, across the Mississippi towards Iowa. We think that fellow in the Taurus went south. You got a map?" She looked at him soberly, "Iowa, can you handle Iowa?"

"I don't know. I'll try to lose myself . . . before I go to Owaceta." As soon as he said it, he knew he shouldn't have. Rosie's eyebrows arched slightly, but she didn't say anything.

Just then Gloria rushed to them, without makeup, and in wrinkled white sweat shirt and pants. To Dis, she looked fresh but disheveled. "I've been sleeping, but my mother just told me. Oh, damn, Gary, do you really have to leave?"

"Hey, it looks like I'm back on the road. Don't worry, maybe this is just what I need; maybe it'll make things happen. But right now I have to go."

"And you're going on a rinky-dinky bicycle?"

"I tell you, Gloria, I can go places on a bike where a car . . . well, let's just say, a car has real difficulty."

Rosie broke in. "Good-by, Gary. You better get rolling. Come back, you hear."

"Absolutely, Rosie. Hey, I can't thank you two enough. I'm going to get this matter straightened out. That's a promise." He said it quickly, but a stone rolled through his conscience when he said it; this time he swore he was going to face it.

"Hey, I have to. I fell in love with this wheel right here." He swept his hand toward the looming red and yellow cylindrical construction, it's shiny rivets and interior silver struts reflecting starry points of light from the morning sun. "I'll be back to ride it. You look for me. One of these days, I'll sneak under that counter over there." He nodded toward the ticket booth. "And the next thing you'll know is I'll be on the top, yelling and waving my arms like a gawky thirteen-year-old. Thanks you two. What can I say . . . I'll be back."

He was finished with his preparation; all his belongings were on his bike. Gloria walked with him as he rolled it toward the gate; Rosie and Carl heading off in the other direction. Gloria spoke, in a subdued, throaty way, "You know, Gary . . . Gary? Terry, Barry, Larry . . . whatever your name really is. Jesus, I was making out with someone and I don't even know his right name. Boy, Gloria, you're really becoming carnie, rolling around on the floor with someone you don't hardly even know."

"Dis said, "Yeah, we hardly know each other. You're right. But I do know this: I got carried away last night, but it happened before we went into the spook house. Gloria, my soft Gloria . . . Jesus, I'll be back. I have to be." He grabbed her arm and pulled her to him, even though balancing the bike with the other hand. "Just let me get this straightened out." He kissed her, lightly, almost just a caress, and then turned to the entrance gate.

She watched him soberly, "Iowa, where in Iowa?"

"I don't know. I'll try to lose myself." He got on his bike. He didn't mention Owaceta to her. "Hey," he grabbed her hand, "just as I told Carl and Rosie, I'll be back sometime – when this thing blows over and I get things straightened out. OK? I'll be back." He squeezed her hand, let it go, and pushed off with his leg, setting the bike in motion.

Gloria stood still, grimly watching as he passed through the gate and wheeled down the road.

Dis looked back when he was about a block away. Gloria was still there, watching. Looming behind her was the Ferris Wheel. In the morning sun, it glinted like a constellation of dancing stars - red, yellow, and pinpointed glints of silver. It was still and strong, and Gloria was there, bright and white in the sun, immovable and solid.

Now, on the county road, he knew that he had to return. But first he had to face Owaceta. And he didn't want to do it in the company of the gray man. It had to be just himself; confronting whatever the past gave him. He was tired of living a lie. He wanted to free himself. The road had become anxiety to him; never knowing what danger was in store. But, paradoxically, it had also given him the most happiness he had experienced during his adult years. At least when he stopped and met people. Gloria and Lorn. Ah, yes, Lorn. What about her? He had loved her – and he still did. Or did he?

If he did, what was he doing with Gloria last night? He was confused. Gloria wasn't just a one-night stand. His feelings for her were true. Or were they? Maybe he wasn't in love; he didn't know her well enough. But the possibility surely existed. Was Lorn just a memory? If he solved his Iowa problem – and his Washington D.C. problem – would it be Lorn or Gloria he returned to? With both of them, time was the problem. He needed time to know them and to possibly love them.

Right now, churning up a medium grade hill about half way to the Mississippi, he was filled with just too many insecurities. He had to get them resolved.

And resolution, he knew, was in Iowa – specifically, Owaceta. If he kept going directly west, he would put the most distance between himself and the gray one, but eventually, he knew, he had to turn and head for the town that beckoned him.

He didn't know exactly what he would do once he got to Owaceta. He didn't think he should go to the law, because somehow, just like Rosie, he had a suspicion that the gray man was associated with the law – maybe a detective, a private eye, investigator, someone with knowledge and connections. How could he keep on my tail, if he didn't have experience – know what he was doing? A rank amateur would still be back in Kentucky.

Dis thought: Maybe if I just appear in town, my looks will bring things to a focus. Rob Clemmon clearly was from Owaceta. All I'll have to do is hang around town for awhile and whoever is after me will find out that I'm in town. I'll go to one of the town's downtown cafes, and I'm sure it won't take long for the word to get out.

Small towns have message networks that work quicker than AT&T's.

But do I want that? Will it mean I'll be arrested for suspicion of murder and hauled back to D.C.? Will I have to face Ruth again? Boy, it seems like so long ago that I faked that buying trip and left her, but it's been just a few months or so now. It's what? – the end of July right now. Wednesday – the carnival was set for a long booking, five days of wholesome, free-spending crowds. And I was just getting set for . . . Gloria.

He crossed the Mississippi at Fulton, Illinois, and then found a good country road out of Clinton, Iowa – straight and without much traffic. But now it was approaching noon; he was hot and sweaty – and hungry. The vacuum in the bottom of his stomach was increasing by the minute. Dis searched for a place for lunch, but the best he could find was a field road that punched through a line of bushes, row shrubs, and gave him some protection from being observed.

He leaned his bike against the field side of the bushes and groped in his left back pannier for the lunch that Rosie had given him. She must have known that he'd be starving when he opened it, because it was filled with just what he needed – three thick-sliced wheat-bread sandwiches filled with cold roast beef, lettuce, and peppers, cool bell ones. A plastic sealed pint of leftover red Italian spaghetti filled the bottom of the bag. And two apples and a plastic fork – and a square of paper towel – filled the remainder.

It was a lunch fit for a hot Iowa day, and Dis went at with aplomb, silently thanking Rosie and his good fortune to have met her and her entourage. He devoured the first sandwich, ate the second, and saved the third. But he also ate about half of the spaghetti, and finished up with one of the apples. The leftovers would make a good afternoon snack. He had started out in the morning with his two water bottles filled, but by the time he finished this meal, he had finished one and was half way through the other. He knew he would have to stop for water, since July in Iowa on a day of sun would drain him like a moist towel on an ironing board.

The road he was now on was a blacktop county road, two lanes wide with no shoulders – very typical of the roads in the area. It headed directly west through a farm country of occasional rises and drops. The wind, as it picked up in the afternoon, was westerly, and the sun was hot on Dis's face.

He rode through a hamlet called Altimount and stopped at a convenience store, a Jiffy Lift, and bought an ice-cold Sprite. He finished it in one gulp almost, then went into the washroom and filled his two bottles with cool water. Ice water would be nice, but he knew that under this sun, ice didn't have a chance – maybe fifteen minutes at the most. The middle-aged woman at the counter hardly interrupted her yawn when he bought the soda; perhaps she wouldn't remember him, certainly not after a day.

By mid-afternoon Dis had covered about 60 miles and was according to his map a moderately sized town, Coreville, was ahead of him about ten miles. Beyond it another ten miles, according to the map, was a fairly large man-made lake. Since he was somewhat out of shape, the sun was hot and merciless, and he really didn't have a goal for the night, Dis considered going into Coreville, or at least its perimeter, and checking to see if camping was available near the lake.

But as he approached Coreville, he could tell something just wasn't right. For one thing, cars, pickups, and vans suddenly became ubiquitous. Parked, moving, stopped at intersections, they dominated. Dis experienced a minor spatial shock; from almost complete isolation while riding on his county road, he was now, almost in an instant, inundated with vehicles of all sorts.

The first thing he thought about was carnival. Perhaps the town was having a festival or celebration – or a county fair. But it was Wednesday afternoon close to the end of July; not a likely time for this sudden convergence of traffic.

Within a block, however, he knew the answer to this mystery. It was a case of deja vu. Bicycles – another bike tour. He was coming within the path of another organized bicycle tour. Bicycle paraphernalia swamped almost every vehicle he observed: bike racks on top and in the rear, bumper stickers and hand written signs, bikes and camping gear looming from the vehicles' windows.

As he rode on, he noticed that the sides of the streets became more and more filled with parked cars. Occasionally townspeople rested on their front porches or sat inappropriately in their front yards, eyes looking attentively at the constant stream of people and vehicles. Quickly, bicyclists appeared; some riding his direction, others on the opposite side of the street. He heard music, a country and western tune that he didn't recognize except for the nasal twang of the woman singing. Rock music, coming from the distance, filtered through his helmet.

Up ahead a crowd of people on foot had gathered across the road he was coming in on, almost closing the street. Dis had to stop; too many people were packed into too little space. He thought: Maybe they're having a parade or something like that. His bike was an encumbrance in the crowd, but the jammed people melted away in front of him, seemingly giving importance to his bike rather than if he were a mere pedestrian.

When he came to the front of the crowd, he was astonished. He was facing the town's main street and it was almost literally a one-way river of bikes. Streams and streams of bikes maneuvered slowly through the confined space, going slowly, cautiously, because they were so closely packed. On the edges of the street, eddies of slowing and stopping bikes formed; while other bike riders used the slowing bikes to gauge their entrance back into the mainstream.

The volume of bicycles was so heavy that Dis had great trouble in simply pushing into this wider street with his bike and walking with it through the crowd. He didn't even think of getting on and riding, not here at least. But he joined the current of bikers by walking his bike through, as it turned out, the main street of Coreville.

On his right, a huge crowd packed the front of a makeshift ice cream stand built of saw horses and lumber. A big sign hanging over it proclaimed, "Welcome BABI riders! Homemade Ice Cream Right Here!"

Dis read it, and in an instant it registered. BABI. My god, that ride through Iowa. He had heard of it; every biker in the country had. And here he was in the midst of it. He remembered vaguely what he had heard: it was large, one of the largest in the country; he thought it was a week long and that it went in various directions in Iowa; and it was supposed to be fun, fantastic fun. He remembered a bike club member back in Maryland a few years ago who spoke about it and showed slides of it at one of the few club meeting he attended. The guy had emphasized the crowds, and the parties, and the fact that it was somewhat grueling at times – and not much scenery, just corn fields relieved by soybean fields. But the guy had been ultra enthusiastic about it. He said that every small town they went through put on spectacular displays of small town friendliness, that the food and drink were great, that you met lots of outgoing people, and that every town where they stayed overnight hosted a gigantic beer party.

And BABI – it stood for something, but he couldn't remember what.

And Dis was now in the midst of it.

The first thing that hit him was that, just as down in Kentucky, he could be swallowed up in it. No gray man could ever find him in the midst of this never-ending stream of bikers. He looked over at the middle of the street; the river was rolling as full and as steady as before. Even if the gray man stood on the side, where Dis was, there was no way he could recognize individual bikers as they bubbled down the way. They were simply too diverse and too many. And even if Dis were afraid to mix in with the crowd as it flooded through a town, he could always skirt around the perimeter of the town and avoid the possible searching eyes.

Dis was in BABI and, for now, he figured it was his salvation.

And, for everyone else, it was a celebration.

They were having a blast! Coreville was jumping. In front of one of the town's bars a country and western band, with three female singers ricocheted high volume nasal tremors through a large crowd surrounding an impromptu stage. Riders, some still with their bikes, bunched closely together listening, watching, drinking, eating – enjoying. Some danced, swinging partners, two-stepping, or just swaying closely with an opposite sex counterpart.

At the bar's outside makeshift drink counter, Dis bought a large paper cup of Sprite for a dollar. He was thirsty, but he also needed the break – and he wanted to just listen and find out as much as he could about the ride and where it was going. So he inched into the crowd keeping his bike with him, although many of the others had parked their bikes. He found an opening close to the bar's building, almost in back of the performers.

Next to him on his right were two riders, probably in their 30s, standing with glasses of beer in both hands. They were dressed for the ride in regulation outfits: clipless pedal biking shoes, Performance socks, multi-paneled and multicolored Lycra biking shorts, Lycra jerseys swirling with color panels of plastic fabric, golden and red hued, with brand names prominently printed on the sides. One jersey bore the brand name "Capagnolo," and the other's front and back blared a large cartoon expansion of Mickey Mouse wearing sun glasses. Dis listened to them:

"What a brewsky, huh? Tastes good, doesn't it?"

"Yeah, I was getting famished about five miles back. Chugged in here with enough thirst to fill up a horse trough. You know, this singer's not bad, even if this music's kind of corny."

"You got that, buddy. Hey, we've been doing all right. About 15 miles left before we hit Summerdale. Not bad, ol' buddy, about 60 miles so far, we each got two beers, only 15 miles left, and then the whole night ahead of us."

"This music's getting to me. How about going down the street and see what's happening. I need some food, anyway. Something to tide me over before we hit some church basement tonight. Do you think they know how to make a decent slice of pizza in this little berg?"

The two left, moved off into the swirl of constantly shifting riders. But Dis now knew a little bit about the drift of the ride. He had 15 miles to go before the overnight town, Summerdale, which, if he could remember from his map, was north and east from here. That meant they weren't staying around the lake, which made sense. A crowd of this size could only be handled by a fairly large town.

As he stood in the midst of the cacophonous music, swirling his cup of soda, he pondered his options. Should he join the constant line of bikers and flow with them to, what was the town, Summerdale? Or should he do what he originally intended to do – take his chances on finding a place to camp around the lake. To go with them meant to be a part of an anonymous large crowd, to be almost indistinguishable; but yet, just as before, the gray man would undoubtedly be drawn there for much the same reasons. On the other hand, at the lake he would probably be free of the gray man, but, since it would probably be relatively empty, he would stand out to anyone around. They would remember him and be able to identify him.

As he debated these two options on the side of the crowded street, now devoid of cars but awash with bicycles and with light, sound, smell, and color pleasantly assaulting his senses, he noticed a woman in front of him. Actually, it wasn't her face or body he noticed, but the back of her T-shirt. It was a BABI shirt and its back was covered with a map of the state of Iowa traced with a line of the route of the ride. The shirt said BABI - XXII, but that didn't help Dis much, because he didn't know if this was the 22nd one or not. Right below, in smaller letters, was the name of the ride – Bicycle Around Beautiful Iowa.

That's right, thought Dis, and he remembered the speaker at the meeting saying, "It's spelled "B-A-B-I" but pronounced "BABY." And let me tell you, it's a real baby of a ride, one big bouncing baby!"

And he did notice, as he stared at her back, that the map showed the Wednesday stop to be Summerdale. She evidently had this year's shirt on.

And then he saw it – Owaceta. Two stops away from Summerdale was Owaceta. BABI was going through Owaceta.

Fate. Dis didn't believe in fate. But he couldn't deny that somehow things were pushing him to the confrontation that he knew he had to make, but was very reluctant to do.

He thought to himself, "The hell with it, I'm going to go with the crowd. They'll suck me right with them into Owaceta. Jesus, when this crowd hits that town, who knows what will happen, what I'll find out?"

The nervously slow line of packed bicyclists was unrelenting. It had no end. Masses chugged into the town, hit tottering velocity, slowed to a two-wheeled crawl, and then gave up and walked their bikes. Then many of them stopped, adding to the congestion. Every concession stand was a massive rock in the river of two-wheeled humanity.

It was actually dangerous. Occasionally a bicyclist, used to the relatively open road, roared into the congestion much too fast and precipitated a hit or a near miss. Dis saw a shirtless teen riding into the crowd on his mountain bike stop abruptly just inches away from a unobtrusive woman and her little girl. The teen's companion, who was riding behind him, a girl in a neon Lycra top, didn't have as much control. She hit the shirtless one's rear tire, lost her balance, and fell to the pavement almost in slow motion. People around them skittered to get away, but one man rushed to the girl as she was falling and almost caught her, getting one hand on the spokes of her front wheel before the girl hit the pavement. She was hardly injured, a grimy and slightly bleeding knee hurting less than her dignity. Her one remark pierced the immediate crowd, "Christ, Jimmy, you got brakes up your ass."

But Dis couldn't believe how friendly the crowd behaved. People were taking a break after some strenuous exercise and they were in no mood to be nasty; just the opposite. Possibly the exercise caused a false euphoria, but, whatever the case, good feelings floated through the crowd like flower fragrance from the front yard garden of a lone residence in the midst of the businesses on Coreville's Main Street.

Most riders were drinking; many, beer; many more, soft drinks. But drunkenness was nonexistent, although Dis noticed some rowdiness in front of a tavern on a side street, two doors from Main. Because of the crowd, he couldn't really tell what was going on. But, when he stood on tip toes, he could make out three bronzed youths, shirtless, doing traffic stands on their bikes while drinking plastic cups of what Dis presumed to be beer. A crowd around them was cheering, and Dis guessed that it was a BABI modified chugging contest - gulping beer while balancing on a stationary bike. It looked like fun for the crowd, and it was – even if in normal times it would be put down as a sophomoric, hey-guys-look-at-me, fraternity party stunt.

He crept through the crowd, pushing his pannier-clad bike down the street in the direction of the bike travel. He passed a small park that was almost completely packed with bikes, bikers, and townspeople. At one end, according to a banner tied to the trees, the Coreville Capettes – whoever they were – were selling hand squeezed lemonade and fudge brownies topped with ice cream. That sounded good to Dis, but when he tried to make inroads into the crowd, he gave it up and reached into his pannier and took out Rosie's last apple instead.

He was biting into it when a biker about his age, a man with both sides of his stretched-tight jersey lined with sweat, guffawed at him: "You got everything on there but the kitchen sink, buddy. What are you gonna do, camp here tonight instead of Summerdale?"

Dis, caught up in the camaraderie of the moment, replied, "Just might do that – I'd tent down next to those brownies, if I could get close to that stand, that is."

"Hey, come tonight this park'll be as empty as all those pop cans in that trash can over there. The only thing around here full will be the pockets of all these townspeople and the taverns where they'll be celebrating our comin' through. This place'll be just another oasis in the corn fields a few hours from now."

"You're right there, my friend." Then Dis thought he'd see if he could find out a little more about the ride. "What's on the docket for tonight, once we get into Summerdale?"

"Who knows. I didn't get one of those newspapers yesterday. But someone said something about cowboys and shoot-outs and all kinds of Western things. Hey, how'd you like yesterday – all that Hawaiian stuff. Boy, these Iowa towns really go out to take care of us, right?"

"You said it. You camping or what?"

"Sure am. I'm with the Waterloo Bike Club, and we're getting pretty close to home. But we've got a whole mess of other people on this here ride . . . in fact, there's one right now. Hey, Missy, what's up? Where's that old buzzard you normally ride with?"

The man moved away from Dis, which was all right. At least now he knew that BABI was a camping tour. It hit him. He remembered that long ago bike club presentation. The guy had showed slides of immense campgrounds, tent after tent after tent, literally acres of tents and bikes. Shoot, he wouldn't have any trouble in finding a nice anonymous spot for the evening.

He threw his apple core into a trashcan and again tried to maneuver into the rushlet of bikes. He made some progress in getting to the edge of the crowd, but now that the initial excitement of suddenly being emerged in this sea of bikers had died down within him, he realized that he was still hungry. Rosie's half finished lunch was still in his pannier. He couldn't find a place to sit down with his bike, though. So he pushed off from the thinned out edge, and entered the biking mainstream.

The traffic was still heavy. Moving bikes covered the entire width of the street's two lanes, while people and parked bikes filled the parking slots and every available space adjacent to the street. Cautiously and very slowly, Dis inched his way down the street, surrounded by fellow riders. He melted into the slowly moving pack. Beyond a few blocks of the town's main business district, however, the bike stream began thinning out. With open road ahead of them and no need to be cautious about sudden stops and enterings, the bikers accelerated at incremental rates.

They moved now through typical small town Iowa, residential neighborhoods. Wood frame houses dominated, some still retaining their original wide front porches. Most had a garage in the back connected by a driveway to the street in front, and wide and deep-set front and side yards. But more modern homes, some expansive and some little more than expanded trailers, also appeared at random. The mix was eclectic, unplanned, and almost pleasing. If anything, it certainly showed the democratic nature of the small communities: these people lived together – poor and not so poor (the truly rich weren't here), middle and lower classes, managers and blue collar workers, country club set and Main Street tavern group – they all lived here and next to each other too.

Many of these homes were in business today. They knew BABI was coming through and they planned for it. They knew as many as ten to twelve thousand cyclists from around the world – riders starved for good, nourishing food and for good, nourishing hometown talk – would be riding past their homes on this day, and they were ready to capitalize on the opportunity.

Ovens had worked to capacity on the previous night – baking cookies, brownies, cakes, muffins, anything that the homeowners thought would catch the whimsy of the passing crowd. Earlier in the week, these potential BABI concessionaires had caused an unprecedented run on the local grocery store, Dick's Food Supreme, for cases of soda pop and bags of ice. Two days before, not one single case of Pepsi could be found in the entire town – until, of course, a telephone call brought a full truck from Des Moines with an emergency supply. But within two hours that supply was completely sold out. The townspeople whose houses would be passed by the bicyclists were experiencing a modified "feeding frenzy." They weren't hungry themselves; they were hungry for the profits to be made.

So the street was lined with tables and chairs and food and drink. Kids camped behind the makeshift counters, but it was the housewives who ran the shows. They were not idle; the demand for consumables was too great. Every stand had customers, even after many bikers had loaded themselves up back on Main Street. The women ran back and forth between their kitchens and their rickety card tables covered with plates of cookies and pieces of cake, each dutifully wrapped in Saran Warp – and whatever "specialty of the house" they prided themselves on: gingerbread cupcakes, Rice Krispy squares, whipped Jello and Dream Whip, ham and American cheese sandwiches, gorp made of peanuts, raisins, and M & Ms. Nothing sophisticated, just mainstream Americana – General Mills and Kraft Foods – variety.

With so many homemade stands in such a short distance, advertising, surprisingly enough, became vastly important. Bikers needed a reason, not to stop, but to stop at a particular stand. The advertising standard was pricing. How much for pop, for three cookies, for a slice of pie? This worked, but only if the prices were remarkable – fifty cent Pepsi, or one dollar for a piece of shortcake.

But since these people weren't out to lose money, they quickly honed up on other advertising. For one, they blatantly used their kids, especially small, cute ones. They dressed them in costumes, had them carrying placards, even had them carrying food through the crowds in front of their stands.

For another, they tried sloganeering. Most of the efforts in this direction were awful – "Stop for a Drink with Rinky-Dink," "Have your Cake and Bike it too," or "Stop Wheeling and Squealing, Come in for a Mealing." But sometimes the true nature of Iowa surfaced on the homemade signs fluttering above the bikers and food sellers: "The Hopkins Family Welcomes You to Stop and Sit a Spell," "Have a Pop before you Drop," "From Smelly Pig to Spicy Pork: an Iowa Miracle," or "Meat no Beans in our Chili."

One thing they didn't use was sex. No bikini-clad beauties posed in front of the apple pie stands; no posters featured sleek women eating pork chops; no homespun beauties in low cut halters bent low while cutting wedges of watermelon. This was small town Iowa, and to be so crude would mean recrimination for years after the bicyclers had long passed. The big cities and commercial establishments could be blatant, but these comfortable neighbors didn't even think of it, much less try.

Chapter 19

After passing two blocks of almost house-to-house food stands, Dis pulled over to a modest one – nothing more than an old door on top of two trestles. A sign overhead written on a white sheet proclaimed: Fresh Cut Lemons in our Lemonade – One Dollar." He'd finish his roast beef sandwich and spaghetti with a cool, thirst-quenching lemonade. The crowd here, almost out in the country, had thinned out, so he was able to wheel right up to the table without getting off his bike. A pert teenage girl with plain features was running the stand. She had her arms folded over her chest and her fingers picked at the edges of her checkered blouse. She wore shorts and a tiny plastic pin inscribed with a golden guitar. She was not smiling. She seemed to be staring straight in front of her, her eye focused on a twig or a fence post on the street opposite.

Dis smiled and asked for one lemonade.

She didn't respond, just continued to stare.

"Excuse me. How about a lemonade?"

Now she shifted. Slowly her eyes turned to him and for a split second continued to be as blank as a bucket of still water on a hot afternoon. Then life ebbed to them and she focused on Dis. "Yes, may I help you?"

"You're back with us, great. I'll take a lemonade."

Her face immediately flashed into color and action. From pale, her cheeks flushed instantly red and her voice cracked with disdain, "Lemonade, sure mister, lemonade is what you want, lemonade is what you'll get." She held his eyes like a freight train engine bearing down on a defenseless whistle-stop. "You want extra sugar or extra ice?"

"Can I have both?"

"You can have as much as you want, mister, for all I care." She picked up a wax coated paper cup, 16-ounce size, and opened up a plastic picnic thermos. She dipped the cup in the thermos and filled it half full with ice, all the time never looking at the cup, her eyes, like a magnet on a refrigerator door, fixed on Dis. On her left was an electric juicer connected by a long extension cord to the open front window of the house behind her. She, again automatically, found a lemon and a serrated-edge paring knife and deftly sliced the lemon in two. The juicer was perched on a wooden platform so she could put the cup under its spout to catch the juice. She started the machine, and pressing one of the lemon halves in a stainless steel half-globe, flipped it on top of the ceramic corrugated pulverizer, causing juice, lemon pulp, and a few small seeds to flow down to the cup.

Again with vacant eyes, she opened the machine's top, grabbed the paring knife, and jerk-stabbed the splayed out lemon skin. It slipped off the knife. She stabbed again. It didn't come. She stabbed in earnest, sliding it underhanded back and forth, more aggressively each time, until little of the skin remained intact. Her expression never changed, her voice either, but her words did: "You God damn lemon. You son-of-a-bitch. Jesus, nothing works right."

Dis looked around, subconsciously looking for help. But the girl was alone, stabbing and cursing – and alternately staring at him with eyes skinned over with opaque hate. He was tempted to stomp on his pedals and just take off, leaving her to her stabbing, but something about her made him stay, almost balancing on his bike, trying to comprehend this cool, but frenzied youngster. He desperately tried to think of something to say and, his eyes noting the tiny pin with the golden guitar, blurted out: "Hey, I like your pin. Can you play it for me?"

The girl put the knife down, and in a soft, hard voice, almost whispered, "Jesus, fellow, what a pick-up line." Her demeanor completely changed. The vacuum in her eyes filled with bits of life; her upright posture slumped into that of a normal teenager; more color flowed into her cheeks, giving her plain face tentative beginnings of beauty. "I mean, I thought you old guys from the big cities would know how to get a girl going with better things than that, 'Can you play it for me?'"

She tossed her head back and repeated it to the fluttering leaves of the hackberry tree overhead, "Can you play it for me? I don't know if I ever . . . Jesus, what a line. All these young guys riding by, without any shirts on, just their tight shorts, and you come along with, 'Can you play it for me?'"

By this time Dis was a little perturbed. He wasn't on the make; all he wanted to do was to stop her from stabbing the lemon skin. "Ah, excuse me, but I did want a lemonade. Right there." He pointed. "A lemonade."

The girl picked up the paper cup, half full now with ice cubes and pure lemon juice, and swirled it. Dis thought she might be going to throw it at him, but she didn't. She turned her back to him, and started doing something to the cup. Dis could see a line of pimples on the back of her neck, under the line of her short-cut hair. He saw that she was putting sugar into the cup, three scoop fulls, then filling it with water.

She turned back, her mouth a hard line of pressure. She placed an aluminum cap on the cup and said, "So you want me to play it for you? Well, if that's what you want, old man, you just watch out." She started to shake the capped lemonade filled cup. She started primly, with the cup held close to her chest, her arms making slight, jerking motions. But as she continued, her eyes became more and more vacant, her shaking became more and more flamboyant. "You like this, old man? Is this what you stopped here for? Did they tell you in town to stop at Rita's; that she'll play if for you?"

She pushed the gyrating cup to the front, to the side, she even turned around, and in an awful parody of a chorus dancer, started twisting and twitching, the cup of lemonade held aloft by her purple-white arms, now dappled by the sun through the overhead leaves. She softly intoned, "Play if for me, oh, play it for me."

Dis, again, didn't know what to think. Mainly, he just wanted to leave. He stared at the back of her pimply neck, watched his cup of lemonade floating through the air, and listened to the girl's immature rasping voice repeating his phrase, "Play it for me, oh, play it for me."

He decided to stop the nonsense. "O K, that's enough. The lemonade's done. Here's your dollar." He placed a one on the table. "I'll take the cup, thank you."

The girl stopped abruptly, turned to him and dropped her arms, almost losing the lemonade. "You don't like it, do you? Every time I try to do something different, people get mad." She gave him the moist cup. "Where you from, mister?"

Dis took the cup and spit out the first city name to come to mind, "Bowling Green. Bowling Green, Kentucky."

"Bowling Green. I'd like to go there. It's a nice name. Sounds so neat, so old fashioned. Bowling Green. Maybe someday I will."

"Well, I hope so." Dis took a sip of the lemonade. It was very sour, almost bitter, but he wasn't about to ask for more sugar. He had had enough of this strange, evasive girl-child. "Umm. . . lemonade's good. You take care."

With one hand holding the lemonade, he slowly walked the bike down the street, looking back only once to the girl, who was standing as before, staring vacantly ahead, but now was slightly singing in her low voice, "Oh, play it for me. Oh, play it for me."

He came to an intersection that he realized marked the edge of town. Beyond it lay fences and farmhouses, pastures and fields of greenery lightly nodding in the late afternoon breeze. He stopped at the opposite side of the intersection, where a low ditch cut down to the first line of growing corn, and laid his bike down. Then finding his delayed lunch, he sat cross-legged on the grass and started to eat what was left of the roast beef sandwich.

When he took up the lemonade cup, he was pleasantly surprised: what was once sour was now sweet.

A young rider on a slick Trek composite bike pulled over and stopped just down the road from where Dis was eating. He had brilliant blue lycra shorts on – and nothing much else. He was eating an ice cream bar that had half melted and was now sticking to his fingers. When he finished, without getting off his bike, he flicked the bar's stick away into the cornfield and leaned down to wipe his hand in the grass. He leaned too far, lost his balance, and went down – with more embarrassment than harm. For just as he was falling, a slim young female rider in a BABI JUMPS tee-shirt rode by and, noticing him, yelled out, "Nice crash, Dude." The ice cream eater tried to see who had yelled, but with his head in the grass he gave up. He just lay where he had fallen, licking his sticky hand, staring straight into the sun.

Dis yelled over to him, "Hey, you OK?"

"Yeah, no problem. Just resting, OK?"

"OK, suit yourself. Enjoy the sun."

Dis opened the plastic container of spaghetti and was hit by its hot, spicy aroma. He wondered if it was still good, having been figuratively baked for much of the afternoon. But then he decided he had been at more risk by eating the roast beef just now, and it hadn't tasted bad at all, although the lettuce and peppers were decidedly limp. He tasted the spaghetti and it was still delicious. He pictured the rotund Rosie puttering around in her kitchen, Carl drinking coffee outside under the flapping patio canvas. He pictured Gloria and remembered their passion in the Spook House.

He thought of her softness beneath her carnie facade, and realized that life with her could be agreeable. She was a warm, caring woman, attractive, and possessing a smoldering sensuality beneath her sometimes-hard exterior. And he wouldn't mind her line of work. The carnie life had its compensations. He didn't even mind her mother.

Sitting at the crossroads, watching bike after bike pass him by, eating Rosie's homemade Italian spaghetti, Dis resolved to return to the carnival if he ever solved his personal problems.

But what about Lorn. It had only been a relatively short time since he had spent the night in her moonlit bed. Even though the memory of almost every minute stayed with him, still time and distance and danger, he knew, were taking their toll – plus the fact that he was meeting other attractive people out here on the road. He remembered the warmth of Jeffrey, the convenience store, and Lornaree and her daughter, Chrissy. But he also couldn't forget the adventure of Gloria, her passion, her way of life, and the glittering stars of the Ferris Wheel.

He finished the spaghetti, upturned the cup of lemonade until he had finished it, poured the remaining ice cubes into one of his water bottles, and stowed the garbage temporarily in his pannier. Then he wheeled his bike onto the road, leaving the prone biker-in-blue still lying on the ground, and joined the bikers of BABI as they streamed down the road.

This week long ride had so many participants that it was literally impossible to bike without accompaniment. Oh, there were lone bikers, to be sure – people riding by themselves, not in pairs or groups. But a rider was never alone on the road. Someone was always around. The sponsor of the ride, the Healthy Life hospital chain, provided maps with the registration fees, but they were hardly used, except as reference points for figuring out how many miles between towns or how many miles before the end of the day's ride. They weren't needed for following the route. All riders had to do was to follow the long line of bicyclists riding ahead.

So Dis, mildly tired, spun down the road at a speed slower than his normal, but still about 15 to 17 miles an hour. He occasionally passed riders and people passed him. He noticed the almost complete absence of cars on the roads used by the ride. But after passing a few country intersections, he knew why. State patrolmen were stationed at each crossroads, directing motorists across, but not onto the roads used by the bikers.

But occasionally a lone car, or a farmer's pickup, would slowly come up behind the riders, to the constant call of "Car Back." Local farmers who lived on the roads were still able to use them; and, of course, there were always the curious, although they were kept down drastically by the state cops.

Personal support vehicles were a problem. These were cars and vans driven by friends or relatives of riders. They drove from night location to night location, but some of them tried to follow the biking route and have contact with their riders along the way. Because of problems and overcrowded roadways in the past, this now was strictly forbidden by the sponsor, but still some drivers tried it. The ride's organizers gave them alternate routes, but some of them went out of their way to get close to the bicyclists.

Almost every country intersection had a number of these vehicles – some bearing signs or logos. The drivers and helpers would most often be sitting on the obligatory folding chair or lounge in front of their vehicle, talking to others doing the same thing – or the state policeman stationed there – and continually watching the cascade of riders going by.

The small towns along the route – like Coreville - that had set up special facilities for the bikers were inundated by these vehicles. The drivers and their passengers could savor much of the flavor of BABI without riding one revolution on a bike. In fact, a significant number of the more flamboyant revelers – dressed in the latest biking wear, and some even sporting helmets and sweat – never rode a bit. They opened up a town; drank, danced, and partied; then took off in their vans or buses for the next town to continue the same thing. They spent a full week of almost non-stop partying – day and night – without exerting a bit of riding muscle. Instead of BABI they did PABI – Party Across Beautiful Iowa.

But most of the vehicles did a real service for their riders, who could resort to these vehicles for every manner of support – water, food, repairs, rest, even sex. With daily rides in the 70 to 90 mile region and many of the days hot, muggy, and sometimes rainy – typical weather for the end of July in Iowa – many of the riders needed help and assistance.

However, these riders were certainly in the minority. Most riders did the whole route, from mile 1 to mile 525, or whichever it was that year. They complained constantly – it was the major source of their conversation – but secretly they reveled in the ride's extremes. When the winds were in their faces, they gasped and lowered their heads. When the sun beat down unmercifully, they gulped water and slathered on sunscreen. When the hills didn't let up, they shifted to the lowest of their lowest gear. When the road turned to gravel, they shut their mouths and breathed grit. When rain swept over the roads, they squinted, splashed, and eventually became soaked – even through Gore-tex. When early morning or storm-driven cold numbed their hands and faces, they wrapped themselves in any available cloth, from T-shirts to old socks. When Iowa pig farm smells assaulted their noses, they spat, sneezed, and joked about the "smell of money." When slower riders surrounded them, they braked and started temporary conversations. And when the need for bodily elimination became acute, they joined long lines at porta-potties or found an open fence leading to a cornfield.

Most riders of BABI transformed the physical problems of the ride into personal psychological victories.

All of these things about BABI slowly worked their way into Dis's consciousness as he rode through the crowded roads with the variegated riders. From snippets of overheard conversation, catcalls back and forth, and some direct answers to questions, the ride started to gel in his mind. He started to sense the pride that most of the riders took not only just in their participation, but also in being a part of a worthwhile and memorial group experience. He started to realize that BABI was unique.

He had only about an hour's ride to the evening's town, Summerdale, but he kept his ears open and made the most of it. He learned that most people were camping at the county fairgrounds, but that many were going to be placed in school yards around the town – and some were just going to knock on doors and get permission to sleep in front yards, and possibly catch a shower from the acquiescent householder. Food would be available all over the town, in restaurants and in almost every church basement or community hall. The town had plans for a major party in the evening. Summerdale's downtown party motif harked back to a hardly known fragment of Iowa trivia – Summerdale had been a minor starting point for a northern branch of the main Oregon trail which started in Missouri. So the party tonight was based on the town's Western past. He also learned that the ride on the next day was about 80 miles, ending in Cedar City, the location of the state's main university.

Dis rode swiftly, but cautiously. He could not go as fast as he usually did, simply because of the congestion of bicyclers, and because he didn't want to stand out. Even now, with his panniers, he felt somewhat conspicuous. One man yelled to him as Dis passed, "Hey, Legs, that's quite a load you've got there." He had conversations with a few riders – and one four-person group who came every year from Ohio – but for the most part he rode silently, observing and listening.

By riding a little faster than most of the bikers, Dis became – he hoped – only a fleeting impression to them, someone they could not identify, and whose image in a few hours would be washed from their memory. Even though the die was cast – Dis was going to Owaceta – he still was fanatical about his security. He didn't want to be exposed before he got there, and he wanted to try to find out things by himself with no interference from the gray man or anybody else.

As Dis approached Summerdale, he could see some confusion up ahead, since the approach to the city was by a long but very gradual downhill. Gradually he was able to discern that some sort of welcoming ceremony was taking place as the riders crossed an intersection and entered the town proper. Many non-bikers milled around the side of the road, and the biking traffic slowed down considerably. Dis had to brake a number of times, gradually slowing down to an almost dangerously slow pace.

Surrounded by tired, hot, hungry, and thirsty fellow bikers, Dis could almost feel an uplift in the air. The riders had finished another major riding day, and they were ready to get off their bikes and find some rest, some food, and some fun. Now they were being funneled close together into another small Iowa city, whose residents had gone all-out to welcome them and then take care of all of their needs.

The welcome consisted of, first of all, a large arch constructed over the street leading into town. It resembled a wooden log entrance to an old fashioned Western coral. Hanging from it, a sign, painted on rough-hewn boards, proclaimed, "Howdy, BABI. Welcome to Summerdale's OK Corral."

Right past the arch, in a fenced off section at the side of the road, a mechanical "cowboy," on a bicycle that was artistically embellished to resemble a horse, was "shooting" every bike as it crossed a line on the street. The bikes actually triggered the cowboy's mechanical arm to flip up and shoot a large squirt gun in the general direction of the street. The "cowboy's" response was so slow, however, that hardly any of the bikers got wet, except for those following closely behind another bike. The gadget did provoke much good natured laughter and joking, and the tired riders were buoyed, for the most part, by the fun, rather than put off by the occasional wet "bull's-eye" delivered by the machine.

Beyond this, four or five "cowgirls," local teenage girls dressed in Hollywood's vision of frontier female costumes, were dispersed across the road giving tokens and brochures to every rider as he or she passed. The tokens were wooden nickels, that, the brochures explained, were worth 25 cents at almost all of the stores located in a selected area of the downtown, called for this ride, "Dry Gulch." Maps and advertisements for the city's eating places filled the brochures.

The last feature of the welcoming consisted of a flatbed truck decorated in Western style with haystacks and rough, wooden, twig furniture. A Country and Western band was set up on the truck's rear platform, and two vocalists, a man and a woman, were doing their best to add to the levity of the occasion. Their twangy voices sang out. "Oh, take me back to my Red River Valley," while the three-piece band behind them tried to follow their somewhat erratic rhythm. The female singer was actually quite pretty, but her blonde hair twisted into twin pony tails and the garish freckles painted on her face made her a parody of the American West – especially the media view of it. Her male companion, sporting standard Western clothing but no painted face, seemed natural, and almost rugged – but his voice could hardly compete with the more strident sing-song of the woman's.

Dis maneuvered his way through the crowds. He, like all the other riders, had to walk his bike through the confusion and congestion, but he enjoyed it. He kept an eye on the sideline spectators, but didn't let that interfere too much with this sudden and unexpected welcoming. Later he found out that almost every overnight city had some sort of similar activity, but now, to him, it was unique.

He took one of the "wooden nickels" from a pretty teen and didn't even use the "don't accept" cliché. She smiled nicely at Dis, but positively beamed at the young guy next to him. Dis noticed that he veered off and went through the line again, this time grabbing her hand and holding it as he took another of the tokens.

The street was filled with bicyclists, some walking their bikes, some riding, after a fashion. No parking was allowed, but, still, many of the personal support vehicles were present – with someone either inside them, or people milling around them. Dis noticed that, indeed, many rider's tents were set up in the front lawn's of the homes along the street. He thought momentarily of doing the same, then realized that he wanted just the opposite – to become invisible in a large group of campers.

Dis noticed an extraordinary number of signs posted on almost every available surface easily read by the riders. Some of these signs were for the homeowner's concession stands and for dinners and breakfasts put on by community groups, but most of them were somewhat cryptic to Dis – until he realized that they were direction arrows imprinted with bicycle club symbols.

Most of the thousands of BABIers camped with bike clubs that through long established rules got blocks of "tags," the basic tickets to travel on BABI. The clubs then set up camping enhancements for their riders who wanted to camp. Typically a club would bus and truck the riders to the start of the ride, then provide trucks for carrying baggage from one overnight town to the next. Each morning after the last camper's baggage was stowed, the trucks would race off to the next overnight town and try to get the optimum site within the overall campgrounds assigned to it by the ride's organizers. A site with easy access and closeness to the restrooms – and especially the showers – was a prize, a shiny goal in front of the truck drivers' eyes.

After a site was settled on, moreover, one of the driver's first jobs was to "arrow" the way to that site with the club logo signs. This was essential, since there were so many campsites and so much confusion, that without signs, riders could almost take hours to find their campsite and their luggage. Clubs also had huge logo-printed banners, which they hung on the side of the trucks, and some clubs erected high poles topped by club flags or helium-filled balloons emblazoned with the symbol of the club.

Dis was at a loss, since he didn't have a club with which to camp. He didn't know if there would be areas for non-club riders or how rigid clubs would be in regard to non-club members camping near them. But he guessed that in the confusion of biking and setting up tents, he could very conveniently become an indistinguishable grain on the BABI beach.

So he went with the flow of riders, surmising that they would lead him to an acceptable camping spot. The sidewalks and boulevards here, in this city of about 15,000 people, were not as crowded as back in Coreville – reflecting probably the small area of the first town and the fact that Summerdale was more "sophisticated" and accustomed to events happening within its borders. After all, it was the county seat and the site of the county fairgrounds.

But the flow of riders was unquenchable. At a slow pace, they almost overwhelmed the curb-enclosed street. They came to a major, stop lighted intersection with a policeman in the middle directing traffic, since cars and trucks were allowed on the cross street, which was the major highway running through the town. The bicycles were directed through this intersection, and after one block they swept down a low hill and around a curve where a large open area spread out in front of them. It was the site of an elementary school, and it had been commandeered by a host of bicyclers.

Dis stopped, pulled off on the sidewalk, and checked the map to see if he should try to find a space here. No, the center of town was still about eight blocks away, and the main campgrounds, the fairgrounds, farther still, on the very edge of the city. Still, this place wouldn't be bad; it was crowded and seemed to be open to anyone.

But Dis went on. Soon he was slowly balancing his way through the city's central business district, the main street of which had been swept clear of vehicles, even those brought by the riders. Here, as in Coreville earlier in the afternoon, masses of bikes and bikers milled around numerous food stands, displays, taverns, and sundry other attractions. But Dis, who wasn't that hungry or thirsty, was more interested now in finding a place for the night and in not being recognized. He continued through the area, following the arrows and the flow of bikes.

Soon he encountered bicycle traffic coming at him also. Early arrived bikers, already set-up and showered, were seeking refreshment and entertainment downtown. The closer he got to the fairgrounds, the more the bicycle traffic increased. Soon he was enveloped again in so many bicycles that he started worrying about his personal safety. But almost everyone was patient and some were even polite.

The entrance to the fairgrounds was mass confusion. Signs everywhere; constant two-way traffic; some tents; curious spectators; numerous vehicles, including trucks, crowding the lanes which ran through the grounds; and people – people riding bikes, walking bikes, just walking, some even just sitting, sprawled with legs akimbo, almost tripping passers-by. Dis was used to this to a degree – after all, there had been times when traveling with Rosie and Carl that some of the same energy, confusion, and elevated expectations had rumbled through the carnival's midway, producing just such an anticipatory high. But this was at a different level. This was a carnival's fun and games accelerated with the euphoria of physical activity, the searching for a "home" for the night, the shared goal-reaching with a mass of people, and the somewhat addled confusion of not knowing precisely the where, when, and, to some, the who, of a temporary aspect of life.

Dis practically ran through the entrance area before he saw, fleetingly in passing, to the right of the entrance, a large yellow tent emblazoned with the official BABI logo and the words, "Information Headquarters." He quickly surmised that if someone were watching for him, this would be the one place to do it. The fairground's entrance was the Grand Central Station of the ride.

So he avoided it. He rolled his bicycle down one of the minor lanes at random looking for an apt place to set up his tent. He didn't want to be isolated on the periphery, but he also didn't want to be right in the center of things. Avoid attraction, he told himself. Stay away from anything likely to draw attention.

Tents were everywhere. No rhyme or rhythm governed their locations. They were scattered as if a giant old-fashioned seed sower had spread them with a flick of an unintentional wrist here on this fertile Iowa prairie. At random points throughout the tents, the rented Ryder trucks bulked up, like orphan yellow sunflowers in a field of soy beans, but even with these, no organization was apparent. Some of the trucks were isolated; some grouped together, even though they had different club's logos taped or flown from them.

As Dis moved along, he realized, through his short experience on the carnival circuit, that he was in the midst of the fairground's usual midway area – a vast, acres-wide, stubble covered field, crisscrossed by barely discernible lanes – clay mixed with dirt, sometimes gravel, harder packed than the nondescript surface of the land in between. He stopped and looked around, knowing that if this were a usual Midwestern fairgrounds, it would have open barn buildings and animal grazing areas. Perhaps that was the way to go; camp in the shadows, in a nook or cranny, away from the huge crowds, but still a part of them.

He moved off to his left in the direction of a large, slightly decrepit building, past the multitudinous variety of tents spread over the uneven ground. But when he got to the building, one of the animal barns, he found it locked – except for the toilets, which had outside entrances close to the building's entrance. That was OK. He didn't want to camp inside anyway. He wondered if they would open it if a major rainstorm came up. Probably not; too much chance for liability problems.

But around the back of the building the ground became grassy and the tents thinned out. No truck was close by, although several station wagons and vans were scattered over the available grounds. Dis decided, why not? He could wheel around for hours and probably not find as nice a spot – somewhat protected, not isolated, and not "belonging" to a bike club.

He picked an open spot. With no trees or fences or anything to support his bike, he just laid it flat on the ground and stripped it of its panniers. He was practiced in putting up his tent, and, the tent being small and uncomplicated, it was less than five minutes before he was stowing his pad, sleeping bag, and panniers in it. He locked his bike with a cable to one of the tent's nylon tie-downs, and now he lay on his unopened sleeping bag and contemplated his next moves.

He wasn't particularly hungry, but he knew he would be. He could check the brochure given at the town's entrance for places to eat – although, for all he knew, there could be an eating place here on the fairgrounds. That would make sense; surely there would be buildings already set up for food. He also needed a shower, and he wondered how so many people with the same need could be accommodated. Oh, well, he could always just wash up; he was sure he could find some water.

He was lying propped up slightly, his head on a rolled up jacket and his feet at the tent's entrance. The flaps were open, but the insect screen was zipped together, keeping the flies out but also keeping observant eyes from looking in. He knew that the gray man couldn't recognize his tent because he had never seen it, and even if he had gotten a description of it, it was so common – an inexpensive pop-up circular tent that Dis had seen everywhere, and that had as many different brand names as the Chinese economy could devise – that he would be hard put to select this one.

He was thinking about his luck in finding BABI, about food, about security, and about the physical exertion he had enjoyed during the day's ride, when he dozed off.

He woke, not just because his belly was beginning the tussle between fullness and cavity, but because of a shrill female voice. A middle-aged woman was declaring for all the immediate area that, "Yahoo, girls, here's a neat place."

Dis opened his eyes. It was still light, but the sun was reaching for the west, and it took awhile for his eyes to adjust to the rarefied light. He figured it was about 7:30. When he focused beyond the tent, the woman came into view immediately in front of him. She had her back to him, and she was loaded down with a huge backpack.

"Come on over here, girls. I like it here," she shrilled at the world. Soon two other middle-aged women struggling to carry rolls, packs, and various packages joined her. They dumped everything unceremoniously, and one of the women sat down, almost falling into a heap. She sat up and moaned, "Oh, I'm so damn sore. Why did I ever even consider this?" She lapsed into silence, with her hands kneading her puffy and chunky thighs.

Dis moved around in his tent until he could stick his head out the flap. He discovered that tents surrounded him, and that the women who had woken him had occupied about the last open tent space around him. In fact, he wasn't sure they would have enough room without sticking some of their tent poles through his tent. He found one of his water bottles, took a swig, rinsed out his mouth, and then stooped out of this tent and stood up.

He was adrift in a field of tents. While he was sleeping, almost every available space had been taken and tents bloomed everywhere. Some were so close together that their tent stays interlocked with one another. Some were perched right next to the barn building. Some had canopies that now shaded neighboring tents.

If all of these belong to strangers, Dis thought, some strangers will be sleeping very close to other strangers tonight - perhaps their heads less than a foot apart, separated by only two sheets of lightweight nylon.

He checked the periphery of his tent. Other tents were close – and the one on his left had a corner just inches away. He thought momentarily, "I hope he doesn't snore." And then he added to himself, "And he's probably hoping the same about me."

He stooped back into his tent and took out the brochure because now his stomach was making itself know with a vengeance. Most of the restaurants and community meals were located downtown, a distance Dis didn't particularly want to travel. But a few places not in "Dry Gulch" were mentioned, including an all-you-can-eat spaghetti meal sponsored by the Summerdale Home-Farm Club costing $5.50 and located "in the big green tent at the fairgrounds."

After Rosie's pasta, Dis longed for something else, but the place was right and he was suddenly becoming very hungry. He grabbed his toilet kit and headed off for the toilets in the front of the barn. The place was a mess, but since porta-potties were spotted throughout the grounds, it wasn't too crowded. Dis was able to get one of the three sinks and do a quick cold water wash-up of his upper body and legs. He decided he would forgo a shower unless he could find one available in the vicinity.

He went back to his tent and changed clothes, noticing that the three women still had not even started to put up their tent. He kept an ordinary pair of shorts and a pair of canvas sandals for after-ride wear, and these, along with a fresh T-shirt, were "it' for tonight.

Soon he was snaking through the maze of tents, moving in the direction of the entrance, looking for the "big green tent" and the promised food. He found it without too much effort and for his $5.50 stood in line with a plastic plate and utensils waiting for a clump of overcooked spaghetti, a scoop of bland tomato sauce, as much cold white French bread as he could pile on his plate, a separate plastic dish of chopped iceberg lettuce covered by the dressing of his choice – French, Ranch or Thousand Island – and a paper plate of either white or chocolate cake and frosting. Fortunately Dis noticed containers of crushed red pepper, garlic, and oregano near the drink pickup, so he was able to put some spark into the pasta.

He sat at a table near the edge of the tent with many other cyclists, his back to the crowd. When he was full, and without speaking a word to his eating companions, he sneaked back to his tent – the women gone, but their tent still not up – and fell asleep again – this time for the night.

Chapter 20

The sun rose furiously back in Morrison, Illinois. Heat swept in early, pushing away the cool morning breeze like a stream of warm root beer melting through a root beer float's ice cream. It awakened Gloria in her tractor loft at the fairground's carnival. Her mother slept in her loft, below her, oblivious to the sudden light from the sun and the increased heat and humidity. Gloria let her mother sleep and peeked through the dark, mauve curtain next to her bunk to look outside. Nothing had changed, except for the unsettling prospect of a muggy day shown by the slight dew on the window and the harsh sunlight vaporizing it.

She arose, softly and silently, and eased through the back transit. Soon, in her sleeping sweats, she was pouring water into the coffee maker and slicing the segmented membranes of a grapefruit. When she was finished, she took the dish of grapefruit through her nylon kitchen door to the eating area outside. It was too early for bugs, so she sat at the round, white table and woke up with the sharp, acidic bang of the grapefruit.

She looked over at the Ferris Wheel and immediately thought of Gary. He was a mystery, a mystery that inexplicably troubled her. She hadn't wanted to get involved with him – or with anybody. Her independence was as important to her as the seeds were to the grapefruit she was enjoying. But he attracted her and confused her. Somehow she had a sense of his presence in her past – but she couldn't grasp it. The memory almost became defined at times – times like this morning, quiet and muggy with only a faint hint of breeze.

She rose, sensing that the coffee was ready, and instantly the elusive Gary-memory almost came back. The coffee smell and the morning heat must be a part of it. But she couldn't knock it down and bring it back. "Damn," she said to herself, "What do I remember about sweet Gary? There's something. Something back there. I know it."

She noticed movement behind the Ferris Wheel and caught a glimpse of Rosie moving through her patio with a cup of coffee. The memory-mystery of Gary came on strong within Gloria when she saw Rosie. It wasn't Gary working at the Wheel this past week and her looking over at him in the morning as he arose from his tent rubbing his eyes and his armpits before accepting coffee from Rosie. No, that wasn't it, although that was a pleasant memory to her; no, it was something else – something more in the past.

She picked up her coffee cup, listened to see if her mother was awake yet – no, she wasn't – and strolled over to Rosie's. "Morning, Rosie, mind if I have a cup of coffee with you?"

"I'd love it, even fill you up if you're so inclined. Gonna be a hot one, eh?"

"Guess so, the way the curl in my hair feels. Did you have the air on last night?"

"No, but might have to tonight. Carl can't take too much heat."

Gloria looked over at the spot, still half-way pressed down, where Dis had pitched his tent. She mused about him to Rosie. "What are you going to do now, without Gary?"

"Carl's going to have to find another helper, that's all there's to it. He'll have to go downtown today. It's too bad. That Gary certainly was a nice fellow – hard working and clean."

"Yeah, I know. You want to know the truth, Rosie, he was one of the best you've ever had – even better than that Spanish guy who was with you a couple of years ago. You know, Senor Gabon, or something like that."

"Oh, yea, Gabby, the quiet Mexican. He was all right. Could use him now, but – don't you know – he had a wife here and another in Mexico – and he was traveling by himself with us. But, you're right, he was a good man, a good worker."

"You know, Rosie, I liked Gary."

"You don't think I couldn't see that? Tell me about it! Fixing relays in the mirror room, come on, Gloria!"

"Hey, you weren't up. How'd you know about that?"

"What do you think? Guess who even had a piece of peach pie yesterday for lunch?"

"Why you . . . that Pete . . . wait till I see him. What did he say was going on, huh?"

"Well, he mentioned you said relays, but he himself thought it was really about . . . connections."

"Oh, he did, did he." She purred in mock umbrage for a moment before getting quiet and bringing up what was on her mind. "Yeah, Gary was all right – better than just all right. But, you know, there was something about him, something I just couldn't place."

The large woman, looking cool and straight even in the morning's rising heat, broke in: "I think I know what you mean, Gloria. He had a hard-to-put-your-finger-on kind of class that you don't find in the usual guys you can hire to work a ride."

Gloria replied, "Yes, that's true. But there was something else, something in me, something I knew. What do they call that, you know on the TV talk shows, deju vu? You know, where you try to remember something that you're sure you've experienced before, but you just cant remember it?"

"Well, Honey, that's not exactly deja vu, but it's mighty close. You know, that man who was looking for Gary didn't come back. That's a good thing. Still, it makes you wonder about what was going on in Gary's life. I guess everyone's got lots of past, right?"

"I guess you're right." Gloria looked over the rim of her coffee cup. "Except you and me."

Both of the women laughed, enjoying for this morning moment the snug pocket of comfort that they gave each other.

Rosie took a long sip of coffee and then said, "Well, he's in Iowa by now. At least I hope he is. And I hope that guy with the picture is where? Arkansas? Kansas? California, for all I care."

"Yeah, Iowa. Did he say anything about where he was headed in Iowa? Later on this summer, I've got a couple of weekend dates over there - when their fair season gets going."

"No, I don't remember him saying anything – except he was going to lose himself. That's what he said, 'I'm going to lose myself.' Wait a minute, he said something about one of the cities up there. Let me see, what was it? Shoot, I can't remember, didn't mean that much to me."

The pool of memory was slowly moving within Gloria. Dis's face flashed within it only to merge with an earlier face – a face associated with pain and hurt. What she had been struggling to remember was coming back. "It wasn't Owaceta, was it?"

Rosie looked at her with a quizzical expression creasing her face, "How'd you know that? Because now that I think of it, that's what he said. He said, 'I'll try to lose myself before I go to Owaceta.'"

Gloria wilted, but not from the heat. Pain returned, making her face hot and her breath choppy. "Damn that town!" spurted from her tight lips.

Rosie was quick with her hand, grasping Gloria's, feeling the heat within the younger woman's skin. "Wow, you've got something powerful wrong against that town. I don't think I've ever seen you react this way. You're going to have to tell me all about it."

But she couldn't, at least right now. Memories and mergers had come together. The dam had burst. The waters raged – bringing Dis back to her, but not as the bantering lover rolling on the mirror room floor, but as a man – a witness – at the trial. That was him! He was there! Damn, the man she had crushed to herself the night before last was the man on the witness stand, the mechanic. But was it him? They looked one and the same, even sounded alike – although she had trouble remembering the words of the man on the witness stand. Did he have a Western accent, a twang? But no, they were different. They had to be; they just had to be.

She finally felt Rosie's hand on her's. She looked at Rosie and blurted. "Gary's from there. He's from Owaceta. At least I think so. I'm not sure . . . there's still something different, but – oh, my gosh – I've met him before . . . in Owaceta."

Rosie softly caressed the tightly clenched hand. "Calm down, compose yourself. I'm gonna go get my pot of coffee, and when I come back, you can tell me what all this nonsense is about Owaceta."

With fresh coffee steaming from her cup, matching the steam rising slowly from the land, Gloria almost squinted at Rosie as she said, "I've never told you, Rosie, but I've got a brother in prison." She hesitated, "For life."

"Oh, my God." Rosie, the wise counselor, didn't continue. Her eyes spoke – "Tell me; get it out; it'll be better."

"He's in the Iowa State Penitentiary at Fort Madison for murder – murder one. They say he killed a little girl . . . in . . . Owaceta, Iowa. Let's see, it was more than two years ago, in the spring. I remember it was before the season got booming and my mother and I went up there for the trial. That's where I remember Gary from – the trial." She stopped, not looking at Rosie, looking into her cup instead.

Rosie whispered, "You can tell me, you know that, Gloria."

Gloria straightened up, drew a breath, and almost smiled. "Yeah, I should be over it by now. Only thing is, I know Barry didn't do it. I know it as sure as I know that this is coffee in this cup. Barry's my brother, younger brother, four years younger. There were only two of us, me and Barry. After dad died, and, well, things were up in the air, Barry just sort of drifted away from mother and me. He drifted and never returned. Every so often we'd get a letter from him – or a phone call. But, you know, being on the road like we are, it's hard to keep in contact. We hardly ever saw him. He didn't like carnival life – said he had too many bad memories.

"Eventually he got into trouble with the law. He was never violent – just drunk . . . disorderly . . . sometimes drugs. We'd get a call from a little town over in Illinois or Tennessee or somewhere. He was in jail and he needed bail. Generally I'd drive over, leaving mother with the House, and pay the bail, and take him home with me.

"The thing of it is, he was always so gentle. He couldn't hurt a flea. Most of the time it was someone hurting him. He was drunk – or drugged up – and someone would beat him up and just leave him there. Then the cops would find him and arrest him, and I'd go get him and then mother and I would take care of him for awhile.

"We'd nurse him back to health, even get him off the bottle. And, you know, he'd seem to be happy. Sometimes we'd even rent a motel room for him instead of having him live with us here at the ride, and he'd like that. He didn't really like the carnival. Maybe he was too gentle for it – maybe that was it. Maybe he couldn't see through the hardness on the outside of most of these people.

"Whatever it was, he couldn't take it. We never knew if he'd be there when we woke up. And eventually he'd fulfill our worries – he'd be gone. Oh, shoot, I'm talking so much about him, when all I'm really saying is that I know he wasn't guilty of murder, of murdering a little kid, a pretty little seven-year-old girl."

Rosie said simply, "I believe you."

"But at the trial they said he did it – and they had witnesses. And." She looked at Rosie and couldn't help the tear running down her cheek. "And one of the witnesses was Gary."

Rosie cupped Gloria's hand again. "Hear, hear. Tell me."

"They had Gary on the witness stand. At least if it wasn't Gary, it was someone who looked exactly like Gary. He was a mechanic working for a used car dealer. Let me see if I can remember . . . the name was almost a joke . . . the Deal . . . no, the I-Deal Car Sales, that was it, I-Deal.

"Anyway, they had Gary on the witness stand and he testified that Barry, my brother, worked for him for a few days right before the murder. He washed cars, cleaned them up, things like that. I guess that's what Barry did when he left us – hired on for day jobs and such. Gary said he was a pretty good worker, but that he had to fire him when he came in drunk the third day. He hadn't slept a bit the night before and he was messed up – dirty and even a little bloody. Said he might have been beaten up on.

"But Gary testified that he liked my brother, that he thought he was harmless. He said one time he bought him a coke and they sat down and chatted a bit. Oh, yeah, then it did come out.

"I gotta stop here for a moment and think this over. Gary and my brother talked about Gary's daughter. That's right, Gary was married and he had a daughter, a daughter about the same age as the girl who was killed. Jesus, Gary – married and with a daughter."

She paused, letting her Gary and the Owaceta Gary swirl around in her mind, entangling themselves in tendrils of memory. Then she looked up at Rosie and said, "You know, Rosie, Gary isn't his name. I don't remember the man on the witness stand's name, but it wasn't Gary. Something like Tom or Ron – just one syllable. But anyway let me get back to the trial. While they were having the coke, they talked about," she paused, "Gary's daughter and Gary remembered that my brother said, 'I like little girls. I wish I had a daughter.' He said that. I remember, because they repeated it. Especially the prosecutor when she was summing up at the end.

"But Gary said he didn't take offense with the remark. My brother, to him, was harmless and the remark was honest. Gary repeated that a couple of times, 'He was harmless; I think he did want to have a daughter.'

"Poor Barry. Now he's over there at Fort Madison rotting . . . and . . . going crazy. I . . .we, mother and me, tried everything we could, but they had evidence – circumstantial – but nevertheless, the jury believed it."

Rosie said, "You can tell me about it. Maybe something I know about Gary will turn out to be important."

Gloria replied, after reflecting for a moment, "They found him, my brother, passed out – drunk – near a broken down factory on the edge of town. And . . . thirty feet away . . . was the little girl. She had been strangled . . . raped . . . and . . . Jesus, Rosie, every time I think of this I get so mad and frustrated. You know what the murderer did to that poor little girl? He broke her arms – both of them!"

Gloria couldn't help it. The tears came down. Rosie just looked at her, almost not believing.

"Listen, Gloria, I've heard many things in my life with our ride, on carnie lots and fairgrounds. There have been lots of twisted stories; lots of things that I don't want to remember. And you just told me one of them. I don't know your brother, but I do know you and your mother, and I'll say this simply and plainly – your brother didn't do something like that. Something like that takes so much evil that it can't be concealed, not for long anyway."

Gloria spoke as if she didn't hear the older woman. "The little girl's blood was all over my brother and his fingerprints were on her – on her neck and on a school book they found nearby. Barry couldn't remember anything, well, hardly anything.

"He said after he got fired, he took what little money he had and drank it all up. He wandered around town, ending up late in the afternoon at the factory where he had been sleeping lately. He remembered taking a nap under a tree next to the sidewalk and waking up when a little girl came by. She woke him up because she was skipping and singing, you know how kids do that sometimes.

"He said he talked to the little girl for awhile. She said her name was Star . . . Star . . . that's right, that was her name. While they were talking, a big car pulled up and a rough man got out and took the girl away. Barry said the man told the little girl to get in with him, to get away from the dirty drunk, that he would take care of her.

"The girl didn't really want to go with the rough man, but he almost forced her – and she climbed into the car. Barry found his half-empty bottle of wine and by the time he had finished it, he was passed out again.

"The next thing he remembered was being roughly awakened by the police and taken away in a squad car."

She paused and Rosie said, "Well, what about this rough man? Was he ever identified?"

"No. It was just my brother's testimony. I don't think they wanted to listen, much less believe, anything my brother said. After all, he was just a drunk, wandering around their fair little city, looking disreputable and ugly, I suppose. No, nobody on either side, prosecution or defense, did anything with this rough man. No witnesses. Nobody came forward to report if what my brother said happened really happened. Probably nobody was around to see it.

"I've been keeping an eye on the Iowa papers to see if anything like that's happened since. You know, someone killed her – if not this rough man, someone else – and maybe he'd do the same thing again. But so far nothing. Not a blame thing. It appears like they were right – they got the right man. But, Jesus, Rosie, I know they're wrong. Barry didn't do it. He couldn't do a terrible thing like that."

"I'm with you, Gloria. I believe you."

Both women sipped their coffee. The little morning breeze stopped, replaced instead by the beginning layers of moisture-packed heat. Tiny pinpoints of wetness appeared on both women's foreheads.

Gloria broke the silence. "I'm going over there. There's just too many things that don't make sense. Why are they after Gary? He's just a mechanic in a small town garage, right? No. He's traveling under a made-up name through the Midwest on a bicycle, working at carnivals here and there. What about his wife and daughter? No, this whole thing doesn't add up."

Rosie said, "I think you're right, Gloria. Something bad is going on – something evil. Only thing is, I don't know if you're the one to do something about it. Sure, you had a little fling with Gary in your haunted house, but that doesn't make you responsible."

Gloria interrupted her, "It's not Gary so much, Rosie. It's Barry, my brother. I'm going."

She rose from her chair. "It's going to be a hot one today, miserable, but I don't care. I'm going. I'll get mother up; she'll have to run the ride all by herself today, even if it is Friday. She can shut down if it gets too hot, right? I'll go see my buddy Pete; he'll let me borrow his car. Rosie, keep an eye on my mother, will you?"

"Sure thing, Gloria. You be careful over there. When I think of that man with the picture yesterday, and then the story you just told, a chill comes over me even in this heat. There's evil still around. So you be careful, you hear."

Chapter 21

Dis was awake before the light – but not before the heat. Perhaps that was what awoke him – his light perspiration within the confines of his sleeping bag, the dampness covering his skin, and the feeling of being confined in a space where the air was so pumped up with supersaturated molecules that it moved only reluctantly.

He looked out his tent flap and saw nothing. No moon, no stars, only the hint of artificial lights. All was dark. But he did hear some movement. Off to his left, someone said something is a low tone. Then he heard the unmistakable sound of a long zipper being pulled. To the right, fairly close to him, came the clanking of aluminum on aluminum. He thought, "People are up and pulling stakes; it can't be too early." With his flashlight he checked his watch; it read 4:38.

He did want to leave early, but not when it was completely dark. But by the time he broke down his tent and loaded up his bike, the sun might be starting to rise, and that's when he wanted to be leaving Summerdale. With the weak light of dawn it would be difficult for him to be observed and identified.

However, by the sounds, he figured he should get up and get ready. Not far away he could hear metallic doors clanking, some with a loud bang, most muted. These would be porta-potties, the temporary toilets ubiquitous on BABI. He left his tent and instead of trying for the barn's toilets, which he figured to be crowded, followed the sounds and two overhead lights to a long line of the temporary toilets between the barn building and the open field in front of it.

The one he occupied was surprisingly clean, even stocked with an extra roll of toilet paper. He did not like these plastic, aluminum, and fiberglass cubicles, but when they were clean, they were acceptable – sometimes even better than the rank toilets of restaurants or public buildings. At least the porta-potty company cleaned the rented stalls at least once a day – sometimes even more – which was more than could be said for many establishments.

BABI couldn't roll without these cubicles of relief. In towns, they were the number one necessity. Old BABI hands even had a word for them: Kybos, supposedly the name came from an early – now out of business – company which had reigned during the first few BABIs.

Mornings were particularly important for these kybos. In the evening people did ingest much liquid refreshment to re-hydrate themselves from the long, hot rides. Or, as in many cases, get incidentally ultra-hydrated because of a thirst for cold beer. In either case, much liquid remained with them for the next day's ride; but much of it also simply cried to be ejected – especially after a long night's sleep.

No lines formed in front of the kybos as yet; that would happen with the loosening of the dark, the first soft reds of the glowing morning. On his way back from the kybos, Dis stopped near the side of the barn where a water spigot was open, creating a marsh of water around it, but offering a dab of water for tooth brushing.

That done, feeling now refreshed and hungry, he almost tip-toed to his tent and started packing away his gear – rolling up his pad, his sleeping bag, stowing other loose articles into his panniers. Since he had been living now out of his panniers for months, except during his stay at Jeffrey, Kentucky, it was an easy trick for him to keep them organized. He could handle them in the dark – with only a little help from his flashlight.

The tent came down with hardly a clank. He wondered if he was awakening his closest neighbors, the three women whose tent was now very much up and almost pushing his into the ground. It was large and slightly billowing, even though Dis could feel no breeze whatsoever. While loading his panniers on his bike, Dis wondered how the three women could have erected such a voluminous tent without waking him and without entangling his tent in theirs. He did know that he had slept well and hard.

Soon he was walking his loaded bike through the masses of tents to one of the lanes snaking through the grounds. A diffusion of light petted the eastern blackness, giving him an inkling of direction. He passed an occasional early riser taking down a tent, but it was still too early for most of the tenters, as evidenced by the hard breathing and snoring rumbling through the tents that he passed.

Soon he was riding, very slowly, through the main "road" of the fairgrounds' midway and passing the "big green tent" where he had eaten the previous night. It was now open for breakfast. The Summerdale Home Farm Club, evidently, hadn't slept at all. But, thought Dis, they would probably make enough from these two days to finance their entire treasury for the next millennium.

At the ground's entrance Dis held back. He stopped before he got close and eased his bike into the darkness next to a permanent shed. Dismounting, he searched the entrance area, looking for his gray man – or anyone who looked suspiciously like him. Very few people were there, except for two bikers sitting next to their bikes and periodically looking at their watches, possibly waiting for someone not as eager in the morning as they. Also present was an elderly lady dangling a set of keys in her hand. Dis checked the periphery and could see no one lurking in the shadows watching.

He did notice that the closed-up headquarters' tent had boxes of what appeared to be leaflets in front of it. So, while making his escape through the entrance arch, he swooped and took one of the papers from each of the boxes. He still wasn't confident that he knew everything he wanted to know about this ride. Stuffing the leaflets into his front bag, he swung his leg over his saddle and was off. In the distance he could make out a few riders; following them would be as much direction as he needed.

He considered riding side streets, but people were so sparse on the streets this early and the light was still so dim, that instead he braved his way down the main street, trusting that his follower, if around, would still be sleeping. A number of the ubiquitous private citizen food stands were up and running in front of the owners' Main Street houses. They offered breakfast food, juice, and coffee. Dis was very hungry, but he didn't want to stop; he felt sure that he could find an eating place more isolated out in the country.

The route doubled back through the city, following the same route that it had used the previous day. At the outskirts Dis passed in reverse through the cowboy arch, the band's flatbed truck and the mechanical man with his squirt gun standing off to the side looking forlorn amid debris and early morning misty gloom.

But Dis shot through the arch and was off into the country, although immediately taking a right turn and following a different road than the one that he came in on yesterday. It was now light enough for him to see the road clearly, although its surface was still somewhat obscured to him. He hoped the county maintained this section of road well. On either side of the road, misty and mysterious fields stretched out to clouds of nothingness, a seamless merging of the land and the sky.

It was warm, unusually warm for this early in the day, and humid. Dis had a sense that this was going to be a difficult day for him – and for most of the people on the ride. He was in good shape and had been living "close to the land" for months now. He could live without the sophisticated veneer that encased you, for instance, when you lived with a home, a car, some kids, and a dog. But even he didn't look forward to a day of high heat and damping humidity; of sweat not only constantly on the skin, but also drenching the clothing; of searing sun, dicing the body with penetrating razor-slices of heat.

But for now it was good to be on the road, racing around the occasional early morning bicyclers who were slower than he and being passed by the still fewer speedsters. Dis was hungry, though, and he did like his morning coffee. Almost upon thinking this, he topped a low hill and saw in the distance a group of people in front of a farmhouse, the sign, he knew by now, of a food stand.

He passed the place, checking his suspicions. Then seeing just bikers and farm women, he pulled in and leaned his bike against a tree. Two ladies and three kids were tending the trestles-and-planks table, and just as Dis got to it, a third lady brought out a fresh pan of cinnamon rolls. From their smell and their looks, Dis knew that these were killer sweet rolls. They were pushing each other out of the pan, inflated with whole pecan halves and icy-black spots of juicy raisins all covered with a scattering of sugar. The lady upended the pan on a large holiday platter. When she pulled the pan away, she revealing a large rectangle of crystallized brown rolls covered by melted syrup. Nuts and raisins peeped from the loops of the rolls and the pungent aroma of cinnamon impregnated the air around it. The lady took a huge spatula and slathered the stiffening syrup from the pan over the rolls, filling in some of the crevasses with tendrils of caramelized liquid.

These were indeed cinnamon-pecan rolls fit for a king. Dis, almost kneeling in tribute, ordered two of them, along with a cup of coffee from a large coffee maker, probably borrowed from a church, and a glass of orange juice from a pitcher resting in an insulated container filled with ice. He had to make two trips with his purchases back to his bike, where he settled with his back to the tree and feasted. Homemade Iowa farm food was hard to beat.

After he had finished one of the rolls and all of the juice, he thought of the leaflets that he had picked up earlier. He retrieved them from his front bag and checked them out, while keeping a wary eye out for anyone unusual appearing on the road. One of the leaflets was a long, green sheet covered with maps – the official route sheet for the ride. He knew the day's destination, Cedar City, but now he found out that the ride was a 77 miler which would go through four small towns before ending up for the night at one of the state's major schools, Iowa Central University. The destination for the next day, Friday, was Owaceta, a 69 mile ride from Cedar City. The maps didn't give any indication of the terrain, but this was corn country, part of the great American prairie, and Dis knew that meant flat riding except for the occasional river valleys.

These days, even with the wet heat, would be easy riding for him.

With both rolls gone and sipping his coffee, Dis opened another leaflet, actually an eight-page tabloid newspaper, a special for BABI riders about the next evening's city, Cedar City. Published by the hometown newspaper, this was full of things to do, special events, a map of the city, and many ads directed specifically at BABIers. Every community group sponsoring a meal had an ad, allowing riders to plan their evening meal ahead of time. The map and listings of events were particularly useful for those who still had energy left after a hot day on the bikes. Dis noted, for instance, that he could watch the champions of the Iowa state high school musical drama competition perform a selection of hits from "The Music Man" in front of the Glacier Memorial Library at 7:00 p.m. tonight. On the other hand, he also could dance to "real Buddy Holly style Rock and Roll" on the street in front of Sam's Goodtime Tavern where the Bud drafts were only 75 cents a glass.

This was all very nice for a regular rider, but not for him. Tomorrow he would be approaching what seemed to be his town of destiny and he needed to be cool and collected as he entered it. But he was still almost completely in the dark as to the past of that destiny. He wished he could find out something, at least an inkling about Rob Clemmon, the identify he had taken and the man he had killed back in Washington.

He almost threw the tabloid in a nearby trash can when he had a quick idea. What about the library? They probably had papers from the neighboring towns – maybe. The university library probably wouldn't, but what about the town's? Yes, there it was on the map, the Cedar City Public Library. Dis now was motivated. He threw his garbage away and jumped on his bike.

If he could get into the library, where would he start? He had a name and an address from the driver's license and a physical description, which didn't seem to help much since it almost perfectly described himself. The same for the small Polaroid picture – it could almost be a picture of himself. The date of the license also wasn't much help. It was last year's, the same year Dis had met the licensee in the Washington D. C. parking lot and killed him. Ouch, Dis still flinched when he thought of that encounter. Such an important pivot in both men's lives; such an insignificant event in the real world around them.

But the date did tell him that the homeless bum, Rob Clemmon, probably hadn't been adrift for long. Why would a shabby alcoholic have a recent driver's license? No, whatever happened to the man, he had been living – probably fairly normally – in Owaceta, Iowa, within the last year and a half. In fact, since his death less than a year ago – that's right, it was in September – that meant that he had been living in Iowa during the first half of that year. All Dis would have to do is examine the newspapers from the beginning of February – the date the license had been issued – to the middle of September.

What to look for? Good question. The name, first of all. Rob Clemmon. Anything, any mention of it. A crime, a police report, an accident, anything. A missing person report – after all maybe that's why the gray man is after me – checking out a missing person report. No, if that were true, he would have been up front about it. He would have mentioned it when he was asking questions. Rosie, for instance, would have treated this whole thing differently if she had thought that he was a missing person and that someone who cared was having a search made for him.

But then again, what was the gray man after? Why didn't he use the missing person approach? Was he a cop? If so, what was Rob's crime, and why didn't the gray man use local police help. He seemed to be working absolutely alone. And if he wasn't a cop, just who was he?

All of these questions rattled through Dis's consciousness as he spun down the BABI road. The sun was up now, but he was on automatic pilot, hardly noticing the increased visibility and the increasing heat. He rode through the first of the four small towns on the day's route almost without noticing it. He wasn't hungry or thirsty and earlier he had stopped to relieve his bladder in a cornfield, the rows upon rows of almost identical plants reaching almost eight feet high. He didn't need a kybo, even though the line of them in the city park was almost devoid of users at this early time.

The townspeople were up and about, but not many bikers had come through yet. It was still early and it occurred to Dis that it was a good thing he had that map. He was ahead of the pack, and just might become isolated, with no one ahead of him to show the way. This would give him increased visibility, but he would just have to take his chances on that. He wanted to get to Cedar City and use the library.

Outside the first town, he found he wasn't alone. Riders were ahead of him and some flew past him, many in packs, riding close together in synchronization, their cranks seemingly linked and their legs pumping in perfect unison. These were "racers:" Dis wasn't one of them, but he was steady and reasonably fast. He was almost a tortoise to their hares, for they would stop in the towns and rest and party; he on this day would ride through, stopping for only the necessities, and beat them to the finish line.

Obviously Dis wasn't getting the flavor of BABI. He was missing the camaraderie and friendliness of almost everyone attached to the ride – the participants and the people living on the route. For a week it was one big riding family – and a tired one at the end of almost every day's ride. For most it was a true vacation, if vacation meant vacating the mind from its normal day-in-and-day-out preoccupations. BABI gave so much activity – both around the riders and provided by them – that it occupied them almost completely. Sure, there were some long stretches of hot and straight road through cornfields where there wasn't much to think about except their real lives. But even there, they found themselves thinking about the minutia of daily BABI life rather than the office or the factory. Should they stop for another lemonade? What about switching tents tonight with Bill? Will Sally beat Will in again today? What would be good for tonight – Chinese or the Methodists? Look at that bike there; an Allsop wheel on a mountain bike and riding BABI!

Dis, however, with his life preoccupation was not on vacation.

So he rode on. As he did so, through the cornfields still beaded with millions of dew drops sparkling in the rising sun, he thought of BABI and what he was missing. He was almost apologetic, promising himself that someday he would return and do the whole ride – do it rightly and do it with . . . whom?

That brought a perplexity. The first image to come to mind was Gloria – bright, flamboyant, breezy-mouthed Gloria. But he had trouble envisioning her on a bike. He almost had trouble thinking of her without the carnival and the Spook House. But then he remembered their walk through the darkened fairgrounds, drink in hand, and he could just picture them doing the same here on BABI. But he still had trouble picturing her on the ride itself.

Lornaree, on the other hand – her freckled-chin, green-eyed beauty coming back to him with a rush – was planted in his memory on a bike. That and in the milky moonlight of her bedroom with her silver breast echoing the moon. He would love to do BABI with her, and he knew she would relish it. He thought of the two of them getting up early, taking off in the early morning light, racing through the route but stopping at all the stops and enjoying the ambiance, eating dinner together in a crowded church basement, sharing stories with fellow diners, dancing and having a few beers in the town square in the evening, and later making muffled love, hilariously quiet, in their snug tent.

Yes, the women in his life would fit on BABI. When he thought of it, that quality was probably a subconscious attraction that drew him to them. A pinpoint of memory interrupted: Ruth. In no way could he ever envision her on this ride. At a seaside resort or stretched out on a poolside lounge, yes. But the rough sweat, chaos, and masses of BABI, absolutely not!

A staggering thought hit him. What if she was behind the gray man? On the one hand, it would be like her, the tenacious ferret, to never give up, to keep the search for him on forever, unrelentingly. But on the other hand, how could she know about Rob Clemmon and Owaceta, Iowa? The gray man had his picture from Iowa. That was about all that Dis knew, but he couldn't conceive that Ruth, or someone working for her, could know anything about it.

It was a mystery.

And he was riding to a library in hopes of dispelling that mystery, or at least some of it.

At the second town he stopped at a booth, tucked inconspicuously aslant the main avenue downtown, that was selling thick slices of Happy Harry's pizza. The booth had no oven, but Dis could see thick canvas insulated bags which were obviously used to carry the hot pizza to the booth. Even though it was before 8 o'clock in the morning, Dis had had his breakfast and, having traveled about 25 miles, was in need of something substantial in his stomach. The slice of pizza, one of the first sold from the booth, was delicious – hot, spicy, and loaded with sauce. He ordered another one and drank a full 16 oz. plastic cup of Pepsi with it. The town, Ridge Junction, was still uncrowded; almost the only people on the street were townspeople scurrying to get ready for the onslaught of bikers.

With the taste of pepperoni still lingering in his mouth, Dis continued riding at a fairly fast pace down the almost straight road. He had covered about a third of the day's route and it was now about 8:15. If he continued at the same rate, he could be in Cedar City almost by noon. There was no appreciable wind to slow him, and he knew that as the hot day continued, the wind from the west would pick up, giving him a little boost to counteract the increasing heat.

It was, when he got away from his preoccupation with his problems, a beautiful little morning for biking. He was riding into the rising sun, but it was still hazy with the morning mists rising from the farm fields. Some clouds drifted around and behind him, but they were threads of white against the dim blue of the sky, and they presented no threat of rain – at least for now. Traffic was absolutely nil; it was great to ride on roads protected by policemen at every intersection. And the roads themselves, blacktop, for the most part, were nicely surfaced, with hardly any potholes or corrugated patterns. They undulated at times – the summer sun's fire and the winter's ice had done their bending and shifting – but that almost was a plus, adding texture to the ride.

Dis didn't stop at any of the other two small towns that were loaded for BABI bear. It dawned on him that if he were the gray man and he wanted to try to see everyone on the ride, he would position himself in one of these one-street towns at some high elevation – the second floor window of a store front, perhaps. It would be a tough job, what with all of the helmets and the sheer mass of riders, but it would make sense to do it that way.

Dis laughed to himself thinking of the condition of the gray man's eyes at the end of the day. What would he do about food, drink, taking a break, going to the toilet. Dis thought of the man upstairs in a dismal room peeing in a glass jar without taking his eyes off the never-ending line of bikers. Dis laughed out loud on his bike. Just then a rampaging woman racer overtook him, jerking her head and staring at him as she heard the laugh. Dis laughed again. She probably thought he was a bit crazy, riding by himself and laughing at his own jokes.

By 11 o'clock Dis was hot – hot and wet. His T-shirt was soggy and his biking shorts, made for wicking moisture away from the skin, were damp, especially in the crotch. His face and arms were covered with a thin sheen of sweat, particularly his forehead, where drops of perspiration formed and then took an express route to his eyes. He found himself constantly wiping his forehead with his shirtsleeve to prevent the acrid sweat from blinding him as he churned away down the highway. He had a kerchief in his left back pannier, but didn't want to stop to find it. It wasn't that much farther to Cedar City and, hopefully, shade and rest – and the library.

About then a young man, about 25 years old, in a green lycra jersey and black shorts, on a Trek 4000 titanium racer drew up beside him. The man turned and yelled, "God almighty, no wonder you're sweating so. Your back's more wet than dry. How many pounds you carrying in those bags?"

Dis looked at the guy and said, "You're not sweating? Then what's that stuff dripping off your chin? Those panniers? I don't know, how much do four panniers full of rocks weigh?"

The man laughed, "Probably enough to give you flats in both your tires. But, hey, man, keep up the work. You're really building up your quads. Watch out that they don't explode."

"Naw, I'm not worried. The bags aren't really full of rocks – just balloons. Yeah, blown up balloons. Looks impressive though, doesn't it."

"That it does. Makes you look like Mr. Legs."

Three youngsters, racing together, came up behind them and passed without hardly a glance or an acknowledgment. One of these racers was wearing a spider man helmet, complete with mask and a trailing web.

The green-jerseyed talker waved to Dis and sped ahead. "Nice talking to you, buddy. I'm going to join Spider Head and his buddies up ahead. If I find some good rocks, I'll stop and help you load them in your bags, OK?"

He was off, zipping past Dis like a taxi around a bag lady. For the last ten miles the road was almost empty. Except for the real racers, almost everyone on the ride was behind Dis. He had left early, kept up a steady pace, and, more importantly, had not stopped and dawdled at the small towns along the route – although he would have liked to very much.

When he arrived at Cedar City no tumultuous welcoming celebration greeted him. The road-turned-street was strangely quiet; even the curbside refreshment counters were almost nonexistent. Also traffic was considerable. "I'm probably just too early," Dis thought. "Things'll pick up this afternoon, I bet."

He had no trouble following the posted camping signs to the University, which he remembered from the map was the major site for the night's encampment. The school had a vast gymnasium-field house complex that would be the focal point for showers and food. On the way, while going through what appeared to be the downtown – not really "dressed up" for BABI, but with many signs pasted on windows welcoming the BABI riders – he saw the town's library, his destination. He wondered if he should go there now, but decided against it. He was too hot, sweaty, hungry, and he needed something cold to drink – real cold, not the lukewarm water left in his bottles.

But he did note the library's location and when he arrived at the parking lot of the university's field house, where a big tent emblazoned with "BABI Headquarters" simmered on the pavement, he figured the library was only about six blocks away. It was about noon and the parking lot was blazing, its blacktop almost sticky. Dis didn't want to put up his tent on it, although with his pop-up tent it was possible, since he didn't need tent pegs. He knew that later in the afternoon the heat would make the parking lot intolerable; in fact, the ride's leadership would do well to move their Headquarters tent now if they wanted anyone to visit it later.

He rode on the perimeter of the lot noticing the paths that diverged from it. The one he took seemed to head for a shady group of trees next to an imposing, institutional building, probably full of classrooms. When he got to the trees, he was almost too late; much of the space under their shade was taken – tents placed like gigantic leaves fallen in random patterns. Space in the shade of the trees was at a premium; the campus being new and lacking in mature trees and landscaping.

Dis remembered that he wasn't planning to be in his tent during the hot afternoon, so he looked around for a site with late afternoon shade and soon found it. He pushed his bike to the eastern side of the classroom building, the side opposite to that with the trees, and claimed a section of ground abutting the building. Two other tents were already erected along the building's edge, but no one was around. Off in the distance Dis could see a large, undeveloped field – now studded with Rider trucks and occasional pinpoints of tents. That probably was the major camping site for the night.

Once his tent was up, his bags stowed, and his bike locked to the tent (not the best solution, but it would do for now), Dis went off searching for a shower. His first choice, the field house, proved to be the best choice. He found a massive shower room, with a long line of showers still with hot water, something which he had heard during the ride was almost inconceivable on BABI – a hot shower. Moreover the room was basically empty, except for three teenagers luxuriating under the hot water, probably using up enough water for ten showers each.

Within fifteen minutes Dis was back at his tent dressed in a nondescript beige T-shirt and a pair of khaki walking shorts. He was hungry and somewhat tired, but he had slaked his thirst with icy cold water from a refrigerated drinking fountain in the shower room. He decided to ride his bike to the library, more for security than anything else; he wouldn't have minded the six-block walk.

Soon he was sitting on the front steps of a green and orange Victorian home, set back from the street amid a plethora of oaks, hack-berries, and maple trees, and munching on a turkey and cheese sandwich made with real, homemade bread. A plastic cup of still cold potato salad sat in his lap and a good, three-inch-by-three-inch hunk of chocolate brownie lay beside him, next to a large cup of lemonade. The house's housewife was a talkative sort, but she had captured a young couple still in their racing outfits and was drilling them about their life histories. Dis, who wasn't naturally standoffish, was happy that the couple was there; he didn't want to have to invent still another personal history.

At the library he locked his bike to the bike rack and asked at the desk if they had copies of the Owaceta newspaper for the last few years. A rather attractive librarian with short, blonde hair, a pecan shaped face, and a shapely figure except for legs that hinted of fat, told him the good news. They did collect the Owaceta Triumph since Owaceta was the county seat. They had last year's copies on microfilm, but this year's weren't available, except as actual copies stacked in a storage bin.

Dis asked for the microfilm and soon was sitting in front of the reader's screen scrolling through a year in the life of a small Iowa town and not finding much to interest him. He had a name, Rob Clemmon, and not much else to go on. He was looking for anything that would have any possible connection with Rob Clemmon turning up homeless in Washington D.C.

Dis quickly found that inching through a newspaper's day-by-day issues was a very tedious business. He couldn't look just on the front page, but had to closely examine every page, especially the minor items contained under police reports. Owaceta was a city of about 14,000 people, most of whom, according to the newspaper's reports, did good community work, constantly boosted their fine town, and were enthralled with "progress." Some of them occasionally got into minor trouble – fights, accidents, political squabbling, zoning disputes – but the town rolled through the first part of the year with hardly a negative front-page headline.

Dis found nothing. And working with the microfilm machine was tedious. He had to inch each page forward to the viewing lens, then use a lever to see its entire length and breath. It took him two hours to get through February, and it was exhausting work. He seemed more tired than from riding a bike – although his ride that day undoubtedly contributed to his weariness. After working through the 15th of March, he decided to take a break and returned the microfilm to the librarian, asking her to hold it until he returned.

She asked if he had found what he was looking for, and he said, "No, and it's pretty tedious – like looking for a needle in a corn crib."

The woman's oval face jerked a bit at the slight quip. She smiled a tight, professional smile. "Well, maybe I can help you in your shelling. What are you looking for, if I may ask?"

Dis wasn't sure if he wanted to tell her the specifics – the name Rob Clemmon – so he said, "That's part of the problem; I'm searching for something vague, yet something that must have been pretty important in that town. You don't happen to remember some major happening – an accident, a trial, a scandal – something like that, over there in Owaceta within the last couple of years?

"Owaceta. Well, I hardly keep up with it, except when something appears in our local paper here. Let me see, a couple of weeks ago they had a big accident, a semi and a car full of teenagers. One of the kids was killed."

"No, it has to be around the beginning of last year, or possibly earilier."

"Wow, I'm good at remembering facts, but not that good. Last year. Wait a minute, there's something coming back. A big trial – not in the county, but in Owaceta itself. Oh, yes, I remember now – a little girl murdered and . . . raped . . . on the streets of Owaceta. But they caught the guy who did it – a derelict, a homeless bum. He was convicted, I'm pretty sure. I think he got life. But the little girl . . . people were sure up tight about it, I'll tell you that. We heard about that even over here."

Something clicked within Dis. He could feel heat. God he hoped he wouldn't have anything to do with such a case, but still he could feel excitement, could feel his cheeks getting red. "And this happened a couple of years ago? When, in the winter, the spring?"

The librarian frowned, her short almost windblown hair belying the seriousness of her expression, indeed of her job. "It must have been last spring or summer. They found the guy asleep in the grass next to the sidewalk. I remember that because, well, let's face it, Owaceta isn't New York City. Sleeping in the grass just isn't done in a small Iowa town."

Dis said, "So that'd be last summer. No, that wouldn't work out for me. It doesn't fit."

The woman stared at Dis, looking into his eyes, then abruptly shifted her gaze to the computer in front of her. "Maybe it wasn't last year. No it couldn't have been. It was longer ago. Maybe the year before, or even the year before that. But it was in the early summer I do remember that."

"Well, I'll check that out. Do you have the tapes for those two years?"

"I think so. I'll have to get them for you."

"Thank you, I appreciate that. Listen I have to get something to drink. I'm on BABI and it was a pretty hot ride today. But I'll be right back."

Chapter 22

Dis left the library and headed for a canopy over the entrance to a drug store where a banner proclaimed, "Mountain Dew - Pepsi - Coke - 75 cents -BABI Welcome" Soon he was gulping a second large cup of Coke and swirling the ice cubes nervously. "Why do I think what she told me has anything to do with Rob Clemmon or myself? The time doesn't work out. Rob got a new license at the beginning of last year and he was homeless in Washington by September. What ever happened had to happen last year – in the spring or summer. But yet – God, I know there's something about this court case; there's just something about it. I'll go back and check it out, and then maybe try last year again. That court case should be easy to locate. It probably made headlines."

When he returned, the librarian was busy on the phone. She nodded to him and gave him two small reel boxes. While listening to the phone, she scribbled something on a note pad, ripped it off, and handed it to Dis with a smile, a pretty but placid smile. The note said, "I think the derelict's name was Shoaty. Larry or Barry or something Shoaty."

Dis read it quickly and again something clicked. A rush of heat exploded within his head. Shoaty. Shoaty. He had heard that name before – recently. An image of the carnival charged through his brain. The grounds, the Ferris Wheel, the Spook House. Yes, the Spook House. At its back – a certificate. Owner-Operator: Gloria Shoaty.

He looked at the librarian, knowing that his face was red, but she continued on the phone, nodding and occasionally talking. He went back to the room that contained the microfilm machines and threaded the tape from two years ago into it. She said it was summer, early summer, so he fast forwarded the tape to about one third of the way through, slowing it down and then stopping in late April. Then it was a matter of skipping to the front pages of each issue and checking the headlines on that page. Soon he was through April and halfway through May.

And then on Thursday, May 14, a glaring headline stopped him short. "Girl Found Dead; Man Arrested." Dis scanned the story quickly for any mention of Rob Clemmon, but found nothing. Then he went back and read the story carefully.

The first paragraph threw him for a loop. It listed the name of the murder victim, Star Oatage. Star. Her name was Star. He thought of the curved lens lying in the bottom of his pannier. "We love you, Star." Dis felt himself starting to get light-headed, his face overheating. Star, the name he had wondered about for the last year and a half – could it be a young, 7-year-old murder victim?

Dis felt things coming together but in a disconcerting way. Barry or Larry Shoaty and now Star, the word that was on the lens which the dying Rob Clemmon had thrust into his hand. My God, he was involved in something vile. Star, the opening paragraph said, had been brutally murdered – and what did the librarian say – dismembered? Dis read on.

The story told that her body had been found only three blocks from her home, which was about halfway from her school. She had attended school that day and had walked a few blocks toward her home after school with a friend. The friend left her at the edge of a block that contained only an abandoned factory, the Overton

Forge and Pan Works, overgrown with weeds and debris, and that is where her body was found.

Police had received an anonymous phone call around 3:30 p.m. to check the grounds of the factory, and officer Tom Smithson, who was cruising in the area, found the body about 30 feet from the building in an area of the gravel parking lot that was covered with weeds. Smithson said the girl was dead when he found her, and he would make no further comments until medical examiners had a chance to look at the body.

Smithson also found a man lying asleep, apparently intoxicated, close to the sidewalk in the same area of the block. The man had blood on his person and clothes, and a weapon was found near him. He was taken into custody and later was arrested and remanded to the county jail. The man's name was Barry Shoaty, address unknown.

Dis skimmed through the rest of the paper and came up with nothing related to Rob Clemmon. But drumming on his brain was the question – Barry Shoaty; was he related to Gloria? Her father, her brother, her husband, a distant relative? Dis had to admit that he didn't know much about her – as she, indeed, didn't know much about him – and that quite possibly the man was in no way connected with her. After all Shoaty was, although not common, certainly not that unique.

Dis continued moving through the newspaper stories related to the murder. Why, he was not positive. What connection did he or Rob Clemmon have with the case? None so far. About the only connection was the possibly coincidental link of Gloria's last name with the arrested man. In the days after the murder, no real substantial details altered the basic facts of the case, but the town, indeed, was up in arms.

Much of the newspaper space was devoted to reactions to the murder by community members and groups. The girl's parents, a young couple who had no other children, were incognito and seemingly distraught, refusing to make any statements to the press. But the same could not be said about Owaceta. It was livid!

The PTA from the girl's school sent a letter to the mayor, city council, and the press demanding the clean-up of the factory site and more police protection during the times when students were going to and from school. People in the girl's neighborhood held a block meeting, marked by loud and emotional pleas for more police protection and the arresting of derelicts and bums. The victim's church held a special informational gathering two days before the funeral, trying to dispel rumors; but it had the opposite effect. Three people became so emotional that they had to be escorted from the meeting before they could finish their pleas.

The school had a real problem on its hands. School was canceled the day after the victim was found, the teachers attending a hastily conceived all-day meeting on how to help the kids deal with the death of their classmate. When school opened, three psychiatrists from the state office of education held small meetings with the victim's classmates and one large meeting with the entire school. Still there was much crying and bewilderment, and, one of the psychiatrists stated, "Who knows what the long term effects of this will be."

The owner of the factory turned out to be, by default, a large Chicago bank. Its officers, who admitted they had never seen the site, expressed regret, but at this time, "They did not have the means or the legal right to substantially change their pattern of building maintenance." They did, however, promise to hire a local firm to trim the grass.

Three days after the murder, the police department revealed through the state medical examiner that Star Oatage had been raped before she was murdered. No other details were given. But that was enough to stun the community. "No, I don't believe it. It can't happen here," or a variation of it, was the most common litany spoken by those quoted in the paper when the news came out. Some wanted vengeance, some wanted explanation, some quietly sought consolation in prayer, and some were almost smug with the realization that the arrested perpetrator was a stranger to the town, an outsider.

What the paper revealed the most, however, was the outrage and the sense of innocence savaged. As one interviewee put it, "But this is just a small Iowa town, and to have something like this happen here, just doesn't make sense. Des Moines, Chicago, yes. But Owaceta! Things like this just don't happen here." Another said, "We moved here thirteen years ago to get away from crime and corruption. Now it looks like things have caught up with us. Where do we go now?"

The visitation, or wake, for the victim became more of a public and media event than a means of consolation for the survivors. It was held in a small funeral home in the victim's neighborhood and long lines formed even before its opening hours in the afternoon. The parents and relatives of the little girl held up stoically through the many almost-strangers drawn to the event, but when a man attempted to bring in a hand-held video camera, the father of the girl collected his wife and close relatives and left the chapel area of the funeral home. He then had the funeral director close the home's doors, even though a line almost a block long stretched down the street. He also canceled the remaining evening viewing hours. The coffin, almost out of sight under mounds of flowers, was closed.

The victim's funeral, covered extensively by the newspaper, was also a public expiation of mass guilt that didn't work. For one thing, the church of the victim's family was too small and the parents refused to have the funeral moved to a larger facility. Consequently on the sunny but windy morning of the funeral, hundreds of people couldn't get into the church. They had to stand outside and try, mostly fruitlessly, to hear snippets of the pastor's words. The victim's teacher wanted to take her class to the funeral en mass, but most of the parents refused to give permission for it. So the kids remained in school, and ironically were running, screaming and laughing at recess when four blocks away their classmate was carried from the church and placed in the hearse.

The only dignified public event was the burial itself. At a hillside cemetery in the sun and the wind, and with a strictly closed group of close relatives and friends, Star Oatage, an innocent little girl who had been savagely raped, brutalized, and murdered, was laid to rest.

This, alas, could happen in a little town in Iowa.

The paper did an investigation into the past of the alleged murderer. He was born in Friedricksberg, Missouri; was 28 years old; was a drifter who worked at odd jobs; and had a record of public intoxication and drug use in a wide circle of small towns in the Midwest. He, however, as far as the paper could tell, had never been involved with a violent felony or even battery. When violence was involved, it was usually to him rather than to someone else. He also had no known history of sexual offenses or, for that matter, child abuse or similar offenses.

Dis read all of this with avid interest, looking for any mention of the name Rob Clemmon. But after about two weeks of front-page articles about the rape-murder, news about it dropped off, and Dis was back to scanning the entire paper for mention of Rob Clemmon. He was about ready to give up, although it was still early afternoon, when he caught a small page-three item mentioning that the upcoming trial of Barry Shoaty for the murder of Star Oakage had been placed on the court docket for August 21 and that Shoaty would be defended by the Public Defender, a lawyer named Pete Sacromand.

Just on the chance that there might be something, Dis wound the machine forward to the middle of August. He stopped it on a front page dominated by a story about the ongoing trial, and as soon as his eyes focused, the name Rob Clemmon leaped out at him from the page.

He was almost shocked. Again heat came into his face. Here was what he had been chewing over in his mind for months – the answer, perhaps, to who and what he was, or if not entirely him, at least a part of him. Rob Clemmon had grown into him, like a wild grapevine into a tree.

Rob Clemmon was a mechanic – or at least he had been.

According to the paper's front page story, which detailed the second day of the trial, one of the witnesses for the prosecution was Rob Clemmon, a long time resident of Owaceta, and a mechanic who worked for I-Deal Car Sales, a used car dealer on Front Street. He also acted as assistant manager of the business because the owner, an elderly man named Joe Schultz, was ailing and only occasionally spent time at the business. The business also employed two salesmen, both relatively new, one having been hired only months before the murder.

Rob Clemmon was brought to the stand because he had hired the defendant, Barry Shoaty, to wash and clean up the interiors of cars and to act as a general helper around the lot. Business had increased and Clemmon was finding it hard to do it all himself anymore. He hired Shoaty, not by putting an ad in the paper, but because Shoaty had simply appeared at the lot four days before the murder and asked for work.

Although Shoaty's appearance was less than desirable – he was unshaven and his clothes were disheveled – he actually turned out to be a pretty good worker. He was quiet; steady, if relatively slow; and, at least during the three days he worked, reliable. He came to work on time and did whatever he was told to do. He was paid on a day-work basis, $5.25 an hour. Yes, Clemmon was happy with the drifter's work.

Yet on the day of the murder he had fired Shoaty. The man had appeared for work on time at 7:30 a.m., but in no condition to do any work. His clothes were dirty and his shirtsleeve torn to the armpit; two of his fingers on this right hand were bleeding although wrapped in a rag; and he had a large bruise next to his mouth. His eyes were glassy and his speech was impaired. Clemmon took him to be intoxicated, although he could smell only a hint of alcohol about him.

After half an hour, in which Shoaty basically just stared at a car which he was supposed to wash, Clemmon told him that he would have to let him go. Shoaty gave no protest, but quietly left. Clemmon never saw him again.

On the day before Shoaty was fired, a hot and humid day, Clemmon took a break with the alleged murderer, buying him a can of Pepsi. They talked about the business and the town, eventually even getting into their personal lives. Clemmon mentioned that he had a wife and daughter, and Shoaty, with a glazed look in his eyes, just stared off into space and mentioned, "I like little girls; I wish I had a daughter."

The prosecutor made him repeat that statement, "I like little girls; I wish I had a daughter," a number of times. Clemmon remembered the statement distinctly because he felt sorry for Shoaty not having a good home. He believed that Shoaty was sincere when he made the statement because he next asked how long he could be expected to work at the lot. Clemmon said that if he worked hard and was reliable, he could probably have the job all summer as long as sales kept up the way they were going.

Shoaty mentioned that that was good; that if he kept at it maybe he could even find a place to stay, a place to rent. When Clemmon asked where he lived, he replied, "Oh, around; sometimes at the mission, but most of the time just around, you know, here and there."

That was it, at least that was all the paper reported. Dis leaned back and thought. "A mechanic, but even more than that, a guy managing a business. This was the guy who accosted me in the parking lot in Washington D.C.? That homeless bum had been a rising small town business manager – with a wife and daughter."

Dis stopped. It hit him. The picture he had was indeed right. It was a wife and daughter with Clemmon in the picture. Were they still in Owaceta? Were they the ones who had the gray man on his tail?

A wife and daughter! A daughter! He thought of Lorn's Chrissy. But then his mind went back to Ruth and her refusal to have kids. Now he, or his alter ego at least, had a daughter. It just flashed into his mind, not making any sense, but it gave him a momentary sense of satisfaction – and a sense, now more than ever, that he had to confront this – had to find out what it was really all about.

Why should a responsible and seemingly successful man, a man basically running a business by himself, a man with a stable home life, with a wife and a child; why should he, a year and a half later, be a raging stumble bum flashing a knife and demanding money in a parking lot?

It was too much for Dis. He got up and walked around the library's reading room. The helpful librarian noticed and asked if there was something wrong. He stared at the woman's attractive face and couldn't think of a reply. All he could do was stammer, "It's OK. It's OK. No problem."

Eventually he found himself in one of the bays of the library's reading room, looking out a window into the sunny street, now filling up with BABI bicyclers, both riding and walking. He stared at them abstractly, hardly seeing them, trying to piece together the mystery that was Rob Clemmon. When he saw a rider wearing an immense Styrofoam ten-gallon hat, the brim curled up and at least three feet long, he came back to reality and returned to the microfilm machine.

When he went back to the trial, another shock hit. The headline on the trial's third day read, "Autopsy Report: Star's Arms Broken Before Death." When the coroner testified to this on the witness stand, the Triumph reported, "An uproar took place among the spectators which caused Judge Connor to solemnly warn the gallery that it would be cleared if they didn't cease." Much of the paper's coverage concerned the outrage upon outrage expressed by the spectators and the court professionals when they heard the startling revelations. The paper even intimated that there had been persistent rumors about the heinous nature of the crime and "that now the rumors had proven to be true."

Intensely interested, Dis read about the trial, but Rob Clemmon's name never appeared again in the accounts. Only his remembrance of Barry Shoaty's words, "I like little girls" reappeared. The prosecutor repeated it, according to the alert Triumph reporter, a total of seven times during his summation at the end of the trial.

It must have been effective – only one hour and fifteen minutes after the jury convened, it marched back into the courtroom with a verdict – guilty. Possibly those four words were what put Barry Shoaty in prison for the rest of his life.

Dis had had enough of the microfilm machine – and of the trial. He flipped the rewind switch and as the film rapidly spooled onto its plastic core the realization hit him – somehow he was connected to this crime. Rob Clemmon was more than just a witness to a chance phrase uttered two years ago. He was involved – either innocently or otherwise – but he was involved. He had the prism of glass with the name Star etched on it. What is it? Where and why did he have it? And why did he give it to me?

Dis took the film back to the librarian and thanked her. "I didn't find exactly what I wanted, but I found enough to really help out." As he was speaking, he remembered something from his days with Ruth. She had spent days with city directories, searching their biographic and geographic data for possible real estate purchasers. He knew that these books listed every homeowner and renter who lived in a town during a particular year. He asked the librarian if they had them for Owaceta. She smiled and led him to a room off the reading room, where after a quick search they found the volumes devoted to Owaceta.

Dis started with the one for three year's back. There listed under the C's was the entry: Clemmon Rob T & Mary K; mech I-Deal Auto Sales h832 Willow St (Ow)

So what the trial account said was apparently true. Clemmon was a mechanic for I-Deal, married to Mary Clemmon, and he owned a home on Willow Street.

The next year's listing was identical. But the present year's was changed. It now read: Clemmon Mary K; wait Glen's Swich Shop h832 Willow St (Ow)

So sometime during the last year Rob left. Dis knew that; he had met him – unfortunately – in Washington D.C. When he left, he evidently left his wife and child (if the trial account was accurate – the directory did not list children), who were still living at the family home. Clemmon's wife was now a waitress at a sandwich shop. Dis looked up the address of the shop and wrote it down, 436 Front Street.

He then – after thanking the librarian and getting a lovely smile in return – went out into the heat. Cedar City was steaming. It was a late-in-the-afternoon sauna box, a mid-summer Iowa staying of the hand of nature. Nothing moved – especially moisture, which hung in the air daring to be disturbed by activity. Riders coming in after a long afternoon fighting the supersaturated air looked defeated; their clothing drenched, their hair, when they took off their helmets, matted and limp; their expressions pained and gasping. As they limped down the street, giving only desultory jerks to their pedals, they looked for all the world like survivors, not of war, but of siege, weary empty-eyed waifs looking for nothing more than a place to rest and a chance to stop the incessant need to keep cranking the bicycle.

Dis, with the knowledge that he was so close to Owaceta and the mysteries that he knew were within it, was strangely buoyant as he walked down the hot and sticky street. He decided to leave his bicycle where it was, locked at the library, in plain view but mixed in with about four others. Juggling the names Star, Barry, Rob, and Mary in his mind, he would just take a walk down to the town square, gray man be damned. In a strange way he was looking forward to tomorrow, looking forward to the chance to confront the soul of his alter ego for these many months.

But now, before he became too hot and uncomfortable, he wanted to experience some of the fun of BABI – and he was very hungry. He knew from the brochures he had picked up that the square was "the place" in Cedar City. It was here that the nightly dance would be held and also where most of the special eating spots would be set up. Community groups, however, would be offering meals at selected sites off the square in church basements, community halls, and public buildings.

The library was only a block and a half from the square and Dis covered the distance quickly, walking briskly down a tree-covered sidewalk that met the square. A grassy park, studded with benches, statues, trees, flower beds, and intertwining paths held center attention; it was a square that was truly a square – a square block park surrounded by four streets, lined on the non-park sides by stores and other commercial buildings. Classic small town Iowa.

On this day because of BABI the four streets were closed to traffic, the parking spaces cleared of cars, and booths set up on the street. Vendors were selling everything from corn dogs to ice cream sandwiches to mugs of root beer. Also a number of bicycling companies had booths filled with Lycra shorts, clipless pedals, gloves, water bottles, and all of the paraphernalia of biking.

Of special interest were the sellers of T-shirts and jerseys. BABI really had no official items of clothing. None were given with registration, although the sponsoring health company did have a T-shirt for sale. However, private enterprise filled the gap very well. Many booths sold nothing but shirts or jerseys – in a myriad of styles, colors, and inscriptions. Neon and tie-dye, almost obscene and sanctimonious, humorous and stodgy, sexy and innocent, cute and blatantly propagandistic, the T-shirts were ubiquitous, eye-catching, and a real tradition. Most of them, somewhere, front or back, had the map of the year's ride printed as part of the design, so the shape of Iowa was omnipresent. Seemingly everyone on the ride bought at least one of these T-shirts, many buying two or three, and one of the jerseys.

In the evening after everyone had set up camp, rested, and cleaned up, riders invariably put on one of these BABI T-shirts, either from the present year or one in the past, and strolled through the town to find food and entertainment. The streets of the towns became moving images of Iowa, so many maps adorning backs and chests.

Mixed in with the BABI T-shirts, of course, were the T-shirts that riders brought from their local areas or from rides that they had ridden in the past. Proud riders selected shirts or jerseys from their most difficult rides, or rides with cute names, to take with them on BABI. Every "Ride the Rockies" rider was sure to be seen at least one day on BABI with the ride's jersey proudly stretched over its owner's chest. And those who had done the "Knight-time in Flour" ride in the Kansas wheat fields couldn't resist showing off their shirts, which resembled flour sacks.

Dis was almost tempted to buy one of the BABI T-shirts. But since he hadn't done the complete ride – and he wasn't an official rider – he thought better of it. Still, he was intrigued by the variety and pizazz of the shirts and their sellers. Good old American enterprise was alive and well in Iowa.

And so was food-making.

Dis's stomach was sending messages, but almost too strong to interest him in the fast-food booths of the square. He wanted something more substantial and also with more variety than the standard ethnic threesome of Italian-Mexican-Chinese. While passing a booth where a short Asian woman was loading beef cubes, green peppers, and small whole onions onto skewers, Dis noted a hand-made sign tacked to a tree. It was a simple, but effective sign. Cutouts from magazines of at least 25 different entrees were pasted around the outside of the pasteboard. In the middle, written with a black marker, was the simple phrase: "Eat and Eat." At the bottom, neat writing proclaimed, "$7.75 – Community Methodist Church, 213 Harvard Street (two blocks from the square), 4:00 to 9:00 p.m.

Dis's stomach warmed just at the thought of it. He immediately backtracked, because the street that he had come down, the one with the library, was Harvard Street. As he walked back up the street, checking by reflex for the gray man, he hoped the meal he was heading for would be better than the one he had last night. He had had his fill of filling spaghetti.

A half block from the library the Methodist Church peeked from green foliage shimmering in the heat. Dis followed a sidewalk around the closed front entrance to a church hall directly behind and attached to the classic, towered church. The hall was a nondescript, modernistic box of a building, thankfully hidden away from the street. A short line of T-shirted, tanned-faced people stood waiting to get in. Dis joined it.

He asked the couple in front of him, "What's the word? Is this a good place to eat?"

The man, a short, chunky fellow with a full mustache and a tiny, wispy dark beard replied, "It's Methodist, isn't it? That's enough for me."

"Pretty good, eh?"

The man's companion, a slight, weary-eyed woman wearing a "Tour the Tots" T-shirt, said: "If there's one thing we've learned on BABI, it's this: 'Go with the Methodists.'"

"Oh, is that right? You mean I've been missing out?"

"Hey," the man popped up, "These ladies are incredible. They'll have food all over this hall, and every dish is different."

The woman broke in, "And every one delicious . . . well, almost every one."

Her companion interrupted her in turn, "It's like this, we're Jewish, but since we've been on this BABI, we're thinking of becoming Methodist, OK?"

Dis put a mock serious look on his face, "Really? That good. But what are you going to do about the initiation?"

"What's that?"

"You know, the Methodist initiation. The ham and pork chops."

That broke the couple up. The man through his laughter said, "The pork chops we can live with, it's the ham hocks we have trouble with."

"Yeah," the woman said, "did you ever try to put a ham hock on a bagel?"

They had to stop the joking because the line moved, the couple paid their money, and disappeared into the air conditioned hall. Dis, being a single, didn't have to wait long. He was directed to the back of the large hall where a series of tables were waiting, all loaded with homemade food. He picked up a foam-plastic plate and realized the truth of what the couple, who were half way through the first table, had joked about. It was indeed a cornucopia of down-home food.

The first two table were just salads – salads upon salads. The salad dishes were squeezed together so tightly that there literally was no open space on either of the long twelve foot tables, except around the enormous glass bowl full of cut-up lettuce at the beginning of the table. After the obligatory dressings (heavy on the French, Ranch, and Thousand Island, after all this was Iowa), which included Italian and Blue Cheese, choices proliferated. Carrot, beet, broccoli, cucumber, celery, zucchini, egg plant, onion, almost every vegetable imaginable, even some imported to Iowa, like Chinese cabbage, was present in a multiplicity of salad forms. Many involved pasta, and the permutations of vegetables and pasta were almost astronomic. Dis wondered where these women living in a small Iowa town could even buy some of the fancy pasta shapes. They probably had to go to Des Moines or Davenport to get the pasta shaped like little bow-ties, for example. And why? Did the shape really add that much to the flavor of the dish?

But, nevertheless, pasta salads were only the beginning. Many of the salads involved Jello. The combination of vegetables, fruit, mayonnaise and Jello was evidently irresistible to heartland cooks – or their Jello salads were such a legacy from the past that something almost genetic pushed them to produce the quivering masterpieces. Dis, surveying the second table which was almost completely covered with Jello dishes, wondered how many yellowing magazine recipe clippings with illustrations of Dinah Shore-like housewives had been brought out for this event. Probably none – these recipes were memorized, maybe not even that: they were learned second nature in the process of growing up female in this culinary repository of the basic, the bland, and the bountiful.

Dis looked around and saw three other tables loaded with more substantial food – along with another table where four ladies were fastidiously serving portions of the main dinner entrees: ham, chicken, or beef. He decided to eat salad now and return later for the other foods. So he filled his plate with a mass of raw lettuce liberally coated with both French and blue cheese dressings, a sampling of the pasta combinations, more of the seafood salads, and heavy on the pure vegetable mixes. He liked green peppers and onions mixed with a tangy dressing, for instance. Mushrooms and scallions in vinegar intrigued him, as did sweet-and-sour beets and potatoes, and green beans and artichokes. Soon he had a mass of liquids and solids piled on his plate, becoming indistinguishable as they ran together on the smooth plastic surface.

But Dis didn't care, as he sat down in the one open space in a long table filled with people wearing bizarre bicycling clothing. He was roaringly hungry, almost rudely so. With hardly a hello to those around him, he spooned into the salads like a reformed sinner into a catechism. Only after eating most of the food on the plate did he realize that he didn't have a napkin or anything to drink. He would get them later. But now that he had pumped some fill into his central cavity, he stretched a bit, relaxed, and looked around – while he continued to munch on the acidic wonders spread across his plate.

If there was one common denominator of his table mates it was that their faces looked healthy. It was obvious they had been out in the sun. In fact many had strange markings on their faces due to the vagaries of their use of sunscreens, helmets, hats, covering cloths, and occasionally stencils. One young pre-teen had a skull and crossbones outlined on his cheek by the sun, and another, his seat mate, had multicolored suntan stick warpaint still blazing from his brow.

The riders' faces were healthy looking, but their bodies, under the flashy Lycra stretchings, were another story. Maybe it was the clothing that molded itself to the flesh, but many of the eaters looked more like limpid pools rather than rushing streams. Truthfully, a greater proportion of the bodies in the room were healthier than the general population, but they didn't appear to be. Every bulge was visible; every not-so-straight line, bowed; every superannuated curve, too flaccid; even those lean and trim seemed to have handles and creases and gussets of knobby protuberances.

But they were happy in their fashions of the day. The Methodist ladies scurrying around the tables with damp washcloths and plastic baskets for dirty dishes were as a group much more lumpy and fleshy and out-of-shape than the bikers, but they were the only ones in the group who looked normal. Ironically, they – who couldn't run a block without gasping, or ride a bike for a mile on a bright spring day – appeared to be more healthy than the cycling enthusiasts who had just ridden about 75 miles in blast furnace weather. But, of course, the ladies in their flowered prints and starched aprons were just as much in uniform as the spandex-clad BABIers.

To each his own, Dis thought, as he started small talk with the people eating around him, and finished the salads on his plate. They talked of heat, humidity, showers and food until Dis pushed away from the table with his plate to explore the glories of the other dish covered tables.

He found casseroles unending. Pyrex dishes, each resting on a hot pad, crowded the three tables, almost every dish intriguing, sometimes visually and sometimes because of a spicy aroma. Potatoes and cheese and, again, pasta were used liberally – along with the ubiquitous hamburger – but that was only the beginning. The wealth of imaginative dishes would have strained a cookbook writer's belief. There were dishes steaming with pickled onions and ravioli; cabbage, corned beef and Swiss cheese; corn flakes, tuna, and spaghetti sauce; even one which featured pork sausage rolled in bacon atop a spread of Chinese chow mien noodles and pineapple.

Along with these one dish casserole combinations of sometimes dissimilar food were the staples: huge metal pans, four of them, mounded with potato salads; baked potatoes heaped next to a cooling plate of pure butter; a mountain of mashed potatoes with complimentary tarns of hot gravy; pans simmering with loads of green beans, corn, and peas; fried potatoes spiced with savory browned onions; loafs of homemade bread, both white and dark; crusty brown dinner rolls, mushrooming over their cylindrical bases; bowls of red, meat-filled spaghetti and creamy macaroni and cheese; pans of spicy lasagna topped with crusted cheese; and bread stuffing smelling of chicken and allspice. All these, and more, were overloading the tables, but constantly being replenished by the brisk Methodist women.

The last dinner table was presided over by four of the ladies, three middle-aged and one lissome woman in her mid-twenties. They were serving portions of the main meat entrees, freshly drawn from the ovens in the hall's kitchen. The other food was brought straight from home ovens and stoves. One lady with bifocals tied tightly to her head cut thick slices of ham on demand. Another carved a large turkey; eaters had their choice of any cut desired – breast, thigh, leg, whatever they wanted. Beef, a large roast slow cooked for hours, was cut by the slim younger lady, who even cut off portions of fat if requested. But this was pork country, and the Methodist ladies were anything but disloyal: a stunning pork roast crowned by crinkly browned fat, lightly laced with cascading juices, and succulent with steaming, almost pure, white meat was carved by the presiding mistress of the feast. A visit to this table alone was worth the price of admission; indeed, to big city folks, two or three times the price.

Dis filled his plate again with casserole selections, vegetables, and potatoes and then had the pork mistress place a fresh slice of pure roast pork on top of his mashed potatoes, the only place available. He was still hungry, but this time he didn't forget to stop at an auxiliary table for napkins and a tall glass of iced tea.

He took his time eating now, enjoying the variegated tastes and textures of the food, much of which he hadn't tasted for a long time, although somewhere and at sometime in his past he had sampled them all. These dished were cooked with care and tenderness in small kitchens, that was obvious; no commercial buffet, stamped by canned food and steam tables, here. This was come-in-from-a-day-in-the-fields kind of cooking, and Dis savored – now that he had slaked his initial gluttony – its openness and wholesomeness.

He put his problems and his impending tomorrow to the back of his head and sat back with knife and fork in hand, eating and listened to his meal mates and noticing their idiosyncrasies. Words buzzed through the air around him:

"We're taking a break next week, but the week after we're goin' across Colorado."

"Boy, my butt aches. It's getting worse instead of better. Do you think a massager could do anything about it?"

"I haven't had turkey this good since last year at Charles's on the lake shore, you remember, two weeks before Christmas."

"I shouldn't have had those two beers back in Jesmond; they almost bonked me."

"Did you see that triple tandem with one guy and two babes? And the babes in string tops. God!"

"Yea, tomorrow won't be bad, only 65 miles, but if this heat keeps up. Hey, anyone heard the weather?"

"I gotta have some more water; anybody else want some? Oh, here's the water lady. God, I need this, that sun percolated my body all day long."

"I don't know what I'm eating. When I took it, it looked good – and it tastes good, but I don't have the slightest idea what it is."

"I am going to sleep. You don't know how much I am going to sleep."

"Hey, guess what, I went over 3000 on my computer today."

"Well, George, do you want to go back for more? I might have a little bit more of that cucumber-onion salad; it is so good."

"Guess what, ol' buddy, after you went through three heaping plates of food, guess what is in the back? Dessert. That's right, three tables full of them."

Dis, who was just finishing the last bite of his slice of pork roast and one forkful of green beans and fried onions and who was thinking about one more trip to the casserole tables, looked up; in fact he stood up. The speaker was right; three tables of cakes, pies, puddings, Jellos, cookies, crumbles, fruit, and he couldn't tell what else were positioned across the back of the hall. Dis sat down and pondered; homemade desserts versus some more baked lasagna, fruit salad, and maybe a slice of that baked ham. What a dilemma!

He settled it by going back to the main tables and loading up his plate with samples of much more than he knew he could comfortably eat. Dessert would take care of itself, he told himself.

And it did. But it was almost painful. He realized he shouldn't have been so piggish when he stepped in front of the dessert tables. None of the commercial, hydrogenated, long shelf life cakes and pie crusts here. These desserts were just out of the oven that afternoon, most made with simple ingredients and either fresh fruit or fruit canned or frozen from last fall's harvest.

Dis took a single slice of cherry pie from a whey-eyed lady in a red smock who said, "I hope you like it. I picked the cherries myself. We've got three trees and last year we had a bumper crop. Canned 45 quarts. That's right."

The cherry pie was delicious, but it almost broke the dam. Dis almost couldn't make it. He had to force himself and it wasn't enjoyable. Why, or why, did he do things like this to himself? But he took his time and with the help of a little iced tea and some friendly but innocuous talk with the people around him, he finally did finish the pie – and every bit of its crumbly crust.

When he left, he went out of his way to say a soft thank you to both the pork carver, who seemed to be the one woman most in charge, and the cherry pie maker. The dessert lady's response was, "It was good, huh? I'm glad, but it's just what we have all the time." Dis left through a separate entrance, but he still had to push through a long line of people waiting to get in. Another characteristic of BABI is that food news travels fast – and good food news even faster.

It was still early, not even 7 o'clock. The heat was easing, and the afternoon's humid atmosphere, with its soggy jersey almost thoroughly soaked, was changing into a breezy evening T-shirt, one billowing the mellow statement:"At Last - Relief!" Dis walked to the library, saw that his bike was the only one still there, and so unchained it and walked it through the straggling bunches and occasional large groups of people – most riders, but some townspeople coming down to the square to see the party. When he came to the square, which was already lively with people, Dis decided to at least walk through it and join, if at least momentarily, this BABI rite: the evening party in the overnight town.

He locked his bike in a side alley that was already almost filled with many similarly locked bikes, many more expensive that his, he rightly noted. Two college-aged guys had established themselves at the head of the alley, sitting against the brick wall of the building with a pitcher of beer and a large pepperoni pizza. They didn't have glasses, but were drinking the beer directly from the pitcher and not being too neat about it.

Dis moved out of the alley into the stream of people who in time-honored tradition were copying traffic patterns by walking around the square in two directions – forward on the right and the opposite on the left. The crowd wasn't like the lively carnival crowds that Dis had gotten used to with the Ferris Wheel; it was still too early, too hot, and these people were still too tired – they had ridden far in hot and humid weather and thus were somewhat subdued. Also this was the second last night of BABI and town square parties were becoming somewhat passé to them. But still the lure drew them. They at least, like Dis, had to walk the square and see what was going on.

One of the four streets of the square was snow fenced off, except for a narrow passageway on the sidewalk next to the stores. Within the fencing a rock band was warming up on a flatbed truck stage. Beer trailers were located strategically within the fencing, and two entrances with uniformed officers controlled the underage-drinking problem. This was the party site.

Dis was looking over the fence, wondering if he should go in, when he saw the gray man.

Chapter 23

Sweating, his T-shirt soaked in a V in the front and in a broad rectangle across his shoulders, Dis pulled into Cambridge Mills. It was about 10 a.m. on another hot and humid day, and Dis, about two-thirds of the way through his last ride before Owaceta, was tired. He had just completed about 45 miles of almost nonstop biking, stopping only once for cinnamon rolls and a quick cup of coffee – and a refill of his two water bottles.

Now he was hungry. The street was lined with card table stops attended by teens and kids, for the most part, and supervised by the resident housewives. But Dis knew that closer to town, probably in the business district, various community groups would be offering a more varied selection of food – and he needed a lunch. For a moment he thought about the enormous meal he had consumed the night before, and wondered how he could be so hungry now. But he nevertheless was very hungry – and he had to consider that 45 miles of gear pounding does, indeed, create a vacuum that demands to be filled.

He was right about Main Street. Three stands, especially constructed just for this day, were spaced along the two-block long street, with many small tables and storefront openings filling the space in-between. Cambridge Mills was one long concession stand. Dis rode through the still lightly trafficked street – again he was one of the earliest riders – until he came to the last stand. A large banner over it proclaimed, "Have lunch with the Eagles. We're friendly folks."

Right then Dis didn't care about friendliness, but he was hungry and the word "lunch" caught his eye. He leaned his bicycle – loaded with every single one of his possessions, except some of his money and a few other items which he kept on his person – against the boarded-up front of an abandoned store and walked stiffly over to the stand.

It was offering sandwiches – sloppy Joes, hamburgers, bratwursts, cold ham and cheese, and tuna and olives. Dis knew that Midwestern sloppy Joes were invariably bland and runny and he wasn't up to fried beef or pork just yet. The cold sandwiches, however, appealed to him. He ordered two of them, a ham and cheese and a tuna. He also bought a tall paper cup of ice cube-laden lemonade. The sandwiches, although made with bland commercial white flour buns, both had generous fillings. The tuna was especially good – cool large chunks of tuna, some celery, and tangy olive halves, held together by a non-cloying mayonnaise, and topped by a healthy leaf of iceberg lettuce – so good that Dis bought another one.

While he was eating – sitting down next to his bike, resting his back on a storefront – he surveyed the passing riders and anxious townspeople and reviewed his plans for the day ahead. During the morning ride he had examined three possibilities and settled on his plan of action. First of all, he wouldn't go to the police. If the law wanted Clemmon for anything, that was that; he, Dis, would be immediately detained, perhaps arrested. If he wasn't wanted, they probably wouldn't have time for him today, the day when BABI was coming to town. He also wouldn't try to contact the parents of the murdered girl, the Oatages. They might know something, might be aware of what happened to one of the witnesses at their daughter's trial; but somehow from reading about them in the papers, Dis had the impression that they wouldn't be very helpful, that they would be closed-lipped and drawn inward. He did, however, want to give them the lens that the dying Rob had given him. Perhaps that could wait. We wanted to find out as much as he could before approaching them.

That left Rob's wife. He knew that she still lived in Owaceta and that she was working as a waitress there. She would know, obviously, that he wasn't Rob, and she would know as much as anybody about the circumstances surrounding Rob's disappearance and why the gray man was following him. She might even know who the gray man is.

The downside, however, in talking to her was that to be completely honest he would have to explain his connection to Rob, would have to tell her about the pitiful bum Rob appeared to be in the bar in Washington, and about the horrible encounter in the parking lot. What would she say or do when she found out that he, Dis, was the killer of her husband?

Should he tell her the truth or should he just see if she could answer his most important questions? If he did open up to her, he would have to give up the false identity that he had used to evade Ruth and the whole pre-life that he was determined to avoid forever. He would have to give up the two IDs that he had used these last six months.

Thinking of the IDs and Rob's wife, Dis almost abstractly took out his wallet again and searched in one of the leather pockets for the family picture that he had taken from the dying Rob. The color snapshot, slightly out of focus, still startled Dis even though he had looked at it a thousand times, if not more. The man with his arm around the woman in the picture was he, Dis. The uncanny resemblance was still unsettling to Dis.

But now he studied the image of the woman. She was of average height, average build, with a distinctively narrow face – pretty, with high cheek bones, a prominent chin, and a mouth set in an almost taunting slant. Her hair, cut short and curly, added to her breezy impression – that and the cigarette that she held in two fingers in her cupped hand at her side. Her other hand held the hand of the little girl, whom Dis took to be their daughter, a girl who Dis could see had the potential to be not only pretty, but beautiful, combining the best features of the man and woman. In the picture, though, with a gaping hole in her line of front teeth, a mass of unruly hair, and a large Band-Aid on her knee, she looked just like she probably was – a feisty little girl, playing, fighting, and questioning with the best of them.

If and when he met them – or at least the woman – named Mary, Dis had to think to remember it – maybe he could evade the absolute truth about what happened to her husband and still find what he was looking for. Perhaps he could use the striking physical similarity between Rob and him as an opening for questions. He could tell her he was tired of being dogged by a creepy man who insisted that he was someone named Rob Clemmon from Owaceta, Iowa.

Thinking about the gray man brought back last night and Dis's brush with him. The son-of-a-bitch was inside the fenced-in party area. When Dis, standing on the outside surveyed the space, there the old glue-mule was, about thirty yards away as clear and as distinctive as Dis remembered him from the convenience store back in Jeffrey, Kentucky. Dis slowly walked away along the fence until he was behind three women who were talking together while eating ice cream sundaes from paper containers and looking at the party grounds. Dis stopped behind them and, using them as a shield, looked back at the gray man.

The man wasn't alone. In his blue jacket and nondescript wash pants, he was standing with a group of obvious riders, dressed in shorts and bicycling T-shirts. He seemed to be trying to make some conversation but didn't seem to be having much luck, the group more interested in themselves and the warming up band than this older non-rider. But just then the gray man said something, and the entire group turned to look at him. Then they all smiled and one even reached over and shoved him in a laughing manner.

Then Dis saw another obvious outsider entering the group. A large man, handsome in a pinkish manner, and wearing a plaid sports shirt and tight jeans with low cut boots, came up and said something to the gray man, while nodding and smiling at the other group members, the riders. They were more receptive to him, responding, and one of them even shaking his hand. When he smiled, however, his face became twisted, screwed awry, effectively taking away his previous handsome appearance. With one good look at the man, Dis's mind went back to his days as a shoe salesman: he wouldn't trust this man alone in his shoe department.

And then – there she was.

The woman in the picture appeared from behind the bandstand. Her hairstyle was changed and obviously her clothes were different, but she was the woman – Rob's wife, Mary. Mary Clemmon.

She walked up to the group, causing its animation to immediately stop. In an instant the smiles and the friendly touching and pushing were replaced by silence and reserve. It looked to Dis like one of those unfortunate social situations where two antagonistic people, such as a wife and a mistress, accidentally end up causing undue strain on a group of mutual acquaintances.

One of the three women sundae eaters glanced Dis's way, so he had to move, not wanting to appear as a gawker or some kind of masher. He strolled back away from the fence until he came to an old-fashioned popcorn machine that was drawing, with its pervasive aroma, a fairly large crowd of buyers. He blended into the crowd, then turned back to observe the group within the fence again.

It was as if nothing had changed. The riders were, even at this distance, ill at ease – and not laughing. The gray man was talking, with a thin grin slicing through his mouth, and Mary, Mary Clemmon, now had her arm linked through the large man's arm, even though she was staring straight ahead, hardly looking at the riders in the group.

While Dis watched, the woman tugged at the man's arm and almost pulled him away from the gray man and the riders. The large man didn't appear to want to go and he resisted. When she persisted, he grabbed her hand, which was gripping his arm and wrenched it away, pushing it and her from him. He turned back to the riders while she remained away from the group, rubbing her hand as if it were in pain.

Then while the large man got involved in an animated conversation with the riders, she almost defiantly pulled a cigarette from a pack in her front blouse pocket and lit it. With a puff of smoke in the group's direction she turned away from them, looking across the party area, straight in the direction where Dis was standing. Dis, under a strange whim, was tempted to walk out in front of the popcorn machine and wave to her, but he resisted the temptation. If fact, he turned away, realizing that his image, at that distance, could certainly appear to her to be her absent husband.

Dis, who had halfway wanted to enter the party area and have a beer or two, decided to change that plan. He would wait until tomorrow for a confrontation. He didn't want to have to face the gray man and Mary at the same time. And who was the man she appeared to be with? The man who pulled her hand away so painfully?

So he left the square without looking back at the group. In the alley where his bike was now jammed close to a phalanx of other bikes he heard the band start up, its massive speakers blasting "Born in the USA" through the square, the alley, and probably, Dis thought, into half the homes in Cedar City. He rode his bike carefully – the number of people and bikes on the main street leading to the camping area was almost enough to demand traffic cops. But he successfully found his tent and was asleep by the time the last pastels of dark mauve became just plain dark.

He wasn't awake when in the cloudless night sky, pinpointed with the brilliance of the summer stars, a new white light started brightening the eastern sky. He was fitfully turning on top of his sleeping bag when that light crystallized into a solid luminescence shining through the trees on the horizon. And when he finally succumbed to deep sleep, he didn't notice the almost full moon illuminating not only the finally quiet camping area, but also the entire Cedar City, the surrounding farms and villages, and sixty-five miles northeast, the city of Owaceta.

Now with his stomach OK again and the last inch of lemonade swirling in the paper cup, Dis replaced the picture in his wallet and got set for the last 20 miles before Owaceta. He stopped at one of the Kybos behind the food stand and then was off, feeling his legs strain as he punched himself up to speed, but enjoying the slight pain, working into it.

He tried to ride at a steady 16 -17 mile-per-hour clip, not counting the many slowdowns for hills, crowds of bikers, and intersections. He passed through three other BABI small towns and innumerable farm home food stands without stopping. He passed two BABI institutions during this last stage. One was Tom's Turkey, a large-scale food tent which offered barbecued roast turkey sandwiches slathered with a sweet-spicy sauce, and whole turkey legs, their skin caked with the same cooked-on sauce. And the other was Iowa Pork Chops, another big commercial operation which featured very generous two-inch-thick pork chops cooked right next to the road on a massive rolling grill fired by corn cobs. The BABI riders loved to eat!

He also passed many homemade sign series, another one of the distinctive features of BABI. The old Burma Shave sign idea was used by almost every food stop along the way, so extensively that for most riders by the last half of the ride, the signs became almost a turn-off rather than a come-on. "The pop is cold" – "The candy sweet" – "So stop just ahead" – "And rest your feet" – "Cub Pack 36." But one of these series, about five miles out, featured Glen's Sandwich Shop in Downtown Owaceta and Dis almost stopped when he read it. She worked there. Would she be working today? Probably. Almost positively – on what could be the busiest day in the entire history of the shop.

He arrived in Owaceta, again one of the earlier bikers to finish the day's route, in late morning and tried to follow the signs to the campgrounds, but could make no sense out of them. They seemed to be going in conflicting and opposite directions. Finally, riding the main street into the downtown, he stopped and found an informational flier put out by the city in connection with the BABI staff. Owaceta had no large, self-contained camping space. Campers were to be located all over town – at schools, community buildings which offered bathrooms and showers, and at the town's two parks, one of which had a swimming pool with a shower facility.

Dis studied the flier, especially the map which occupied a two page spread in its middle. He searched for and located Willow Street, a side street leading away to the south from the inevitable Main Street. He counted eight blocks down Willow and placed his finger on the probable location of Mary Clemmon's home. Three blocks away from it was a school, marked with yellow on the map, that was to be one of the camping locations. Another one was five blocks away in the opposite direction. Dis decided to try that one, the Cooper Elementary School, rather than the obvious close choice.

Soon he was putting up his tent in an almost deserted plot of grass behind the school's combination parking lot and playground. A Ryder truck from the Marshalltown Bicycle Club had claimed prime turf in front of the school, but here and there around the school's perimeter isolated tents were visible, sometimes with an occasional bicyclist puttering around or just sitting or lying in front. With his tent erect, Dis found his toilet kit, his beige shorts, a T-shirt, fresh socks, his walking shoes, and his towel, and went looking for the shower, if the school had one. It did. It even had a small, but serviceable gym, which, the janitor explained to Dis, he could sleep in if a storm came up, although that, he confirmed, was not very likely tonight – the forecast saying dire things about tomorrow, not tonight.

Dis was showered and shaved by noon and a few minutes later was riding his bicycle past Mary Clemmon's home, 832 Willow Street. No car was parked near the house, but since the door to the attached garage was closed, he couldn't tell if anyone was there or not. With a deep breath, he pulled up to a small concrete front steps and porch, leaned his bike against a not too solid wooden railing, walked up the three steps and knocked on the door before finding the doorbell. No one was home, just as he suspected.

With resolve, he climbed back on his bike and headed north – for Main Street and the downtown, where according to the BABI sign, Glen's Sandwich Shop was located.

At that moment on the outskirts of Owaceta to the south, on highway 32, away from the now building bicycle traffic coming in from the west, a blue Pontiac pulled into the Hi-Way Plaza's parking lot and came to a stop. The woman driver looked around at the combination café-convenience store and filling station, noted that the parking lot was halfway filled and that two of the cars were state police vehicles, and then emerged from her car.

The woman was Gloria.

Chapter 24

Gloria had just driven straight from the carnival site in Illinois and she needed a sandwich, some coffee – maybe even a piece of pie. But most importantly she needed information. As she had been mulling while she was driving, she needed to find out the real name of the man she knew as Gary. She figured two ways to do that. He had worked for I-Deal Motors; she was sure that was the name of the place. If she could find a phone book with a map, she could locate it and drive to it. Probably someone there would know about and still remember the trial witness and perhaps have more information about what happened to him. And maybe, just on an off chance, the trial witness would still be there. Perhaps the man who looked so much like her Gary had never left – but no, that didn't make much sense. Why was the cop creeping around the carnival, showing a picture of the man, and seeking information about him? Whatever, her first plan was to check out the auto place.

If that didn't pan out, she could still go to either the library or the newspaper office and from the accounts of the trial find out the witness's name and then find out if his wife was still in town. By talking to the wife, she could probably find out something about what was going on. She'd have to be wary. After all, what if Gary really was the witness and his wife had someone tailing him to bring him back to her? How would his wife react to her, Gloria's concern? What if she put two and two together and realized that this stranger was romantically interested in her lost husband, that during the last week or so she, Gloria, had fallen so for him that if it hadn't been for a faulty relay, she'd still have him in her arms, her legs wrapped around him on the floor of the Spook House?

To counter just that, she'd made up a story that she could use with the wife to explain why she drove up here. Gloria's friends, Rosie and Carl, who ran a Ferris Wheel, had a hired man who left a couple of days ago when a plainclothes cop appeared and showed the hired man's picture around. When that happened, she, Gloria, remembered that the hired hand looked very much like the man, the auto mechanic, who appeared at her brother's trial. She didn't think much of the whole thing, but then Rosie told her that the hired hand had left an envelope with her, all sealed up. The man wrote the word – here Gloria searched her mind and memory for some word the wife would possibly remember. She came up with "Star," the name of the little girl who was murdered. The man wrote that word on the outside of the envelope and said what was in it wasn't very valuable except to the right person. Rosie figured the right person was the man's wife. Rosie was bothered about keeping the envelope. She wanted to get rid of it. That's when Gloria volunteered to go to Owaceta with the envelope and see if it indeed was for the wife. Rosie couldn't come because she was ailing, but she, Gloria, could and, besides, she had been here before. It was a cock and bull story, but Gloria hoped it would give her some plausibility in finding out about Gary.

If either of these sources, the car dealer or the wife, didn't work out, she didn't know what she would do. Probably go to the police or maybe just talk to people – ordinary people in town, maybe in restaurants or in the park, or places like that. She was sure that many people had memories of the crime and the trial, and if she didn't bring up her brother, they might tell her what they knew.

But now she was hungry and thirsty. The cafe section of the HI-Way Plaza wasn't much – a long lunch counter with old fashioned, revolving, cylindrical stools and, opposite them, six booths seating four persons each easily, six squeezed. It was after lunchtime but still the place was moderately busy with all the booths occupied and only a few spaces at the counter available. As she entered, she noticed a public phone and she immediately stopped and looked up Automobiles in the business section of the battered phone book hanging by a homemade cord from the phone. There it was, I-Deal Motors, just as she remembered. She quickly took out a pen and an old list she had in her purse and wrote down the address and phone number of the place, which advertised, "I-deal, You-deal; Our-deal is I-deal."

Gloria sat down at one of the stools and looked for a menu. She would have preferred a McDonald's or Hardee's because she didn't want to waste any time, but she couldn't remember if Owaceta had one. She hoped the service at this place was reasonably fast, and she was happy that almost as soon as she picked up the menu from behind a napkin holder, a brisk counter woman appeared with a glass of water. Without even thinking about it much, Gloria ordered a chicken salad sandwich and a cup of coffee.

She looked around the cafe, gazing abstractly at the people lined up in front of the counter on the stools and even spinning a little bit to notice the booth patrons. She didn't recognize anyone, but she didn't expect to; she had spend only two days here during the trial and almost all of her time had been at the court house. She hadn't left her motel either evening.

The service was fast, with the coffee coming before she was finished with her random survey of the place. She heard, from the two men seating next to her on her right, a vague reference to "those gosh darn bicyclers" but didn't think anything of it until the word "BABI" floated through the cafe's clanking dishes and murmur of small talk. Then she thought of Gary. He was on a bike and she knew vaguely that BABI was some big bike ride through Iowa. Probably no connection.

Her coffee was steaming hot and she spilled a little of it at her first sip. When she reached for another napkin, she said to the man next to her, "Excuse me, but I heard you mention something about bicycles and BABI. What's going on?"

The middle aged man, who looked like a small business clerk or office worker, replied, "You heard right, lady. There's this BABI goin' on today and tonight here in town. Ten thousand crazy people on bikes will be stayin' here overnight."

His companion butted in with, "Yeah, and keepin' us awake all night with their dancing and loud music. Five years ago they were here and I didn't get any sleep at all, 'course I live almost downtown, only a half block away from it."

She was about to work around to asking about the trial, but just then the waitress appeared with her sandwich and as she was settling to eat it, the men turned back to their conversation, which she vaguely could hear was about D parts and the best way to ship them to Davenport.

The chicken salad was filling but bland, but she liked its cool texture in contrast to the hot coffee she occasionally sipped. The bill came with the sandwich, so as soon as she was finished, she left a tip, paid her bill at the cash register at the end of the counter, and then decided she had better use the washroom. It could be a long afternoon.

Leaving the cafe, she again passed the phone. It reminded her that she didn't know how to get to I-Deal Motors. She checked the phone book for its map, but it was ripped out; she could see the jagged line where it should have been. Well, maybe the waitress at the cash register could help her out. She took out the paper with the address and was walking back to the counter, when she noticed one of the two policemen in a booth – and recognized him.

One of the few people she had talked with when she was in Owaceta for her brother's trial was a state policeman on special detail providing security because of the emotional nature of the event. At first he was slightly suspicious of her, since she had identified herself as the sister of the defendant. But eventually when the policeman realized that she was harmless – and distraught over the way her brother was being judged circumstantially – they developed a wary, friendly relationship. It wasn't romance or anything like that, but they had talked during breaks in the trial in the lobby of the ancient, crumbling courthouse. Now here was the same policeman.

She stopped at the man's booth, which he was sharing with another policeman. They had finished eating and were sipping coffee. She caught his eye, smiled, and he smiled in return, but it was a polite smile, not a smile of recognition.

"Well, hi there," she said. "I know you don't remember me, but that's all right. Maybe you can help me out anyway."

The man, who had a strangely high-pitched voice in contrast to his healthily muscular build and, yes, his neatly starched state police uniform, said, "Well, Miss, I think you're right, I don't remember . . . wait a minute . . . a couple years ago, right here in Owaceta. I know . . . it was that gosh-darn Star trial. Well, sure I remember you . . . But you're not from here; what are you doing back?"

"That's what I wanted to ask you a question about."

The policeman interrupted here with, "Wait a minute. Fred, move over there a little and let this lady sit down for a spell. Fred, I want you to meet . . ."

"Gloria Shoaty."

"Sure, that's it – Gloria. Now I remember."

Fred made room for her with, "Hi, Gloria, I'm Fred Smathers with the Jackson County Sheriff's Patrol. You want something to drink, some coffee?"

"No thanks, I just had lunch here and was just leaving. Maybe both of you can help me out, though. I'm looking for one of the witnesses at that Star trial, the mechanic who hired my brother right before the mur . . . right before they found that little girl."

The first officer spoke up. "Gloria, and by the way my name is Sam, Sam Shapino, Gloria, you're still uptight about that trial, aren't you? I remember you back during it, when I was doing special security. We used to talk in the rotunda hallway, right?"

"Right. During breaks."

"It was your brother what was on trial . . . Barry, right? Barry Shoaty. He's over there in Fort Madison, right? You were convinced he was innocent, I remember. You know, I was half way with you on that, and I still am." He turned to his lunch mate. "You remember that case. They found this drunk – pardon me, Gloria, but even you admitted he had a drinking problem – real close to the victim's body with her blood on him and his fingerprints on her. But they didn't have any witnesses. It was all just circumstances."

Fred said, "Yeah, oh boy, do I remember that case. I was still working over in Styville then, doin' traffic on those south roads, but we used to read and discuss that case all day long. It was one of the biggest cases we ever had in this county."

While he held his coffee cup to his lips and slowly took a sip, the first officer, Sam, said, "I was with you, Gloria. Your brother looked too harmless to do what was done. That's strange for a cop to say, but he was one of the few that I truly believe looked innocent."

Gloria broke in. "Well, thank you for saying that. I appreciate it. These have been a terrible couple of years – for me and for my mother. But something came up, and I need some simple information. Number one, do you remember that mechanic who was a witness?"

Sam spoke up first. "Oh, yeah, the one who disappeared."

"So he did disappear?"

"Oh, you bet. Let's see, it must of been about a year ago. As I remember from the paper, his wife said he just never returned from work. Left his wife and kid just like that. And as far as I ever heard, no one's ever got a line on him."

The county policeman spoke up. "You're talking about a guy by the name of Clemmon, Rob Clemmon, right?"

Gloria and Sam almost spoke together, "Rob Clemmon, that's it."

"Well, we heard about that at the Sheriff's office. They found his car over in Davenport, but that's the last anyone ever heard of him. Why'd you want to find out about him? You run into him?" This county policeman had a stock of vivid red hair and a bad case of uneven front teeth.

Gloria did a quick shuffle in her head. Should she tell the truth or use the story she was preparing to use with the wife? She looked at Sam, remembered the compassion he had expressed for her brother during the trial, and knew she had to tell the truth. In fact, she was glad to.

"Either he or someone who looks very much like him. This guy, who called himself Gary, was working as a helper on the Ferris Wheel at this carnival down in Missouri. Ah, Fred, I'm a carnival operator – my mother and I run a Spook House."

Fred eyes widened imperceptibly as he looked at Sam, who smiled, "yes."

Gloria continued, "But the other day this older man shows up at the carnival gate in the morning asking questions and showing a picture of this Gary. Well the carnival people, you know, we stick together. And everyone liked Gary and the Ferris Wheel people, so the word was passed to protect Gary. We sent the man on a wild goose chase down to Kansas or Arkansas or somewhere, and Gary took off, probably for Iowa. On a bicycle, he took off. He didn't have a car or anything, and that's how he joined up with the Ferris Wheel people – on a bicycle. Said he was touring the country and needed to replenish his money."

Sam sipped more coffee and asked, "So what made you think this guy was – what's his name, Clemmon, Rob Clemmon?"

"Well, after he left, it hit me. I finally connected him in my mind with the guy on the witness stand during my brother's trial. I mean, they looked alike – even spoke very similar. The whole thing made me start wondering, you know, about the case, my brother . . . I mean why should this guy, if he was the witness, run away from his wife and . . . I think he had a daughter? And what was going on that someone went to the trouble and, I guess, expense to send someone around the country to try to find him?"

Fred spoke up. "Yeah, well, you know, we talked about that when he disappeared. We wondered if it was in any way connected to the murder case. But . . . nothing came up. I mean the guy in prison – your brother, right? – is still there and the parents of the little girl still live in town. But they are real quiet; they didn't have anything to do with the disappearance, according to the Sheriff. I tell you, though, being connected to such a case, well, sometimes it does things to people, changes them, works in their minds."

Gloria didn't think that was true of the Gary that she knew, so instead she said, "So, anyway, to make a long story short, I came up here to try to piece together this situation with this Gary and . . . well, I guess, to see if it connects anyway with my brother. I actually, before I recognized you, Sam, I actually just wanted to ask how to get to the I-Deal Motors – to see if the witness still worked there.

"Oh, and one other thing." She didn't know if she should use her made-up story with these two cops, but she felt she had to justify herself, had to give a reason for traveling all the way up here on a matter that didn't really concern her. Would she be here if she hadn't had her love-tussle with Gary the night before? Very unlikely – even though she did want to do as much as possible to try to clear her brother.

So she told them. "This woman who Gary worked for at the carnival, this Rosie. Well, before I left, Rosie told me that Gary left something with her – a sealed envelope. She didn't know what it was; she hadn't opened it and she wasn't about to. But she did say he told her it was valuable, and he asked her to keep it until he could safely return and pick it up. Well, Rosie didn't want to keep it; you know, she just doesn't want to be responsible. So . . . well . . . I have the envelope. I'm going to ask this Clemmon's wife about it, and if she doesn't know anything, well, I don't know what I'll do. Probably take it back to Rosie and then maybe we'll both open it."

Fred spoke up, "Maybe you'd want to take it down to the police station."

But the state cop interrupted, "Yeah, you could do that. But first try to check with Mrs. Clemmon, if she's still in town. Maybe she knows something about it." He finished his coffee before continuing to speak. "Well, I hate to tell you this, Gloria, but it appears that you've made a long trip for nothing – well, maybe not quite. The local police should know about this; I'm sure they have a missing person's inquiry out on Clemmon. You ought to stop in and tell them what you know. On second thought, don't do it today. BABI's in town today and they've got their hands full. They won't have any time – fact of the matter is, they might not even be at the station, probably have just a clerk there. How long you planning to stay in town?"

Gloria said, "Maybe overnight, but that's about it."

Fred interrupted, "Let me tell you, if you don't have a place reserved by now, you're not staying here over night. These BABI characters have every place booked up solid, had it like that for about six months now."

"Well, I guess that means I'm here just for the rest of the afternoon."

Again Fred spoke. "Tell you what I'll do. I know these cops pretty well. Tomorrow I'll go down and make your report. I can pretty much remember what you just told us. Why don't you give me your address and phone number and if they have any questions, they can get a-hold of you?"

Gloria replied, "Well, that sounds pretty reasonable, but with my line of work, I'm at a different place every week. However I do have a Post Office box in Columbia – Missouri, that is – that I check into regularly. I can give you my cell phone number, though."

Fred took out a notebook and Gloria told him the number of the box in Columbia, Missouri, and her phone number. The two policemen finished their coffee and started to leave. She went out the door with them, telling them she was going to try to find Clemmon's wife – just to talk to her, to see what was going on. They told her that they were in town just for the day, to help with any BABI problems, so they couldn't be much help. Fred repeated that he'd make a report to the city police tomorrow about the missing Rob Clemmon, and, as an afterthought, said that I-Deal Motors was just down the highway, only about two blocks away.

As they parted, Sam said he'd keep her in mind in case he came upon anything. Secretly, Sam was as mildly attracted to her as he was when he first met her during the trial. He now had her box number address and her cell phone number in his memory, although he was sure nothing would come of it. And as she left the parking lot, he also noted her car, a brown Toyota Camry with a Missouri license, RTG 483. He made a quick note to himself with the numbers. He thought he'd kind of keep an eye on her today if he had the chance. These BABI crowds were massive and sometimes intimidating, but for the most part very law-abiding. A few college kids got drunk, but the local police usually could take care of that.

Hell, if he were to find her car around dinnertime, he just might – but, no big deal, he'd let things go their course.

Fred, however, said good-by, got into his three-year-old county sheriff's car, drove downtown and then turned left for three blocks to the Overlook Cafe, a musty, unkempt dark restaurant that also served as the town's bus station. In a back hallway two public pay phones lined the wall, each in a semi-enclosed booth. The cafe was almost empty and no one was using either of the phones. He went to the first one and after three no-answer attempts, made a connection. He spoke low and unemotionally, keeping his hand close to his mouth and his eyes, like a cobra's, watched every movement around him.

Chapter 25

She drove into I-Deal Motors with a grinding slam-brake and an envelope of perfume – cheap perfume – her shockingly blonde hair flying from her head in sporadic directions trying to escape the one band of blue polyester clamped around it. Sunglasses, a windshield of dark amber across a good third of her face, and a ripe red slash of lipstick disguised a pale face turned fearfully ashen. A wrap-around short skirt, canvas slippers, and a silken blouse, buttoned high, but with a mid button open, revealing – when she moved – the side curve of a breast unencumbered by a bra, all gave the impression of edgy haste, undisciplined flight.

She was pretty, sexy, and, Rob could tell, obviously in one hell of a hurry. When she inadvertently took off her sunglasses to rub her eyes, he could also tell she was abused. Two black eyes are hard to come by naturally.

Rob knew her slightly. He knew of her, rather than actually having met her. She was Jack Carton's girlfriend, Louise. Everyone in Owaceta knew Jack Carton, and probably everyone had seen him at one time or another with this girlfriend – that is, had seen the girlfriend, because when they were together, Jack was not the one who was noticed.

It was Louise who everyone, women as well as men, noticed.

Girls in small towns sometimes emerged into womanhood with the aid of tabloid papers and lurid magazines rather than a realistic look at the other women living around them. They copied the cheap, the sensational, and the shocking in dealing with the newly created sexual hormones coursing through their systems. They rebelled into makeup, hair permeation, and abbreviated clothing. They fluttered from the school systems, escaping the drowsy cocoons of classes for days of soap opera boredom and nights of sporadic flirtation and catch-as-catch-can sex, which was often accompanied by out-of-control violence as much as frenzied eroticism. But they usually got their man – or men – and eventually slipped into the fringe life of the town – aging prematurely, usually showing some evidence of being battered, and – together with their man – doing the dirty work of the town for a reward of small paychecks, cheap beer, and a succession of rusty Lincoln Continentals or Chrysler Town & Countries to abandon behind the shed on their overgrown edge-of-town rented property.

Louise had followed that route, but it wasn't working. Sure, the flirting and the makeup and the untoward display of skin and newly curved flesh had brought Jack Carton to her; and Jack, with his prominence in town and with his money, was a glorious trophy to dangle before her still-in-school ex-friends. But that was in public; in private, Jack was becoming, in fact, always had been, a monster – but now a more and more depraved monster.

When she accidentally took off her sunglasses, the whole world could see traces of Jack's brutality. But it could never see the huge underlying reservoir of his rage and hate, of his irrational and strident demands and demeanings. It could never see or know about his bent sexuality or the viciousness that festered at the heart of his pathetic Eros.

He was a monster, and if she didn't get away from him, she would be so too – either that or dead.

But Rob couldn't see all that. All he saw was the flashy clothes, the painted face, and the glints of flesh through her inadvertently opened blouse. To him she sounded like she looked – an ephemeral flash-in-the-pan. He couldn't see or hear the desperation within her breathy voice or gaudy clothing.

Her voice was a long swish scratched with a irritating whine. "D' you buy cars. I need to sell this car."

Rob looked over the car quickly. It wasn't the sleek Camaro that Jack Carton usually drove. But the car, an older Ford Mustang, was not unfamiliar to him. He had seen it around town – with her in it.

"We sure do, Miss. That's our business."

"Good, I want to sell it – right now."

"Well, slow down. We can't do it that quick. First thing, I'm just the mechanic. We got to have the salesman here for an appraisal, but he left about two hours ago – stomach flu, he said."

"Oh, shit. If you can't buy it, I'll just go some place else."

"Whoa. Just hold it there. Let me see what I can do. Hell, I do most of the real appraising around here anyway – after the customer's gone. What do these salesmen know about used cars anyway?"

She gave him a blank look, standing next to the Mustang, dangling the keys nervously on a chain that included a tiny feathered bird and an enameled medal that spelled out "Too Hot to Handle" in searing neon green.

Seeing no response, Rob continued, "Tell you what. This car's a few years old. So that would put it into the . . . well, let's say four thousand dollar price range – that's if it's clean, ya know what I mean? But I'm goin' to have to check it out – under the hood and under the body." His eyes inadvertently went to the slit in her blouse.

She was used to eyes like that. Usually with a man of Rob's age and position, she exploited this sexual advantage. A tug of cloth, a hand smoothing a collar, a deliberately revealing gap gave her attention and, frequently, the man almost sheepishly made exceptions for her that he wouldn't make for anybody else.

"Listen, mister, I got some running around to do downtown here, so why don't you do your checking out real quick so that when I come back I can sell you this. What'd you say, four thousand dollars? You can give that to me right now. I could take that check right down to the bank right now."

"I'm sorry, lady, but if I was to do that, I'd have to take my pay check down to the bank with you – my last pay check. No, I just got to have a couple of hours to check this Mustang out, that's all there's to it. You can take it somewhere else, but, to tell you the truth, they'll probably even take longer. Maybe even overnight."

She moved closer to him, her sticky sweet perfume an irritating net, but even he could sense the desperation beneath her surface coquetry. Some things, like her coy flirting, were so automatic with her that she hardly knew she was doing it. Now, when flirting was the last thing she wanted to do, she couldn't control herself. She put her hand on his arm and said, "I'll be back in about an hour." She pressed her gleaming crimson fingernails into his arm with just enough pressure for him to feel slight pain. "Why don't you have it checked out by then, OK?"

Rob smiled and said, "Give me the keys – and, uh, when you come back make sure you have all the papers – title and everything."

"Oh, I've got that now."

"OK, then. When you come back, if you see a sign on the door that says, 'Closed for Lunch,' just come around the back. I'll be working on it."

She left, looking conspicuous in the hot midday edge-of-the-business district with her out-of-kilter clothing, her gait a slight swagger coupled with a suggestive rolling of the hips. Then about 50 feet from the used car lot, her posture changed into business, strictly business – a worried, fear-laden scurry.

Rob watched her leave and knew he had some easy pickings here. The car, he was sure, was a beaut. He could tell that just from looking at the body condition, but, of course, he would check the obvious, something that would take him, at the most, fifteen minutes. The main problem was the ownership. Was this car hers to sell? Where did she get a car like this? He knew she was Jack Carton's girl. Was this a present from him, or was it really his and she was just using it? And why the sudden rush to sell? Did they have a fight – the black eyes – and she wanted to cash in his car and take a powder?

He was going to have to get on the phone with this one. Damn, he wished Big Jim hadn't faked that flu excuse and taken off. And Jim wouldn't be around; he'd be at the lake by now, getting his fishing gear sorted out. So Rob would have to call the Old Man himself and make sure with him that everything was right with this deal. He'd let the Old Man call Jack Carton. But, damn, he knew that the Old Man wouldn't do that. No, it'd be he, Rob Clemmon, who'd have to take the heat – and the fury. And for what? They'd probably never get the car. He'd work his tail off for a couple of hours and the only result would be that the hussy would end with a couple more shiners and maybe a broken nose.

He walked into the office and hung the "Out to Lunch" sign on the door. Before making phone calls, he would do the easiest thing: give the car a cursory check. Except for a few nicks caused by flying stones and one scratch on the left back wheel enclosure, the exterior was almost pure factory, taking into account the four year natural deterioration. Rob opened the hood and made a visual inspection. Nothing untoward. He wheeled over the electronic ignition analyzer and quickly hooked it up to the engine. Every cylinder checked out OK, except for the third, which showed a slightly lower than normal escape pressure. But that was no problem, normal in fact.

He was just about to move the car into the building's small repair bay and put it on the hoist and inspect its undercarriage, when he decided to first check out the interior. He opened the passenger-side door and saw exceptionally clean floors, seats, and dashboard. This gal might be cheap and gaudy, but if this were truly her car, she at bottom had a clear sense of neatness. He got into the front seat, and bounced it hard, with his legs stretched into the firewall under the dash. He wanted to examine the tightness of the seats and interior. It felt good, although he did feel a slight nick during one of his most energetic pushes. Then he got out, pushed the front seat forward and wedged himself into the back seat. He knew that back seats were seldom used by people without children. He also knew that you could tell the whole history of a car by examining it from the back seat.

No problem. The car, just as he guessed at the start, was a charmer. He was squeezing himself out through the passenger door when he saw it. A little flash of light caught his eye from under the front seats, about midway between the two of them, where the shifting console interrupted. He stopped, reached down, and picked up the round piece of glass. He knew immediately that it was a lens of some kind, a cheap one because the glass was thick and imperfect.

He was about to replace it under the seat when he noticed that something was inscribed on it. He held it close to his eye into the light, and there it was, in tiny neat letters, "We Love You, Star."

Rob almost dropped it. The word, "Star," fused in his mind. The trial; the little girl; the murder. Her name was Star, and Rob knew no other person in his entire life with that name.

What was this piece of glass doing in this car?

Immediately he knew he had to go to the police. Then he almost dropped it again when the idea of fingerprints flashed through his mind. He was sorry he had touched the glass. Perhaps it still held fingerprints.

He found a clean garage cloth and delicately wrapped the glass in it. Wait a minute, what was the girl's name, the blonde's? He went through his memory. Jack Carton's girl? Had he ever heard her name? Didn't remember. And she had left this car here without even giving him her name. Maybe, just maybe – on a long shot – her name was also Star?

Her keys. Maybe she had an identification on her key chain. He reached into his pocket and took the chain out. Besides the metal and the bird, the chain held three keys, a tiny plastic picture holder containing a cut-out photo of a dog, and a tag of the kind meant for luggage. It read, "Louise Gorman, 438 Silmond Street, Owaceta, Iowa 81234."

Her name wasn't Star. But maybe it was a nickname, one of those names that lovers make up for each other. Somehow he couldn't picture Jack Carton making up intimate, romantic names like that, but, still, it was a possibility. And what was this lens for anyway? About 2 and 1/2 inches diameter, it was too large – and too crude – for jewelry. Was it from a camera? That wouldn't make any sense; the photos would be distorted because of the lettering. Some kid's toy? A toy camera, a look-see scenery box, a . . . a – sure, that's what it was from, a kaleidoscope!

As soon as that thought struck his mind, Rob was sure that that's what the lens was from. It was the right size and the right quality. And, Jesus, it fit with the name "Star," if, indeed, it was connected with the murdered little girl.

Rob was sweating, standing in the noonday sun in front of the slightly run-down used car sales building. He didn't know what to do, but the more he thought about it, he knew going to the police was the answer. He would call up his buddy, Pootchie Banarsky; and have him take a look at it. Pootchie, who had started as one of the town's four police officers three years ago, would know what to do about this.

He went into the office and was just about to pick up the phone, when he saw her returning. She wasn't sash-shaying or even walking now; she was running, the way a scared woman in high-heeled shoes runs. She rushed into the office, her throaty voice now a scream. "You got it? You got the money? Give it to me right now."

Rob put the phone down and, trying to be calm, replied, "Hold it now, lady. I haven't had time to look underneath the car yet. I gotta move it in over there and put in on the hoist, take a look-see."

"Jesus, I can't wait. I gotta go . . . the bus leaves in ten minutes or so, and I gotta be on it and I need that money. Here's the papers." She reached into a shoulder bag and took out a wadded fold of black-tinged Xerox documents. "Here. Now gimme the money. I'll sign these right now." She started groping in the purse for a pen. "Listen, while I'm figuring out where to sign these things, will you do me one favor?" She looked at him with a hint of some of the old coquetry. "Will you go out there and move the car around to the back? Will you do that, OK?"

Rob reached into his pocket and took out the keys. "I tell you what, lady, why don't you just do that yourself. You see, I don't have any authorization to buy that car yet. I still gotta finish that inspection and then I gotta call the Old Man and get him to go along with this deal. And I'm not even the salesman, for pete's sake. So put that pen away and sit tight right here. I'll run the car up on that hoist over there," he pointed through a open door into the service area, "and it won't be long while I look it over. Longer than ten minutes, though. If you want the money, you'll have to take a later bus."

She sat down, deflated. "There ain't no later bus. This is the last one out today. Hell, maybe I'll take the car to some other town. But then . . ." The tears started.

Rob did not like this at all. He preferred wrenches, and tolerances, and bearings, not bawling almost-teens with cloying perfume and shaking breasts which he could see almost heaving through the slit in her blouse. He waited for the tears to stop.

They didn't, but they eased. "Hell, it's not my car anyway – which you'll find out when you look at those papers, if you ever do. But I still gotta get away. Look," she took the glasses off, "look what he done to me."

"Couple shiners, huh?"

"Yea, and that's the least of it. Jesus, mister, I'm only seventeen. I mean, you called me 'lady.' Hell, I'm not. I should be in high school right now – sitting in one of those old desks, worrying if I can chew gum without getting caught. Instead I'm . . . I'm . . ." The pause trailed off into silence.

"Well," Rob thought to himself, "just as I thought. No sale here. I just went through a bunch of work for nothing. This gal is going to get up and drive the car right off the lot and that'll be the end of it." Then he remembered the lens and the fact that he was about to call the police, his buddy Pootchie. He thought, "Hell, maybe I'll play a little policeman myself."

He dangled the keys in front of her. "Here, Star, why don't you take the keys?"

She didn't respond, just sat there looking glumly at the floor.

"I said, Star, here are your keys."

She looked up, her face still blank. "It's Louise, Louise Gorman. Yea, I guess I better take the keys and let you go on with your work."

"You mean you're not called 'Star'?"

"Star? What do you mean? No, I'm Louise – sometimes Lou. Never Star. The only Star I ever heard of was that little girl got murdered last year." When she said that, Rob could almost trace the fear returning to her body, moving through her like a deranged hiccup. He was right; Star was no lovey-dovey name that Jack used with her.

Rob decided to go farther. He took out the wrapped up lens from his big left pocket and, holding it gingerly by its edges, showed it to her. "Do you know anything about this?"

The girl's eyes were watery. She had to blink to clear them before she could focus on the piece of glass. "No, I never saw it before in my life. What's it for?"

"I'm not sure, but I found it in your . . . that car out there – underneath the front seats."

"So it's a piece of glass, big deal."

"Here, take a look at what's on it. Hold it by its edges, OK?"

She had to blink some more. She read it out loud, "'We love you, Star.'" Her face was a road map of discovery. It unfolded from blankness, to understanding, to horror. She was too naive to conceal, or even to try to cover up, her understanding of just what the lens meant.

She jumped up and nervously prowled the small office space in front of the counter where the phone sat unused. Then she turned to Rob and almost spat out, "Will you move that car around the back! Jesus, one of them is gonna drive by and see it, and then I'll have to go back."

Rob said, "OK, I'll do it, but first give me back that lens." And then go into this small room here and wait for me."

Rob parked the car between two others, a position that would make it almost impossible to be observed from a car driving down the street. As he walked back to the office, he wondered if he should call Pootchie right then, even before he talked to the girl again. But as soon as he walked through the door, she was at him.

"What am I gonna do? I can't go anywhere. The bus is gone. I got no money. And they'll find me, sure as hell."

"Well, I don't know about you, but I got a friend on the police force, Pootchie Banarsky, and I'm gonna get him here right now."

She almost wailed, "No, don't do that. Who do you think I've been talkin' about? Who do you think's after me?"

"Jack. Jack Carton."

"Yea, sure, him. But that old bastard Leghorn is in with him. Jack can't do anything without Leghorn knowin' about it. Leghorn and Old Jake." She subsided a shade, "No, don't go to the police. Why do you think I was trying to get away? From Jack? You're damn right. But from this pig-ruttin' small town police force too. That's right, damn right."

Rob was at a loss. He didn't know what this was all about. "Listen, get away from that plate glass window. Come into this small office here and tell me what's going on. I don't know, maybe I can help you."

"What the hell can you do?" But she went in anyway, still fuming and excitable and desperate.

Rob closed the door. "What do you know about this here piece of glass?" He patted his pocket.

"Not a damn thing. As I said before, I never seen it before in my life. But it's connected with that murder, isn't it? And you found it in Jack's car, didn't you? But it wouldn't surprise me a bit. He's a bastard, a god-awful bastard. But what the hell is it, anyway?"

"Well, I don't know for sure, but I think it's a lens from a kaleidoscope. You know, one of those kid's toys with all the designs and patterns."

"Designs and patterns." She almost whispered this, but then she was crying – really crying hard, uncontrollably. Rob went into the other larger office and brought back a box of Kleenex. She grabbed some and in a hoarse imploring voice said, "He did it. I know that right now. Two nights ago, when he gave me these." She pointed at her eyes. "Two night ago when he was sluggin' me, hittin' me in the face. You wanna know why I got this buttoned up blouse on? Here, I'll show you."

She unbuttoned the top two buttons of her blouse and it opened like a paper cut. Above the beginnings of her youthful breasts was a veritable battleground of bruised flesh. The skin on her upper chest and especially around her neck was mottled and dark, discolored into abstract patterns of abuse – purple and yellow beginning at the edges, ripening into dark red and black at the center. Finger indentations spotted her neck and collarbone. She had been held and choked.

"I got other things too, things I ain't gonna show you."

"Jesus," Rob whistled.

"No, it's not Jesus. It's the goddamn devil. That's who it is. It's that goddamn devil Jack. Ya know what he was screaming at me when he had me over that sink and was doing this to me? Ya want to know?"

"I don't know. Maybe I don't. I remember that trial . . ."

She cut him off, her voice rising in intensity. "He said he could do it again. He did it once and he could do it again."

"What?"

"He was slugging me and . . . something else . . . holding me so tight by my throat I just about collapsed. He hit me on my nose and I think it hurt his hand. He yelled and said he could kill me. He said he'd kill me. He did it once and he could do it again."

"Jesus."

"I let go when he said that. All I thought about was getting away. I let go and let him do what he wanted to do. But all the time through that pain I was thinkin' – I'm leavin'; I'm getting away."

Rob reached out and touched her arm. "Why don't you . . . ah . . . button up. God, I knew Jack Carton was rough, but, what the hell, we're talkin' about murder."

She whispered. "Murder is right. You see this neck." She was just about to button the last high button. "I was this far from death. I mean, it was terrible. Breathin', I mean, I couldn't."

Rob interrupted, "That little girl, Star, she was choked too, wasn't she? Yeah, she was, I remember reading that. And what did you just tell me he said? He could do it again. He did it once and he could do it again. I tell you, girl – Louise – you're right. You gotta' get away. Let me call my buddy Pootchie."

"Sure, that's a part of it too. Go ahead, call Pootchie, or whatever his name is, and you know where I'm gonna be tonight? I'll be on that bastard's kitchen table with my eyes lookin' up at that big faucet and I won't be able to breath . . . Oh, shit." She stopped. She had been looking out the window of the little room's door.

Rob could see her face register total fear. It became ashen, so drained of blood that her heavy makeup became a garish mask of contortion, her mouth an oval of dried parchment, and her eyes – riveted on Rob – twin points of glowing trepidation.

Rob heard the office's outer door bang open. Five seconds later the door next to him burst in on them and a nondescript older man stepped into the room. Rob knew him. He was Oscar Leghorn, a policeman, who also acted as the town's only detective. He just glanced at the girl on the chair, then started talking to Rob. But he kept the girl in the periphery of his eyesight.

"Hi there, Clemmon. Look, I see you got a Mustang sitting out there in back. It for sale?"

"Ah . . . not really."

"Oh, well, good, cause I think it . . . ah . . . don't belong to . . . whoever might be wanting to sell it. In fact if you've got the keys for it – which I see you do right there in your hand – I'd like 'em . . . so that, well, they can be returned to their rightful owner."

"Hey, wait a minute. That ain't no stolen car. Hell, it's been around town for a couple of years now. This girl's been drivin' it. Hell, I've seen her all over town in it."

The detective still didn't look directly at the girl. "Well, it's not her's. You knew that, right? You're no dummy, right? So gimme the keys and then this little gal and I can . . . Come on, give 'em to me."

Rob would have liked to stand up to the brusque policeman, and he was just about to put the key chain in his pocket when the detective snapped the chain and its garish trinkets from him. He dropped it into his pocket, saying, "Thanks, Bub, I knew you wasn't no dum . . ."

The girl made a run for it, but the detective was waiting just for that. She got to the open door and that's all. Instantly one of his large hands gripped her upper right arm and the other clasped her other hand in a painful grip. "Where you goin', Louise? Out to my car, right? You're sick of driving that old Mustang and wanna take a ride in my car, right?"

She struggled, but it was no use. He had her. Quickly he yanked one of her arms behind her back, then using the old leverage trick almost carried her before him out to the very plain, gray Ford Taurus parked in front of the office. A young guy, a kid barely out of high school, was sitting in the passenger seat, but when he saw the two coming toward the car, he jumped out and held the door open. The cop flipped him the girl's key chain and nodded toward the rear of the building. The kid took off running.

The detective pushed Louise into the passenger seat, but before he closed the door, he leaned in and spoke some words that Rob couldn't hear. Her reaction was immediate. She slumped in the seat like a swimmer being pulled under by something underwater, something powerful.

The kid in the Mustang roared through the parking lot and exited left, away from downtown. Leghorn backed his car in a sweeping half circle, then rolled past Rob out to the street. Rob didn't look at him, though; he was looking at the girl. But all he saw of her was her teased and bleached hair lying limply over her upper face, which was punctuated by two of the most frightened eyes he had ever seen.

Not long after that Rob got a call from his wife – a routine call – occasionally she called him, usually about household matters, groceries, things to pick up and the like. Today was much the same, but when she asked him what he was working on, he hesitated and then blurted out, "A Mustang, Jack Cannon's girlfriend's Mustang." Why he told his wife this, he didn't know, but realizing that he didn't want to say anymore about it, he quickly changed the subject. Yes, he would be home about five thirty or six o'clock unless an emergency came up.

The rest of the afternoon was a nightmare for Rob. He wanted to call his friend Pootchie, a man who he was sure was a good cop, one to be trusted. But Pootchie had just joined the force a couple of years ago, still a greenhorn. This Leghorn was the town's veteran, the cop with the most seniority and one who called himself detective, although an appointed chief of police was above him, technically. The word around town, however, said that Leghorn really ran the police force.

Now, Rob thought as he puttered around the work bay, tuning up an old, warped-piston Pontiac, Leghorn seemed to be in cahoots with Jack Carton. And the girl had also mentioned Jack's father, Old Jake. He, also, was in on this somehow. That was bad because Old Jake ran the only really successful business the town had: a turkey processing plant that employed 600 or so people in three shifts. And Rob knew from town scuttlebutt that Old Jake was about to announce his candidacy for State Representative in the Democratic primary.

Complications and underhandedness, but one thing was becoming certain. These people didn't want a teen-aged, bleached blonde, punching bag running around town telling tales about being almost choked to death by the son of Mr. Big. And she had the upper chest to prove it.

But if that were true, what would they do if they found out what he had in his pocket? Rob had to stop and think about the implications of that little piece of glass. Jesus, if it was Star's, she must have been in the car. How else would it get there?

Jack found it? No, why would he bother to pick it up? It had to be there because she had been there – which meant that . . . and what about Jack's words when he was beating up Louise?

Jack killed the little girl!

It all made sense. Rob never believed that the drifter, Barry Shoaty, could have been so vicious. But Jack was another story. From what Rob knew of him from stories told around town in the past, and now what he had heard today – and from the marks on the girl's chest – god, it just made sense, it fit together.

What the hell should he do? If he went to the police – no good. The police seemed to be on Jack's side; at least that's what appeared to be happening today when Leghorn came for the girl. Oh, hell, the blonde and the murder aren't even connected; Jack just wanted to make sure his car wasn't sold. Then why didn't he come himself? Why did he have the town's top cop do this bit of dirty work? There had to be more to it than just a battered girl friend scramming with her boy friend's car.

There was more to it – the lens.

Maybe he should take it to the murdered girl's parents – see if it really was her's. Just give it to them and let them go to the police. But they had become almost invisible in the town. Guys who worked with the father at the turkey factory said that he was like a closed up clam shell – hardly talked to anyone and never did anything with any of the guys who worked there. The mother, so the town said, was just about the same. She had her church, and that's about all anyone saw of her. Somehow, Rob just couldn't picture himself barging into their lives with the piece of glass. Besides that wasn't the way to go about it. It should go to the police.

What about the state police? He knew one state cop, a decent guy who was around Owaceta often. What was his name? Shoot, he stopped in here occasionally to check up on stolen cars; what was it? Shepherd? No, that wasn't it. It started with an "S," he was sure of that. In fact, both of his names started with an "S." He had his card somewhere. Where? In that cardboard box in his tool drawer. Shapino. Sam Shapino. And here's his number. Should I call him?

But, hell, he's based over at Yankton. All he'd probably do is tell me to take it to the local police. Besides, I hardly know the man, and I doubt if he remembers me.

Questions and debates raged through Rob's mind that whole spring afternoon, but in the end he did nothing about the lens. A few routine repair jobs came in, all of which he handled on the spot. I-Deal Motors did not have much of an inventory of used cars for sale, so Rob spent much of his time working on cars either previously sold by them or driven in off the street by people who knew that Rob was a competent mechanic. The repair business was small, but it brought in a steady income, something for which the Old Man was pleased – so pleased that just three months before he had purchased a used wrecker from a gas station that hadn't lasted through a gas war.

About four o'clock Rob got a call from the police dispatcher to go to an accident out on County 43 and the Old River Road. While locking up the building and unlocking the wrecker, he wondered what was going on. He hardly ever got accident calls, and never from the police department. Most accidents in the area were handled by Dave's Repair, the town's biggest and most aggressive automobile repair facility.

The dispatcher hadn't told him anything about the accident; all Rob knew was that the location was obscure. Old River Road was a seldom-used gravel road, almost a lane, traveled only by a few farmers and an occasional fisherman.

But he dutifully took off, heading out on 43. But when he came to the intersection with Old River, he could see nothing – no accident, no police cars with flashing lights, no people.

He became suspicious. What's going on here? Or did I hear the dispatcher wrong?

Then off to the right, way down the River Road he saw a moving figure emerge from the woods bordering the river. It was followed by another figure. Rob shifted the wrecker and headed to them; possibly they knew something about an accident.

They did. A young lady, a girl really, had evidently been speeding when she lost control, went off the road, and hit a tree head-on.

Suddenly Rob became very nervous.

Down the road he could see a number of cars, including some police cars and an ambulance, parked at a fisherman's opening in the trees. Off to the left, tire tracks led through high bushes to the wrecked car, surrounded now by a number of people, some standing, some milling around. Rob pulled to the opening and got out.

The first person to greet him was Leghorn.

What the hell, Rob thought. What the hell!

Leghorn said, "You know that girl I picked up at your place today, well, I was right. She was trying to make a run for it in that car over there." He thumbed at the wrecked car, and Rob could see through the bushes and trees that it was indeed the Mustang from this morning.

Leghorn continued. "She grabbed it again a little while ago and tromped on it so fast on this here gravel that she couldn't handle it. Ended up hitting that tree head-on. Threw her out of the car and killed her just like that."

Now it was Rob's turn to become ashen. He felt his stomach panicking and the blood leaving his head. He leaned against the truck's front fender and just stared at the wrecked car through the woods hardly hearing the words that Leghorn was brusquely barking. "As soon as we're finished with the investigation, you can back in here and pull that Mustang out of there. I think it's back axle is OK. Front's kinda banged up though. Take it down to your shop for the time being, OK?"

Rob just looked at the man, not knowing what to say, not knowing whether to get back into his truck and leave or to start yelling right then and there.

"Come here, Clemmon, take a look at this." Leghorn grabbed his arm and marched him through the tall grass. He was being tugged along, pulled really, Leghorn's steel grip reminding Rob of how he had almost dragged the girl, Louise, to Leghorn's car earlier that day. They moved through the bystanders, who were being held back by Rob's friend Pootchie, almost up to the mud entrenched car. But Leghorn pointed instead to the ground about 30 feet from the car to the left.

Louise lay crushed in death. Her face was calm now, the eyes open but the pupils unnaturally just peeping from the bottom of her eyelids. Her face, not damaged, was still tough-pretty and old-young, despite the traces of makeup that seemed inflicted upon it. But her arms were out-flung and her left leg wretched completely under her; her skirt driven up to her hips exposed a right leg stretched almost daintily to a bloody canvas shoe.

Leghorn moved to her and kicked at her skirt with his shoe. She was not wearing panties – her dark groin, to Rob's frightened eyes, open and terrible. It was crimson with frothy blood, more startling because of the dark and battered flesh that surrounded and engulfed her lower stomach and her upper thighs. Rob remembered her intimations when she showed him her chest bruises; he had not even guessed then of something like this.

He looked away, catching himself with involuntary bile erupting into his mouth. But the steel arm held him, and the nondescript voice forced him to look back. "Look, Clemmon, look. Take a good look. Hell of a bad accident. Looks like she got thrown and ended up right on her ass. Tore her butt up something bad, right? Hell of a note. I kinda liked her; she was half way pretty – but real young. And she had a big mouth, you know what I mean?"

The grip on his arm was sharply painful now and Rob reached with his other hand to pull it off, but the officer didn't relent. Instead he pulled Rob to him and hoarsely whispered, "She had a big mouth, Clemmon. Too bad."

Then he relented and the claw on Rob's arm became soft, almost consoling. But not so the man's eyes, as they turned to Rob. "You pull that car into your back lot, then wait there. We gotta have a little talk. But first I gotta finish the preliminary investigation. Then we'll talk. OK? You wait there – in the back lot of I-Deal Motors, right?"

"Well, sure, I guess so, but I'm off at six, the place closes then."

"Don't you think I know that. You be there. You wait for me, hear?"

An hour later in the back lot of I-Deal Motors Rob made his decision. He would run.

He had no choice really. If he stayed, they had him. He was sure the girl had told them about the lens. They would want it and they would want his silence. But, Jesus, look what happened to the girl. He'd end up the same way. Or his wife would. Or his daughter. Maybe they'd use the threat to his family to hold him – to shut him up. But he couldn't live like that. Knowing about the little girl and now Louise. And Jack Carton strutting around town. Jack Carton doing the same thing with some other youngster. Maybe even his own daughter, Teresa.

No, he had to get away and protect his family. It wouldn't be too much to leave his wife. Since she had started waitressing, he didn't know, but he felt some funny things were going on – things he couldn't put his finger on, but were just not right. They didn't seem to see eye to eye anymore.

But he would miss his daughter. She was in first grade, as cute as a lollipop, and now he had put her in real danger. Damn, she was the one they would go after, would hold over him.

He couldn't take that, couldn't live like that.

He couldn't even risk going to the state cops. If Leghorn was involved – hell, he seemed to be in charge – what the hell could a state cop do? Sure, he had seen movies about courageous fighters for justice going against the system, but that was Hollywood. This was real life, that girl's body out there on Old River Road was horribly real. She was dead – murdered.

And he would be next. Or even worse – his daughter, Teresa.

If he left right now, and no one knew where he went, and he never tried to get back to his family, didn't even contact them ever, why then that would protect them. The only reason he was in danger was that he knew stuff – about the lens, and about the girl. If his wife and daughter didn't know any of that, they would be safe.

But he would have to make a complete break. If Leghorn and whoever was in with him – Jack Carton and whoever – had any inkling that his family was in communication with him, that was it. They could use the threat of harm to his wife or daughter to bring him in and to silence him.

So he had to leave – to leave quickly, with no future contacts planned – and he had to do it now.

He left the wrecker, went into the office, opened the safe, and took every bit of money he could find in it. Luckily for him, before Jim, the salesman, left with the "flu" that morning, he had taken a five hundred dollar down payment and first installment on a used Toyota from a farmer who paid everything in cash. The five hundred was in the safe – that and some petty cash - about forty bucks. Rob took it all – along with the keys to an old green Chevy Camaro that he knew to have a trusty engine. He was about to take one of the dealer's license plates, when he realized that if he took only one, they could figure pretty quickly which one it was and then every cop in the state would be looking for that one. He took all the plates – a dozen at least. He unlocked the back storage room and threw a couple of cartons of candy bars and peanuts meant for the vending machine into an old athletic bag along with the license plates. He also grabbed some extra work clothes and a toothbrush he kept in a locker. He was just about out the door when he thought about telephoning.

Should he try to put them on a bogus trail? He could call his wife and tell her he had to make an overnight trip to Des Moines or Cedar Rapids or Dubuque and then take off for where he was really going – Davenport. But Leghorn would know it was a lie and not even bother with it. What the detective would do is put out a bulletin and pretty soon every cop in the state would be looking for him and his car. Leghorn could sit back and wait for him to be found and brought in. And maybe if he knew about a phone call to his wife, maybe it would set him to try a little intimidation on his wife. No, the best thing was a complete break – quick, fast, and now.

An hour later he was standing at the one bus stop at North Park Mall, a huge shopping complex near the northern outskirts of Davenport. He knew that by then the Camaro would be "hot," but he figured that it would go unnoticed for a longer time if it were one of the jam of cars parked in the massive lots that surrounded the mall. Someone would probably notice it during the night when the lot cleared, although he did park it near the entrance where an all-night Italian restaurant was located.

When eventually the bus came, and he joined the few passengers, most laden with parcels from an afternoon of shopping, he took it until it pulled into the bus station a block from the Mississippi River. He wanted to get to Illinois, hoping that the cops there wouldn't be as likely to respond to an unimportant robbery and stolen car case from a little town in Iowa.

He lifted his bag of clothes and candy and walked east on the street bordering the river. On his right was a park and the embarkation point for a gambling riverboat that kept the area alive with people, garish banners, and loud music. He crossed the river on foot on a bridge system over an island that contained the Rock Island Arsenal, and soon was in an area of older buildings, warehouses and some small commercial and service businesses in Rock Island, Illinois.

His next goal was Chicago, from where he figured he could get transportation almost anywhere without being conspicuous. But how to get there? Fly, rent a car – he'd have to show identification. Take a bus – he knew he'd have to wait until tomorrow, and even then he would stand out. Hitchhike – he thought about it, but the risk of being picked up by the cops was too great, besides he wasn't sure about hitchhiking along an interstate highway, the most direct route to Chicago.

That left stealing a car. He could do that easily enough, having had to break into any number of keys-locked-in cars over the years. Rock Island also had a thriving gambling riverboat, and a downtown lively with night entertainment and activity. After eating a bowl of chili at a small cafe, he stationed himself about two blocks from the gambling boat, near an off-street parking lot. It wasn't long before he had what he was looking for – two couples in a Hyundai who got out with much noise and headed for the boat. Rob followed them and made sure they entered the boat. He was in Chicago in three hours and in Washington D.C. two days later.

Chapter 26

The county deputy's voice on the phone was hoarse, raspy, and nervous, as if irritating dust was in his throat. "Listen, Jack, I'm glad I got a-hold of you. I don't know much about what's going on, but your father told me to keep a watch out for anything like this."

Fred, the county cop, paused. When he began again, his pained voice pushed through the dust. "I just met a woman – by accident – a woman who runs a carnival ride, I guess someplace in Illinois right now. But she claims to know Rob Clemmon."

"She what?"

"Yea, she said he was working – hired help – at this carnival. He was biking, on a bicycle, and he needed money and stopped and went to work for a Ferris Wheel or something like that. Then she said the other day, a guy came looking for Rob Clemmon and he had a picture of him – and she said the picture looked just like Clemmon. Anyway, you and I both know that guy was Leghorn, right?"

"You said it, pal. I didn't."

"Well, anyway, these carnival people, they protect each other. So they set Leghorn on a wild goose chase, and Clemmon, he took off on his bicycle. He went west, over here to Iowa. But she didn't say where. She probably didn't know. Maybe he didn't know where he was going. But he probably could be traced pretty easily – except for all these BABI bikers – he'd stick out like a seed cap at a garden party."

"Get to the point, Fred. This woman's in town now?"

"That's right, Jack. And here's what gets me. She's got something. It's in an envelope that Clemmon left at the carnival, and she says it's valuable, but she doesn't know what it is because she hasn't opened it. She's gonna try to find Mary and then the both of them can open it."

"Jesus."

"And that ain't all. You're probably wondering how this lady figured out to come here, here to Owaceta. Well, come to find out, she was here for the trial – the trial of her brother. That's right, her brother was that wino who went to prison for the little girl's murder. This lady's name's Gloria, Gloria Shoaty. Her brother's in Fort Madison. She was here for the trial and that's how she came to recognize Clemmon when he appeared at the Carnival. Well, actually, she didn't recognize him at first; it was only after Leghorn appeared and Clemmon left, that it hit her that he, Clemmon, had been at the trial."

"OK, OK, I see. So she's up here today in the middle of all this BABI shit – and where's the old man and Leghorn? – and she's got something valuable? Did you see it?"

"Nope. She said it was still all sealed up. She was gonna ask Mary about it – if she found Mary – and if she didn't know anything about it, she – this Gloria – was gonna take it back to the carnival lady and they'd open it together."

"Listen Fred, you're my friend, right? And you're the old man's and Leghorn's friend, right? Well, I don't know where they are just now, but I think they would say that they might want to open that little envelope. Get the picture?"

"Listen, Jack, I tried to get ahold of your old man and Leghorn both. Before, you know, they told me to watch out for something like this. I don't know what it's all about, but neither of them is around, but, Jesus, BABI's here and the Sheriff's got me doing all kinds of crap today. I ain't got time today; some other day, sure. but not today."

"What'd I just say? Didn't I just say, 'Get the picture?' Didn't I?"

"Yea, I heard you. I'll have to shift some things around, but I'll try to find her. Where you gonna be so I can call you?"

"Forget about me. You find that lady. And you find Leghorn. You hear me? What did this lady look like?"

"Kinda pretty, actually. Kind of an oval face with nice blonde hair. Average body, but, you know, shapely. I'd say about 35 years old. Wearing white slacks with a blue top. Hair's cut about average – kinda straight with curls in front. She's driving an old '95 Pontiac – light blue, with Missouri plates."

"OK, OK, I got ya. But you get a-hold of her. And when you do, get a-hold of me. You got this cell phone number, right? You find her and that package, and then you call me, hear?"

Jack got out of the big, disheveled bed in the messy, all white bedroom. It had a set of wide windows that looked out over the town's only golf club, the Owaceta Country Club. The sun was just beginning its decline, but it was still bright and shiny outside – and hot; inside with the automatic air conditioning the temperature was unvaryingly moderate.

He dressed quickly, then walked through the kitchen, where he grabbed a banana, before entering the attached garage and his car. He pressed a button and the garage door rolled down, letting him out into the hot and sticky town.

Chapter 27

Carl's Cafe in downtown Owaceta was crowded, as crowded as it had ever been. Every one of its twelve tables was occupied, along with most of the stools in front of its long, slightly curving main counter. Dis boldly entered and sat down at one of the three open stools. He picked up the plastic enclosed menu from the clip in front of him, gave it a desultory glance, and then started looking around. The place was filled with bicyclers – only a few people in ordinary clothing, not talking but looking, sat scattered throughout the place. Two waitresses scurried through the crowd, but none of them even remotely resembled the picture of Mary Clemmon that rested in Dis's billfold.

Then Dis heard a discordant female voice from behind the counter right in front of him. "May I help you." It was Mary Clemmon. She was the woman in the picture. Dis knew her instantly.

But he took her completely by surprise.

Her pretty but weary face slumped as she hissed almost in a whisper. "Jesus, you've come back. But why today of all days? Hey, I can't handle this. Five thousand customers and now you. Where the hell have you been?"

Dis was taken back by the virulence of her greeting, but he tried to stay calm: "When is your break? I want to talk to you?"

"Wait a minute; who are you? You don't sound like Rob. Just who are you?"

"I'm going to be out back – in the parking lot. When you get a break, come out there. We have to talk." He got up and left, the place too crowded and noisy for him to have a chance to really level with her. He had to wheel his bike completely around the block until he came to an alley in order to get to the back of the cafe – and even then he wasn't quite sure which of the alley entrances was the one he wanted. But he found a fence to lean his bike against and started thinking about what to ask her.

The primary question: Was it she who had the gray man looking for him? If not, who would be after him? Did she know anything about the lens? He didn't know if he would ask her about the rough man from last night, but it might come to that.

From the two glimpses he had had of her, he did not like her. She seemed to be harsh and coarse, superficially pretty, but like sandpaper underneath. He decided that if Rob Clemmon had to leave a wife, she would be an easy one to leave. But she and Rob had a daughter. Dis wondered where that daughter was now.

He was just getting ready to sit down on the ground and lean against the fence when she appeared. Her hand digging into her waitress apron for a cigarette, she came up to Dis with a scowl. "Who are you? Just who the hell are you? I mean, you look just like my ex – my runaway husband – to be him. What . . . what's going on here?"

"Are you having me followed? Do you have someone on my tail – a gray guy in a gray car?"

Still with a sneer on her weary face, she said, "Do I have someone on your. . . . Oh, you must be talking about Leghorn. But no, he's not doing anything for me. Well, I mean I turned in a missing person report last year when you . . . Rob . . . when my husband left, but I don't think anyone's been doing anything about it for awhile now."

"Who's this Leghorn?"

"He's the police detective around here. We got a chief, but it's Leghorn who's really in charge – when he's around. Come to think of it, maybe that's the reason he ain't been around much recently. You said he's been following you?"

"Why would he be following after me, asking about Rob Clemmon?"

"Honey, you look like the spitting image of Rob Clemmon – you don't talk like him though. Hey, do you know what happened to him – where he is?" She was smoking by now, her hand curved around the cigarette just as in the picture resting in Dis's wallet.

For now Dis was going to ignore that question. How would she react if he told her that her husband was dead and that he had killed him?

Instead Dis reached into his pocket and brought out the lens, wrapped in the square of Styrofoam and rubber bands that he used to protect it. While he was loosening the rubber bands, he asked, "What do you know about this thing?"

She looked at the lens, held gingerly by the edges in Dis's fingers. "Never seen it before in my life. What is it?"

"Well, I don't know for sure, but I think it's a lens from a kaleidoscope, you know, one of those kid's toy viewers."

"So?"

"Here look at it, but don't touch its surface. Read it."

She took the lens in her nervous waitress fingers, nails chewed short and cuticles ragged. "Read it? What do you mean, read it?"

"Look through it into the light."

She raised her hand and squinted at the shimmering glass. She turned it around and Dis saw a shadow engulf her face. "Where'd you get this?"

"I got it from a man named Rob Clemmon. Don't ask me the circumstances, but it was in the possession of Rob Clemmon – of Owaceta, Iowa." He put his hand out and she returned the lens to him.

Her face became a mask of distraught muscle. She took a quick puff of the cigarette and rattled, "What are you saying, huh? That Rob took this from the kid, the little girl that was killed a couple years back, Star, Star Oatage? You're saying that Rob was the one who did it? Is that what you're saying?"

"I don't know. All I know is that I got it from Rob Clemmon of Owaceta, Iowa."

She was pacing now. She stopped to light another cigarette, but just then another waitress appeared at the cafe's back door. "Hey, Mary, you better get in here right away. The place is going crazy. People are waiting in line."

"OK, OK, I'll be right there."

Dis spoke up. "If Rob Clemmon didn't get this from the little girl herself, where do you suppose he got it?"

She almost screamed, "Jesus Christ, oh Jesus Christ." She went to him and grabbed him by the arm. "Listen, I never told nobody before – cause it didn't mean anything. But, Jesus Christ, it sure does now. Right before Rob left I called him. I used to do that almost every day. And one of the things he said was that he was working on a car owned by Jack Carton. I didn't pay much mind to it, but I never forgot it either."

"So?"

She was almost imploring him now. "He found that in Jack's car I bet. That's why he left. He found it in Jack's car. Listen, I know this. Rob and I had our outs, but one thing I know about him for sure – he could never of killed that little Star.

But Jack Carton, oh, Jesus Christ."

"What about him? Do you know him?"

It was almost a wail. "Do I know him? He's my boyfriend now. He's even living some times with me." She paused, then erupted when the thought hit her. "Jesus, he's been looking after my daughter, my Teresa, while I've been working."

"Could he . . . ah . . . could he be capable of . . ."

"Christ, do you expect me to know that? That's just the thing that I don't know. I don't know, but . . . but . . . maybe." She reached up and unbuttoned the top button of her waitress smock. Dis could see the discolored flesh underneath – purple and black, yellowish on the edges.

Now it was Dis's turn to say: "Jesus Christ!"

She threw the cigarette away and ground it into the dirt with her heel. "I . . . I have to go in now." Her harsh, but pretty face softened, and she reached out to Dis's arm. "Help me, will you? Watch my daughter, will you? Jack . . . Jack is supposed to pick her up this evening at school. Her summer school class is staying late, helping with the meal they're serving there for BABI. He said he'd pick her up and take her home. Seven thirty, that's the time. I gotta go, but watch her for me, will you? And come back later, I gotta talk to you."

"OK, OK. Where do you live and . . . and . . . what's the name of the school?"

"I'm still living where I lived before, 832 Willow Street, and she goes to Lincoln School. It's about eight blocks away.

"This Jack Carton, is he the big guy who was with you last night, over in Cedar City?"

"Yeah. Hey, how'd you know about that, that we was over there?"

"Never mind. What about your daughter. . . Teresa? I think I know what she looks like, but what's she wearing?"

The voice came through the crack of the back door again. "Mary, get in here, for heaven's sake."

Mary yelled, "I'm comin', I'm comin'. As she retreated to the door, she dictated to Dis. "Shorts – pink, no peach. A T-shirt . . . with a bike on it. Yeah, she wore it on a-counta' BABI. Peach shorts and a T-shirt with a bike."

Dis watched her disappear through the door. "I'll go over there and keep an eye on her. Is she supposed to go home or come down here?"

"Come down here," echoed through the back alley.

Dis looked at his watch. It was five to seven. Enough time. He took out the city's BABI brochure and looked at the map. Lincoln School was clearly marked; it was one of the overnight camping sites. He was surprised that they were using one that had a summer school session, but they probably needed every space they could find – spaces with bathroom facilities, that is.

The school was on Spring Street, a street that diagonalled southeast through the town, eventually turning into a county highway at the outskirts. Dis wheeled his bike on foot back to the town's main street, Front Street, where now more and more bikers were congregating, and where city workers had moved construction barriers into place to close off the street to vehicle traffic.

He walked the bike east on Front until he came to the five points intersection where Spring met Front. There he jumped on his bike and soon was racing down the fairly busy street. His mind was a whirl of conjecture. But things were dropping into place. He remembered the dying man in the parking lot in Washington D.C. imploring him "Don't touch it. Don't touch it." If the lens still had Star's fingerprints on it, and the lens came from Rob, and Rob had been working on Jack Carton's car that afternoon, then some pretty good circumstantial evidence linked up Jack Carton to Star Oatage. What was the lens doing in Jack Carton's car if she was a complete stranger to him, if he was just another man in town?

She must have been in his car.

Why, how, when? He'd probably never know the answer to any of those questions and it dawned on him as he was waiting at a stop light intersection, "Why should I care?" In fact, why was he racing to the school of a child he didn't know and had no relation to? Why was he getting himself involved in some relatively obscure happenings in a small town in Iowa, which had no connection to his life or future?

The answer hit him: he was involved. He had the lens and someone wanted that lens dearly – enough to send a city detective scouring the countryside looking for it – and for the carrier of it. He was involved because he could testify where he got the lens, could link the lens with the identity of Rob Clemmon. And that, some how, was threatening to some powerful forces here in this little city.

He thought of Mary and the way her sneering composure had evaporated when he showed her the lens. And her neck and upper chest – the ugly purple and black bruise that she implied was done by Jack Carton. Brutal. If he could do that, could he do the same – or worst – to little kids? To Star Oatage? My god, dismembered! That's a psychopath, a maniac, a. . . Dis thought of the man he had seen with Mary Clemmon last night, the big man with the brutal hand on her arm.

It all fit together.

Chapter 28

Gloria was tired – and frustrated. She had spent most of the day in an unrewarding search for elusive tendrils of knowledge and had come up with nothing – or not much. First off, at I-Deal Motors, Rob Clemmon was a dead issue. The two people there, a salesman and a mechanic, both in need of haircuts and dentistry work, had never know him, since they were both recent hires. They had heard about him vaguely. Their boss, "Old Man" Benson, had mentioned him in passing a few times, usually with a snort of mild anger because of Clemmon's abrupt departure. But Benson wasn't around today, in fact wouldn't be around for another week. He was on vacation.

Gloria left and drove aimlessly through the town, finally ending up where everyone does in a small city in eastern Iowa, in the downtown. But on this late afternoon it was crowded and she had to park two blocks away from the main concentration of stores. She had tried to drive through the main street, but had to detour around it. And, of course, she noticed the unusual number of bicyclists, almost all of them dressed in colorful and tight biking clothing.

Having drawn a blank at the used car dealer, her next option was Rob Clemmon's wife. On foot, she found a telephone – and an abused telephone book – in a drug store. Mary Clemmon's name was listed, but when Gloria called, no one answered the phone, and no answering machine talked to her.

Where did she work – if she did work? Gloria had no idea. She walked back to her car and drove to Mary Clemmon's address. After ringing the doorbell to ascertain that no one was home, and waiting in her car for another fifteen minutes, she decided to see if any of the neighbors knew where Mary worked. That also was nonproductive. Only at one house of the eight on the block did anyone answer the door, and the elderly lady who appeared only knew that, "That wild Clemmons lady comes and goes at all hours of the night and day. I don't know where or if she works, but I heard tell that she's some kind of waitress. She's got a little girl, though; a cute little kid."

So Gloria was back in her car, waiting out the increasingly hot and humid afternoon, and wondering more and more what exactly she was doing there. The block was not an appealing place to be on an uncomfortable afternoon. Small frame bungalows dominated by driveways and looming garage doors set the tone. Only a few small trees gave a hint of shade to the baking and browning grass. The few flower gardens or plantings around some of the houses had long since withered to hard brick-like soil or had been taken over by hardy but suffocating weeds.

She had to move. Waiting was getting to her. Perhaps, despite what the county policeman had said, she could find something out at the police station, which she assumed to be downtown. It was, but the county cop was right. A clerk held sway at a reception area on the ground floor of city hall. No one else, not even the chief of police, was present; they were all out policing the increasing crowds of BABI riders who were either just arriving into the cordoned off Main Street or who had returned to it after taking care of their night's accommodations and cleaning up. The clerk had only a vague memory of the trial and the witness, Rob Clemmon. She did look through the missing persons file, not a very thick one, and confirmed that, indeed, he had been reported missing by one Mary Clemmon, a waitress. It did not tell where she worked.

Gloria asked the clerk, a shivering, thin, middle aged woman, if anyone from the police office was actively investigating Clemmon's disappearance; if anyone, for instance, was out with his picture asking people in other states if they recognized him. The clerk said not that she knew of – in fact that idea was preposterous; they didn't have time for non-criminal investigations like that. Their chief investigator was so busy with a fraudulent cattle sale, in which he had to travel all over the country, that he could hardly concern himself with a guy who simply left town.

Gloria wondered if she should report what she had told the two police officers at the restaurant, but decided against it: the county cop would likely report it later, but probably nothing would come of it.

She left the office, hitting the blast of hot, late afternoon air as she emerged from the building as an increasingly petulant woman. She was getting nowhere, and with the heat, the overflowing crowds, and her frustration, she was about to give up, get back in her car, and head back to Missouri.

Before she would do that, however, she would stop at a local restaurant and have a cool drink. Who knows, maybe one of the waitresses there would know Mary Clemmon, or where she might possibly work. The first likely place she came to turned out to be bedlam. Every table and stool at the counter was filled, and people in lycra were even waiting in line at the entrance.

Gloria mentally detoured. As she turned around, she caught glimpses of two of the waitresses, both unsmiling and preoccupied. One was a gritty, sharp-featured woman, superficially attractive, who presented a vague sense of recognition to Gloria. But Gloria dismissed the waitress, who was indeed Mary Clemmon, as just another waitress who had served her when she was up here at the trial two years before. Indeed, Gloria had a blurred sense that she had eaten in the same place then, Carl's Cafe.

She left the crowded place. If someone had been behind the counter at the cash register, she would have stopped and inquired about the names of the waitresses, but with the crowds and the confusion and her by now dim sense of purpose, she was glad to escape to the street, even though it was almost as crowded and confusing.

Feeling self-conscious in her normal clothing (Even though the majority of bikers had showered and changed clothes by now, their standard clothing was still bicycle enhanced T-shirts and shorts.), she stopped at a open-air booth and purchased a paper cup of lemonade. It was cold and tart-sweet, but tasted too artificial to be completely natural, a fact confirmed when she watched how the operator squeezed a small amount of real lemon juice and pulp into a powered base before adding water and crushed ice.

The sun was beginning to slant, and a quick glance at her watch, moved Gloria out of her heat-enhanced stupor into action. She had better get on the road if she wanted to get back to the carnival late tonight. She knew from what the cops said and from the masses of people surrounding her, that she wasn't going to spend the night in Owaceta. Then a momentary idea edged into her consciousness – a small closed-in tent, Gary, no sleeping bags, no covers, just themselves.

She realized why she was lingering so long in this little town with only a cursory reason to be there: Gary. He was a bicyclist and this place was like a gigantic magnet, drawing bicyclists from all over, including, she realized, the possibility of Gary – or Rob – or someone.

So, with the realization that she would probably spend the night either on the road or in a motel room on the road, she moved through the crowd reluctantly, searching the faces of anyone who even remotely resembled her memory of Gary. After three loops from one end of the roped-off street to the other, she gave up in frustration. He wasn't there. Still she stopped at a pizza stand, ordered a slice of pepperoni pizza and a Pepsi, and while standing next to the booth and eating it, she continued to survey the masses of people moving across her vision.

Then it hit her. Gary wouldn't be here, even if he was using BABI as a cover while on the road. He would probably be at a campsite now, cocooned, with his tent protecting his identity – whatever it was. She had noticed many sites filled with tents scattered around the town, so she knew it would be impossible to find him – if indeed he was there.

So Gloria, dumping her empty plastic and paper eating paraphernalia in a large trash can, left the downtown and started back to he car. She was tired and defeated, and she realized that she would have to drive at least to Interstate 80 in order to find a place for the night. And the place would be lonely, and she would be lonely, and – oh, damn – why had she even bothered to come up here anyway.

Getting away from the center of Owaceta was another matter, however. Cars and campers and vans and bicycles swirled together in an undisciplined medley of vehicle crunch. She was only able to edge very slowly out into the bumper-to-bumper stream of traffic on the street where she had parked. And once into the parade, she felt like a commuter in the stories she had read about gridlock in Chicago or Kansas City. Eventually, after a very long two blocks, she was able to gain a little momentum and almost travel at normal city speed.

She found herself on Spring Street, going south, the direction she knew she wanted, but she couldn't find a highway sign, and she knew that this was not the same street on which she had come into town. At a stop sign she debated whether she should turn off Spring, but couldn't decide whether to turn left or right. Then two things happened that took the decision away from her.

The first was that the state cop, Sam Shapino, who was parked on the side of the crossing street, saw her and decided to follow her.

And the second was that she saw Gary.

Chapter 29

About 15 minutes earlier, when Dis had arrived at Lincoln Elementary School, he had parked his bike with a group of other bikes in front of the building and entered the lobby. Bikers were standing and sitting all through the lobby, since the building's large open doors and windows created some moving air – hot and moist though it was – in the tiled entrance. The building was not air conditioned since for the most part the school was little used during the hot summer months.

He strolled purposely to the card table blocking the entrance to the school's gym where the food was being served; smiled at the haggard lady sitting behind it with a cash box and a check list of indecipherable notations; and, after a quick, desperate glance around the tables filling the gym, asked her if he could just go in and talk to that guy right there, the one with the "Just Do It!" T-shirt. Dis motioned in the general direction of the receding end of the gym.

The lady, whose wire rim glasses hung from her neck by a gold chain, looked sweetly at him and said, "Sure, but don't sit down. We're doing this for charity, you know."

Dis didn't know, but he winked his eye at her and moved quickly through the tables, watching, not the bikers – most of whom had finished their meals and were now lingering over iced tea and slow conversation – but the people who were putting on the meal. No kids were visible, only ladies – brisk, efficient ladies in dresses or starched blouses and skirts. Dis wondered if he were too late.

Near him was an elderly lady wiping off a table with a damp dishrag. Dis asked her if a little girl named Teresa Clemmon was still around. "My lands, little Teresa, why sure she's still here. She's such a sweet thing . . . was helping put silverware into napkins just a few minutes ago. No wait a minute, I think she just left. I thought I saw that Jack Cannon a little while ago telling her to get her things together, that he had to take her to her mother. She's a waitress downtown at the cafe, Carl's Cafe."

Dis almost exploded. Brushing against people, he rushed out of the gym, grabbed his bike, and fairly leaped onto it. He rode through the school's parking lot, searching for the big man he had seen the night before and a little girl wearing a peach colored bike T-shirt. No luck; all of the cars were empty.

But not the car that was at the lot's exit, waiting to turn right into the unusually heavy bike and car traffic. A light green Saturn, it was being driven by the man who the night before had seemingly crushed Mary Clemmon's left arm at the BABI gathering. Dis recognized the large head, the neatly clipped hair, and the pursed full lips of Jack Cannon. Next to Cannon, he could just see the top of a small head, covered with light brown curls.

The car jerked into the traffic

And Dis responded like an bird dog in a duck blind.

He was off – streaking through traffic, cutting in front of cars and fellow bikers, threading in and out, ignoring stop signs and delays, careening over curbs onto the sidewalk at times, trying to catch up with the green Saturn.

At first he thought it would be easy, but the traffic soon eased, most of it turning left toward the downtown. The Saturn, about half a block in front of him, kept to the right and therefore wound through the clogged streets fairly quickly. At the intersection with Spring Street, it made a right turn on the red light and sped off south away from the town's mid-center.

Dis scrambled. He jumped the curb to get around the cars in front of him, cut around the intersection on the sidewalk, and almost lost sight of the Saturn by the time he was on the road again. The car was way ahead, almost a faint green lump, and gaining speed. Dis shifted to his highest gear, and pushed his legs desperately. He hoped there would be some stoplights, or at least stop signs, before the city limits. He had to stop that car!

But he couldn't!

It picked up speed and soon was but a dot, misty and out of focus, on the horizon of the road ahead. But Dis kept on pedaling as hard as he could. He was in his fastest gear, his bike unencumbered by bags or any extra weight, but still he lost ground to the rapidly vanishing car.

Dis looked down and checked his speed on his bike computer: about 30 mph. Fast for a bike in town on flat roads, but piddling for a car.

Within a few minutes he noticed that he had traveled out of town, passing cornfields and pastures, with just a few suburban homes intermixed. Where was Jack Cannon going? Wasn't he supposed to just pick the girl up and take her to the restaurant?

Then Dis lost sight of the car. It either sped up too much or went down a hill – or perhaps turned off the main road. He couldn't tell. But he kept on pounding as fast as he could.

The sweat was a deterrence now. It ran into his eyes, obscuring his vision, hurting his ability to search ahead, to try to pick up the vanished car. He reached with his right hand and swiped across his forehead and eyebrows, then used his thumb to gouge the perspiration from his eye sockets. It helped – but only temporally.

But in the interval before more sweat occurred, he caught a glimpse – way in the distance – of what he took to be the Saturn. It appeared to have slowed or stopped.

He increased his speed, fractionally, and seemed to gain somewhat on it. Yes, it had stopped! But only momentarily. Now Dis could see a stop sign and a car crossing the intersection perpendicular to the stopped car. But as soon as the car passed, the Saturn accelerated and started picking up ground on Dis.

The chase began again. Dis approached the intersection and knew why Cannon had stopped so completely. It was a blind crossing; a stand of trees on the right obscured the crossroad. Dis made a snap decision not to stop. He would take the risk of being hit by an approaching car. He took a deep breath and sped through the intersection without hesitation. In his peripheral vision no car appeared, but Dis hardly had time to dwell on his good luck. The Saturn was just about out of sight.

Dis almost lost it, but then about a half-mile after the intersection the car slowed again – or at least it stopped receding from Dis's vision. Its dot appeared slightly larger than before. But then, when Dis looked up after scanning his front wheel and computer, the car was gone! Disappeared!

Had Cannon noticed him in his rear view mirror and tromped on the accelerator to get away? Did he somehow turn off the road? Where was he?

Dis careened ahead, now actively scanning the side of the road, but seeing nothing but fields, fences, and an occasional row of trees. He passed a farm, with house and outbuildings, but no Saturn and no driveway circling around to the back.

But then, as he continued pumping away, off to his right, he saw what appeared to be smoke – a line of yellow-brown mist seemingly hugging the ground. Dust from gravel. Cannon had turned off on a gravel road. Sure enough, a few moments later Dis could see an intersection sign looming in the distance and then quickly he came upon the crossroad.

The gravel road was serviceable, but rutted and patchy. Dis let caution fly and roared after the car. Good – the road would slow Cannon down, and Dis could still go almost as fast as he had been. Sure, the going was rough, but if he kept in the packed-down wheel tracks, he could probably at least keep up with the car.

Dis wondered if Cannon had noticed him and had gone down this road to evade him. If he had, it wasn't working. Cannon should have stayed on the paved road.

So what was Cannon doing out here in the midst of nothing much but corn fields with little Teresa in the passenger seat? Dis had a momentary vision of the little girl – he had only seen her in the picture and the top of her head in the car – furtively trying to hide something – her favorite possession – something that could be found – her birthday present! The image of the lens, which was with him right now in the left front pocket of his shorts, leaped into his mind.

God! Had this happened before? Is this the same scenario? Is this madman repeating himself?

Up ahead, Dis couldn't see the car – but he could see the line of dust that it stirred up. He seemed to be just barely keeping up with it. The terrain here was Iowa flat, but the road did undulate slightly with the natural swells and turns of the underlying land. The road followed the land rather than pitched through it. And the land was corn land – some of the best in the world.

That's why he couldn't actually see the green Saturn ahead of him. When Dis craned his head as high as he could to see over the forest of tall corn stalks, however, he did notice that the dust was losing its power and getting closer. As he careened along the increasingly grit-filled path of the car, he kept expecting to see the source of the dust. But it was gone. Racing as fast as he could on the difficult surface, he soon found himself out of the dust, even though the road's basic gravel covering had not changed.

Where was Cannon?

Getting more perplexed, Dis suddenly had to make a decision. To his right a farmer's lane led to a small farmhouse and a couple of outbuildings; just past the lane, a weather-beaten sign proclaimed "dead end." Dis skidded to a stop. Was Cannon here? He cautiously rode down the rutted double track lane leading to the farm. He could see no one, not even the inevitable dog. No car was visible. He left the track and slowly rode around the side of the house. Nothing stirred and no car was visible. The place seemed abandoned, a casualty of this age of consolidation.

Dis was perplexed. How could he have lost the car?

He rode out to the gravel road and continued down the dead end section. It was indeed a dead end – and showed no evidence of a recent car's presence. In fact, a large tree branch lay across it fifty feet before the road stopped abruptly at a field of corn. No one had ridden down there recently.

Dis started back down the road slowly, looking from side to side intently, searching for any place where Cannon could have turned off. Then it hit him: maybe Cannon had noticed him and turned into a cornfield somewhere just to dodge him? By now he could be back on the highway, heading wherever?

Dis immediately accelerated, the sweat still profusely pouring from him. He had not even taken the time to wipe it off. As he sped along, he kept an intense watch for any disruption in the line of growing corn along the side of the road. Cannon had had to pull off somewhere, and he was either still there or he had used it to get away from him.

Dusk was deepening. The sun had gone down, but ambient light, aslant and yellow-amber, still gave enough illumination for Dis to make out the configurations on the side of the road. It wouldn't last, however. When it got really dark, Dis didn't know what he would do.

But now, as he rounded a slight curve, he noticed something that he had missed earlier – a track leaving the gravel. It was surrounded by corn, but it was more than just an access point to the fields. It led, curving and slightly elevated into the corn, a discernible two-tracked trail. His speed carried him past it, but he slowed, came to a halt, and returned to where it branched from the gravel.

In a hurry, but still wary, he biked down its grass covered surface. In the fading light Dis soon realized that the track led to another abandoned farm. A falling-apart farmhouse lay before him, in front of a burnt-out shell of what had probably been a barn. Weeds surrounded the place, except for the ruts of the track, which curved around the house, ending where the plantings of corn began.

There, obscured from the gravel road by the tall corn, was the light green Saturn.

It was turned facing the entrance and illuminated by the faint glimmering of light left by the defeated sun. Through the windshield Dis' worst fears were being enacted. Cannon was far over on the passenger side of the vehicle. He was staring intently at something very close to the passenger door – something that Dis knew to be Teresa Clemmon, although he couldn't really make her out. Cannon's arms were positioned in front of his turned body gripping something, possibly the little girl's head or neck.

Dis didn't hesitate. He leaped from his bike.

He ran to the car. But his abrupt movements caught the eye of Cannon, who stopped what he was doing, his arms dropping to his side like dead weight. He turned his head and stared at Dis through the windshield, his face changing instantly from skewered intensity to surprised anguish.

Simultaneously, Dis heard the cry – through the 20 yards or so between him and the car, through the car's closed up windows, through the abandoned tranquility of the place. The cry cut and bled. It was a little girl's cry of excruciating pain and desperation. And it was accompanied by tremendous sobs and intakes of breath. It rattled Dis's mind and psyche as nothing he had ever heard.

It was the cry of a little girl who had just escaped death.

Jack Cannon heard it too, of course, and it snapped him into action. In duo motion he shoved the gear level with his hand and hit the accelerator with his foot. The car had been idling with its air conditioning on. Now it shot right at the running Dis, swerving as Dis angled to avoid it. But it came right at him, accelerating. Dis leaped as it brushed his calf.

As he flung himself through the air to the left of the rampaging car, his eyes latched for one compelling moment on the tear-strung face of the girl. Dis had never seen horror and terror before; now he saw it – vividly. Her face was a mask of extreme human desperation, a baby's innocence turned into a wail of strained flesh and tears.

He hit the ground and rolled, miraculously ending up on his feet near the edge of what once was the farm's front yard. But the car was gone, skidding around the edge of the cornfield down the old farm lane. Dis chased it momentarily, just enough to see it round the right angle turn onto the gravel road. It was gone.

He ran to his bike, grimly determined to follow as fast and as hard as he could. The bike was unharmed; Cannon probably hadn't even seen it in the overgrown grass. Dis leaped on the bike and began the chase again.

This time the cloud of dust was very visible. Cannon evidently was charging down the road pell-mell, desperate to get away and not get caught. But he still had the little girl, the gasping, almost strangled six-year-old. What would he do?

Dis charged too. He pushed as hard as he had ever done in his life – even through the rutted, gravely surface. He bounced and chattered, almost losing control when a washout or a deep pit slammed his bike ajar or knocked it askew. But he didn't relent. He was the only one who knew what had happened back there and if he didn't stop Cannon, he didn't know what would happen to the child.

But Cannon was far ahead of him and increasing the distance between them. When Dis came to the intersection with the blacktop county road, he was at a loss. Which direction to go? Would Cannon go back to town or race away from it? Dis didn't know, and as he was slightly slowing for the intersection, he made up his mind almost without hesitation. Dis would go back to town. He knew he couldn't catch Cannon on the blacktop and in town he could get help, he could go to the police and tell what had happened.

So Dis turned left and raced in the fading late evening light toward the town, which in the distance even now appeared as a faint glow on the horizon, lit up as it was for all the evening BABI festivities.

About a mile down the road Dis heard the faint strains of a siren that then stopped abruptly. Almost simultaneously he picked up a flashing red light way off in the distance ahead of him. Perhaps there had been an accident, he thought. But there wasn't much traffic on this county road, except when it entered the city. He also sensed, perhaps through his hearing because he didn't look back, that another car was off in the distance behind him.

As he sped on, he saw that the light was a police car emergency flasher and that the car was pulled up on the side of the road. Another car was in front of it, and when Dis swerved wide on the road, he could tell that the car was light green – and that it was a Saturn.

Fantastic! The cops had him!

He raced up to the two cars and the various men who were standing between them, Cannon one of them. He yelled "Hold him. He's got the girl!"

But another man turned around and faced him, police pistol in hand, a familiar man in an gray suit and a nondescript face. He said very simply, "Let's have the lens."

Chapter 30

Gloria had tried to catch up to Dis, but it was no use. The traffic was maddening. She did, however, follow as well as she could, trying to watch ahead of her as she slowly crept out Spring Street. Once past the last few residences, she sped up because traffic almost magically decreased. But nothing on the roadway up ahead was visible. Although it was still light enough to see fairly well, she turned on her lights, hoping to cut through the slanting shadows cast by the occasional clumps of trees.

She accelerated more.

Soon she was speeding down the well-paved blacktop road, keeping an intent eye on the road ahead and any possible intersections. She passed one break in the road, a unprepossessing gravel road, but in an instantaneous decision decided not to take it. She did notice, however, a slight beige mist to the right as she passed the road, but didn't connect it with dust spun into motion by a passing car.

Ten minutes later she knew she had missed the bicyclist she knew as Gary. He could never have biked this far out in the time since she had seen him speeding through the intersection in town. She slowed down just past a bridge, at a farm entrance, and turned around, moving now at a more moderate speed, but with an increasing visibility problem – she was now traveling at an angle to the sunset and it played tricks on her eyes.

About half way to Owaceta, she noticed a flashing red light way ahead of her. Her first thought was that her Gary had had an accident, but she put it out of her mind and continued searching the side of the road for any place where a bicyclist could turn off. She passed the same gravel road as before and noticed that what appeared to be a mist was now enfolded over the entire intersection. She slowed, wondering if she should turn, but the lure of the flashing red light ahead drew her on.

Soon she came upon two cars pulled over to the side of the road, a nondescript gray Ford with a portable flashing light stuck on its roof and a light green Saturn. She slowed behind them, almost coming to a stop. When she noticed the bicycle lying next to the left-hand side of the road in front of both the cars, she braked abruptly.

Her first thought was "Oh my God Someone's run into Gary."

She was ready to leap from her car when she saw him. Her beautiful Gary was standing upright between two men. All three of them were looking in the direction of her car, probably trying to penetrate through her headlights. Gary did not look injured in any way.

Then as she was about to turn her lights off and stop her engine, Gary abruptly broke away from the other two men and ran down the road away from her. The two men, startled momentarily, gave chase. The younger of the two, a big and burly man with a closely cropped haircut, soon disappeared into the faint darkness. The other man, older and moving cramped and awkwardly, soon stopped and waited at the extreme edge of Gloria's vision. He seemed to be shifting his attention back and forth between Gary's disappearance and her headlights.

Gloria became immediately suspicious. She didn't like the older man at all. In her white headlights he was a pasty gray vision of incongruity. Just then the younger man appeared, almost dragging Gary. He had Gary's arm wedged behind his back and was almost lifting him off the ground with the levered arm. The man almost shoved Gary into the older man when they approached him.

Words were spoken and the older man started walking towards her. She heard, "Turn off those lights, will you, god dammit!"

With her carnival experience behind her, Gloria knew that the lights were to her advantage. She could see them; they couldn't see her. Her mind was a-whirl with options: how should she handle this?

She settled in an instant. She turned the lights off – and turned them on again a long two seconds later.

She caught a glimpse of the older man instinctively raising his hand to his eyes, but her attention was immediately drawn to the two men behind him. The big younger man was doubled over clutching his groin area and her Gary was free again. He wasn't moving toward her, however.

It was his bicycle he wanted.

All at once a bicycle leaped out from in front of the first car. In the light of the first car's headlights, Gloria could see, frozen momentarily before he exploded down the road toward the town, a frantically moving Gary on his bike.

Chapter 31

As soon as the car with its blinding headlights started to slow down, Dis made his decision. He was taking off; he didn't care what happened. The little girl in the car was OK; she had stopped crying. Cannon seemed to be cowed; it was the gray man who was in charge; he was the one who had demanded the lens.

Well, he wasn't going to get it!

Even in the iron-tight clutch of Jack Cannon, Dis was determined to run. Any distraction and he would be gone. When the third car's headlights snapped off, he wretched away from Cannon and kicked as hard as he could in the general direction of Cannon's midsection. He caught him squarely in the groin, the quick pain enough to cause Cannon to relax his grip and for Dis to make his move. He raced to his bike in the darkness and almost as the light came back on again, he jerked it upright and leaped on it.

Dis took off, standing on his pedals, pushing with all the force in his body. He didn't look back, hoping that the newly arrived car would be enough of a distraction to give him a chance to cover the mile or so before town. Once in the city, he could go almost anywhere to avoid the cars – side streets, alleys, even backyards. Plus, he would be covered by the myriad of BABI riders in town.

So he pumped, the muscles in his legs moving quickly to the straining point. They ached, but he didn't let that affect him. This was not an endurance race; it was an elemental sprint.

And it was dark now; almost all of the last glimmerings of natural light gone. At first it didn't bother Dis, distracted by his sheer need to get space between him and the cars. But as he moved farther and farther away from the receding light of the car's headlights, he realized he was almost flying blind.

He concentrated on the constantly moving sight frame shrinking in front of him. He knew the blacktop was smooth and good; but he also vaguely remembered some disruptions in the surface, not major potholes, but minor rippling and some torn-up layers. Whatever, he wasn't going to worry about them; the main thing was to stay on the road and get to town.

Soon the car lights that he sensed behind him faded into nothing, smothered by the night's dark. The cars weren't moving – unless they were driving in the dark! No, he hadn't noticed the blink of their headlights being extinguished. But the absence of light was a problem. He wanted to look back, to see if he could sense any movement coming behind him; but if he did, he might lose his sense of direction in the almost complete darkness. At the speed he was traveling, he could be in the ditch instantly – with who knows what kind of injuries.

Just then he hit something and his bike lurched. He felt himself propelled in the air, both wheels off the ground. The back wheel touched first, then the front; and he found himself skidding, aslant to the road. He leaned and with an effort brought himself back to an upright position. Was he going in the right direction? He had to be. At his rate of speed, if he weren't, he would be in the ditch by now.

He didn't know what he had hit – perhaps a pothole, maybe some road kill – it could have been anything. But he didn't slow down. He had to get to town with the lens.

The faint glow in the sky that he took to be the lights of Owaceta seemed to be getting brighter. But he only saw it in flickering moments as he roared down the road past large bushes, trees, farm buildings, each of which obscured the light momentarily. But the faint glow confirmed that he was headed in the right direction and that he was gaining on his pursuers.

Then through the sweat still poring down his forehead into his eyes he noticed another light to his right. As he passed a level field, this light seemed to be embedded in the ground, but it disappeared as the road went uphill between two larger hills. But when he started leveling off and felt himself picking up speed in his descent, the light to the right was stronger and seemed to be emerging from the ground.

Then Dis realized, bumping along the irregular road, that what he was seeing was his old friend – the moon. It was rising on a shimmering, heat encrusted evening; it wasn't as pure and as ivory as he remembered; it seemed to be more golden and tarnished. But it was his moon, his light – and now, when the road became increasingly more bouncy, his savior.

He could make out the road now, even see its imperfections. He could dodge them, weaving around them when necessary.

He passed a line of trees, the edge of a small woodlot around a swampy stream, causing him to drop into darkness again – except for an alarming light in the distance behind him. The cars – or a car – were on the road!

The light behind was coming up fast and he knew he still had some distance to go before the beginning of the town. Soon, when he quickly jerked his head and looked behind him, he could make out two lights, two headlights. He wasn't sure who it was, but he wasn't taking any chances. He braked sharply, skidding almost to a stop, and leaped off the still rolling bike. He ran with it into the ditch on the right side of the road.

It was very dark, but Dis could make out some trees on the other side of the ditch, which he found out immediately was both wet and muddy. But he didn't care. He raced through the cold muck, almost carrying his bike across the ditch, and dragged it with him into the trees, which thankfully were not protected by a fence. He flopped down on the ground, crushing some small underbrush, with his bike right next to him.

The car's headlights increased in intensity. It was more than one car. In fact, all three cars were racing down the road, their headlights filling the area around Dis with the unnatural light of high intensity focused power. He tried to melt into the ground, realizing as they came up so quickly, that he did not have good cover. He was out in the open, in a clump of trees, to be sure, but not behind any of the trees. He could be seen by an observant eye and, quite possibly, be betrayed by his bike – its reflectors were designed just for occasions like this. But it was on the ground, hopefully the reflectors wouldn't be in line with the beams of light.

They were, though!

The first car's brake light started pulsing as soon as it passed Dis's sprawled body. It skidded, braking to a stop, almost causing the car behind it to smash into it. But the second car, the Saturn, caught itself in time and skidded to the left, swerving but stopping. The third car, which had been farther behind, stopped safely, more than a hundred yards behind the other two.

Dis didn't know if they had seen his reflectors, had picked up his form lying on the ground, or even had seen him go into the ditch. He just knew that he wasn't going to be around to ask. He jumped up, grabbed his bike, and carrying it over his head, ran through the cold ditch and onto the road. He came out behind the second car, which Dis could see now was still driven by Jack Cannon. The little girl was either hiding or was not in the car. But Dis didn't have time to ponder. He ran with his bike, wheels to the ground, made a flying leap onto it, and hit the pedals pushing. Before Cannon could get out of his car, Dis rushed past him.

Chapter 32

In the light from the almost completely risen moon, Dis boomed past the end of a cornfield where it abruptly stopped and became a neatly trimmed suburban lawn, complete, as he could see for just an instant from the corner of his eye, with a flower bed protected by a concrete birdbath and a plastic statue of a winsome fawn.

He hardly noticed the items though. But almost unconsciously, he did realize that he had made it to town. A minor victory, but – with his face still covered with streaming sweat, his clothes dirty, saturated, and steamy, and every muscle in his body screaming in pain and strain – still a victory.

He sensed the town's light rather than consciously noted it. The soft illumination in the stifling night was filtering through the murky, super-saturated air, and combining with the golden glow from the almost completely risen moon to give light to Dis's path.

He passed another field, a small one, not of corn but of something that he couldn't recognize if he wanted to, before another home reared out of the murky darkness. This one was a tumbledown shack of a place with a rusting car next to it and children's toys strewn in its front yard, they also rusting. Next to it a line of towering yew trees shielded it from its neighbor, a more respectable small bungalow.

Ahead of him, Dis could see an intersection with a stop sign. An overhead streetlight illuminated two cars waiting for another car to cross the intersection. He wondered if he should commandeer one of them if he could get there before they moved away. He would have the protection of a car and an innocent driver as a witness. They could find a policeman – or the police department – and he could stop this interminable chase.

But some indefinable caution in the back of his head told him not to do it. That was the gray man back there and he had had a gun and a car with police lights and a grim, almost bitter authority. Dis knew without analyzing it that he was a cop in this town and that the last thing Dis should do was to go to the local cops. State cops. State cops would be the answer. Would they be in town tonight? Very likely, what with BABI's 10,000 extra overnighters swarming all over the place.

And Dis also checked himself by remembering how he had left the town chasing after the Saturn. His bicycle had been an advantage in the congested traffic, which would probably still be as bad, if not worse, than before.

Wondering who was in that third car, which had given him the chance to break away, he made his decision: he would ride through town looking for a state cop, going back to Carl's Cafe and Teresa's mother as a last resort.

Teresa! God, he thought of that piercing wail and sped up even more. At least she was safe – or he hoped she was. She had to be – too many people and cars involved now.

God! He should stop right now and when the cars pulled up to him, tell them what he had seen at the abandoned farmhouse. The third car – even the second with the gray man – would certainly listen and stop this nonsense. Surely they wouldn't protect a man like Jack Cannon!

But the gray man wanted the lens – with a drawn gun, he wanted the lens. He was in cahoots. Hell, maybe even the third car was also.

Dis veered into the intersection. It was empty, the last car 30 yards away and accelerating towards Owaceta. Dis followed it without stopping, hardly shifting his eyes, knowing that any car would be stopping at the four-way stop signs. Behind him, the three cars closed the gap. Headlights slowed at the stop signs, then burst forward.

Dis raced toward the car in front of him, which was obeying the in-town speed limit. If he could pass it, it would protect him from the relentless three. He rose to the occasion and soon was slipping around the car's right side. The street here wasn't busy; it was largely a semi-industrial area of small companies, warehouses, and trucking depots. But up ahead, Dis made out more traffic, even a few bicyclists amid the more residential streets shaded by trees ghostly illuminated now by streetlights and some overpowering front yard and porch lights.

Behind him, the car he had just passed – driven by a young mother with three kids bouncing around the back seat – was slowing to make a left turn. The three cars behind it had to slow too. But the first car, the Saturn, swerved around it to the right, almost clipping its fender, and continued after him in high pursuit.

Dis was almost drained. He felt himself involuntarily ease up. Perhaps because he was in town, or maybe just reaching his physical limits; whatever, he was slowing. The Saturn was catching up to him – even on the relatively slow city streets. He pushed harder, but found himself losing the battle of the gap. The Saturn gained on him.

He had a momentary vision of losing the race just when he was so close to his destination. He pictured big Jack Cannon pinning him to the ground and going through his pockets – a mob of onlookers around them, but the gray man with a drawn pistol and a determined authority giving legitimacy to the scene.

He sped around another car, this time on the left. But seemingly within seconds, the Saturn screeched around it also, and – still gaining – crept up behind him.

Traffic.

It was traffic that came to his rescue. That and his bicycle's maneuverability. The street led straight to the downtown, the prime destination on this night for what appeared to be everyone in town – BABIers and townspeople alike. Just when the Saturn sped to where it could almost bang his back wheel if it wanted to, the traffic engulfed them both.

A double line of cars, creeping along at a low gear pace, dammed the rushing street. Dis sped between them, not caring about safety, courtesy, or the law. The Saturn and the other two pursuing cars had to slow down, even stop – and then try to creep through the cars and bikes converging on the central focus of the town. But Dis had freedom. He squirreled through the throngs of vehicles and bikes like a pickpocket in Times Square. He jumped the curb, whisked down sidewalks, veered around vehicles and pedestrians, even took to the grass. At one point he almost plowed into a makeshift cool-aid stand run by two overwhelmed 8-year-olds.

But he got away.

When he careened to the stoplights where another major street merged with the one he was on, his peripheral vision told him that the three cars were nowhere in sight. But as he was lurching through the intersection, going through the red, his ears belied his relief.

Maybe he hadn't gotten away. A siren began its quickening wail. It came from behind him, and a quick jerk of his head told him that the chase wasn't over. Flashing red and blue lights were slicing through the haphazard traffic.

The intersection with its stoplight had momentarily eased the congestion; Dis had a chance to gain some momentum and speed. But just as he met the packed traffic again, the gray car with the flashing lights burst from the intersection and roared after him. Now the traffic around him really stopped, the motorists obeying their automatic response to sirens and police lights.

But that was good for Dis. He raced through the massed cars and bikes, bumping through the barricades where his street met Front Street, which was all blocked off for the BABI party, with uniformed police or auxiliary officers handling conflicts. But bikes were carte blanche on this night. In fact, the street was filled with them, most parked, but some being ridden on the margins of the street by die-hards and showoffs.

Dis leaped off his bike and with both hands on the handlebars, swept through the crowds in the general direction of Carl's Cafe. He was also searching intently for a state cop. In his haste and still covered with sweat as he was, he soon realized that the possibility of meeting a state cop in the midst of the crowd was minimal. They wouldn't be in with the swirling masses; they would be outside, looking in – in a command position.

So Dis charged through the strollers and standees as quickly as he could, looking behind him constantly and warily. As he approached the other side of the street, the side with Carl's Cafe, he noticed a commotion behind him.

The crowd yielded to a flurry of running men, one brandishing a weapon.

God, he's got his gun out in the midst of this crowd!

Dis exploded. He leaped onto his bike, yelling at the same time, "Out of my way! Out of my way!"

He charged through the masses of surprised walkers and gazers, heading straight for the edge of the street. But stores walled the street in at this point, so Dis had to make a lateral turn and try to pedal through the crowds until he found an outlet. He saw a parking lot ahead, but when he approached it, he saw that it was blocked by snow fencing. One small fence opening remained, however – manned by two men in orange vests evidently taking tickets or checking I.D.s or something. Dis made an immediate decision to bull his way through it.

He yelled, "Watch out; I'm going through!" and when the startled walkers in front of him parted, he accelerated and aimed for the opening. Just then he heard from behind him in a voice of commanding authority, "Stop him! Stop the man on the bike!"

The two vested men by now were looking in his direction. When they heard the yelled command, they reacted quickly. One of them reached behind him and pulled a section of snow fence across the opening. The other man grabbed it from him and held it taut across the gap.

But it was too late for Dis. He didn't stop. In fact, realizing he had to get out, he put everything he had into a final burst of speed and power. He hit the makeshift gate with a crash. The end held by the second man snapped from his hands. The fencing flew, giving way to the onrushing Dis. But the contact wasn't pure. Dis had to smash the fencing down to the pavement, then roll over it. And the fencing resisted. After his front wheel passed the top edge, the fence surged upward, catching his bottom bracket with the wire that held together two of the wooden slats.

Dis reeled to the side, almost upended by the sudden stopping force. But his last burst of acceleration saved him. The wire snapped from the force of his momentum and he caught himself before the suddenly jerked bike could hit the ground. He twisted the handle bars, righting himself, and with both legs up and pumping, he was off down the completely filled parking lot, riding his still usable bike as hard as he could.

Still yelling, "Watch out! Watch out!" he rammed through the narrow passages between parked cars, trusting that walkers would scramble out of his way. By now, however, he was being chased by a multitude. He didn't look back, but he could hear the commotion behind him – hard running, yells of "Stop him! Stop him!" and some high-pitched screams from startled people squeezing through the parking lot.

But somehow he managed to get through the tightly enclosed spaces. He erupted through the lot's edge, leaping over a concrete-edged, grass filled barrier, hitting the street like a cat escaping a dog through a second floor window. The street paralleled Front Street, but an alley ran away from the downtown opposite the parking lot. Dis headed for it through strands of people moving towards the center of attention, the BABI party on Front Street.

Unfortunately he had no time to notice the small sign to the right of the alley's entrance: Dead End.

He sped up the alley prodded by the commotion behind him and his need to escape and get help. After about half a block, the alley turned to the left, Dis scrambling on the slightly gravely surface. But then it stopped – abruptly, a looming garage door an imposing barrier across the entire width of the pavement. Fences and hedges bordered the alley sides, and in the semi-darkness of this cul de sac behind a mixture of businesses and residences, Dis could see no outlet.

He could, however, hear pursuit. It galloped behind him.

He screeched to a stop, almost jumping his bike to turn it around. Just then he saw an opening. A chest-high hedge opened on a narrow, three-foot width of concrete sidewalk. Dis didn't hesitate. He bulled his way through the opening, tearing the hedge with the two ends of his handlebars. Inside was grass, with the concrete sidewalk leading to the small back porch of what appeared to be a residence.

Dis searched for a side opening, but couldn't see any. "Damn!" he thought to himself, "I'm trapped!"

Just then he heard the yelled words, "Stop right there. There's a gun on you!"

Chapter 33

Gloria did not like the sweat and the puffing. She was not used to it, except on hot set-up days at the carnival; but then she could control her pace. Not now. She was trying to catch Gary, and he was scrambling.

She had followed him and the two cars, chasing them all through the town, dropping her car when the two others did and following them – a big, young man with a short haircut, and a nondescript older man – as they chased after Gary through the crowded streets. She did not know what exactly was going on, but she knew in her heart that Gary was in trouble – serious trouble.

She knew it even before she abandoned her car in the traffic surrounding the main street. At a lull, while waiting for the car ahead of her to move, she had taken her pistol, the little .22 she usually kept in her bedroom in the trailer, from the glove compartment and put it into her handbag, her trusty cloth bag with the strap that went over her neck. Something was going on that she didn't know about, and she felt more than just a vague sense of apprehension. In fact she was downright scared, but she had no other course. Gary needed help. And just maybe, her pistol would be needed.

As the pursuers ran through the clogged streets, the short haired guy outdistanced her. But she kept pace with the older man, following close behind him as the crowds melted in his advance. He, following the young guy who crashed through the crowd with unapologetic bluster, was not saying much – just an occasional, "Stop that man!" – but he seemed to have an invisible authority that caused the walkers to stop in their tracks and let him through. A few people followed her, but most stared in bewilderment and then continued with what they had been doing.

It was hot and sweltering and almost pitch dark away from Main Street and the streetlights of the other streets. The only natural light came from the just risen moon, a glorious full moon, now just high enough over the city's houses to cast its weak light. Sweat claimed the surface of her skin, staining her blouse in front below her bra and in back on her shoulder blades. She hardly noticed, except that some of it ran into her eyes, stinging her, and she had to brush it away while she was running.

But she was game. She had always been a determined woman, and she wasn't letting up now. She would see this through to its end.

The older man in the gray pants stopped abruptly just as she was rounding the corner in the alley. He was on the left side of the alley, looking over a hedge, breathing heavily, but speaking with authority in a voice that was hardly more than a whisper, but that could be heard clearly throughout the whole alley – by her and by the other few spectators who out of curiosity had stayed with the chase.

And he was pointing across the hedge – pointing with a gun.

Gloria ran up to the hedge about ten feet from the gray man and in an instant saw what he was pointing at – her Gary with his hands up, the big guy to his side, patting her man's pockets furiously.

All at once the big guy yelled, "I got it, Leghorn. I think this is it." He reached into Dis's left pocket and with some difficulty pulled out something. Then he held it up in the air triumphantly. In the dim moonlight, it seemed to be nothing but a small paper-wrapped flat square. The guy said to the older man, "This is it, baby, this is it."

Just then the man she knew as Gary yelled, "Hey you out there. This man's a killer, a baby killer! He killed Star –"

That was as far as he got. The big man smashed him in the stomach with his free hand, and then quickly clutched Dis around the neck. All that came out of Dis's mouth were muffled words and a low rasping.

The man continued to hit him in the lower body, each smash punctuated by a corresponding "uff" from Dis, while he yelled to the older man, "Come here, Leghorn, take this thing while I beat the shit out of him."

The gray man didn't move. He just said, again in almost a whisper, "That's enough, Jack. Quit hitting him; just make sure he doesn't say anything."

"One last punch, OK?" With that he hit Dis as hard as he could in the solar plexus.

Dis slumped, tottered, and slipped to the ground. He ended up on his back, his eyes fluttering, trying to stay open, but losing the battle.

Gloria, who by now was at the opening in the hedge, reached into her cloth handbag and grasped her pistol. She didn't quite know what to do, but she knew she wasn't going to let them hurt her Gary anymore.

The big man, Jack, glanced sideways at the gray man, and then looked down at Dis, whose head was lolling and his consciousness fluttering. A sneer crossed the face of the standing man with the close cropped hair and he moved his right leg back. It was pointed directly at Dis's head.

Gloria didn't hesitate. She jerked the little .22 out of the handbag, pointed it at the big man, and yelled, "You kick him and you're dead!"

Her voice carried and Jack got the message. His foot stopped abruptly. He looked in her direction, a questioning grin on his face.

"Shit, lady, this guy's gonna be arrested. He's a wanted man."

Dis didn't know what was going on. His eyelids still moved randomly. But he wasn't out. He fought for consciousness.

Gloria yelled again. "You hear me. Kick him again and you're dead." She kept the gun aimed at the big guy, but shifted her eyes back and forth between him and the older man who she had followed through the crowd.

Then she added, "And bring whatever you took from him over here. Yeah, that package wrapped in paper. Bring it here."

The big man was in a quandary. A sickening puzzlement spread across his wide face. He looked at Gloria, trying to gauge her determination. Then his eyes shifted to the gray man, seeking a command, instructions, some idea of what to do. But the man stood behind the hedge, his face an implacable mask.

Jack's eyes shifted back to Gloria. "Hey, Lady, you ain't got no right to pull that gun on me. Now put it away while I take this guy down to the jail."

He started reaching down to Dis, but before his hand got half way to Dis's body, a shot rang out, the bullet whizzing through the humid night air and smashing into the house immediately behind Jack with a splintering crunch. Jack jumped back. The shot hadn't hit him, but he knew that it had come dangerously close. He stood up straight and backed away from the prone Dis.

The shot, however, seemed to revive Dis. His eyelids stopped their movements and he moved his head up slightly, enough to try to see in the direction of the shot.

Gloria moved towards him. With her pistol held firmly in her hand, she advanced into the yard away from the hedge, separating herself from the increasing number of onlookers who were watching and trying to figure out what was going on.

With one quick glance at Dis, Gloria walked up to the big man, her unoccupied hand out. "Now give me what you took."

Jack seemed to notice for the first time that he was clutching the paper wrapped glass lens. "No, I got it, and it's mine. I mean, I got it . . ." His voice dwindled. He didn't know what to say. He stared at Leghorn, beseeching him wordlessly for help.

"Give it to me." Her voice, insistent and authoritative, drew him back to her demand. He didn't know what to do, but the memory of the spinning bullet flashing by him was fresh. He raised the hand holding the lens and extended it toward Gloria.

"Don't give it to her." The gravely voice was a sound from a dead rock quarry. Both Gloria and Jack looked at its source. Leghorn's shoulders and head loomed over the hedge, but more importantly, his hand, holding a .38 police special, was now pointed directly at Gloria.

Gloria's gun was still pointed at Jack – and Jack still had his hand out, cradling the softly wrapped package.

No one was watching Dis – and that was all he needed!

He pushed himself up with every aching muscle in his body. But because of the beating he had just taken, it wasn't enough. He was able to raise his upper body, but his legs refused to respond.

So he literally threw himself with his arms at Jack – at Jack's legs. He tackled him, both of his arms grasping the big man's legs below the knee. Then Dis rolled into the man, his arms pulling Jack's legs together. The suddenness of it made Cannon lose his balance. He crashed to the ground – and the lens went flying!

Went flying – right to Gloria.

In fact it hit her in the chest then rolled away onto the grass, its brown paper covering flapping for release from the deep creases acquired through months of tight confinement in Dis's panniers and on his person.

She stooped down and deftly grabbed the lens, yelling, "I've got it, Gary. Whatever it is, I've got it!"

Dis's voice came muffled from the ground. He had a death grip on Jack's legs, but Jack was struggling with all his might to break free, and he was a big, muscular man who was becoming very irate. Dis had all he could do to keep his arms around the squirming legs.

"State cops," he blurted. "Get it to – state cops." The voice was hardly more than a rasping whisper, but in the stillness of the moon-lit night it penetrated.

Now Gloria was in a quandary. Should she stay and try to protect Dis or should she take off and somehow do what he had just commanded?

She leveled her .22 at the struggling forms of Dis and Jack, but their tightly moving conflict gave her no stationary target. From under Jack's thrashing legs, Dis had a momentary glimpse of her standing above them, her pistol in her hand. He rasped again, "Go! State cops! The lens!"

She took off, running towards the opening in the hedge.

But the opening was blocked – by Leghorn. And his imposing .38 revolver.

She had to slow down. She had no place to go. But, no, she wasn't going to stay in this cul-de-sac. She put her head down and bulled right into the opening, only one glance at the gray man betraying the terrible dilemma of this decision to put her life in jeopardy.

The gray man, however, refused to move.

So she ran right over him. Actually, she ran between him and the side of the hedge opening, scratching her leg and tearing her blouse, but also knocking Leghorn to the side and almost causing him to lose his balance.

But he recovered and as Gloria scurried through the perplexed crowd he raised his pistol and said, his gravely voice a pitch higher than before, "That's it, Lady. Stop where you are."

But she didn't stop.

So he shot her.

He shot her in the back, the force of the bullet knocking her instantly to the ground. The jarring as she crashed released the lens from her hand and it sailed across the alley's pavement, ending up in front of a young man in jeans, T-shirt, and an improbable Dixie Cream Donut cap on his head. He stepped forward and almost casually retrieved the bouncing paper-covered lens.

Gloria was dead instantaneously; the bullet ripping at close range through her lungs and a corner of her heart, emerging through her left breast, tearing through her brassiere and her blouse, and hitting the ground, spent from its deadly mission, next to an alley fence. Blood poured from her – both back and front as she lay lifeless on her side in the middle of the moonlit alley.

The crowd, including the Dixie Cream man, was aghast. Things like this didn't happen in Owaceta. New York, yes. Chicago, yes. But not Owaceta!

The Dixie Cream man now noticed that he had the package in his hand. He looked at it in amazement, as if he didn't know how he had acquired it, as if it were a rare bird that had somehow fluttered into his hand. But when he looked up, he looked straight into the barrel of Leghorn's .38. Without a moment of hesitation, Dixie Cream dropped the lens. It landed flat on the alley in front of him, its brown paper covering still hugging it securely.

"Pick it up and give it to me." The gravely voice was the epitome of command. So the man stooped and retrieved the lens, then stepped forward with the lens in front of him, as if making an offering to an irate prehistoric god.

Leghorn advanced towards the lens, but he wasn't fast enough. Jack beat him. The big, younger man had finally wrested himself from the clutching arms of Dis, and had made a bee-line through the opening in the hedge, past the bleeding body of Gloria, up to the extended hand of Dixie Cream, where he grabbed the lens.

"Give me that thing! It's mine! Mine!" He turned to look back at Leghorn with a triumphant smile on his face. "I've got it!"

The smile vanished, however, when he saw movement behind Leghorn – rapid, accelerating movement. Dis was up and his legs were moving!

He was running as hard as he could right at Leghorn. When he came up to him, he had the momentum that with one push with both hands sent Leghorn careening to the ground, the pistol falling from his hand. Leghorn landed face down right on top of the revolver.

Dis didn't hesitate a moment. He swooped as hard and as fast as he could at the ugly figure of Jack.

But Jack reacted with the innate ability of a natural, but out-of-shape athlete. He took off like a rabbit from a hawk. He ran down the alley to where it met the street. On the other side was the parking lot behind Main Street, filled now with the mobs of people. So he made a right turn and ran down the street, which was almost just as confusing – filled with a mass of slow-moving cars, pedestrians walking back and forth to and from the festival, and criss-crossing bikes.

The heavyset Jack could run! Dodging cars and people, and almost crashing into skittish bicycles, he leap-frogged and scampered down the street, his hand tightly clutching the paper covered lens.

Heat escaped from the street after being trapped there all afternoon. Humidity hovered in the air like a water-sodden mist. But the moon was up. It was up fully, above the houses and the trees. And it was full!

As Dis turned the alley corner, all he saw was the fleeing Jack careening through the traffic, silhouetted in front of the moon. He followed him pell-mell, his legs moving quickly but painfully now; his body aching from the beating. But nothing was going to stop him from getting to Jack and retrieving that lens. Nothing!

But still Jack moved away from him. Dis ran as fast as he could, but Jack scrambled faster – a leaping, side-stepping black figure in front of the moon.

In desperation Dis caught his breath, slowed momentarily, and yelled out, "Stop him! He's a killer!"

People paused, surprised by the chase more than the hoarse words.

With another gasp of air, Dis blurted, "A killer! He killed Star! A little girl! He killed her!"

One man started running with Dis, saying, "Hey, that's Jack Cannon up ahead. What'd he do?"

But Dis was too exhausted to answer while he ran. The man, however, continued to run with Dis. Two other men – teenagers really – joined them.

By this time Jack came to the intersection with a street, Spring Street, which was completely blocked by traffic. And just when he erupted from the street he was on, a team of about a dozen bikers, riding in file next to the curb clogged the intersection even more when they bunched together because of the slowed traffic ahead. In their camaraderie and joking, they effectively put a plug into the intersection, preventing any movement across it.

The raging Jack was stymied. But his quick eyes saw some openings, some less dense traffic, to his right. He changed directions in mid-run, pushing off from a pair of teenage lovers, arms entwined together. The girl didn't even notice, but the boy took immediate umbrage; it was too late, however, to do anything about this violation to his body: Jack was gone, sidestepping and dodging down the street.

When Dis raced toward him, however, the boy was prepared. "Hey, watch where you're goin'!" he yelled even before Dis approached him directly. The boy put his arms in front of him, preparing for a defense.

Dis saw the movement and yelled, "That guy! He's a killer! Catch him!"

The boy gave a swift glance at his girl friend, and jumped with Dis, almost colliding with him in the process. "OK! He pushed me; let's get him!"

The boy was fast – faster than Dis. He started picking up on the fleeing Jack, leaving Dis slowly falling behind. Other passers-by also followed, but more discretely, not wanting to get closely involved.

In desperation, Dis used his voice. He bellowed, "Stop that man! He's a killer. He killed Star, Star Oatage. You know, that little girl. He's the real killer. Stop him!"

People reacted. They stopped and looked behind them at the fleeing figure of Jack. Locals, especially, bristled. The words "Star Oatage" hit some of them like a powerful punch. They remembered. A few joined in the chase. One twenty-year-old, riding his mountain bike to the downtown festivities, even turned around and followed Dis, wondering just how involved he should get.

Between the streetlights and the now risen moon, Dis could make out almost everything on the crowded street as he ran. He saw Jack about a half block ahead, the teenager pursuing him and gaining on him. The side of the street was completely filled with parked cars, but Dis, looking hard, noticed that one double parked car was a cop car. He could see the dual set of blinkers mounted on the car's top.

And Jack was running toward it, was almost next to it. Now the teenager yelled something about "killer," and Dis could see some movement in the car. The driver's side door opened and an officer stepped out. He wore the quasi-military uniform of a state trooper and he had his radio microphone in his hand.

Dis ran as fast as he could. Jack was past the cop car. Maybe it was too late for him to be stopped. And by the time Dis arrived at the car, he could hardly talk, so heaving was his breathing. "The guy's . . . a killer! Star Oatage! He's . . . the killer!"

Officer Sam Shapino couldn't believe his ears. Two times in one day! First the pretty blond lady whose brother was in Fort Madison and now this wild man chasing a big guy who was vaguely familiar to him. Well, let's see if we can get this straightened out.

He dropped into the driver's seat and immediately started the car, the flashing red and blue lights on top and the siren erupting with sudden violence. He also pushed the interrupt button on his radio mike and barked, "State Officer Shapino. Got a situation here at Spring and Second. A citizen's being chased by someone calling him a killer. I'm going to try to follow him. Give me some backup."

The street, parked on both sides, was too narrow for him to make a U-turn. But up ahead a driveway was open to the street, and it wasn't long before he had turned around and was warily making his way down the street, lights flashing and siren screaming, bulling a path through the groups of BABI attenders.

He passed Dis and the people who were running with him. Up ahead he could see Jack, now sprinting down the middle of the street, the teenager following closely. With fewer pedestrians, cars, and bikes on the street, and his warning devices opening a path, the officer sped faster and soon was almost upon Jack.

He clicked the PA button on his mike and hurriedly barked, "Stop right there. That's enough. Don't move." Then he reached over and found the controls to his spotlight, snapped it on, and aimed it at the panting Jack.

Jack jerked his head around, squinted at the blinding light, and stopped.

Just then the officer's police radio crackled into action: "I've got a lady shot. Look's pretty bad. Shot at close range and she's not moving. Just south of Forthright Street, in the alley between Spring and Comanche. This is patrol officer Darnell — and the detective's here, Leghorn; but get an ambulance here real quick, and I need some backup for the crowds."

Shapino didn't know what to make of what was going on, but suddenly he became very wary. With his revolver drawn, he opened his car door and stepped out, keeping the radio-PA mike in his other hand.

"Don't move, there, fellow. And get your hands up in the air."

Through his gasping and heaving for breath, Jack did as he was told, his right hand, raised overhead now, still clutching the paper covered lens tightly. Through his convulsions, he blurted: "Not me. That biker's the one. Get him. I'm Jack Cannon!"

He was framed in a perfect circle of light from the car's spotlight. The teenager whom he had pushed ran up to the police car and blurted, "He's the guy, officer. This man back here says he's a killer. And he shoved me – me and my girl."

Officer Shapino was in doubt. He knew vaguely of Jack Cannon. His old man was important in this area, wealthy with connections. But right now, he just wanted to get this whole thing straightened out.

"Stay right where you are, Mr. Cannon. Don't move."

A cloud, the first of the night, passed in front of the moon, darkening the street imperceptibly, but enough to register subconsciously with Dis. But the moon of light from the cop car ahead was more than enough for his focus.

He ran even harder and arrived at the scene – and didn't hesitate in going right after Cannon. He didn't stop, running right for the heaving big man. He tackled him in an almost perfect football tackle, knocking him off his balance and sending both of them to the pavement. Dis clambered for the lens, and in Cannon's surprise, was able to wrench it from him.

Lying on the ground, still wrestling with Cannon, he raised his arm with the lens clutched in his hand, and through his heaving breathing yelled, "Take this, someone."

The authoritative voice from the police PA boomed: "That's enough. Both of you – up. With your hands up."

Dis tried to rise, but Cannon had him pressed to the surface. "Let me up! Officer, this is evidence – about Star, Star Oatage, the little girl who was killed. Don't let him get it."

He looked directly at the powerful white light, pleading through his convulsive breathing, "Please, someone, take this."

But it was too late. Cannon, who was on one knee by now, reached and deftly grabbed the package from Dis's hand. He threw the package to the ground, then leaped at it, attempting to smash it under his foot.

But he missed – and that was all Dis needed. He pitched himself to the ground and fell, trying to retrieve the lens. But his outstretched arm knocked it instead, sending it skittering across the pavement, out of the circle of light from the cop car. Both men jumped for it, Cannon on his feet, Dis rolling across the ground.

A shot rang out, but Dis didn't care. All he cared about was the lens. He scampered toward where he thought it was, the darkness more vivid because the light had been so bright. But he couldn't see.

He heard Cannon in front of him, and he followed that sound. Cannon was stomping heavily on the pavement, trying to smash the fragile glass. And Dis was lost; he couldn't see. He rushed toward the sound, throwing his body where he thought the foot would stomp next. He caught Cannon's smashing foot on his leg and felt a sharp needle of pain.

But he couldn't see the package; he couldn't find it.

Then the moon came out from behind the cloud.

And there the lens was, right in front of him, its paper still intact. Dis reached for it, but at the same time heard a sharp impact next to him. Cannon in his blind rage was jumping up and down on the street trying at random to smash the glass, which he knew was close by.

But Dis knew where it was – and his hand was now on it, his fingers around it, clutching it, protecting it.

Before he passed out, two things registered on his sorely charged brain: the shoe coming down directly on his hand, and another pistol shot exploding through the now soft moonlit air.

Chapter 34

It was about two months later and Dis was sweating and panting again.

But he was not being chased – and he was not running after anybody. Not directly, at least.

He was on the road again, on his bike, heading back into his past, but on some of the same roads that he had used to try to get away from it.

Right now he was pedaling rapidly on Highway 156 between Novelty, Missouri, and Quincy, Illinois. And the wind was on his back. It was glorious to have a tailwind. His memory of his odyssey included a constant wind in his face. It was as if even nature had been trying to push him back, and now with things more whole, it was rushing to help him return.

And return he would. He had vowed to himself to do just that.

His destination was Jeffrey, Kentucky. But that was beside the point; his real destination was Lornaree McAbby.

He had talked to her; had called her from his motel room in Owaceta after he had been released from the hospital, and after he had talked with his wife, Ruth. Actually Ruth had called him. As she told him, she almost accidentally was reading a copy of U.S.A. Today in a client's office, when his name, Hal Disberry, had leaped out at her from a small item in the section about news from the states. Under Iowa, the short paragraph told about a "lookalike" who precipitated the arrest of two Owaceta men, one a police officer, involved in the murders of three young women. An elaborate cover-up was also a part of the murders.

What Ruth didn't tell him was that when she saw the words, "Hal Disberry," she almost fainted. She rushed out of the office and found a cubical in the restroom where she could privately lower her head to counteract the sudden exodus of blood from her face. She was stunned – knowing without a moment's hesitation that Hal Disberry was really her Dis, her husband, the man she had lived with for more than ten years and then disappeared – just like that – from her life.

She was sure that the man in the paper was the man who had vanished into nothing, more than four months now, leaving her with – well, a sweet setup: a home, a good job, a lover (whom she quickly got rid of), and a couple of "boy friends," each able to further her goal – infinitesimally or expansively, in her mind – of becoming "Multi-Million Dollar Agent of the Year."

And now, like a ghost from the past, Dis was back in her life.

Damn! Just when she and Jesse Holmgren, the newly widowed owner of the Nissan auto dealership out in Bragtalia, were just starting to hit it off – just after they had spent the weekend together on the beach at Annapolis, and both were still rosy with the expectations of each other. Damn!

She was over Dis – finished with him. His departure, enraging her immensely at the time, was now a part of the past. It was something that had taken place that she had learned to live with.

And, as it turned out, to actually be glad about.

She did not want Dis back.

But she needed to know, to find out where she stood in this sudden development in her life. So within hours of reading the newspaper item, she was on the phone to the Owaceta Police Department, asking if there was any way she could contact the Hal Disberry who was connected with the case involving the murdered women. The clerk said that this Hal was staying at a local motel, that he had no personal phone there, but that he had been stopping at the station every day. She would deliver a message to him.

So Dis, that evening, in a phone booth in the lobby of the Oasis Motel, made the one phone call that he had sworn he would never make.

It turned out, however, to be one of the best. He and Ruth were actually amiable, if reserved. He told her somewhat of the recent events in Owaceta and of that night long ago, it seemed to him, in the parking lot close to the bar in Washington D. C. She, in return, told of her adjustment to her new life style, and that she was over her adamant refusal to consider a divorce. In fact, she would actively welcome it.

"Ah, Ruth, I don't have a tape recorder handy, but can I really believe that? I mean, the reason I left so secretly was that you were so adamant about no divorce – and about making the rest of my life so miserable."

"I guess I was a bitch, wasn't I? But, you know, we were going nowhere, you have to agree to that. You with your shoe clerking job and me, well, you know, Dis . . . Hey, do you remember those Catskill Apartments over in Royal Oaks, the ones that I represented exclusively, well, I got them. I sold 'em, and it put me in the running for the silver shield. I didn't make it, but I came awfully close. And this year . . . but you're not interested, right? You never were, were you Dis?"

"What do you mean, don't you remember how I used to grab the real estate section of the Sunday paper before the front page? How I used to keep track of which agent sold which property? How I used to . . . well, anyway, Ruth, what you're saying is sounding good to me. When I finish up with this mess around here, I'll be returning to Rockhurst. I don't know when, but I'll keep in touch. Is there any hurry?"

"Ah, not right now, Dis. But, then again, you never know."

"You know, that's the same with me, now that I think about it – you never know."

After more than a slight pause, she responded with a bit of the old cutting edge in her voice, "That's right, Dis, you never know. But anyway, it was good to hear from you again – to know that you are still alive, for god's sake. And I'm really sorry about all the trouble that you . . . er. . . fell into. It must have been really bad."

"It was. It was. Someday I'll tell you about it. But for now we better say goodbye. Let's be friends, Ruth, we can be that, right?"

"Sure."

"I'm going to be on the road, but I'll get back to you. You'll hear from me. Then when I get back there, we can start making arrangements. It might take me awhile . . . I've got a few things to straighten up back up the road."

"Oh?"

"OK then. I'll get back to you. Goodbye Ruth."

The conversation had been cool, but cordial. He hadn't thought much about Ruth for months now – she was slowly being relegated to that vague part of the memory filled with once important people now on hold. He did know that her voice had not been pleasant to him; it stirred up too many negatives of his past, too many images of self doubt and mutual frustration, too much time alone when they were together.

He did not want to spend the rest of his life listening to her voice.

But he wouldn't mind doing the same thing with the hush-puppy voice of

Lornaree.

He almost couldn't wait to call her after finishing the call to Ruth.

"Hi, remember me?"

"God, it's you, Rob! Rob, oh my god, Rob, I recognize your voice. Where are you, I mean . . . I thought you . . . "

"Oh, it's so good to hear your voice again, Lorn. You don't know how good you sound to me."

"But. . . I can't believe this. . . where are you? Is everything all right?"

"Did you get my letter?"

"I did just exactly what your letter said. It's gone, but I remember it. Was there another?"

"No . . . I . . . as I told you . . . I couldn't take the chance. Listen I've got so much to tell you. So many things have happened. But I'm going to wait until I see you in person. Is that going to be possible? Are you . . . ah . . . still . . . free?"

"Yep. I'm still free. Still riding. Still ready to patch up every poor road-rashed rider who can't handle the big hill we have here in Jeffrey."

"And Chrissy, how's she?"

"Well, I'll tell you, I'm pissed at her right now. That little snip went out and . . . hey, what am I talking like that for. Rob . . . I just can't believe that I'm talking to you again. After your letter and then nothing for so long, well, I . . . you know . . . hey, were you ever in Eagles Gap on TOCRV, you know, that big bike tour?"

Dis made a vow to himself right there and then to tell the truth about everything. "Yes, I was. That is I traveled with it for a couple days. Hey, I bet that guy with the loud jerseys, what's his name . . .?"

"Knobby?"

"That's him. Yeah, good ol' Knobby. He saw me and tried to strike up a conversation. Caused me fits, he did. But I got away from him, pretty easily as it turned out."

"Yeah, he's bugged me about that for a long time now. Keeps kidding me about you popping up unexpectedly some time. Hey, we'll have to surprise him if and when you ever come back here."

"That was what I was going to ask you about, Lorn. After the way I treated you, what would happen if some day this very bedraggled bike rider found himself going so fast down a certain horrendous hill coming in to Jeffrey, Tennessee, that he . . .

She laughed, "Oh, Rob, you know I'll be here to welcome you. I hope you know that."

"Well, I'm on my way. All that mess, all those things that caused me to leave you in the middle of the night, well, that's all cleared up – most of it anyway. Needless to say, I've got some real stories to tell you. Some I don't even believe myself yet. But I'm free – free from my past – free for my future – with you."

"God, Rob, I don't know what to say. This is so much of a surprise."

"Well anyway, I'm still working out what happened to me. That's why it'll take me a little bit of time to get to you. I'm in a little town in Iowa right now, Owaceta, and I think I'm going to return to you by bike. I've got some stops to make, but most of all I've got to take some time to work things out for myself, to get things settled in my mind. I just need the time, and some good mileage on by bike will give it to me. Besides, I should have tailwinds all the way, right?"

"Oh, Rob, whatever. You take the time. I'll be here – well, around here somewhere. You'll call me every once in a while, won't you?"

"You bet. I will. God, Lorn, just hearing your voice brings you so back to me. I'm so glad you're still willing to take a chance on me. After all, I wiped myself completely out with you – told you to do the same."

"And I did – but I suppose not completely. I always kept a part of myself open – open to . . . well, you, I guess. To your return."

"And I'm going to be doing just that. I . . . I . . . what can I say. You've been with me all through my travels, my dodging, and my horrible time up here. God, Lorn, you've been with me. I just couldn't let you go."

"I was the same, Rob. Oh, God, I think I'm going to cry. I hope Chrissy doesn't come back right now and see me like this. Hey, I'm supposed to be in control – you know the mother who knows how to handle any situation. Rob, come on back here, will you. I need to hear your stories . . . I need you."

"I need you too, Lorn. And I'm on my way."

"OK, Rob. But keep in touch. Call me."

"I will. Ah, what the hell. I want to be completely honest. You call me Rob, but I'm not Rob."

"You're not! You're not Rob? But, Rob, then . . . then who are you?"

"Dis."

"Dis?"

"That's right, my name is Dis. Actually it's Hal Disberry, but I've always been known as Dis. And that's what I want you to call me – Dis. No more lying, Lorn, no more some other fake life. I'm Dis."

"OK . . . Dis. You know it's hard for me to say that. My mind has been filled with Rob. But whatever – it's been filled with you – you, Dis, whatever your name is."

"It's Dis. And, well, I have to say goodbye now, Lorn. Goodbye. I will be back."

Back in his dumpy motel room, dominated by a mass-produced picture of Carlsbad Caverns that was peeling from its backing, Dis stared at the cheap picture and positively beamed. He didn't really see the picture; he didn't see Ruth or even Lorn. All he saw was an expanse of silver-black clarity with a dim light opening up in the distance. He stared and laughed and the dim light slowly expanded – enlarged to a circle of pure silver amid the dissipating darkness around it.

He rebounded back to reality because of the throbbing in his left hand. It switched off his mind-light like a roll-up window shade snapping and surging all the way to the top. He should go back to the hospital. The emergency room.

He remembered after he came to in the emergency room late on the night of his encounter with Jack Cannon. The intern in the emergency room, a Doctor Effan Ewalt, after X-raying and examining him and especially his crushed hand, the fingers still tensed as if still clutching the lens, had wrapped it in elasto-bandages, gave him some pain killing pills, and told him to, "Come you back. You come back if it hurts too much or it's two days from now."

The short, but efficient doctor continued, "Nothing is really damaged. Just a lot of laceration and pushing around. But, no, nothing is broken. Your hand is OK. You were lucky that that piece of glass didn't break. It could have really cut you up. Oh, sure your hand's going to hurt, but just take it easy with it and it'll come around. You use it much? What you do for a living, yeh?"

Dis didn't know what to reply. He could say shoe salesman, convenience store clerk, carnival attendant, or even detective, but all he said was, "Well, right now, nothing. I bike. Bicycle, you know. Gotta have a good hand when you bike."

The doctor opened his mouth to continue the conversation, but he was interrupted by the police officer who strode into the alcove of the emergency room and went directly up to Dis. He was the same officer, a state policeman, who was at the scene of the last encounter that Dis had with Jack Cannon, the officer to whom Dis had so desperately appealed for help. With resignation in his look, he quietly said, "Did you know a woman named Gloria Shoaty from Columbia, Missouri."

Dis replied, "Gloria. Gloria Shoaty?" It all came back, the scene in the blind alley. The gray man and Jack Cannon. The crowd. And Gloria. Gloria with a pistol. Gloria shooting in his direction and bringing him back to consciousness. He remembered Gloria grabbing the lens and running through the hedge opening, knocking over the gray man. And then – oh, God – and then. It all returned. The blast from the gray man's pistol. Gloria being instantaneously jerked into the air and then thrown to the ground. The lens rolling and a kid picking it up and then Jack Cannon demanding it. Dis remembered his rush at the burly Cannon and the resulting chase. But what happened to Gloria, his Gloria?

He looked at the officer and said, "Yes, I knew her. She worked at a carnival where I worked. How is she?"

The drawn and gaunt state policeman looked at him for a long instant before saying, "You have any . . . relationship with her?"

Dis was in a quandary. He thought to himself, hell yes, I had a relationship with her. The memory of that night on the floor of her spook house returned. He opened his eyes wide and was about to speak, when the officer interrupted. "You knew her, didn't you? I'll bet that's one of the reasons she was here."

"Yeah, I knew her. We were . . . friends."

"I figured. Did you see what happened to her – in that backyard over there by that BABI party?"

Dis could see it coming. The ache in his hand increased with the blood draining from his head. Oh, Christ, no! He slumped. Luckily he was standing in front of a chair and he naturally fell into it. The shot! Gloria!

He looked in desperation at the officer, his face almost as defeated at Dis's. "She didn't make it. She's dead."

Time and light stopped for Dis. He was out, falling from the chair to the floor with the grimness of dead weight, his eyes fluttering, his lips a parched crackling of pale.

The doctor didn't hesitate. He also jumped – reaching Dis before the officer. He grabbed Dis's shoulders and almost threw him on the examining table in the room. When Dis came to, it was with the sharp remnants of an acrid taste in his mouth and a profound anxiety in his mind and heart.

Gloria was dead. Shot and killed. Why? What did she do? Why was she even here?

It took awhile, but eventually Dis found out what the officer, Sam Shapino, knew about the events that took place earlier that night. Shapino was cool, calling in a stenographer to take notes of Dis's testimony. No, Dis wasn't under arrest, not at all. He wasn't even under suspicion. But Shapino did want to find out as much as he could about what lay behind the confrontation at the BABI evening community party, Shapino's arrest of Jack Cannon, the subsequent arrest of J. Oscar Leghorn, and the killing of Gloria Shoaty.

But Dis had a big blank to fill, also. What happened when he passed out with the lens in his hand and Jack Cannon 's broad leather shoe smashing at it? It turned out that just before Dis lost consciousness, Shapino had fired the second shot from his service revolver. The first had been a warning to Jack Cannon to stop; the second had been for real. The blast penetrated Cannon's right arm midway between his elbow and wrist and nicked the side of his hip. It knocked Cannon to the ground, so shocked was he at the wave of velocity and sound engulfing him.

From then on the bully-boy, bouncer-from-hell side of Cannon oozed out of him like runny whipped cream from a stale cream puff. Holding his arm with his left hand, he tried to kick the lens from the hand of the unconscious Dis. But as soon as Shapino fairly tackled Cannon and had him on the ground in a hammerlock, Cannon – with a clouding of his eyes – gave up. He rested quietly on the ground and, while staring at the blood seeping from his arm, started crying.

At first his maudlin rambling didn't make any sense to Shapino. He talked about a "gas station creep" returning and causing all kinds of trouble – a guy who was supposed to be taken care of by Leghorn. He accused Leghorn of not doing his job, of letting down both Cannon and Cannon's father, who was now "gonna be really pissed at him, really pissed."

He rambled on about "that Star, that little bitch who wouldn't be quiet" and about the "loud mouthed blonde, Lou, the lip," who tried to run, "but she couldn't run fast enough." This blonde, Louise, was connected somehow with what he called a "toy piece of glass."

By this time at the scene of the encounter on the street in Owaceta, an off-duty emergency medical technician had brought Dis back to vague consciousness, enough for him to realize that he was out of danger and that his lens was safe, clutched still in his battered hand, which was just beginning to throb in pain. When Dis realized that Shapino was a state policeman, and only then, he relaxed his grip on the paper-wrapped package and give it up to the technician who brought it over to the policeman.

When Shapino, under Dis's instructions, held up the lens to the light and saw the inscription, "We love you, Star," Shapino started seeing the depth of all these events. He had been at the trial of Star Oatage; he had just talked earlier that day to Gloria about the trial; and now he was hit with a number of things that went right back to that trial.

One was the lens from a child's kaleidoscope. Another was an exhausted man who looked very much like the used car serviceman who gave some nondescript testimony at that trial. And, although Shapino didn't know the details at the time, another was a pretty woman with an enormous bullet wound in her back who lay dead a few blocks from the scene.

Dis had enough energy to say, "Don't touch the surface of that lens. The guy who gave it to me said that two times before he . . . well, before he gave it to me. I think he meant fingerprints."

By now they were taking Cannon away to the hospital on a stretcher. But he had said enough to set Shapino's mind reeling with strategies and investigations.

Dis found out later that by the time Shapino went to sleep that night in a downtown rooming house behind the jail, he had sent the lens to the state crime lab under a rush order to find out everything it could reveal. He had called upon State's Attorney Carl Rathman, a man who he knew personally, to formally charge Jack Cannon with malicious assault. And informally he had told Rathman about the ramblings that Cannon blurted. He suggested that the Owaceta police force not be included in the subsequent investigations because of the suspicion that its chief investigator, an officer named J. Oscar Leghorn, was activity involved in a number of major crimes. He also suggested that Rathman immediately question Jack Cannon as to the events of the evening and other things that he had mentioned in his ramblings.

Chapter 35.

In the morning two days after the encounter, Dis walked from his motel room down to the county court house to continue being interviewed about all of the events leading up to the death of Gloria and the fight over the lens. He didn't exactly have to fight his way through a mob of press people, but a number of reporters were waiting inside the court house and when Dis appeared, they ran out to try to interview him.

They were friendly reporters, but Dis was very reluctant to give them any significant information. He, to a certain extent, still felt like the man-without-an-identity that he had become for so long. And certainly in regard to the press, he still felt that way. He had no advantage in becoming a "media celebrity," and he wasn't the sort who relished the limelight just for the sake of the attention it would give him.

He had too much on his mind to have to worry about giving conflicting information to the press.

So he smiled and said innocuous things like, "It's great to be free and to see that justice is being done."

Inside the courthouse, after he was led to a basement arraignment room by Officer Sam Shapino, Dis quickly found out what had happened since they had talked earlier.

Police officer J. Oscar Leghorn, who was booked for first-degree murder, and was being held without bail in protective custody in a neighboring county jail, was absolutely silent. He would not say a thing, not even to the lawyer from Des Moines who appeared three hours after he was booked.

Jack Cannon, however, made a complete confession to the murder of Star Oatage, even though he was represented also by a lawyer from Des Moines. He confessed after he had been confronted with the state crime lab report that indeed one of the two fingerprints on the lens was his – the other was that of Star's. Although obviously circumstantial, nevertheless, the report caused the burly Cannon to break down and tell the whole story.

He had picked up the little girl on her way home from school by supposedly protecting her from a dirty drunk who was half-asleep on the sidewalk by the muddy and broken up parking lot of the abandoned factory where later the drifter, Barry Shoaty, was found.

He had taken her out to his favorite "make-out place," a farmer's turn-around in the middle of a corn field, and when she had fought off his demands, had lost his temper and – but he didn't remember what happened right after that. He did remember sort of waking up and finding the lifeless body of Star in the car, both her arms wrenched akimbo behind her back, and large bruise marks on her neck. She wasn't breathing.

He had "kept his cool" and driven back to the place where he had picked up the little girl, being careful to use side streets away from people who could identify him. Luckily, the girl's lifeless body was not bloody – but the arms dangled from the girl's blue blouse in such an abject fashion that it gave him heart-pounding trepidation. At an intersection, he pushed his hand over to the body and slowly lifted her skirt away from her scratched knees.

What he saw took his breath away. Torn panties, clotted blood and massive bruises filled the area between the little girl's legs.

He replaced the skirt while noting that the blood did not seem to have seeped onto the car's upholstery due to the fact that the underside of the skirt was bunched up under the girl's pelvis. If he was lucky and could get rid of the girl quickly, he might be able to get away unscathed.

When he noted the equally lifeless body of Barry Shoaty lying near the sidewalk where he had first seen him, Cannon almost grinned with his good luck. "And there was nobody around either. Just that sack of pig shit asleep next to the sidewalk – hardly moved since I picked the girl up."

This confession, recorded on both a tape recorder and by an authorized state police stenographer, was enough for his immediate arrest on a charge of first degree murder.

But Cannon wouldn't shut up. When asked about the kaleidoscope lens taken from Dis, he told the whole story about his old teenage girlfriend Louise Gorman and the car accident that killed her.

They were a "red hot" couple until she started getting real touchy about sex, downright distant and skittish. He lost control with her a couple of times – and once even blurted out something about Star – about how if she, Louise, didn't behave she'd get the same thing that "that little girl, Star," got. When he realized what he had said, he really got serious and made her swear that she would not ever say anything about what he had just told her.

But then the next day she and his car were gone. He had to get his dad and Leghorn involved because they both knew about what he did to Star and now he had gone and blurted it out to someone else. They were madder than hell at him, but what could he do – he just seemed to lose control with women, especially "bitches, talky bitches. . . and little crying ones."

Luckily Leghorn and he found his girlfriend Louise before she got away or told anyone of importance. But it was Leghorn who did what had to be done. He took her down to the basement of Cannon's house and tried to find out just how much she knew.

It didn't take much – just a couple of kicks to the stomach – for her to promise never to say a word to anyone, especially any officials. She also promised to obey Cannon and do whatever he told her to do – and to not try to run away ever again.

Something in her eyes must have hit Leghorn then. He lit into her furiously when she confessed about going to the used car place and trying to sell the car for enough money to take the bus and get away from Owaceta. Leghorn must have had an inkling somehow that she wasn't telling the complete story, so he took a broom handle and pushed it into her face.

When she still held back, he moved the handle lower.

Pretty soon she told them that the used car man had found a round piece of glass with Star's name on it.

Leghorn roughly clutched the broom handle harder. Within seconds, through choking sobs, she told them that she told the man about what Cannon did to her the other night and what he told her about killing someone.

All Leghorn said was "shit." But he took the broom handle and snapped it in two. He looked at the jagged point and without saying anything else made sure that Louise Gorman would never say another word – period.

They carried her out and put her in Cannon's Ford Mustang – in the passenger seat – positioning her so any leaking blood would be close to the drivers' seat. Leghorn said they were going to take a drive out to Old River Road and stage an accident. Cannon drove and Leghorn followed. Cannon pushed her body down in the seat and took out-of-the-way streets as much as possible on their way to the gravel track close to the small river.

After insuring that nobody was around – checking for fishermen, especially – they stopped the cars on a section of the road that was atop a slope leading down to the tree and brush covered riverbank. They parked Cannon's car close to the edge, facing the side of the road at a 45-degree angle. Then they pushed the dead weight of the teenager into a sitting position behind the steering wheel.

After Leghorn started the engine and positioned the dead girl's foot on the accelerator pedal, it was an easy matter for him to release the emergency brake while the muscular Cannon gave the car a big shove from behind.

It was almost as if they had practiced it before. The car rolled down the slope, picking up some speed as it careened over small bushes and saplings. It crashed through an opening in the thicker woods as if it had been aimed, and ended – going fairly fast – by smashing dead center into a silvery tinged cottonwood.

The crash threw the body of the girl through the unlatched door and onto the muddy ground about ten yards from the car. The crash also immediately stopped the car's engine, but did not puncture the gas tank.

The two men then went back to Leghorn's unmarked police car and left the scene for about ten minutes. When they returned, they did everything as if they had just happened inadvertently upon an accident that had just taken place. They went down to the smashed car, "found" the body, walked around obliterating their earlier footprints, and then Leghorn called in for the usual support – more police, emergency medical vehicles and personnel.

Cannon confessed that he had wanted to stop at I-Deal Motors and get the piece of glass from the mechanic and tell the guy to keep quiet about what the girl told him. Leghorn, however, insisted that they call the mechanic to come out and pick up the car and that while he was there they show him the body. "Nothing like a bloody butt to scare the shit out of someone," Cannon reported him saying.

They got the mechanic to come out – a man named Rob Clemmon – and he indeed did become scared when he saw the girl's abused and battered body. Trouble was he became too scared. He ran – took off.

By the time they could get away from the accident investigation and drive to I-Deal Motors, the man had flown. He was not at work, not at home, and nowhere in town. He was gone.

After that Leghorn had his work cut out for him. He had not only to protect himself, but also Cannon' father, old Milo Cannon, the owner of the largest turkey processing plant in the state of Iowa, and a man with ambitions to become the Iowa delegate to the U. S. House of Representatives from the 32nd District of Iowa.

Milo insisted that Leghorn do nothing until he had traced down this Clemmon and had "taken care of the problem."

It took Leghorn awhile, but he was good at investigative work and eventually, after about four months, he was able to trace him to Washington, D.C. It took Leghorn a few days in the Capital City to locate the man, who had fallen to the life of a homeless, alcoholic drifter.

When he did find Clemmon, Leghorn, however, stumbled into another item of bad luck. He confronted the man in a shadowy parking lot in downtown D. C., after locating him in a seedy bar where he had been drinking. He grabbed him from behind, stuck a knife point through the back of his coat, and demanded the piece of glass. Just then a man leaped over the parking lot chain in front of Clemmon, evidently scaring him so much that he involuntarily jumped back – to his death. Leghorn, also startled by the intruder, held the knife rigidly – its blade slipping cleanly through Clemmon's back muscles, between two of his ribs, and into his lung. It stayed right there, since Leghorn let go of it as he crouched to the ground and stealthily crept backwards.

He melted into the shadows of the parking lot, hiding behind a car directly behind the floundering Clemmon.

The stabbed man, who seemed to be acquainted with the stranger, almost tackled the man in his agony. They scuffled. At one point Clemmon somehow reached behind and wrenched out the protruding knife from his back. They exchanged rasping words, which Leghorn could not discern, and then the knife was spinning on the pavement, knocked out of Clemmon's hand by the stranger, who picked it up quickly and pointed it in front of him to fend off the onrushing Clemmon.

But Clemmon was dying – no more in complete control of his body. He abruptly stopped in front of the thrust out knife – but only momentarily. Without a warning his body pitched forward, collapsing on the surprised stranger – and on the tightly held knife.

Leghorn wanted to leave his hiding place and scare the stranger away, but he didn't have a chance. He noticed three people walking on the sidewalk across the street from the parking lot, so he slinked away from the scene of the murder, scooting from one isolated car to the next, ending up at the inner edge of the lot next to a dilapidated warehouse.

When he had a chance to survey the scene, the three walkers were gone and no movement came from the place of the crime. But just as he was considering returning, the stranger appeared – stood up – and with brisk steps gingerly made his way through the parking lot, leaping over the chain again and disappearing in the direction of Union Station.

Leghorn returned to Clemmon's body and searched it thoroughly. He did not find a fateful circle of convex glass or a wallet.

He also had not heard the last words of the dying man – words rasped to the stranger who had just ripped open the man's dirty shirt and found, strapped to the man's chest, a wallet and a hard, flinty package wrapped in cloth held in place by rubber-bands. The man reached out to the stranger with a clutching hand, saying, "Here, take it. Star Oatage. Don't touch it! Don't touch it!"

Chapter 36

One week after the climactic chase and altercation at the Owaceta BABI party and the shooting of Gloria, Dis attended the funeral of Gloria in Columbia, Missouri, a town selected during a series of phone calls to Rosie, who Dis located playing a weekend city festival in nearby Hallsville. According to Rosie, Gloria's mother was beyond making the funeral arrangements, being absolutely distraught not only over the death of her daughter, but by the complexity of living without the guidance of the caring Gloria. "The Spook House. What can I do? I can't even drive our rig, much less set it up and take it down."

Gloria, Rosie and Dis concluded, was a citizen of the entire state of Missouri – and some of the neighboring states – so Columbia, located close to the center of the state, was a logical place for her burial. Rosie's network produced a church, cemetery, minister, and an entire church-full of carnival and amusement ride people on the Thursday morning of the funeral.

Dis was not only given permission to attend the funeral, but was also driven there by the very attentive officer Jack Shapino. They stopped at the penitentiary at Fort Madison – somewhat out of their way – to pick up Gloria's brother Barry, who in light of the recent Owaceta events and Jack Cannon's confession, was to be released from prison on a temporary court order to attend the funeral until a permanent order could free him completely. He was technically in the care of Shapino, but as soon as he entered the police car, both Shapino and Dis knew there was no need for apprehension.

Prison had helped Barry Shoaty. He was no longer a wan-faced, ineffectual alcoholic. Somehow – or someone – in the ancient brick prison had forced him to confront himself, and he had come out alive and blinking – and looking good physically. That was the first thing the two men noticed about Barry; he had bulging muscles, a brisk air, and a positive resolve in his movements. He had probably spend much time in the prison's work-out spaces – much to his advantage. He fairly bristled with energy and zest.

But what had the time in prison done to his character and values? Both Shapino and Dis wondered if he had learned the typical lessons that prison teaches – negative criminality, profound resentment against life on the outside, and an ability to dissemble to outsiders the real nature of the inmates' convictions about honesty, values, and character.

After two hours in the car – with Barry in the back seat with Shapino – and Dis driving, Dis felt he knew the "new" Barry Shoaty. At least Dis was convinced not only that Barry did not have the mind-set of a criminal, but that he just might be able to change his life style from drunken loser to something different. In fact, a changed Barry just might be the solution to two problems. He could take over the suddenly rudderless Spook House and at the same time take care of his equally rudderless mother.

Shapino brought up the subject: "Hey, Dis, what's happened to that carnival ride that Barry's sister operated? I mean, where is it – what's happened to it?"

Dis replied, "Rosie had it packed up and put it into storage in Columbia. And your mother, Barry, is living for the time being in a motel in Columbia. Rosie's at a festival in Hallsville, which is close-by to Columbia, and has been looking after things, but – you know – she can't stay there forever. She and Carl have commitments; they've got a schedule of bookings for the rest of the summer and most of the fall."

Barry didn't say a thing, so Shapino chimed in with: "What about you, Barry? What happens if you get out of that crumbling pile of brick and stone at Fort Madison?"

With surprising strength in his voice, Barry replied: "I don't know. Looks like that Spook House is just sitting there waiting for me. Trouble is, I never cared for it or – you know – being on the spot all the time. Every day, up and at 'em. Same time, same station."

"Hey, come on, Barry," Shapino retorted. "That's the way life is. You had to do that in the Fort didn't you? Was it that bad?"

"Man, that's one gigantic thing I'll really enjoy if I get out permanently. No time schedule; no hourly do this, do that."

"You mean you'll go back to just kind of drifting along, doing your own thing at your own time. Christ, man, you'll be back drowning in your own spit on another sidewalk like that sidewalk in Owaceta before Thanksgiving – probably Halloween, for that matter."

"No, no. I'm not going back to that. My buddies in the weight room in the Fort taught me that. Big Jerome used to say it this way, 'You got two eyes and only one life. Don't waste the one by clouding up the others. Hear me, keep those eyes open and clear. Who knows what you'll be able to see.'"

"Amen," escaped from Dis's lips.

Barry continued. "So I got my eyes open now. I'm going back to my sister's funeral. I'm gonna try to deal with that. She was one of the only people who ever saw anything in me – and I don't know, I don't know if I can handle it. But I'm gonna try damn hard. And I'm gonna try damn hard to take care of Mom too. Won't that be funny. Ol' Barry comes back and takes charge of Momma Minnie, the movie freak. But, hell, I can do it – even if I don't particularly like that kind of life."

"What kind of life do you like?" this from Shapino.

"Whoa, stranger, let's not get too personal. We've just met, don't cha know."

"Come on, Barry, get off it. What do you really want to do?"

"What do I want to do? Just what? I want to go to the Statue of Liberty and climb up that torch just like in that Alfred Hitchcock movie. I want to continue to read – I started to do that in prison. Let's see, I want some sex. It's been too long and all those guys in prison do is talk about it. I never had any good sex. I'm due. Busting for it . . . I don't know, maybe what I really want to do is travel from town to town in Missouri with a live-in van pulling a flat bed truck loaded with enough stuff to scare the pants and panties off anyone with a sweaty buck in their wallet . . . or purse."

Shapino interrupted. "You know, Barry, you probably could get yourself some sex if you did just that. You're not a bad looking guy, but you probably have to wear a mask, right? – in the Spook House, I mean."

"Yeah, Gloria used to hire guys to dress up like Frankenstein, but I wouldn't do that. Come to think of it, though. A guy in a cop uniform might be real scary . . . ah, you know with dark glasses and a club. Oh, forget it."

The talk turned desultory, but Dis could see that the Barry in the back of the car was not the Barry that he had read about in the library file or the Barry that Gloria had told him about. This Barry just might come through.

And, as it turned out, he did come through the funeral without any major problems, although at his first sight of the body in the coffin, he did look around helplessly and frantically for a few seconds until Shapino caught his arm and strongly directed him into the family room. After about a minute, they both emerged, and respectfully viewed the remains of the once vibrant Gloria. Barry even ended up in the small receiving line with his mother – who hardly recognized him – and a very reluctant but perfect-for-the-job Rosie.

Dis reacted even more strongly to the sight of the dead Gloria, unnaturally still and covered with the cosmetics that morticians inflict upon the helpless and lifeless bodies entrusted to their care. Her presence came back to Dis like a physical bludgeon from a hammer. Upon seeing her face, unnatural though it was, Dis could not help himself. His eyes glazed momentarily, confusing the sedate face in the coffin with the animated features of the energetic Gloria he had known.

His imagination almost clouded out the reality of the morose funeral home. In a mist, he sensed the dead woman's pale face puffed back into color, and the lips opening, emitting a penetrating but pleasing, "Hey, buster-buns, keep your hands off the merchandise, even if I'm laid out here like a cold buffet at a delicatessen. Just watch, but don't touch. Well, Gary, one little touch, I suppose will be all right. Right here on my cheek, but that's all."

Dis almost lost it. He could feel his legs weaken and the blood drain from his head. He reached out a hand and steadied himself on the wooden edge of the coffin. He almost spoke, so vivid was his impression that Gloria was speaking.

"Well, Jesus, don't touch me then. That's all the thanks I get for following you up to Bike Town, Iowa, eh? Well, Gary-Berry, what can I say, it almost happened, didn't it? We almost had it, didn't we?"

His legs bent involuntarily. He could not control himself. He found himself kneeling next to the coffin, his eyes barely able to see over its edge, saying softly, almost to himself, "I'm sorry. God, Gloria, I'm so damn sorry. Why did you have to get involved? You never should . . ."

Shapino was on one side of him and Rosie on the other. They gently, but forcefully raised him to his feet and silently walked him away from the coffin and into the family room. There, after finding a chair, and looking back and forth at the two who helped him, his color returned with a blast – from pale to embarrassed red.

But the words were the same. "I'm sorry. I'm just so damn sorry."

He couldn't help it; tears beaded up and rolled down his cheeks. He looked at Rosie. "Christ, Rosie, I could have fallen in love with her – maybe I had already. I could have married her. She was so . . . so alive. And now she's dead. Dead in Goddamn Owaceta. Because of me. Jesus, what a world . . . what a world."

Rosie's words were as large as her frame. "Shhh. Be quiet, Gary . . . or whatever your name is. Just be quiet. It wasn't your fault. Not at all. She went up to Owaceta for her brother – oh, well, if the truth be known, you were in her mind too. She liked you . . . she liked you very much, to tell you the truth. But she didn't run off up to Iowa just to chase after you. Some of her last words to me were, 'I'm not going up there for Gary, so much, but for my brother, for Barry.'"

"How'd she know anything about Owaceta?"

"Just be calm, Gary – or whatever, Dis – when I last spoke to her, she said she recognized you – you were someone who testified at her brother's trial. Let me think now . . . a mechanic. Yea, a mechanic who Barry worked for right before the murder of that poor little girl. She said you were him . . . well, almost him. Not quite, but real similar."

"Yea, our resemblance is what got me into this mess in the first place."

"But she also sensed something else. She said there was evil around, powerful evil. She couldn't make out the whole picture, but with her brother, and you, and that man looking for you, well, she just knew something was powerfully wrong. That's why she went to Owaceta. And you know what, Gary?"

"What?"

"She was right."

Dis didn't reply to that. He just looked into her eyes and nodded.

He had nothing to say about evil. It had been around him. He had been a part of it – in his own way. And now he was finished with it.

Gloria was dead and evil was dead. And he was alive.

Recast, reinvented, alive to life. Himself once again.

He opened his arms and embraced Rosie, then eased her away with his hands on her shoulders. "You know, Rosie, she was a great person. I thank her for . . . for well, just so much. But Rosie, you too. Thanks. You and her, you brought me to life. Thank you so much."

He pulled her to him, kissed her cheek, and left the room and the funeral home.

He found a patch of grass behind the home, sat down, but all he could think about was getting on his bicycle and pedaling. He wanted to climb and grind and spin and crank. He wanted effort and exertion; up long, steeply graded hills; through cornfields and river valleys; sweat pooling on his back and butt aching in his shorts.

Distance and speed and physical need.

He was ready to bike. To go east. To recovery and life. To Jeffrey, Tennessee, and Washington, D.C. To Lornaree McAbby. To the real Hal Disberry.

To ride and pedal.

Chapter 37

The wind was sharp and clear now in late August, but it was at Dis's back and he was rolling, approaching the hilly western outskirts of Jeffrey, Tennessee. He hadn't expected to be this far this early, but the miles had just floated away with the wind, or so it seemed to him.

Last night he had camped – almost for old times sake – and because he still carried his tent and sleeping bag on his back rack above his twin back panniers. About six o'clock he had noticed a small city park with a faded sign saying "Overnight camping allowed" on the outskirts of the sleepy town of Westford, Tennessee. He circled the town, finding three restaurants amid the two blocks downtown near the courthouse.

That was enough to have him back at the park, putting his tent up, and trying to decide which restaurant to visit: Smokey's Made-Rite, which had a sign in its window proclaiming, "Our Five Buck Buffet Can't Be Beat;" The Pizza Pit; or Susie's Cafe, a storefront with somewhat shabby and unclean curtains.

A process of elimination sent him to a meal of pizza. He had become very distrustful of small town cafes during this long bicycle trip. Many of them had slow service, bland food, and squeeze catsup bottle ambiance. Susie's looked from the outside as if it also had almost empty mustard bottles on each table. As to the buffet, he had stuffed himself the night before at a Bonanza – slaking a need to sample too much of too many breaded or mayonnaise coated food items.

So he ordered a small double crust pepper and pepperoni pizza and an Italian salad at the Pizza Pit, and ate it with relish – along with drinking almost an entire pitcher of ice water. It was small town, homemade pizza, commendable for its spicy and thickly spread sauce. Dis liked heavily sauced pizza; it was even more important than cheese or other embellishments. And this pizza was good – somewhat surprising considering Westport, Tennessee, was hardly an ethnic Italian enclave.

Later, in the fading twilight of the small campsite next to a slowly meandering river, he spread his maps out, and while tracing his most direct line to Jeffrey, wondered if the next day's riding would be his last long bicycle leg for a while.

He felt the need to end his long odyssey back and forth through mid-America.

He wanted Lornaree – her silvery image was in front of him constantly, even though he had tried to push it away during the long time when he saw no hope in ever seeing her again. Now with almost daily telephone conversations with her, and the tantalizing expectation of seeing her on the next day, he could hardly contain himself. He wanted to ride off into the night to get to her, but he held himself in check.

He wanted a job. He still had about $500 of the money he had saved while working for Rosie and Carl, and two one-hundred dollar bills still remained in his front seat tube from his initial home-leaving funds. He wasn't broke, but he wasn't much better off. He wanted security and that meant money – income, savings, even investment. But more than that, he felt the need to settle in and create some economic niche for himself – and a social niche too. He knew he could work well with people, could help make them happy or satisfied, and he almost unconsciously relished the thought of finding a position where he could help people while making a respectful living. Salesmanship was all right, but he wanted to go beyond selling shoes in a department or specialty store. He could do it – temporarily – could even go back to the We Got It store for awhile, but he knew that somewhere out there he had a career waiting to be discovered.

He also wanted a home. With Lornaree; with Chrissy; with a kid – or, who knows, kids of his own. Deep down he knew that his life wasn't complete just for himself. He needed to share it with others and to create and nurture new life. He didn't care where the home would be located, or what it would look like physically. To him, a home was human closeness and family. Hey, he thought to himself, I could even live in a carnival van if it were a home.

On the map, the most direct line between where he was now, Westford, and where he wanted to be the next night, Jeffrey, was, he estimated, about 100 miles. But that was the major highway route, including a super highway for about half the way. He started plotting out a route using less traveled roads, not county roads, which in Tennessee he knew could be elevation killers, but state routes and local highways. He concluded that if he could do 125 miles, he could be in Jeffrey by tomorrow evening. He would try.

And after a good night's sleep and an early morning start, try he did.

Now, here he was just a few miles from Jeffrey, 126 miles already racked up on his computer, a healthy tailwind pushing him, and the shadows of twilight just hinting behind his back. He was using the state highway, coming into Jeffrey from the west. The road had steady traffic, but its shoulder – about three feet of asphalt reasonably clean – was usable for a bicyclist. He had been on it before, but it was hardly a bicycling goal such as Raintree or some of the other two-laned county roads which interlaced the area. But it could get a bicyclist to where he wanted to go, and that was perfectly fine with Dis.

Although tired, he picked up his cadence, moving up a steadily rising hill at a 15-17 mph pace. He moved through an area of trees, and twilight descended with the suddenness of a light switch. His watch said 6:30, but the rather densely packed woods, which at places overreached the road, limbs meshing overhead, cut off the descending sun's light – and in Dis's mind seemed to cut off summer just like that.

Unconsciously it hit him: his long summer of flight and invisibility was deepening into the longer twin shadows of mature responsibility and satisfaction. The deepening darkness was not clear and obvious, but its suggestion of enveloping closeness was, nevertheless, comforting.

And when he reached the top of the hill and could see the outline of the town of Jeffrey, a water tower rising up on a hill behind it, lying like a rumpled quilt of stout green interspersed with lines of glowing yellow, he slowed down. Without knowing why he came to a stop.

And that is how Lornaree, riding out to meet him on her bike, found him: stopped on the side of the road, looking intently at her as she approached and also alternatively gazing out, past the town placid in its burnished solemnity, in its silvery heavenly light.

She reached him just as the white orb slipped completely over the town in the distance, and with not so much as a word, they both rode down the gently sloping hill into the bicycle moon.

A memory surged in Dis's consciousness. Words from a long ago campfire: "You get a bicycle moon, and you can go on forever. You got eternity just awaitin' you down the road."

****

This book is dedicated to the many fellow riders who have accompanied me as I traveled throughout this great land and in foreign countries on a bicycle. You won't recognize yourselves, but impressions are lasting and they sometimes transform into the stuff of storytelling.

Certainly do note that this book is fiction, a product of the imagination, not of real people, events, places, even times.

By the way, as a first time novelist, I'd appreciate any feedback you care to give – good, bad, constructive, destructive, what ever. Just email your comments to me at chuckace2@gmail.com.